ADMIT THE HORSE

P.G. ABELES

OAK LEAF
PRESS

This is a work of fiction. Names, characters, places and incidents are either the product of the author's imagination or are used fictitiously, and any resemblance to actual persons, living or dead, events, business establishments or locales is entirely coincidental. Actual historical events depicted reflect the author's research and opinion.The publisher does not have control over, or responsibility for, any third-party websites or their content.

Oak Leaf Press
5576 Norbeck Road
Rockville, Maryland 20853

ADMIT THE HORSE

Cover Design by Tony Greco & Associates
Cover Illustration: "The Procession of The Trojan Horse In Troy" by Giovanni Domenico Tiepolo, 1773
Interior Design: Pequod Book Design

ISBN: 978-0-9840314-3-6
Library of Congress Catalog Card Number: 2011942011
Cataloging-in Publication Data is on file with the Library of Congress
Political Thriller/Mystery
Visit Oak Leaf Press on the World Wide Web at www.oakleafpress.net

Manufactured in the United States of America
Published simultaneously in Canada

"This novel is fiction.
Except for the parts that aren't."
Michael Crichton

For my parents...

Comment pourriez-vous etre perdu
quand vous etes toujour trouve dans mon coeur?

Admit The Horse

‘O wretched countrymen! What fury reigns?
What more than madness has possess’d your brains?
Think you the Grecians from your coasts are gone?
And are Ulysses’ arts no better known?
This hollow fabric either must inclose,
Within its blind recess, our secret foes;
Or ‘t is an engine rais’d above the town,
T’ o’erlook the walls, and then to batter down.
Somewhat is sure design’ d, by fraud or force:
Trust not their presents, nor admit the horse.’

The Aeneid, Virgil, Book 2 (translated by John Dryden)

CHAPTER ONE

July 2007
New York, New York

SINCE ITS FOUNDING IN 1923, Tolero Star Securities had weathered economic and international crises with aplomb. The Stock Market crash in 1929, World War II, even the September 11th terrorist attacks, had only tested its financial stability and solvency. Other firms were dragged under by the weight of those events. Tolero Star had survived; some might even argue, it had prevailed—listed as one of the "most admired companies in America" by a popular business journal. But Tolero Securities had a problem—more specifically it had two problems. Tolero's High Quality Investment Fund and High Quality Leverage Fund had promised their investors low-risk, high-grade investments with a negligible 6% invested in mortgage-backed securities. The funds had enjoyed a record-shattering forty-month 50% return; but the truth will out. The hedge funds' investment in the pooled mortgages of credit-risky borrowers was not 6%—but 60%. And, as the Wall Street broker dealers were reevaluating the pricing of those securities, returns were collapsing. Investors wanted their money back. With few other options to forestall a major panic and massive sell-off, Tolero Star Securities announced it was suspending redemptions. Nobody was getting out.

CHAPTER TWO

August 2007
Hilo, Hawaii

IT WAS RAINING OUTSIDE. She slid off her high heels and pushed them under the desk cubicle with her toes—savoring the moment of freedom. From her bag she pulled out a pair of impressively logo-d flats: a sidewalk knock-off that cost approximately one-hundredth the price of the original. No sense ruining her good shoes in the rain.

In a workplace characterized by Hawaiian shirts and flip-flops, she dressed like she worked in a New York law firm. She didn't invite confidences from her co-workers and she didn't share any. With her perfect tawny skin, expensive-looking suits, and exquisitely manicured hair and nails, it was no wonder she was a source of interest and envy within the island bureaucracy.

The effort was worth it. She was determined no one should guess what she considered her embarrassing origins—a mother so swollen and fat on Spam she had to turn sideways to fit through the door of her battered mobile home—popping blood pressure pills like candy. So much for the royal blood of Kamehameha, she thought.

Taking a covered elastic from her desk drawer, she pulled her glossy hair into a high ponytail. There was no one left in the office to see her; she might as well be comfortable. More than once, she'd looked for an excuse to stay a few minutes after the others had left so she could savor the day-end freedom. But today she wanted to get home—to pack. She turned off her computer. This was a dead-end job on a dead-end island. She hadn't bothered to make any friends in the office; there was really nobody here worth keeping.

There was no need to lock anything. The building was secure, and, anyway, the cleaning service would be making their rounds within the hour. As she exited the elevator on the ground floor, her shoes padded softly against the intricately veined marble floor. What he'd asked her to do was easy. With the polyglot ethnicities of Hawaii, she'd had no trouble creating a birth certificate for a multiracial child. She'd mailed it to the P.O. box specified in the envelope, but with a brief note of explanation that there had been no way to create a record in the database as they'd directed—either their password information was outdated or someone had blocked the code. She'd been instructed not to contact them, so she hadn't. She supposed if they checked the system, they'd figure it out for themselves. In the meantime the money they promised her should be waiting.

She unlocked the car door and slid behind the steering wheel—throwing her purse on the passenger seat. The wheel felt a little sticky. She grabbed a handiwipe from her bag and wiped her palms as she eased her car into the traffic on Aupuni Street.

As the first waves of nausea hit her, she tried to remember what she had eaten that day—just a quick candy bar from the machine and a couple of diet sodas. She should have eaten something. Her mother was always after her for not eating. She was too skinny, her mother said. Men did not like women that were all bones and sinew. Well, maybe not men on the islands—but there was a confirmation on a flight in her name to LAX on her computer, all bought and paid for. She had decided long ago—she wasn't staying on the island.

She suddenly realized she was sweating—pouring sweat. There was a metallic taste in her mouth that was strange and familiar at the same time. There was something in her mouth—something wet and salty like tears. Was she crying?—she wondered absently. She was confused; there was no reason to cry. She had her whole life ahead of her. Finally, after years of waiting, she was escaping, unfettered, unbound.

But she wasn't crying; it was sweat from her forehead. It felt like she was drowning—in—what?—what was in her mouth?—filling her mouth—almost suffocating her? She opened her mouth and saw it spill to the passenger seat. In the dark it looked black. Now it was pouring out of her mouth, even as the car headlights and traffic lights started to blur and coalesce. Even after she could no longer see, she heard the horns and the sirens and the voices; but it didn't have anything to do with her anymore. She was free.

Chapter Three

September 2007
Arlington, Virginia

This time they needed to be sure. Two men mounted the brick stairs, checking that they had the right address on Vernon Street, North. Twenty minutes earlier they had been trying to open the door at the similar sounding North Vernon Street when the irate householder almost called the cops. They used the office key to open the black lacquered door. As they entered the nondescript brick townhouse, they could hear the phone ringing. Consulting a page torn from a notebook, they disabled the security system. The office had been trying to reach him for hours after he missed an important committee meeting. The senior staff had been slow to worry. Most of them were still readjusting to work after the long Labor Day weekend.

The house was still; quiet. "Congressman?" one called out. No answer.

"Anyone home?"

They moved into the house by inches.

"Probably, you know, he just went home to Ohio for the long weekend and forgot to tell us." The other staffer nodded, it made sense. "Did we try the number at the lake house?"

"Kiera did. No answer."

Both involuntarily looked up at the large brass chandelier in the foyer.

"Well, no panties. I guess that's a good thing."

Both staffers were nervous. Neither had wanted this assignment. Discovering your employer involved in any activity that was worth missing a Congressional hearing was not generally considered good for your career. They steeled themselves against unpleasant discovery, armed with the knowledge that Donald Gilchrist was a family man with five children at home in Amlin, Ohio. He was not a man with secrets. But he was also not a congressman who missed important meetings.

Beltway insiders scoffed that he looked more like a plumber than a politician, but, in truth, he looked like what he was: a doughy sixty-five year old man with a big nose, small teeth, and enough hair to say he had it; perfectly at ease with his fellow Masons and Rotary Club members and always ready to hit a few balls on the golf course. He'd now been returned to Congress ten times from his socially conservative, new-money Ohio district, and if other men might have been tempted to consider his 57% share of the vote in his most recent contest as an invitation to seek higher office—Gilchrist was not among them. He liked where he was, liked his job.

And he was not without influence. He was the ranking Republican on the Financial Institutions and Consumer Credit

Subcommittee and his staff was working on an investigation of the alleged fraud that was going on in the sub-prime lending market sponsored by a voter advocacy group called SEED. SEED was the acronym for Self Empowerment through Economic Development and was one of the primary movers behind the *Community Reinvestment Act* or CRA, which encouraged banks to make high-risk loans to customers with poor credit to increase home ownership. It had been done in the worthy name of ending discrimination in the lending industry, but like so many government programs, it had become vulnerable to special-interest pressures.

For years now, any bank that wanted to merge or expand had to demonstrate that it had complied with the CRA—and an application for approval could be sidelined completely if SEED or other community interest groups filed complaints or staged protests. Making the banks more responsive to consumers, and their lending practices more transparent, should have been a good thing. But bank officials increasingly complained to a sympathetic Gilchrist that SEED was using the bankers' fear of their "rent-a-mobs" as a form of extortion to force them to ignore standard industry risk ratios. Few people realized that banks were now required to accept food stamps as a source of income on mortgage applications.

Few of these loans were in the best interests of the borrowers—most of whom would be hard pressed to keep their homes when the usurious rates charged by the mortgage brokers reset skyward, but there was little question that they devolved to the benefit of SEED. If the mortgage were written directly by Fannie-Mae or Freddie-Mac, SEED received 4% of each and every mortgage underwritten by the quasi-governmental agencies. It wasn't a small chunk of change. In 1992 Fannie-Mae was making $1 billion in loans to low income families, by 1999 that figure had grown to $80 billion; by 2003—the last year for which figures were provided by Fannie-Mae—the loans had reached a staggering $600 billion dollars. SEED declined to provide hard numbers, but even by the most conservative estimates these loans were generating $50 million dollars a year for the organization; and possibly much more.

The banks complained that with so many questionable loans on their books, they were prevented from transacting business they wanted and needed to do with low-risk investors—a situation which, they claimed, threatened to stall the commercial banking industry. Luckily, the investment banks had a solution. Congress could resolve the issue, they suggested, by instructing Fannie-Mae and Freddie-Mac to package the loans with other less risky mortgages—theoretically reducing the risk—and Wall Street could profitably sell them to investors as "mortgage backed securities." As far as Gilchrist had been able to ascertain, the U.S. government was now unwittingly operating as a guarantor of a pyramid scheme.

Most disturbing for Gilchrist, who was Catholic and pro-life, was the way SEED, and its notorious use of satellite and front organizations, had apparently hoodwinked the Catholic Church. For decades, every Sunday before Thanksgiving, in dioceses across the United States, parishioners had been provided with pre-printed envelopes to donate to the *Campaign For Human Development*—an initiative, they were informed, of "The Catholic Church working to end poverty and injustice in America."

Unbeknownst to most American Catholics, in the last ten years CHD had given more than $7.3 million dollars to SEED. Money, paradoxically, used by SEED to support pro-choice candidates.

Not only would Gilchrist's investigation discredit the ranking member from Massachusetts—a pompous, openly gay blowhard despised by the homophobic Gilchrist—but its links to one of the democratic candidates for president would likely prove equally embarrassing to the Democrats—the possibility of which, Gilchrist was honest enough to admit, he savoured. Apparently, one of the Democratic contenders, Congressman Okono, had long-term ties to SEED. Pictures had surfaced of Okono teaching a Power Training seminar for SEED from sometime in the mid-1990s. Based on the idea of "power analysis" formulated by social agitator Saul Alinsky, it was a cynical strategy to identify relationships built on self-interest and find a way to exploit them to the organizer's advantage. Gilchrist imagined it would come as a surprise to his idealistic, kumbaya-singing backers that the soft-spoken, professorial Okono had been *teaching* the brass knuckle tactics of intimidation, disruption, and extortion that had proved such powerful tools for SEED's "community organizers."

Of course, it was early days yet. Gilchrist was not one to count his chickens before they hatched. Even among his own staff, Gilchrist was notorious for being close-mouthed. Last weekend, he'd been concerned when Josh Stein at the *Political Insider* had called him, and seemed to have some information that Gilchrist staffers had been sniffing around SEED and the home loans. Gilchrist had had a few drinks by then, and had been afraid he'd revealed more than he meant to. But nothing about the investigation had appeared in Stein's column, so he had relaxed.

Both young staffers were trying to pretend, for the benefit of the other, that they weren't nervous.

"Congressman?" their voices were intentionally loud, but low, strained.

"HELLOOOOO? Anyone home?"

"Uuuuck. It smells poopy in here."

"Did you just say: 'it smells poopy in here'? Seriously? Like, how *old* are you?"

"Whatever. I don't like to use bad language around the Congressman. Anyway, something's not right. We should call the police."

"Hold up. Let's just look around, first." said the other. "We don't want to do anything to embarrass the Congressman."

"*Something* smells like shit in here."

"I thought you didn't say shit."

"Shut up."

Past the small entryway, they could see the staircase in the living room beyond. The Congressman's corpulent body sprawled brokenly on the marble tile, his head pillowed by the bottom stair. His eyes were open, staring.

The staffers looked at each other, wide-eyed with shock.

Stepping around the pool of fluid that had collected under the body, the younger staffer pulled out his cell phone and took a picture of the late Congressman Gilchrist before dialing 911. The older staffer finally gave up any pretense of being cool and ran retching toward the door.

Chapter Four

October 2007
New York, New York

WITHIN FIVE DAYS OF EACH OTHER the CEO's of the world's largest brokerage firm, Shirlington Securities, and the world's largest financial services company, OmniTrust, resigned under pressure from their boards. Only two short weeks before, Shirlington CEO's announcement that the firm's estimated write-off from losses in subprime mortgage-backed securities would be in the neighborhood of $5 billion had sent shock waves down Wall Street like an atomic blast. OmniTrust had announced it anticipated similar losses—of $5.9 billion.

However, by month's end, as devastating as those losses had seemed at the time, it was apparent that both men had seriously underestimated their company's risk. Shirlington reported a devastating $2.4 billion loss in the 3rd quarter and a $8.4 billion write-down in asset value. OmniTrust was now advising nervous investors that the firm would experience a 60% decline in 3rd quarter profits and a write-down somewhere between $8 and $11 billion.

Analysts at the 24- hour cable financial stations, spouted sage maxims about how unforgiving Wall Street could be. Apparently, when your annual compensation is in the $50,000,000 range, you're not supposed to be off by a few billion.

Chapter Five

December 2007
Chicago, Illinois

The door of the South Side apartment building showed its age even more acutely in the grey of the December afternoon—chipping paint, gouges where the wood had been damaged by contact with untold furniture and electronics, and planes sufficiently out of plumb to be consistent with the multiple instances of domestic disturbance to which it had been an unwilling participant. He really should move to a better place. Most of his friends had moved to the more culturally lively North Side for its restaurants and galleries. Maybe he'd check out the apartments in Lakeview and Andersonville this weekend.

He let himself in, stamping the dirty snow off his boots, noticing that someone had draped some raggedy dime store tinsel over the mail slots. He checked his mail. Nothing. That was curious—the other residents' slim metallic boxes were overflowing with circulars and pizza promotions. He had been expecting to hear from Sinkowski. After their last telephone call, he'd been pretty creeped out—Sinkowski seemed to believe he was being followed, his telephone tapped, even. But how likely was that, really? O. had asked him to contact Sinkowski; find out what it would take to shut the guy up—maybe dig for a little info on whom the guy had spoken to. O. said he couldn't ask anyone from his office to do it; he needed to keep the situation at arm's length. But Sinkowski was just a lonely middle-aged queen with mental health issues. O. had been wrong to ignore him; so much easier to just talk to the guy—he only wanted some attention.

The drug thing was a non-issue anyway. Sure, O. may have done some lines if someone else was paying, but O. was by nature an ascetic—always tightly under control, sometimes eerily so. Was O. even gay? Who knew? For all his handsome good looks and easy smile, that cat was cold. If someone was offering to blow him—he wouldn't refuse—it took a lot of stroking to assuage that limitless ego—but it was always the same with him—nothing reciprocal. O. was a taker. He'd learned that himself the hard way.

As he started down the long hallway, he thought he saw his apartment door close. Could it be? Was Kevin back? He hadn't given up hope Kevin would return to him. He was young, taking time to find himself; so beautiful. Kevin had been in love with O. or maybe just in lust. But there had been too many calls to the office, too many people starting to ask questions, get suspicious; an ambitious young politician on the 'down low' with a young family couldn't have that. Talk to him, said O. Explain to him. Get him to calm down. But Kevin was unheeding, threatening to march over to O.'s house, talk to his wife, talk to the press, expose him.

"I'll deal with it," said The Minister. And he had; he sent Kevin on a vacation, The Minister said. Caribbean, warm sea, soft sand and (he privately suspected) lots of nubile boys happy to get friendly with a well-paying tourist. But even after talking to The Minister, something was nagging at him; something in The Minister's manner. It seemed weird that Kevin hadn't called him, especially as he'd always claimed to distrust The Minister. The Minister told him he'd received a postcard from Kevin a few days ago—"Weather is here. Wish you were beautiful"—typical gay humor.

As he reached his door, he was still hopeful. The key turned easily in the well-worn lock. If he's here—if he's come back, I'll take him away, he pledged to himself. He'd find another church looking for a choral director. After twenty years, he was certain The Minister would give him a reference; somewhere far away from O. He'd made good money, been careful. They could be happy. They would forget everything and start fresh; just as The Minister had advised. And then he opened the door.

CHAPTER SIX

New York, New York

ON THE DRIVE IN FROM THE AIRPORT, Appelbaum had watched as the storm started to build; the sky darkening and the wind rising as if the elements, held in check for a time, were now restless for adventure. It was precisely the kind of weather, he thought, that alerted ordinary people that they might be called on at any time to be very brave, or very quick. But from up here, it was all different. Now he was so high, the building so insulated from the elements, the sheeting rain glimpsed through the broad expanse of tempered glass might as well have been happening on Mars, it was so far removed. In New York, weather was what happened to poor people. Oh, perhaps a stroll down Madison Avenue on a warm spring day to observe the hoi polloi. But mostly, the New York elite's experience of weather was something that happened on the way to, or from, somewhere else—with a helpful doorman or driver to provide protection and insulation on the twenty steps between building and chauffeured car.

It was different, of course, in Chicago. Chicago was still new enough, still Midwestern enough, to pride itself on braving the elements. The buildings weren't uniformly as tall, the inhabitants not quite so pampered, the elite not quite as arrogant. The power center in New York was Wall Street and money. The power center in Chicago was City Hall and influence.

But, really, in the end, it made no difference. David Appelbaum wasn't by nature an introspective man and his profession did not encourage second-guessing or regrets. He was here today to pick up money—lots of money—as much as Wall Street had ever given any candidate for president. And they—these eager, arrogant wizards of finance—were there to give it to him.

Oh, of course, they paid lip service to a lot of crap about a new direction and a change for the future. Of course, they couldn't get enough of O.; that winner's circle smile and elegant reserve. But the reverse psychology with the moneymen, and the right-brain emotional appeal of telling everyone the candidate's "story" as The Professor had advocated, had worked exactly as he had predicted. The laughable, staggering, untraceable amounts of money that came pouring into the campaign on the internet (best not to examine the sources too carefully), only made these financial guys want to contribute *more*.

That's what politicians in this city never understood, he thought to himself with a rueful smile. All these piggy financial guys looked down on their politicians because they had no dough. Most of them were so grateful for the measly hundreds or small bill thousand dollar contributions Wall Street secretaries wouldn't consider acceptable as bonuses. On Wall Street, the barometer of success was making money, and the barometer of intrinsic value was cost. Influence, as it turned out, was cheap.

At first, fresh from Chicago, Appelbaum had expected to be impressed. But as it turned out, despite the accident of their eye-boggling wealth, these Wall Street guys weren't particularly exceptional. Most weren't that educated; Appelbaum thought. They weren't cultured (that's what wives were acquired at great expense to provide). God knows they weren't handsome. And let's face it, Appelbaum thought, most of them weren't even that smart. But they knew how to make money—not in and of itself such an accomplishment, when you consider that it was really more about taking other people's money. And, that, after all, was no big deal. Appelbaum knew all about taking other people's money.

In the end, the commuter helicopters, and the hurry-scurry, got-to-get-to-the-office lifestyle was kind of a sham, Appelbaum reflected. The guys on Wall Street weren't producing anything; they weren't inventing anything. What they were *really* best at was leveraging (and sometimes liquidating) assets that had belonged to other people—and miraculously, legally, taking them for their own. That's why they respected O. They could see he was a rainmaker. And they suspected that, like themselves, he was an opportunist—defined by the more cynical among them as someone who was concerned more nearly with what was legal than with what was right. O. pulled in the dough—or more precisely, Appelbaum pulled it in for him. In the whacked psychology of Wall Street, the less O. needed them, the less he respected them, the more eager they were to jump on board and show the love. And Appelbaum was there to see O. got plenty of love.

Even then, O. wouldn't play the game; wouldn't pander. O. held himself apart: arrogant, aloof. Unlike the usual political candidates—back slapping, blow-dried sincerity drones who paid their dues at soup kitchens on the weekend and endless weeknight fundraisers (and had to account for every measly penny of contributions and expenditures); O. didn't work it, and he didn't account to anybody.

The media would end up crowing over the clothing expenditures of the Republicans—without bothering to notice that the only reason the press knew what those expenditures were, was because their books (unlike O.'s) were open. The vent-less Canali and Zegna suits, the wife's expensive designer duds—no one asked questions. The political idealists impotently wrung their hands over O. not accepting public financing as he had promised to do. What they didn't realize, was that there was never really any choice. With public money came public scrutiny...and public audits.

What Appelbaum knew that the public did not was that the Federal Elections Commission, tasked with ensuring fair elections, was already sending documents in the hundreds of pages detailing "problem contributors" to Okono campaign headquarters. Donations that the FEC had tagged as suspicious for a variety of reasons: either because the contributor had exceeded the $2,300 personal limit, or the contributions originated from foreign addresses or foreign bank accounts, or the contributors used obviously fictitious names and addresses. The infractions were so extensive and so bald, it would be hard to make the claim the campaign hadn't been aware of wrong-doing with a straight face. The FEC accountants were paper tigers, of course, nothing would happen until after the election, and even then an audit could only take place if it had bipartisan support. Appelbaum had ways to make sure that wasn't going to happen.

No. No audits.

When they'd come to him fifteen years before and told him to set this guy up, brand him, make him marketable, he'd been astonished. Back then O. was so uncomfortable meeting with constituents, so maladroit, he looked like he was going to crawl out of his own skin. The people in those housing projects looked at O. like he was an alien—so divorced was he from their experience with his thin skin, private school elocution, and tight ass. But the money was there, and at the time Appelbaum had not been quite so picky about his clients. Sell him like a box of Cheerios, they told him. Make us a star. So, he had.

He controlled the information. No school transcripts would be provided—O. was a bright guy but an indolent student. No test scores—O.'s scores would never have qualified him for the top tier schools to which he'd been admitted. No college pals to interview—some of the groups those guys belonged to might sound a little too radical. Appelbaum shook his head with amazement—some kid, just graduated from Harvard, without a pot to piss in—and no one wondered where all the professional photos from the "early years" came from? He'd hired a photographer to follow O. around; that cost dough. But dough had never been a problem for O.—there was always plenty of dough.

Appelbaum had heard rumors of plastic bags filled with money delivered to campaign headquarters. He'd never asked about the rumors for the simple reason that he didn't want to know. It was certainly true that the community 'get-out-the-vote' organizations were always breathing hard for O. Those people didn't get off their fat asses for less than a hundred grand, he knew. Somebody was paying them, and paying them well.

Then there were the state and federal tax credits—worth hundreds of millions of dollars—to all the real estate developers on low income housing projects—more than a hundred in O.'s district alone. These developers had received tens of millions in tax credits, low-cost financing on loans and community investment dollars. Those 'innovative partnerships' O. had sponsored between the public and private developers were now slums. The absentee landlords just absent. A little bit of a dust-up when a heavy gate rusted off its hinges and fell on a toddler—killing the child—yet these developers remained some of O.'s closest associates and friends. And still, no one asked any questions.

Thank God for Antoinette—at least she gave the guy a little game. Okono's wife was the tough one, the brass knuckles. Her family knew Chicago politics; knew what it took to get the deals done. If O. demurred, she'd give the nod—well, to pretty much anything. Of course the proverbial chip on her shoulder, was, in her case, more like a boulder—but her "do-it-to-them-before-they-do-it-to-us" philosophy had made Appelbaum's job much easier on more than one occasion. When challenged by a local reporter about her $195,000 pay raise within a week of her husband's election to Congress, Antoinette hissed at the guy like a junkyard cat. The reporter all but ran in his haste to get away. Appelbaum chuckled at the memory. Antoinette was tough, but she wasn't *just* tough; she was *mean*.

Of course, he'd had to rein her in from time to time when Antoinette got a little too confiding. After all, Appelbaum couldn't have her telling folks as she did at that speech in Iowa, "See I'm not supposed to be here. As a black girl from the South Side of Chicago, I wasn't supposed to go to Yale because they said my test scores were too low. They said maybe I couldn't handle Harvard Business School because I wasn't ready..." No, none of that. Appelbaum was selling brilliant, and brilliant people don't have shitty test scores. But Antoinette was right about one thing. She was ready. She'd been born ready.

Appelbaum was still amazed at the unbelievable ease of it all. He had handed it to O. on a platter, showed him how to get it done. Challenging the nominating petitions in his first race so O. was literally the only candidate left, then engineering the disclosure of the primary challenger's messy court-sealed divorce. Not one to discard a trick that worked, Appelbaum pulled another rabbit out of the hat in the general election by taking out O.'s Republican opponent in the same way—as sympathetic journalists again, "miraculously" gained access to court-sealed documents relating to the Republican's divorce, including made for prime-time revelations of the would-be senator's inclination toward threesomes and bondage. *Very nice.*

Appelbaum wasn't surprised it had worked; *of course* it had worked. What he was surprised by, and would always be surprised by, was the fact that no one had asked any questions about O's "too-good-to-be true" or perhaps just "too-easy-to be accidental" rise to influence and fame. He sure hoped they weren't going to start any time soon.

Well, maybe it wasn't so complicated. People created the myths they wanted to believe. His son was telling him this morning about a report he was doing in class on Benjamin Franklin. His son had a point: if you considered all Franklin's accomplishments, it was surprising he hadn't been lionized by the young nation instead of George Washington. Sure, ol' George had the physical advantage—but, as Appelbaum's son pointed out, Franklin had everything else. A brilliant scientist and inventor, a successful businessman, the founder of the first hospital, the first fire company, the first library—the list of his achievements went on and on. Franklin was smarter, more socially adroit—and perhaps, more to the point—genuinely involved in the discussions of democracy in a way that Washington never was.

Washington was a good man, a person of enormous courage and discipline, but he wasn't much of a tactician or strategist. But to lionize Franklin was to celebrate the role played by the French—without whom Washington's rag-tag army never stood a chance. To celebrate Washington was to highlight the role played by the Americans. Framed in that way, Appelbaum thought, it made sense—the psychology of the choice was easy to understand.

The Professor was right. O. was easy to sell because people wanted to believe in the myth of O. But, Appelbaum considered, it was almost more than that. Appelbaum had seen the hungry look in people's eyes when they looked at Okono; they were starving for him. This clean-cut, handsome guy with the photogenic young family, who spoke about his high ideals of fairness and service, was as irresistible as a drug.

Chapter Seven

Rockville, Maryland

It was raining. Lacey Houghton turned the Lexus into the long, tree-lined driveway, just as violence erupted from the back seat over the ownership of some Bakugen transformer toys. Attack, wrestle, smack, silence, scream—she could almost time the sequence from initial struggle to final retribution. Mostly, the boys—eighteen months apart—got on famously. But between episodes of what her overworked pediatrician called 'friendly cooperative play' was plenty of testosterone-fueled territorialism.

A Labradoodle bounded out from the bushes, joyously racing the car up the winding drive. As she swerved to avoid him, her phone rang.

"Hi Honey—I'll be late tonight."

Hooray. She adored her husband, but in simplest terms his absence meant a quick dinner for the kids and early to bed. Maybe she'd order pizza.

"Don't order pizza. We've got tons of stuff in the fridge, okay?"

"Hmmm," she responded.

"That's not an answer."

"I'll see what's there. Gotta run, Lovey—we just got home." He signed off, grumbling.

"Well, I'll look," she thought. But the honest truth was that her husband lost a lot of credibility on the whole leftovers issue because he was unwilling to concede anything was past saving—or indeed—(sell-by date to the contrary)—eating. Odds and ends of old salads, casseroles, and meat carcasses would be meticulously wrapped and saved, slated for some future combination, with no consideration of initial origin. This mostly happened on the weekends, with Sunday night dinner frequently devolving into a test of civility and endurance, and everyone ravenous and grumpy Monday morning.

Well, she laughed to herself, I suppose it gets them out of bed Monday morning. The fact that they practically came to blows (or tears) over who received the first serving of toast and eggs notwithstanding.

She entered the house to a ringing phone. As she struggled to carry mail, grocery bags, and backpacks into the kitchen, dodging the delighted dog, and a wet and annoyed cat, she made a grab for the phone. It was Connor. He'd been to the McCracken presidential campaign headquarters today and was calling with a report. The ever-optimistic Connor was subdued—a bad sign. "It's very discouraging," he said.

According to Connor, older volunteers were milling around headquarters waiting for some direction from 22-year-old "supervisors" more interested in flirting and making communal runs for their double cappuccino 2% foam lattes than actually getting down to the hard work of winning the election. As far as strategy, the McCracken campaign consistently catered to the lowest common denominator of risk. Twenty people were routinely included in top-level policy calls—conference calls that should have been limited to three or four. To others, the campaign manager seemed to endlessly seesaw between options and tactics. The intention was to be collaborative, to "think outside the box"—but the problem wasn't the intention, it was the thinkers.

Surrounded by what the Okono campaign termed "concern trolls"—people endlessly terrified of offending one special interest group or another—the McCracken campaign lost all its spontaneity—all its mojo. The campaign was being run by superbly educated, shockingly self-satisfied... hacks. Fundamentally, these were not people looking for, or suited to, the adrenaline rush-rush unpredictability of a brass-knuckle political campaign. They wanted to work in the White House, even saw themselves arriving each morning with a wave to the marine at the gate, Starbucks in leather-gloved hand. It wasn't simply that they had the wrong skill-set; they had the wrong mind-set. Connor was clearly frustrated: "No effort is being made to utilize the people that are coming in...you've got doctors and lawyers, small business people—why are they not networking them? Why is no one coordinating them?" There was no answer. The campaign was disorganized, dysfunctional.

On the state level, the recently graduated, with no business, sales or marketing experience were directing, not just more-experienced volunteers, but strategy. At the national level, the campaign employed pollsters and campaign veterans whose aggressive take-no-prisoners advice was fundamentally at odds with the concern troll culture. After all, why pay someone big bucks to advocate a slash-and-burn strategy—if you knew that neither the campaign or candidate would ever act on their advice? It was an idiotic way to run a campaign. The political brutes were despised, and ultimately ignored, by a supercilious senior staff, who claimed to be forging their own path, pirouetting on eggshells.

The problem was, even as this was all playing out, the momentum was starting to turn against them and they all knew it. Despite having started with an estimable lead in support and money, the McCracken campaign was now floundering, due to the combination of a savage media and an incompetent and arrogant staff.

And the two big primaries they'd been counting on to turn the tide in their favor—Michigan and Florida—were infamously cited by the Okono-loving Democratic National Committee for 'rules violations' in moving up the dates of their primaries. Most of the media gave reports of McCracken's big wins in both states short shrift—if they covered them at all. It appeared to be bias on an historic scale, approaching journalistic malfeasance. McCracken supporters were left shaking their heads in amazement. That, of course, wasn't even addressing the opposition.

The McCracken volunteers referred to the Okono campaign as the "Borg"—an allusion to the ruthlessly single-minded extra terrestrials from the Star Trek movies, whose ferocious discipline overwhelmed and then enveloped everything in their path. Everything animate in the Borg's way was absorbed into their mass collective. McCracken supporters wrung their hands with dismay, but the simple truth was that a fawning media that never reported or apparently cared about Okono's slim résumé and toxic personal and professional associations, and a campaign fueled by untrackable internet campaign contributions that had reached staggering proportions, left the McCracken volunteers little choice but to fight a rear guard action.

What was so disheartening for the McCracken volunteers was that they had by far the best candidate. Other candidates relied on teleprompters for even whistle stops. McCracken could speak extemporaneously for hours. People came to McCracken events because they wanted to hear her speak specifically to the issues. People were lured to Okono's huge events with the promise of free food (or in the case of some college campuses, free concert tickets) to pack the place to the rafters. Okono only talked about the issues in the most general terms.

It didn't matter. The whole thing was wonderfully self-perpetuating. The more the media reported large crowds for Okono, the more people came—fascinated to see what all the fuss was about. Elaborate stage sets with carefully branded faux-presidential symbolism convinced people of Okono's qualifications visually in a way they would never have been persuaded intellectually. He'd never done much, true—but he looked the part. It was the ultimate mind-fuck. The guy looked "presidential"—therefore, people started to think he was qualified to be president...after all, to quote the old saw: he played one on TV.

Claire McCracken, on the other hand, was pretty extraordinary. Throughout her life, she'd stood out among her peer group as a leader, as an intellect and as a worker. When she visited a small town in South Carolina or Michigan or North Dakota—wherever she was—she knew the local problems and issues. She appeared at mid-sized high school auditoriums, not cavernous sports arenas. The demographics of her constituency were working class people—these people were punching a clock, they couldn't necessarily take the day off to attend a rally. The size of her crowds was respectable, but not overwhelming.

She'd appear 'onstage', usually just a small platform in the middle of the room with a cordless microphone, a stool, and a bottle of water. Sometimes she carried a single index card with the name of the person introducing her. As much as forty-five minutes were devoted to answering questions from the floor, and people asked her everything. That was it: no stage and light show, no dramatic theatricals, no thumping backbeat of pop songs, just her speaking simply, directly, and matter-of-factly to the people she was asking to be her constituents.

It should have worked. For decades, the press had been lamenting the lack of "authenticity" in the political process. In every broadcast of the Sunday morning political shows, pundits lobbied wistfully for some bygone day when politics had been conducted without all the hype and handlers and hairdressers—real politics *à la* Lincoln v. Douglas—*mano a mano*. Politicians who would speak directly, straightforwardly, to the American people, without all the layers of spin-doctors, pollsters and consultants.

The local press who covered these events loved her. The national press eviscerated her. Where was the magic? Where was the sparkle? The wonky emphasis on Q & A devoted to local (to their mind) minutiae drove the national press to distraction

(*WTF*? Who cares about the water quality in Roanoke, Virginia?). The campaign was lackluster, they reported, tired, bereft of new ideas, running on entitlement.

Whatever the reality was, it was irrelevant. If the national press reported something as being true, everybody believed them. When the McCracken campaign denied it, they were dismissed as flat-earth fantasists. So the McCracken campaign started stumbling over themselves to revamp, reinvent, and reinvigorate their campaign, in an attempt not to win the people, but to impress the press.

They were wasting their time. The press already had their preferred narrative (spoon-fed to them by the Okono campaign). McCracken wasn't likeable enough, they were told. She was too polarizing, too political. Whether they were complicit, or just compliant, the press parroted the Okono talking points so perfectly they could have been working for the campaign. "It was over," they said, shaking their heads, "for McCracken."

With the pizza box carefully stowed in the garbage, and the kids washed and in bed, Lacey Houghton concentrated on what had become her real job in the last few months: organizing and coordinating a group of volunteer bloggers in 50 states. An early supporter of McCracken, she'd never done anything vaguely political before, but after realizing that the Okono campaign had paid bloggers to trash McCracken on the internet and build up phony grassroots support for Okono, she'd drafted a group of pals to leave online comments in local papers before primaries.

The Okono strategy was based on a controversial marketing practice called "astro-turfing" developed to an art form by Okono's political mentor and consigliore, David Appelbaum.

Whether it was creating, then building support for a municipal project or a breakfast cereal, the principle was the same. Few people realized that the recently opened downtown Chicago children's museum had anything in common with Illinois' new rising political star—but both were being marketed and sold in the same way—to the same unsuspecting populace, and by the same puppeteers.

It started simply enough: a client with a problem. In the case of the children's museum, problem real estate the client was desperate to get off his books. But with problems came opportunities. And in real estate, opportunity means only one thing: money. So Appelbaum went to work. It was easy enough. It started small intentionally, under the radar. Seed local newspapers, radio stations, and internet sites with some seemingly unrelated buzz about the project. Throw some money to a community group (or create your own) that could garner some local PR with events and literature. Spur other advocacy groups, throw them some money, and encourage them to hold meetings. Invite the press.

Enlist some local educators to talk about the importance of the project for "the children of our city" (Who could be against building a museum for children?). Question the lack of resources being given to children in "underserved and underrepresented" districts. Subtly introduce the question of racism: why were inner city children not being given the same access and opportunities as the white children in the suburbs? Ignore all the evidence and statistics that showed that socio-economics drives attendance. Attendees would still be suburban children regardless of where the museum was built.

It didn't take long before City Hall pricked up its ear; the State Assembly, then the governor's office would be behind it. The pragmatists would argue that the children in the city would be better served by staffing the libraries, cleaning up and fixing the schools, buying the promised books and athletic equipment. But even as they raised them, their objections were drowned out. They had already lost. They didn't realize that they were standing in the way of new, sexy, progress. The momentum was all the other way. If they got obstreperous, their commitment to the community would be questioned. They would back down.

The end result? Some worthless and unsalable inner-city property inhabited by drug addicts and the indigent, and riddled with gang warfare, was generously "gifted" to the city—among much publicity and fanfare—for an enormous tax write-off by one of the largest and most corrupt developers in Illinois. With a new multi-million dollar municipal project under way, the adjoining lots became not just commercially viable, but very valuable.

After the first drawings were approved, the city discovered it would need—well,—more land! Additional space would be required for a parking garage and gift shop, property purchased from the developer at newly inflated prices. More property was sold for some cute, slick eateries. And more again for a few in-and-out retail stores selling books and jeans and the quasi-English, multi-flavored, fruity smelling body lotions beloved by teenage girls. Pizza slice shops and upscale lard-laden boutique ice cream retailers discovered the central plaza with its Jeffersonian arches, brick sidewalks, and tinkling fountain created the perfect urban ambiance and resting place for weary shoppers. They were happy to rent the "cuteable" narrow restored townhouse storefronts for exorbitant sums.

Between sales and rental income (why sell a cash cow?), the property generated hundreds of millions in profits for the developer. A developer, not coincidentally, whose hands were never seen on a $13 million dollar investment—money paid to Appelbaum's company, that the developer would later write off as "community reinvestment."

The city had rehabilitated and reclaimed part of the inner city and created a new and beautiful cultural attraction that looked fantastic in the city's glossy tourism brochures. Gentrification was happening (albeit more slowly than optimistically prognosticated by city planners). And if the mostly poor, mostly black, mostly elderly inhabitants of the neighborhood could no longer afford to stay? Well, some of them, at least, owned their homes and could sell for a profit. All very tidy and profitable...a victimless crime.

Except, perhaps, for how the money wasn't used, and the necessary social services which the city was forced to cut as it approached record deficits.

What made astro-turfing so effective for the Okono campaign was that it was so subtle. At first glance, the on-line comments had seemed innocent enough, as if they might actually have been left by authentic Okono supporters. But the Okono bloggers were too arrogant, too sure of their strategy passing undetected. And, like most arrogant people, they got lazy. They began not just leaving the same comments—paper to paper and state-to-state—they were actually using the same user names.

The other striking thing about the Okono campaign's bloggers' online politicking was their remarkable sameness—in virtually every case they were not pro-Okono, they were anti-McCracken. The attacks were never focused on the policies she advocated or even on her résumé—they were *personal* attacks—on her looks, her laugh, her family, her person. The McCracken supporters who came to their candidate's online aid were immediately (and strangely) vilified by the Okono bullies as "shills" and "campaign workers"—in an unintentional revelatory projection and "tell" of their own activities. If a McCracken supporter persisted, the Okono supporters would hunt her down online and expose her personal information on the public forums. "Are you the Leslie Webber that lives at 395 Williams Avenue in Newton, Massachusetts?" they would ask online. "How is your son enjoying the new PlayStation you bought him on Amazon?"

It was creepy. The implied protective anonymity of the internet instantly dissolved. The McCracken supporters—mostly women and older people (and security conscious to start with)—were immediately intimidated, which was, after all, precisely what the Okono supporters had intended all along. Some McCracken supporters tried to fight back—but the Okono supporters with the wanton maliciousness of a mob, made punch-drunk and fearless with their own power, "flamed" any blog comments in support of McCracken—effectively ending her supporter's ability to participate in the online discussion.

Isolated, and believing themselves alone—many of the McCracken supporters had eventually given up. Okono had trained community activists using Saul Alinsky's *Rules for Radicals* as his guide. The first objective was to single out and personalize the attack ("Pick the target, freeze it, personalize it, and polarize it. Cut off the support network and isolate the target from sympathy. Go after people, not institutions. People hurt faster than institutions." Rule #12). By going after McCracken supporters one-by-one all over the Internet, the Okono campaign followed a coordinated strategy to isolate her supporters so that they would not coordinate, volunteer, or give money.

It took months for the McCracken supporters to realize that this was no spontaneous outpouring of grassroots support; what they were facing was a coordinated, orchestrated assault. But by then, many feared it was probably too late to regain the momentum, anyway. It was axiomatic that winning political campaigns was all about momentum.

But the miracle of the internet was that as ruthlessly as the Okono supporters had driven the McCracken supporters from the huge parallel blogging universes of the *Huffington Post* and the *Daily Kos* (which had become so unashamedly partisan that both had ceased to be regarded as reputable news sources by objective observers)—a McCracken resistance movement started to build and grow.

McCracken supporters developed networks of email correspondents, which grew almost overnight into the thousands. User groups banded together, new websites and chat rooms and blogs supporting McCracken started springing up everywhere. The Okono campaign monitored them and went after those they could identify as possible leaders. In one case, having media partisans and internet outliers accuse one McCracken supporter of being a racist and another of embezzling funds. One of the men leading a large network was savaged on television by a reporter who claimed the McCracken supporter had inflated his fundraising expertise —not usually considered a major offense by news organizations that regularly employ scandal-tinged commentators.

The online attacks were spiteful and shocking, directed as they were, not against paid political operatives, but private citizens and fellow Democrats, regular people who had somehow ended up involved. But the McCracken sphere—wary at first (could it be true? they wondered, worriedly), rapidly grew skeptical and then downright distrustful of the attempts to go after their leaders, particularly when it was pointed out that these were the same tactics the Okono campaign had employed against McCracken herself.

McCracken supporters started to see the Okono game for what it was—a cynical strategy to discredit and distort, and to leave the nascent resistance rudderless and confused. The mainstream media, so seemingly eager to support Okono at every turn, wisely stayed away from these attacks. Perhaps, some of them wondered, even if they refrained from publicizing it, how the McCracken websites were routinely being taken out and rendered inoperable—sometimes for days—by some malevolent unseen internet powerhouse strong enough to send millions of untraceable spam messages and overwhelm the servers in the space of a few minutes. After all, not many amateurs had the capability to pull something like that off—at least not without "borrowing" the capabilities of multiple data centers of a major network.

CHAPTER EIGHT

Atlanta, Georgia

MIRIAM CARTER WAS NOT SOMEONE to whom people said "no", or at least not easily or with any regularity. Carter had made a career as someone who was hard to distract or talk down to. Before she had gone into politics, she had been an effective civil rights lawyer. When it dawned on her in her forties that the elected officials she was trusting to make wise decisions for her community were not very smart, and more frequently motivated by self-interest than a call to service; she decided to run for Congress.

Atlanta was only one hundred and twenty nine miles north of where she grew up, but it was worlds away. She was born in 1945, the fourth child of Georgia sharecroppers who wanted something better for their only daughter. Her parents had never even completed elementary school, never mind college or law school—and they were delighted when all the boys made it through high school. But right from the start, Miriam's parents were determined she would have opportunities they had been unable to provide for the others. When her brothers and most of the other kids were earning extra money for their families working full-time to bring in the harvest, her father insisted that she go to school.

But even before Miriam was born, her father had sought a connection with a wider world. Electricity had come to Oglethorpe in 1931, earlier than other places in the rural South. Miriam grew up hearing stories about how it took Big John four years to save the $7.80 (20%) down payment to buy a radio; a mind-blowing extravagance to some in the community. But it hadn't been just any radio. Big John had no interest in the cheap Philco radios sold by the traveling salesmen to the other croppers, where the much-touted "wood surface" was just a painted, paper-thin decal.

As the man said on the radio advertisement "There is no substitute for quality. And when you're buying Atwater Kent, you're buying quality." The Atwater Kent 145 was a five tube beauty with a cathedral shape, burl walnut veneer and illuminated "aeroplane" dial. With a balanced superheterodyne nickel-plated chassis—its rich bass and treble resonated bold and sweet. With three tuning ranges, Big John could listen to broadband, police band and even shortwave radio broadcasts from Europe. The other cropper children used to come in just to look at it.

The first consequence of the purchase was the rearrangement of the parlor to accommodate the extra visitors who dropped in for a quick chat and a long listen. The radio could be heard throughout the small house, but for some unexplained reason, people wanted the set in full view; the nearer they sat, the more honored they felt. Therefore, all the chairs were rearranged to face the 15-inch set, which sat on the parlor table like a little walnut deity.

It was hard to overestimate the way radio changed the family's point of view. Of course, being church-going people, they already knew what every neighbor in the county was doing. But, for all of them, it was their first real experience of themselves as part of a nation or larger world. Every morning after taking care of the animals, her father turned on the radio to hear *The Farm Hour*, courtesy of KDKA radio in Pittsburgh and rebroadcast by the local station every morning at 6:30 a.m. Breakfast was eaten silently; the scraping of fork tines against porcelain the only interruption as the family listened almost breathlessly to the agricultural reports (with musical intermissions provided by the big band sound of Slim Bryant and The Wildcats). It was on *The Farm Hour* before Miriam was born, that her parents had first learned of the Japanese attack on Pearl Harbor.

Most mornings, as soon as the program ended, her father and the boys were back in the fields or tending to chores on the estate until dinnertime. When the men returned from a day's work, her quiet, gentle father would wave his enormous calloused hands and ask Miriam about her day: "Tell me something I don't know," he'd say—and she would.

He liked current affairs best. She remembered how amazed her father was to learn that former President Franklin Roosevelt had spent most of his time in a wheelchair, and how he had insisted she keep that to herself as if it were a secret too dangerous to share. But Big John was interested in everything. He was fascinated to hear how scientists were beginning to develop rational explanations for meteorological phenomena—weather patterns that as a farmer he'd been hostage to his whole life. "Well, I'll be," he'd say over and over, asking her to explain, again, about earthquakes and tornadoes and how weather patterns in Southeast Asia might affect cotton plants in rural red clay Georgia. She was always surprised at how much her father remembered about what she'd told him, and his intellectual curiosity never left him. She often wondered how Big John's life might have been different if he'd had the opportunity to get more than a fourth grade education.

Saturday was bath night for farming children across Georgia. But once in her plain cotton nightgown, Miriam would lie dozing on the parlor rag rug, as her parents and older brothers clustered around to listen to the *WSB Barn Dance* on radio station WSB out of Atlanta. WSB had a powerhouse 50,000 watt clear channel, and the hillbilly sounds of Boudleaux Bryant on the fiddle, Harpo Kidwell on the harmonica, Kid Clark on the accordion, and Boots Woodall on the steel guitar came through the wooden box like those fellas were raising the roof in the next room. Miriam's favorites were three sisters: Bertha, Irene and Opal Amburgey who called themselves the "Hoot Owl Holler Girls." So many Georgians flocked to the Atlanta station for tickets for the *Barn Dance*, the station started to host the show at auditoriums around the state just to accommodate everyone. At the end of every program, Master of Ceremonies Chick Kimball would intone:

"It's about time for us to get off the wind now, but we've had a fine time at your house tonight and we hope you'll let us visit with you next Saturday night at the same time— 9:30 p.m— when we'll be broadcasting from the High School Auditorium in Forest Park, Georgia. The 'WSB Barn Dance' is a regular Saturday night feature of WSB, "the Voice of the South", Atlanta, Georgia."

Every Sunday after the whole family attended services at the Whitewater Baptist Church, Big John drove them all over to Smitty's in nearby Ideal to pick up the *Macon Telegraph*. Miz Tummy started right in, clipping out the coupons from one of the big new grocery stores in Macon. The Piggly Wiggly! So wonderful, even its name sounded like entertainment! The store was the brainchild of Clarence Saunders, who in 1917 had patented the idea of a self-service grocery. Previously, shoppers had presented lists of items they wished to purchase to behind-counter clerks. The Piggly Wiggly changed all that. For the first time, shoppers with baskets were invited to browse through attractively presented aisles of merchandise (the prices clearly marked) and pay cashiers in the front of the store. By 1932, the idea was so successful that Piggly Wiggly had 2,660 stores in more than 29 states and was doing $180 million dollars in business—and retailing would never be the same. For the cropper wives, their Saturday excursions to the Piggly Wiggly, with its intoxicating rows of shiny canned goods, brightly packed boxes and elaborate store displays, was almost like going to the theatre.

While Miz Tummy was clipping coupons, Miriam started on the front page of the *Telegraph* and read the whole thing to her parents—end to end. Sometimes her father would ask a question about a story: "Well, why didn't so-and-so do such-and-such?" he'd ask. If she didn't know, he'd just shrug his shoulders and keep on rocking in his chair. "Well, that's all right, child. I expect we'll learn more about it next week."

Years later, on her parents' black and white TV, they'd watched the troubles in Alabama and Mississippi when the authorities had turned fire hoses and dogs on black people who wanted basic access—to drinking fountains, to schools, and to cafeteria lunch counters. One of Miriam's proudest moments was explaining to her father what the civil rights legislation of 1964 meant to him. For 20 years, starting in 1945 when the state of Georgia had eliminated the $3 poll tax, Big John had gone to vote. For most of those years, he'd been turned away.

For a time, her father had been hopeful. After the war, things felt different. When, in 1946, Primus King had challenged the legality of the Muscogee Democratic Party refusing to let him vote—and won—more than 125,000 black men registered to vote in Georgia within a few months—the highest registrations of blacks in any southern state. But the euphoria was short-lived. Within months, the state inaugurated Herman Talmadge as governor, and civil rights activists learned to their injury and detriment what happened to those who criticized or defied segregation.

Twenty years later, when Big John learned that he now had protections to ensure he could cast a ballot in an election, he started to cry. Not that he hated whites—her father was among the most tolerant people Miriam had ever met. "Black folk and white folk just mostly misunderstand each other, and they both are afraid because of those misunderstandings. And their fear makes them dumb, and dumb makes them frustrated, and frustrated makes them angry."

Her mother was known universally as Miz Tummy, but no one remembered why. The little brother who had named her had died from the arsenic dusted on the cotton fields. Miz Tummy never forgot the brilliant blue-green sheen of his skin after his accidental exposure to the pesticide. For many years, she and the other children believed that he hadn't died at all, but had become a leprechaun. She told Miriam once that she still believed it, preferred to believe it.

But if she was sentimental in some ways, for the most part Miz Tummy took a clear-eyed view of things. One time, Miriam asked her mother why she never tried to vote. Miz Tummy put her hands on her hips and hooted with laughter. "You ever see any black woman go to vote?" she asked.

Miriam thought. "No, ma'am," she replied.

"You ever seen any white woman?"

Miriam bit her tongue and tried to remember. "I don't think so."

Her mother picked up a big rolling pin covered with flour. She waved it emphatically at her youngest child and only daughter. "Miriam you remember this." Miriam watched, eyes wide. "When man slaves were counted as three-quarters of a person...women—black or white—weren't counted as nothing. Women in this country, black or white, don't go upsetting everybody by doing no voting, because they know they don't have no rights except what their men-folk decide to give them."

But on a rural southern farm, the distinctions Miriam saw every day between male and female, black and white, were so ingrained it took her a long time to understand her mother's warning. On some level, she began to realize that though her father treated her mother with respect and cautious affection, few of the other women—black or white—enjoyed the same degree of independence and equality.

For both of her parents, it was a hard life. Her kind and quiet father worked as a sharecropper because that was the only job on offer, the only job he knew. Sharecropping had existed as long as anyone could remember, but began in earnest in the U.S. during Reconstruction. In a more perfect world, sharecropping should have been a wonderful, synergistic arrangement benefiting both partners. After the Civil War, plantation owners had rich farming land, but no money to pay laborers to farm it. Former slaves and poor whites were skilled at agricultural work, but owned no land. The idea was that owners and "croppers," as they were called, would share in the risks and rewards equally. The benefit to the sharecropper was that he was, perhaps for the first time, his own master—master of his time and the method and form of his labor. The benefit to the landowner was that he received a 50% share of the crop produced. By the 1930s, 3,000,000 African Americans and 5,500,000 whites were sharecroppers.

But sharecropping yielded another dividend for the corrupt landowner—the insidious introduction of the institution that has created misery from time immemorial for human beings of every color on every continent—"the company store." Farms were located in rural areas, often quite remote from big cities. As the population began more and more to rely on purchasing manufactured goods, a savvy planter came up with the idea of stocking a commissary to sell durable goods to his croppers. For some landowners, perhaps, it was intended as a means of supplying necessary goods, foodstuffs, and even medicines to a captive population. But on too many farms, the commissaries soon became a lever of control, some planters insisting their workers purchase goods only at their store. Lack of competition enabled cash-strapped landowners to charge exorbitant rates, and lack of alternatives required the sharecroppers to pay.

After settling their debts with the commissary, many croppers, regardless of the success of their crop, made only five or ten dollars for a year's worth of work. Others found themselves mysteriously *owing* hundreds of dollars—with their next year's labor (and crop) held as ransom toward paying off their "debt." Croppers had little or no education, could seldom read or write, and the planters used this circumstance to calculate the debt to their advantage. For the cropper to challenge the word of his landlord would be to risk losing everything: his house, his livelihood, even the crops he'd cultivated in the field. But if he did, it mattered little. A poor white man in the South had no recourse to the law that would be honored; a poor black man had no recourse to the law at all.

The other problem for the croppers was an ugly little grayish-brown beetle that had crossed the Rio Grande somewhere around Brownsville, Texas in 1892. In 1913, the fuzzy beetle with the prominent snout was decimating cotton fields all over Missouri. By 1915, the quarter-inch insect had reached southeast Alabama, and by 1922, it had reached the Carolinas. Traveling an estimated 40 to 160 miles in a year—depending on conditions—it had wreaked havoc across the entire cotton-growing portion of the Southeast by 1926.

Scientists identified the beetle as "anthonomous Grandis." But to the desperate farmers, who painstakingly removed as many of the pests by hand as they could, it was simply the "boll weevil." But the farmers' frantic efforts were of no use, and by the mid-1930s the boll weevil infestation in the cotton belt had reached almost Biblical proportions. One pair of boll weevils could produce 134 million offspring before the first frost —and that was assuming the frost even killed them. Winter temperatures in the cotton-farming South rarely reached the 23 degrees Fahrenheit necessary to destroy the rapacious insects. It would take almost seventy years before scientists figured out how to minimize the devastation.

CHAPTER NINE

Oglethorpe, Georgia

THE PLANTER FOR WHOM BIG JOHN WORKED was a brutish and puerile man named Drew Jackson. Jackson routinely raised his fist to workers and was known for his violence and drunkenness. When discretion or sobriety stood in the way of his hitting his workers, he beat his dog, a self-consciously dignified big-boned poodle named Cotton. "Goddamn, no-account dog, never even barks," he would say when asked about the good-looking dog. The only thing Jackson was known to care about was his car—a 1955 Buick Century convertible, "the banker's hot rod"—eight cylinders and 236 horsepower of sheer trouble. There was nothing Jackson appeared to enjoy more than pretending to run people off the road and leave them choking on the car's dust.

Very little was known of his family life; his wife was rarely seen. Drew Jackson's wife was "county"—folks said she came from a grand family in Virginia. And that's all most folks knew about her. Amalia Jackson would appear some Sundays in church, a fine, elegant-looking woman. Then she would disappear for weeks at a time, just a fleeting shadow of a face glimpsed from behind an upstairs curtain.

Riverview, named for the sweeping vista it commanded of the nearby picture-perfect Flint River, was incredibly fertile farmland. But the steamboats that used to carry all the local plantations' cotton to market had ceased operations in 1928. The big riverboats were simply too expensive to run for so few trips. Their owners either found more lucrative routes, or were 'done in', the farmers lamented, by the weevil.

The large antebellum plantation house on top of the hill had seen better days. The paint on its longleaf pine clapboards was peeling, and the pigs and chickens routinely broke their pens and wandered around the enclosed back yard. Despite all the entreaties of land agents sent by the Department of Agriculture, Drew Jackson distrusted the "Yankee government." He refused their no-interest loans, refused to mechanize, refused to rotate crops. Beetle or no, Georgia was the South, and in the South, cotton was king. Stubbornly ignoring declining prices (and losing a third of the crop each year to the weevil), Jackson, like many other landowners around the state, continued to plant cotton right up to his front door.

One midsummer night, when Big John arrived to work in the yard, he quickly noticed all the electric lights in the house were out. The day had been long and hot, the sun pregnant and heavy in the Georgia sky. But the turn to twilight was hardly better, the air so heavy and damp it made a man's lungs beg for every molecule of oxygen. Over the ridge, sloe-eyed alligators floated purposefully in the lazy river current, watching, waiting.

Everything around the house was strangely still—even the fool chickens had been penned—as if the world itself was holding its breath, waiting to exhale.

Someone with a soft, cultured voice holding a lantern called out to him from the wide-columned porch. "Are you called Big John?"

"Yes, ma'am," he replied, as struck by her sudden appearance as if she were a spirit. She gestured for him to follow her into the dark and silent house. He climbed the staircase behind her, still holding his hat.

"Mr. Jackson," she explained, had "taken sick very suddenly," and she required his assistance. As he entered the upstairs bedroom, he noticed for the first time a large, angry bruise on her cheek and a bloody handkerchief tied around her hand. Drew Jackson was sprawled on the wide-planked wood floor of the elegant upstairs bedroom with a gunshot wound to his head. Dead. In the flickering light of the lantern Big John noticed that the dog Cotton sat silently by his master's body, as inscrutable as ever. Amalia Jackson looked steadily at Big John, her wide-set intelligent eyes never leaving his face. Her voice was soft, but determined, as if daring him to disagree.

"Mr. Jackson was taken ill very suddenly. I fear it was the fever, and therefore it would be best to bury him immediately."

Big John knew better than to ask questions. "Yes, ma'am," was all he said. A hundred years before, the town of Oglethorpe had been wiped out by so-called "river fever." State health officials were still arguing about whether it was smallpox or malaria that had done it. It didn't matter to the 'new' settlers. With so few doctors, fear of the unknown—of contagion—was still palpable.

No one would voluntarily risk himself by checking on Drew Jackson.

In the dark, Big John went down to the hay barn, found some wooden planks and fashioned a simple casket. He placed the body in the casket and nailed the lid shut. He put the casket on the old wagon and carried it to the plantation's ancient family graveyard, where he dug a hole in the red Georgia clay, and buried it deep.

The dog Cotton had followed the coffin's meager little procession, as if he had somehow nominated himself chief mourner. When Big John placed the last spadeful of red clay over the grave, he turned to see the big white dog regarding him stoically. He was in the habit of talking to animals, so as he took a break, leaning on the shovel, he spoke to the dog.

"I didn't have nothing to do with this—and don't you think I did. But I ain't sorry just the same, and you shouldn't be sorry none, neither."

When Big John returned to the house, the dog followed silently, positioning himself alertly on his haunches by the back door, as if in readiness to greet some foreign queen or potentate. Miss Amalia had laid out a cold supper for Big John in the kitchen. He could see she was trying to shield her bruised face from his view. "I want you to eat all you want, Big John, then I need you to leave here and tell everyone to stay away—that we have the sickness here—that I myself am sick unto death and that the master has died of it. You hear Big John? That's exactly what you tell them."

He nodded, dropped his eyes, and continued eating, not sure what to say. They both knew if he told anyone, she'd fry in the state's electric chair, like poor Lena Baker from Cuthbert over in Randolph County. She'd raised her hand against an abusive white man, too. The trial that sentenced her to death by electrocution had lasted four hours.

Unexpectedly, Miss Amalia placed her hand on his shoulder.

"Big John?" He looked up.

"Things will be different around here now. I promise."

As she turned to leave the kitchen, he could see the weariness in her, but a new resolve, too. She turned her head.

"Come on, Cotton; I guess you belong to me now."

The stately, silent dog rose quietly to follow her, and for the first time in his life, Big John saw him wag his tail.

Things had been different. Miss Amalia sold the commissary to a local man, who ran it as a small general store, even the poorest croppers now preferring to do most of their shopping on weekly trips to town, anyway. But Miss Amalia saw to it that accounts were presented at the end of every month, and for the first time in their lives the Riverview sharecroppers felt that if an accounting mistake was made, they could point it out without fear of retribution.

Despite her genteel upbringing, Miss Amalia showed a surprising head for business. But what she discovered could not have failed to dishearten her. The situation was nothing short of desperate. It was hard to find good men to farm the land. So many had left in search of better jobs and more money working in one of the factories up north. The planters themselves were forced to borrow money at a ruinous 15% for the seed, animals and equipment they needed to supply the croppers who worked their land. Even worse, under the terms of the agreement signed by her husband, she was contractually obligated to sell to certain Nashville cotton brokers who were notorious for not giving a fair price. Louis XIV had famously said: "Credit supports agriculture as the rope supports the hanged." Riverview was hanging all right, hanging by a thread.

Most of the southern planters were victims of the innocuously termed "crop lien," whereby the future cotton crop was pledged as collateral to merchants in exchange for desperately needed necessities. Consequently, planters all over the South were driving cotton production to historic levels—causing the increased supply to make the price drop still further. When the weevils got in, it was even worse: they lost everything.

One day, Miss Amalia drove to Big John's tidy farm. No one had ever seen her drive before. She emerged from the long, elegant car, Cotton by her side. As she stood in the little yard, she shielded her eyes from the sun's glare with a gloved hand. "Good afternoon, Big John. Afternoon, Mrs. Tummy. Afternoon, Miss Miriam." Miss Amalia always spoke to the children.

"Afternoon, Miz Amalia. Afternoon, Cotton."

Cotton thumped his tail on the hard ground.

Miriam ran up to give the big white dog a pat. Cotton licked her little hand with silent decorum.

"Mrs. Tummy, do you grow any goober peas in your back garden, by chance?"

"Well, yes. Yes, I do."

"Would you be so kind as to show them to me?"

As Miss Amalia started to follow Miz Tummy, she noticed the big white dog held back. "Well come on, then, Cotton," she said with a wink at Big John and Miz Tummy. "We might as well see what you think of them, too."

With self-conscious dignity, Cotton padded after them on silent feet.

Miz Tummy was justifiably proud of her back garden. Runner beans were carefully staked, shiny-skinned red tomatoes basked in the rutilant Georgia sun, and lettuce and cabbage burst from the neat rows like green flower bouquets. In the back, planted almost as an afterthought, were the goober peas.

Goobers came from the Kikonga word "Nguba" and had been brought to North America by African slaves. An unusual plant—it was known by a variety of names: earthnuts, goobers, pandas, jack nuts, monkey nuts. By any name, they were difficult to grow and harvest due to their unusual growing habits. Most croppers grew them as subsistence crops, food of last resort. White folks mostly grew them for their pigs, allowing the hogs the task of uprooting the below-ground beans.

Miss Amalia surveyed the short row of bushy, broad-leafed plants. The plants stood about a foot and a half high with a small yellow flower.

Miss Amalia directed her questions at Miriam's mother.

"Mrs. Tummy, how early may they be planted?' she asked politely.

"Late April, early May, depending on the year, Miz Amalia," Miz Tummy replied.

Miss Amalia nodded. "And how long until it flowers?"

Miz Tummy cocked her head to the side, making the calculations. "I reckon about another month and a week."

"And after it flowers, this part," Miss Amalia gestured at the flower stems with a gloved hand, "...will push its way under the ground, is that right?"

"Yes, ma'am, right into the dirt," Miz Tummy replied, nodding her head.

Miss Amalia regarded the plant quizzically. "It's quite a peculiar plant, isn't it?"

Miz Tummy replied with a smile. "Mighty peculiar, Miz Amalia, but good to eat, keeps fine, and plenty fortifying to the blood."

Miss Amalia smiled. "And then, Mrs. Tummy, how long before the goober nut appears?"

Miz Tummy considered. "Well, let's see. Perhaps two more months in the ground, depending on the season."

"So planting to harvest is about five, six, months, is that right?" asked Miss Amalia.

Miz Tummy responded, "Yes, ma'am, I reckon that's mighty near."

Miss Amalia looked unconvinced. "So how does one get at the nut?"

Miz Tummy chuckled. "Well, that's the funny part. You got to keep them goobers out of the dirt..."

"Even though they grew *in* the dirt...?" Miss Amalia questioned.

"That's right," Miz Tummy said with a chuckle. "So first ways, you gotta pull-up the plant, then you turns him over, upside down- like, and let the goobers dry. Then after four days or so, you pull 'em off the stalk nice and easy."

Miss Amalia considered the strange plants. "My great grandfather ate these fighting the Yankees. He called them peanuts. The soldiers used to roast them, or eat them right out of the shell."

Big John was burning with curiosity. "Why you so interested in goobers, Miss Amalia? This here's food for rich man's pigs and poor folks—ain't never gonna bring the kind of cash cotton do, if we could just keep them weevils off."

He could see she was torn.

"Big John. I understand your hesitation. I do," she said, swatting away the late afternoon no-see-ums attracted by the carbon dioxide of their breathing. "...but we can't keep the weevils off. We've done everything the land agent advised—burning the old stalks, hoeing the rows, cleaning up the leaf cover..." She paused, looking at him sympathetically. "I see how careful you are in your own fields, Big John. I believe all the farmers are doing their best. But none of it has made a bit of difference, has it?"

"Not much, I reckon," Big John replied, shaking his head sadly.

Miss Amalia nodded. "Times are changing, and I expect we must change right along with them. They've got new machines now, not just to plant the goobers but to harvest, shell, and clean them, as well."

"Is that right?" Big John had seen the big combines at work in other plantations, but only from a distance.

"I'm not sure I can altogether believe it myself," Miss Amalia said with a laugh, "...but it's what the agricultural agent tells me, Big John."

Miriam's father had a great deal of respect for Miss Amalia, but he was a plainspoken man. Since the late 1930s, farming all over the South had been changing rapidly. Largely as a result of the catastrophic depredations of the boll weevil, the federal government was offering incentives to landowners to replace cotton with livestock and feed crops, including subsidies to mechanize. However, machinery was still expensive and could only be efficient on consolidated farms—not patchworks of ten and twenty acres all independently managed. The consequence: mules and tenants were being replaced by tractors and wage hands all over the state. Croppers had been evicted, or their holdings reduced to a few acres—inadequate to provide for their families, but a sufficient incentive that many would stay. Croppers had no choice but to augment their incomes by accepting the 75¢ a day for working the plantations' "home farms." And, with an ever-declining labor force, the landowners had little choice but to mechanize and consolidate.

When rumors started to fly among the croppers that Miss Amalia wanted all the croppers farming her land to switch over to peanuts and livestock, Big John felt he needed to make her aware of their concern.

"Miss Amalia—folks around here...Well, can I speak plain with you, Miss Amalia?" he asked in his deep voice.

"I hope you always do," Miss Amalia replied simply.

"Well, you ain't a man, Miss Amalia."

Miss Amalia regarded him seriously, waiting.

Big John noticed her reaction and nodded. "Yes, ma'am—but people 'round here, they like to follow the history of things and ain't no history of things with a nice genteel lady running no dirty farm."

"I see," Miss Amalia replied, her voice expressionless.

"I'm not saying you ain't been doing a fine job—all I'm saying is that when you try to change people's course—when it's a course they've been on their whole life—they ain't easy to move... so when you tell folks we're all going to do better growing no-account pig food," Big John paused, "well, those folks may not be so easy in their minds about some such thing like that."

Miss Amalia looked past Big John at the tilled fields.

"Big John, years ago, did you ever see a *Carver Bulletin*?"

"Yes, ma'am, I know of Professor Carver," Big John said proudly. One of the first things he'd asked Miriam to read to him was the Reader's Digest autobiography he'd been saving for years about Professor George Washington Carver of the Tuskegee Institute in Alabama: *A Boy Who Was Traded for a Horse.*

Miss Amalia continued: "I've been reading some of the old bulletins about the work he did with peanuts. Not only is there a growing demand for peanut products—particularly in candy and so forth, but he claims planting peanuts will actually improve the soil. If we have to go back to cotton, we'll be none the worse for it."

Big John considered: "Professor Carver was a fine man, Miss Amalia," Big John said slowly, "...but folks 'round here just want to be sure they can feed their families and put a little by. Understand..." he paused, thoughtfully. "I hear what you're saying—but one bad year is all it takes to wipe some folks out. Some of them sure to be thinking if we can get some of them cotton bolls—leastways, there's a market for whatever crop we git."

So, Miss Amalia threw a party...and she invited all the croppers on her land. Of course, her farmers knew all about goober nuts as a subsistence crop, but none were as yet awake to the commercial applications of the strange legumes. Was there really a market if they grew them, they worried? And was the market too new? Too new to ensure that a reliable buyer could be found—season after season?

So Miss Amalia set out to make her case by providing a demonstration. She put out heaping bowls of Cracker Jack (created 1893), and Planters roasted peanuts (created 1908), salvers of Oh Henry! bars (created 1920) and silver trays stacked with Babe Ruth bars (created 1920). Next came silver Revere bowls full of Butterfingers (created 1923) and Reese's Peanut Butter Cups (created 1925). And as they were eating, she told the croppers they were all going to start growing peanuts—and perhaps under the mellowing influence of all that chocolate, they agreed. All, that is, but Muncie, who might have agreed eventually, but apparently had an undiagnosed peanut allergy and died of anaphylaxis on the ride home. Of course, ever the pragmatist, Miz Tummy observed to the preacher at Whitewater Baptist that his loss probably would have been felt more keenly if he had been a better farmer.

Chapter Ten

Chicago, Illinois

As the detective entered the apartment, he was struck by the urgent smell of decomposition. The victim was male, early forties, African American—but he would have known that any way because the church was involved.

"Our choirmaster," The Minister had said. Long dreadlocks, manicured nails and a complexion as even and cared for as a woman's, Harrison noticed.

"A nice young man, a schoolteacher during the week, perhaps not as selective as he should have been about his companions," said The Minister. "Gay" was left unsaid, because to The Minister's conservative African American congregation, homosexuality was the unmentionable sin. Perhaps because of the great fear that some men in the community were on the "down low" (perhaps even, rumors suggested, The Minister himself), the church carefully disassociated itself from outreach or involvement in the GLBT community. Even the nutty Catholic priest—queer as a three-dollar bill, inexplicably joined in the condemnation.

The Minister had been reserved, cautious on the phone. Apparently, he felt an obligation to a former member of his congregation. But clearly, too, he had bigger fish to fry than becoming entangled in any sordid goings-on of the homosexual population of Chicago. Harrison had done some checking: the choirmaster was charismatic and well liked by all accounts, if a little flamboyant. But Harrison found it hard to believe anyone would have held that against him. He had attended the church on a few occasions, and those guys all played to the back rows. The cavernous concrete barn was famous for being more theater than church; every sermon more a test of The Minister's showmanship and acting ability than knowledge of the scriptures. Flamboyant was what those guys were all about. Flamboyant was what financed The Minister's expensive lifestyle, kept the fannies in the seats, kept the lights on.

The fact that the victim was a teacher also told the lieutenant something. In Chicago's "pay to play" culture of patronage and corruption, the unions were all-powerful, and the most powerful union was the teachers'.

In Chicago's ruined school system, the teachers union called all the shots. Most of the schools only went half a day; the teachers were too expensive for the city to be able to afford an ordinary afternoon school closing. As parents and city administrators and the school board fought over books and basketballs—too many things in too short supply—no one mentioned the union wages that crippled the system from the start.

Union negotiators had essentially secured Chicago public school teachers a sinecure for life, including a lifetime pension that sometimes ended up paying a teacher a salary in retirement for more years than he or she had worked. Many, if not most, of the teachers hated the system, which promoted union loyalty above teaching ability or commitment to the students. But the teachers were themselves powerless against the corrupt bosses. The union system rewarded its own: essentially guaranteeing some of the least-credentialed, least-accomplished teachers in the nation the highest salaries. But in a one party town like Chicago, no one was willing to take on the union.

Many rationalized their decision to remain mute, hesitant to criticize. If the union had perhaps overbalanced, they reasoned—in consideration of teachers' long history of being under-appreciated and underpaid–the pendulum swinging in the opposite direction for a time was no more than delayed justice.

Whatever the principles involved, in actual practice the combination of high wages, guaranteed employment and generous pensions, meant the teaching jobs were sought after — and in Chicago's pervasively corrupt system–shared out among the favored few like sugarplums. It was almost impossible to get inside the system without doing favors for somebody.

The victim was lying face down on the floor. A burgundy circle of viscous fluid surrounded his head like a halo. The man's long dreadlocks had been undisturbed by the explosion that took off his face. In addition to the single gunshot to the head–from the back, Harrison noted without surprise–the young tech lifted the sheet from the body and pointed to the left side of the victim's back– a single gunshot wound to the heart.

"Insurance?" said the tech with a ghoulish smile.

"Looks like," Harrison replied.

Harrison ticked off a mental checklist of what he already

knew: no sign of forced entry, no struggle, no prints. The techs had been all over the apartment, were still there trying to find something. The place was wiped clean—too clean for an amateur—not even the decedent's fingerprints were on anything. And, of course, nobody had heard a thing. Maybe it would turn out some cash and some credit cards were missing. But if they were used, Harrison was willing to bet, it would be by some homeless guys living under an underpass—celebrating the sudden turn their luck had taken with the acquisition of some rotgut wine and a couple of packs of smokes.

Stuff was dumped out of drawers, scattered around the apartment in order to make the case for a burglary gone awry, but the gunshot wound to the back of the head told the story. This was not an unpremeditated crime of robbery, not a crime of passion. This was an execution-style hit on someone who knew too much about something—or at least somebody thought he did. Somebody was cleaning up.

When Harrison's father had been a cop, the police had solved nearly 90% of their cases. As gang and drug violence became more prevalent in the intervening years, the solve rate had declined, but what most people whose knowledge of crime solving was based on hour-long TV dramas didn't realize, was that it was still around 70% in most major metropolitan areas. What that should mean to the average perp looking to take out a girlfriend was that you get caught a lot more often than you get away with it.

Most murders were pretty uncomplicated. When you considered it logically, deciding to kill someone was an enormous commitment. For regular people, there were actually very few people who had sufficient personal interest in their life– one way or the other–to justify the enormous risk of killing them. Most people simply weren't important enough for lots of people to want them dead, a fact which narrowed the potential universe of suspects considerably.

First to be suspected was the victim's family. Next, were the victim's co-workers or people with whom he had business dealings. Now, of course, this could raise the number of suspects dramatically, depending on your profession. A drug dealer, for obvious reasons, was more at risk from his "workplace" associates than a computer programmer, for example. Last was the person's social group. Virtually all murders–something approaching 85%–were committed by someone the victim knew.

Crime scenes told a story to experienced cops. Scenes of great violence were most likely between people who knew each other well; too well, as it turned out, for one of them. Stabbing was a "personal" way to kill someone. The impulse to get close enough to cut someone, to make them bleed–was an impulse of passion, of anger. A gunshot wound to the back of the head told the opposite story–the killer was dispassionate, all business–there was no inclination to make the victim suffer or seek a confrontation, only to make sure the job was done. In most cases, it was because the murder was a business arrangement, occasionally it was powerful evidence that the murderer was afraid of the victim.

Real robberies had a different feel to them than staged robberies–where it was more likely the victim's stuff would be trashed–again mostly because it was acting as a cover for a crime of passion. Real burglars were methodical, professional; the last thing they wanted was an interaction with a human or animal that might complicate things. Burglars didn't spend a lot of time emptying drawers and piling stuff on the floor—dead-giveaways to the returning homeowner that they'd been there. The longer it took for a burglary to be detected, the better. So they kept it clean, they kept it quiet.

"Lieutenant?" A young uniform called him over. "Victim's name was Antwone Green. Wallet is missing. Some jewelry seems to be missing from a box in the bedroom, presents taken from under the tree. The uniform gestured to a garishly decorated feather tree in the corner of the apartment. "Neighbor next door knew the vic well—said he was like a son to her—wanted to wait for you, sir. She's over here... Mrs. Dendra Jones, sir."

Harrison stepped out of the apartment to where an elderly woman with an enormous scoliosis hump hovered in front of the hallway door. She looked like a question mark.

"Mrs. Jones?" inquired Harrison politely, extending his hand, "I'm Lieutenant Harrison." He could see the elderly woman had been crying.

"Antwone was the nicest boy," she said, a sob catching in her throat.

"Yes, ma'am," said Harrison, respectfully. He noticed there was an intelligent glint in Mrs. Jones' eyes.

"I just can't believe this has happened. He used to buy my cat food, you know. A special brand. You can't buy it at the grocery. Organic. My cat has diabetes...like everybody else around here," she said, waving her hand impatiently to include some of the elderly African American residents gathered in the hallway. "The store's too far for me to walk. He used to go all the way out there in his car to get it for me. Did you know cats get diabetes, Lieutenant Harrison?"

"No, ma'am I did not," Harrison replied courteously.

"Well, now you know," she said, nodding her head.

"Yes, ma'am."

There was a pause.

Harrison leaned toward the elderly woman, his voice low: "Did you notice anything unusual, Mrs. Jones? Any reason someone might want to hurt your...ah.... Mr. Green?"

Dendra Jones cocked her head to one side. "Well, sure I can," she said, as Harrison and the plainclothes taking notes straightened with surprise.

"It was that crazy young fella Antwone was always mooning after that was causing problems for people," she paused. "People at the church," she said knowingly. Dendra Jones could see that Harrison was disconcerted.

"I didn't tell the other one when he asked," she said gesturing to the detective inside the apartment. "And may be I'd be better off not telling you now. I'm sure that's the sensible thing. But the sensible thing ain't always the right thing. He was a lovely boy, you know," she said, and she started to cry softly.

Harrison knew he needed to press her. "Mrs. Jones, please, I need to understand who you think might have done this," he said.

Dendra Jones turned her tortured spine to look Harrison in the eye.

"He was a sweet boy, you understand?" she said, as if challenging him to disagree. "Always taking care of people, doing his best. Kind. That was Antwone Green." She paused for a moment, as if wondering how much she wanted to say. She looked at Harrison levelly. She considered him a moment appraisingly, then she spoke. "Didn't like girls, you understand?"

"Yes, ma'am," he replied, with studied seriousness.

She nodded, pleased that he hadn't interrupted.

"Liked boys...funny like that from the time he was just a little guy—always getting into his mother's things. Didn't choose nothing, you understand? It was just the way the good Lord made him."

"Yes, ma'am," Harrison replied deferentially, nodding his head.

Dendra Jones had something on her mind.

"Gay—they call them gay! When I was growing up—well, gay meant something different—happy, fun, joyful," she laughed without mirth—a great sadness in her eyes.

"What was so gay about it? Looking for men to have sex with in public toilets? There wasn't nothing gay about his life—you understand me?" Again, she looked Harrison directly in the eye, challenging him to disagree or demur.

"He should have gone someplace—someplace where they would accept him—maybe he could have been with someone—had a real relationship. You know, a partnership—like Oprah and that nice Gayle. Been happy. But his whole life was being choirmaster of that church, so he kept it under cover. But you could see it was eating at him just the same." She shook her head sadly. "Antwone was never himself, you see. Then he lost his head over that young man—some runaway he found at the bus station. Before you knew it, he got him a job, got him cleaned up and had him singing with the choir." She paused, considering:

"Oh, Antwone was crazy about him." She closed her eyes as

if remembering. "Handsome is as handsome does, they say—but I'd be lyin' if I told you different. He was a mighty good-looking boy." She sniffed dismissively. "But *that* one. He was just no good. He had his sights set on an altogether bigger fish. Took up with somebody he shouldn't have." She looked at Harrison meaningfully. "Somebody that can't have any talk." She paused, considering. "And now, most likely, they're both dead."

Harrison exchanged glances with the plainclothes. He noted with approval that the man was taking detailed notes.

"Mrs. Jones—Do you know the name of the young man?" Harrison asked quietly.

"Kevin. That's all. If he told me the last, I don't remember it. Didn't have no reason to. Good looking," she replied, "but trouble, just like I said. Everybody 'round here knows him. Disappeared about a month ago, supposedly on a fancy vacation in the Caribbean." Her waggling eyebrows expressed the full measure of her skepticism of this scenario.

"And you have reason to believe that's not true?" Harrison asked pointedly.

She harrumphed. "Only the sense the Good Lord saw fit to give me after 86 years, I guess. A 22 year-old boy who ain't got two cents to rub together starts making a fuss about being in love with an older man. A married man. A connected man. A man with a lot of hard friends that have big plans about how he's going to help them get ahead." She paused, her voice full of cynicism. "And all of a sudden with no goodbyes to anyone, he's gone for a long vacation on some island?" she questioned. "Who's paying for that?"

She paused, as if considering: "Who around here has money

like that?" She shook her head, looking like a wise old owl.

"More likely, he's wearing a pair of concrete shoes in Lake Superior than swanning around sipping umbrella drinks in the tropics, if you ask me."

A black and white cat with a black patch over its right eye walked down the hallway and started winding its tail between the elderly woman's legs. She passed a trembling hand over her eyes, obviously exhausted.

"Mrs. Jones—would you prefer to sit?" Harrison asked solicitously.

She brushed aside his concern with a weary attempt at a smile.

"Don't make no never mind to me—this spine pains me something terrible, one way or t'other," she replied.

The plainclothes brought her a chair. Harrison continued

"And the victim..." he quickly consulted his notes.

"....ahhhhh Mr. Green. He suspected somebody at the church?"

Dendra Jones shook her head in disgust.

"That boy," she replied, her voice pregnant with motherly aggravation. "He didn't suspect nobody. Never did."

She paused thoughtfully. "But he would have figured it out, I expect—same as me...given time." She thought for a moment as if struck by an idea.

"And he wasn't the quiet type when there was trouble, neither."

"Yes, I gathered that," Harrison said with a smile.

Dendra Jones laughed, remembering.

"No, sir, Antwone Green was not quiet. Antwone Green was

brave like a lion. Always stood up to the bullies. If anyone did a bad thing—well, he'd have his say around it." She shook her head sadly.

"Antwone loved him; that Kevin, he was a bad boy— but Antwone loved him just the same."

Harrison waited politely as Mrs. Jones dried her eyes with a rumpled tissue. "Mrs. Jones, I need you to come down to the station with me and make a statement. Will you do that?" Dendra Jones shook her head, tiredly.

"No, sir. This has been a long day and I'm an old woman with a friend to mourn." Her eyes were filled with a deep sadness.

Harrison persisted. The statement was important.

"You could come with me right now, which I would prefer..."

Mrs. Jones smiled and shook her head, 'no.'

"...or I could send a car for you tomorrow, if that would be better."

He hated to delay, but it was late and the elderly woman was nearly fainting with fatigue.

Dendra Jones nodded her head slowly.

"That would be best," she said simply.

May I have Sergeant Timmons see you to your apartment?"

"Well, I would take that very kindly," she answered almost coquettishly. The sergeant escorted her to her apartment next door, the cat keeping stately pace beside them.

Harrison turned to the plainclothes. "Fisher—please get all Mrs. Jones' information and have her sign a preliminary statement. Make arrangements for her to come down to the station tomorrow. Let's make sure she's comfortable, okay?"

"Yes, sir. No problem."

"Have you guys been interviewing the other tenants? Anybody else coming up with this line?"

"No, sir, not that I've heard, sir, but I'll get right on it."

"Good. Oh, and Fisher? While you're at it, see if anybody's seen any of The Minister's ahh...security team around here lately."

Fisher looked at him knowingly, but his voice was carefully expressionless. "Yes, sir. Right away, sir."

Chapter Eleven

Chicago, Illinois

To Harrison, and many others in the Chicago Police Department, The Minister's private security force, known as the "Guard," were goons plain and simple, never mind their choir boy expressions and buttoned up uniform of coat and tie. These guys were tough, repeat offenders schooled on the mean streets. They had very little in common with the conventional muscle-bound, overfed, and slow-witted men who usually found jobs as 'security' to the rich and famous. Harrison had had reason to run into them on more than one occasion. What worried him, when it didn't infuriate him, was that The Minister's "bodyguards" were allowed to carry concealed weapons anywhere they wanted. Sure, any celebrity might have a bodyguard or two—but The Minister basically operated a private army who made it their business to be as intimidating as hell. Nobody else would ever get away with it. Of course, it hadn't started out like that.

Initially, they had refused to carry weapons. Calling themselves the Guard of Jehovah, they claimed to believe they were protected by their righteousness. Less well publicized, but perhaps equally useful, was the judo and military training they received at Elijah Farms–a 5,000-acre training facility and commune the Guard operated in southwest Georgia. Regardless, their role was controversial–even among African Americans. It was true that most of the guards were recruited from prisons and detention centers. However, in a very real sense, the Ministry had demonstrated its ability to reform men on whom the criminal justice system had given up. Clearly, too, the Guard had repeatedly succeeded where conventional police forces had failed, and failed miserably.

The Guard's 24/7 strategy of remaining on-site in the projects where they were deployed allowed them to clean up areas that had been hopelessly drug-infested for years—sometimes in a matter of weeks. More than that, their policy of not using weapons in the residential projects caught their adversaries off-guard. If they found people within the complex selling drugs, they evicted them. They went through basements, laundry rooms, hallways, and stairways and cleared them of loiterers or suspected bad actors. People in the projects were more likely to perceive them as the "good guys" rather than just another armed band. They practiced abstinence, famously refraining from alcohol, tobacco, or drugs. In the early mornings, they appeared in the central courtyard and did calisthenics in unison. Later, in the afternoons, they jogged through the projects, chanting. Lastly, they had provided the community with powerful male role models of civility and respect (addressing the project's inhabitants as ma'am or sir –or if younger—brother and sister), initiative, and in a very real sense, power.

Typically, men with power were not hanging out in the projects unless they were drug dealers. Success for kids in the projects meant finding a way out—and unless they had a talent for sports—that pretty much meant running drugs. The Guard gave the kids an alternate version of success to aspire to. These guys were tough, they were respected, and they were enforcing the law. It was as if the Lone Ranger had appeared on the South Side of Chicago, and he was black!

Of course, there had been problems. Allegations of abuse and heavy-handedness had surfaced over and over. One suspected drug dealer, who had shown a disinclination to absent himself from the projects, was beaten nearly to death by seven guards with flashlights. The regular police claimed, with some justification, that the Ministry's forces were responsible for flagrant instances of brutality that would never have been tolerated had they been committed by a municipal police force. However, community outcry was muted. Possibly because the project's residents saw the Ministry's forces as being a part of their community, instead of something controlled by outsiders, the residents kept silent. It spoke powerfully to the reason the Chicago P.D. continued to hold so little sway in the community after years of outreach. Harrison hated to admit it, but it was true. The Guard was viewed as an integral part of the community in a way the police never had been. You don't rat on your own. And you don't rat on people who are trying to help you.

Lost amid the accusations and finger pointing, Harrison knew, was the harsh reality that the police didn't want to secure the projects. Chicago housing projects like Cabrini Green and Robert Taylor were war zones. New Year's was celebrated by hundreds of gang members firing their guns in the air, forcing the police to block off entire neighborhoods whose residents would otherwise be at risk from falling bullets. Balconies intended for the residents' tomato plants and plastic beach chairs had to be enclosed with steel fencing to keep the residents from disposing of their garbage—or each other—over the edge. By the 1990s, most members of the Chicago Police Department refused even to enter some of the projects. Called to investigate a robbery or rape, policemen were being killed by snipers waiting in ambush.

But, in the end, the positive actions of the Guard didn't matter. When the bureaucrats started to receive the inevitable complaints from the Anti-Defamation League, the fact that the church was virulently anti-Semitic had eventually caused the Guard to lose their government contracts to police the projects. As news of the contracts seeped out, public outcry picked up, and the governmental decision makers who had quietly awarded the contracts realized immediately that the Guard had outlived their usefulness. True—they could be a powerful force for good in the community, but it was also true that they preached a doctrine of empowerment that was only partly focused on self-reliance. Critics alleged it was focused in equal measure on advocating revenge and retribution for perceived racial wrongs, and that ended up scaring a lot of nervous white folks in Winnetka.

While acknowledging that the Guard had, at times, been overzealous, supporters countered that if the Guard had sometimes played a little fast and loose with civil rights, they had also restored law and order in what was essentially a war zone.

More than that, the Guard's advocates argued, the Guard was responsible for rehabilitating dangerous felons into productive members of society and providing the oft-cited inner city "youth" with positive role models of industry and discipline. Well, so – the Anti-Defamation League argued—did the Nazi brown shirts. Creating an alternate power structure in a democracy—state sponsored vigilantism—was always a dicey proposition. Creating one that might be preaching hate and supporting racial cleansing was particularly problematic.

What they really feared creating, Harrison thought, was what the pro-western or moderate governments in the Middle East were experiencing today. The Saudis had used the radical Wahhabi groups as a means to control a restless, disenfranchised segment of the population—believing that by doing so, they could bring them into the society, make them productive. The planners had been confident that these men would see for themselves the benefits of an open and free society.

But somehow it had gone badly wrong, and what any observer of the news would deduce, Harrison thought, was that the Middle Eastern oligarchies had begun to realize that they did not control the movement, the movement now controlled them. They had taken the most economically and socially disadvantaged—and therefore the most psychologically vulnerable—and turned them over to leaders who demanded total, unquestioning loyalty. The loyalty of this private army was to the group and their leaders, not to the state or the democracy.

It was axiomatic, Harrison thought, that any revolutionary group would end up taken over by their most radical members. And make no mistake, he thought, African Americans agitating for civil rights had been revolutionaries. Eventually, advocates of moderation were swept aside in virtually every revolutionary movement in world history—the French and Russian revolutions, communists in China, Korea, Vietnam, the Khmer Rouge in Cambodia, the Islamofascists in Iran—all had started as moderate movements seeking reform—sometimes from within the existing governments. However, inexorably, incrementally, the bourgeois leaders were replaced and the group's goals and objectives became increasingly more radical over time. In virtually every instance, the "founders" found themselves brushed away, pushed aside to make room for men with more far-reaching and game-changing agendas.

Harrison considered himself a history buff, and he knew from the survey courses he'd taken, that historians considered the American Revolution as one of the singular exceptions to the rule. Their argument was that it served as a model of (relatively) bloodless regime change—at least the victors did not turn on the population for ritualized 'cleansing', as had taken place in other countries. That the revolution did not precipitate class warfare —perhaps with the sole exception of the Whiskey Rebellion— was largely the result of the American colonists' perception that the "class" that was persecuting them was an ocean away. After all, large landowners in Virginia were just as inconvenienced by the stamp tax as yeomen in Boston. Class distinctions in America were not institutionalized the way they were in Russia, China, or India.

One distinction America did observe, however, was that of color—specifically any color not white—and that had always been, Harrison thought, the fault-line of the American democracy.

People were fond of saying that the Founding Fathers, who in the Constitution guaranteed equal protection for all men under the law—counted some of those men as only three-fifths of a person. But that promoted a profound misunderstanding of the three-fifths provision, Harrison thought. Counting the slaves never conferred any rights on those fractionated people, nor was it ever intended to do so. In any organization run by majority rule, numbers count. Counting the slaves —by any metric—served as a mechanism engineered by southern slaveholders to secure the equal dominion (and voting power) in the new nation of the darkly populated south with the more whitely populated north.

Of course, as Harrison's sister was fond of reminding him, women—slave or free— were simply not counted at all. So, in a very real sense, the other fault line of the American Experiment was gender. Abigail Adams had urged the irascible John to "remember the ladies"— but probably like so many admonitions of wives to husbands—this had fallen on deaf ears. Historians liked to make note of the comment—not to applaud it, as they did an abolitionist minister castigating Jefferson about the evils of slavery—but to show what a 'character' Abigail Adams had been. Apparently, even great men like Adams had been forced to contend with a nagging wife.

The Founding Fathers were rightly faulted for not considering more closely the morality of keeping millions of the new republic's black citizens in bondage, and yet seldom had these same moralists stopped to consider that the mothers, wives, sisters, and daughters of those esteemed and learned men had virtually no rights at all.

But, Harrison reflected, history had shown that perceptions

could change. "Red" Indians, who had been scorned in the days of Jackson (when their armies of warriors could still decimate white colonies), were sentimentally eulogized—even revered—by the time of Roosevelt and the new century. The explanation was simple: they had ceased to pose a threat. A hundred and ten years after Culloden, Queen Victoria decorated her castle in wall-to-wall plaid (plaids, whose appearance on a Highlander would have meant death seventy years before). Eighty years after the Civil War, even the antebellum South was rehabilitated with popular fiction and movies devoted to the graceful beauty of a system many had reviled as putrid and decaying decades before. Why, Harrison reflected, do people memorialize, even idealize, what they've worked so hard to destroy?

Harrison wasn't really worried that the Guard was fomenting revolution. He thought fears of the Guard as anti-Semitic 'Black radicals' probably missed the point. His concerns about the Guard had more to do with the way they currently operated than any incendiary statements they'd made in the past. Because, despite their idealistic start, by the 1990s the Guard of Jehovah had morphed into a good deal more than volunteers policing the mean streets, or the Ministry's personal security detail.

They had become an autonomous paramilitary security service—a virtual army—frequently hired by high profile African American entertainers, lawyers, and underworld kingpins. They were everywhere, in major cities across the United States: Baltimore, Boston, Chicago, Dallas, Dayton, Detroit, Los Angeles, New York, Philadelphia, Pittsburgh, and D.C. And they were packing. The U.S. Department of Defense had estimated in a memo to the Chicago Police Department that the Guard of

Jehovah had 20,000 'uniformed' troops, all carrying state of the art weapons.

Fair enough, Harrison reflected. Righteousness would only get the Guard so far when well-financed drug runners had arsenals more sophisticated than most countries. But the Guard not only acted outside the law, there were allegations that they acted as if they were above the law, as well. Most people in the projects considered the prepositions irrelevant. To them, the Guard simply was the law.

His cell rang. It was Fisher.

"Sir, Mrs. Jones wasn't at her apartment when we arrived to pick her up today." Harrison was instantly alert.

"No?" Harrison struggled for calm.

"No, sir, and nobody's seen her since last night, either. She didn't have any family, sir. Nobody to see to her—and she was pretty frail."

"Did you check inside?" Harrison asked.

"Yes, sir. Manager gave us the key. No sign of disturbance. Everything neat and tidy," Fisher replied.

"You've checked with the neighbors? Has anybody spoken with her?"

"Yes, sir," Fisher replied. "Nobody has seen or spoken to her her since yesterday."

"Anybody hear anything? See anything?" Harrison was grasping at straws.

"No, sir. As I said, we've checked with neighbors on the whole floor, and we've started canvassing the other apartments in the complex. If anybody saw anything, so far, at least, they're not telling us. But..."

“Yes...?” Harrison prompted.

“All the neighbors did agree on one thing, sir,” Fisher paused.

“Yeah?” Harrison prompted. “What?”

“They’re sure she didn’t leave on her own.”

Harrison considered. “How can they be so sure?” he asked.

“She left her cat.”

CHAPTER TWELVE

January 2008
Georgetown, Washington, D.C.

HE'D DECIDED TO ATTEND THE PARTY AFTER ALL, mostly just to be polite. The primary consideration had been that he was sleeping with the hostess—although, when he thought about it, he wasn't always sure why. Athena Dendridge worked hard at being perfect. First, of course, and perhaps most noticeably—she was one of the skinniest women in Washington. Her tiny little surgically sculpted nose was, in its way, perfect as a nose, and her voluptuous, bee-stung lips were perfectly crafted lips. With her immaculate makeup, and carefully sculpteted coiffure, she looked like an alien construct of the perfect human.

Not as obvious were the obsessive-compulsive issues that had her constantly adjusting everything in her environment. She operated in a state of constant restlessness—always waiting for the next thing, the next person. Generous, but so needy, being around her for any length of time was exhausting. Her divorce from a high-priced lobbyist would have left her comfortable—

her inheritance from a Greek shipping magnate whose exact relationship to her remained unclear—made her rich.

Athena had enough money to do whatever she wanted, and Athena loved to throw parties: mixing the intertwining Washington networks like a cocktail. A few well-known journalists would be invited for color, a few politicians for gravitas, but the majority would be the real power brokers of D.C.—the members of its exclusive clubs who ran all the lobbying, law firms and think tanks.

Oh, well, he thought to himself, he didn't have to stay long. More to the point, Athena would have good food. But as he moved through Athena's large living room, he was genuinely pleased to see an old friend across the room. She was speaking to a group he knew. He watched her animated face as she delivered the punch line to the story she was telling. As the group started to break up, he tapped her gently on the shoulder and assumed his most beatific smile.

"Max!" she was delighted to see him and happily pecked him on both checks. "I've missed you. How are you?"

He'd long since decided that if he weren't such a prick he'd be in love with her; maybe he was a little in love with her anyway.

"Better now that I've seen you, exquisite creature," he said smoothly.

"Tell the truth, you vile flatterer." She looked at him skeptically, her head tilted to one side, pretending to flutter her eyelashes at him.

Lacey Houghton had beautiful eyes.

"Careful, we'll make your husband jealous," he replied.

She laughed out loud. "Impossible."

She took his arm and led him to an open space near the bar. "It *is* good to see you."

"Everything going well? Kids, dog, suburban living?"

"Sure," she replied carefully.

"Where the hell did you move to, anyway?"

She looked at him with an air that told him she was resigned to letting him play this out.

"Rockville, was it?" he continued.

"Yes, dear," she said, still laughing at him. He missed having her in the city. They used to live in the same part of Kalorama and bump into each other with some frequency.

"And, you?" she said, her eyes full of mischief.

"I still get around," he replied with a smirk.

"Ah," she said, with a significant look at their hostess. "So I hear."

He looked at her quickly from the corner of his eye. "You don't approve?" He was surprised to find he was waiting for her answer.

"What is there to disapprove of? You're both consenting, unattached adults." Lacey, paused reflectively: "Actually, I like her enormously. She's very..." She groped for the word momentarily... unusual for Lacey.

"Kind," he supplied.

"Yes," she smiled, surprised but pleased.

Max emptied his glass, and signaled to the waiter for a refill.

He leaned over without looking at her. "You always like the kind people."

Lacey laughed, delighted: "And dogs. I do. It's a weakness. What can I tell you?" she smiled.

He looked at her closely. "I hear you've become a political animal."

Lacey smiled. "Hardly. But Claire McCracken will make a great president."

He shook his head. "I don't like her."

"Maybe you just don't like brilliant women," Lacey teased.

"I like you," he replied.

Lacey considered his answer. "True; but I'm cute....and I don't make as much money as you do." She paused, "Anyway, that kind of thinking is wrongheaded. It's not important that you *like* the president. It's not as if you're all going on a family vacation together."

Max pretended to be affronted. "I'd go if she asked. And for the record—I'd still like you, even if you made as much money as me, Lacey."

Lacey shook her head, laughing. "Not if I got to order you around."

"I dunno," Max regarded her appraisingly. "Try it. I think I might like it." He smirked, she rolled her eyes.

The waiter handed him a new glass from a silver tray. He raised his glass to him by way of saying thanks. He took a sip of his bourbon.

"Anyway, he's an asshole."

Lacey was momentarily confused. "Who?" she asked.

Max sipped his drink. "Okono," he replied.

Lacey was surprised. "Really?"

"Yup. Cold. Full of himself. Lazy as shit—just shows up for the press conferences. Ever heard him speak on the House floor?" Max questioned.

Lacey considered for a moment. "No."

"Me, neither." Max shook his head. "I'm thinking that if this guy were such a natural orator we might have noticed."

"Okay," Lacey replied, her curiosity piqued. "The guy's never done anything of merit and from what you're telling me, he's not exactly knocking himself out to change the planet now..." Max nodded. Lacey continued, "So, why is everybody in the party salivating over him?"

Max rolled his eyes as if she were being intentionally obtuse. "Jesus, Lacey, the guy's black."

Lacey was nonplussed. "Yeah, I noticed."

Max continued as if he were explaining something very basic. "And he's handsome and he went to Harvard."

"So?" Lacey replied, unimpressed, "I could think of twenty African Americans that are great looking and went to top schools who have done more than Okono."

Max laughed, a gleam in his eye. "Yeah? Well, tell them to call me. We need them to run for office."

Lacey frowned "That can't be it?"

Max raised his eyebrows and regarded her. "No? I dunno, Lacey, there's a lot of white angst in the Democratic Party."

"You mean among the rank and file?"

"Naw, they don't give a shit. I mean what you call the mandarins."

Lacey was unconvinced. "But nobody's ever heard of this guy; he's never done anything."

"You know Miller?"

"Former Democratic majority leader, ignominiously defeated in the last election?"

"That's him," Max nodded. "His entire staff are heavy hitters, been with the guy for years; major players, okay?"

"Okay."

"So their guy gets defeated, these staffers could go anywhere, everybody in Congress wants them."

"Okay."

"So, who do they go to work for?" Max took a sip of his drink. "Let me amend that. Who do they, all, *en masse*, go to work for?"

"Okono?"

"Right. Explain that to me, because I've never seen it happen. A freshman congressman with no high-profile committee chairmanships, no status, gets handed the entire staff of the most senior, most experienced Democrat on Capitol Hill."

"You're right," Lacey agreed. "It seems weird."

"It's more than weird." Max lowered his voice, "It's unprecedented, and on Capitol Hill, nothing's unprecedented."

"So what do you think is going on?"

Max shrugged, then reflected a moment. "Well, there *is* something else..." he said it almost as an after-thought.

"What?" Lacey asked.

"Staffers like that get paid good money. They're not 20-year-old kids who can afford to be idealistic. They're older; they've got kids, mortgages. Freshmen congressmen ordinarily never have any dough, they could never afford those guys. But, somehow that hasn't been a problem for Okono." Max shook his head in amazement. "The guy has more money tailing him than I've ever seen in politics."

Max helped himself to a tiny hamburger from a passing tray. Lacey shook her head. "Claire McCracken is more qualified; she's worked hard, she knows the issues. She's the real deal, Max."

"Lesbian," Max winked. He was starting to enjoy himself.

Lacey was outraged. "She's not a lesbian!"

"No?" Max responded, trying to keep a straight face.

Lacey was aggravated "She's not, and you know it. Why can't we embrace the idea that women of intellect and industry come in all shapes and sizes? It should– theoretically– be possible, for a woman to be strong and powerful and ambitious without being somehow–masculinized because she hasn't chosen a traditionally 'feminine' role. And if she were a lesbian, it shouldn't make a difference, anyway."

"Is 'masculinized' a word?" Max teased.

She glowered at him and crossed her arms.

"Okay, okay," he held up a hand in truce.

"We agree," Max replied. "Claire is not a lesbian," he paused for effect, "...but don't tell me all those bull dykes at the DNC aren't lesbians."

Lacey knew when to concede a point.

"No, they're definitely lesbians...but they're all for Okono, anyway," she added a little dejectedly.

"And Oprah, right?" Max persisted.

She regarded him, eyebrow raised. "Max, is it possible that you are still addicted to daytime TV after all these years?" Official Washington always had its sets tuned to CNN–theoretically–so that it was on top of developing news stories, but Hill staffers in particular were notorious for switching the channel to soaps and talk shows when their congressmen were out of the office.

Max looked hurt. "Really, Lacey, you make it sound like... porn."

Lacey laughed: "It is—empowerment porn."

Max almost snurfed his drink. A passing waiter offered him a napkin, which he used to wipe the wet beads of bourbon off his bespoke suit.

Lacey shrugged her shoulders, in mock protest "What is it with everybody's fascination with Oprah's sexuality lately?" she asked curiously. "Anyway, I'm the wrong person to ask. I've seen Oprah's show maybe twice in my life." She laughed. "I'm not really qualified to discuss her personal life."

Max was enjoying himself. "Pretty suspicious with that girlfriend always around and she's been engaged to sensitive Stedman for what—like—thirty-five years?"

Lacey was clearly uninterested. "Something. Look. I don't care if they're all gay, or none of them are gay. It shouldn't make any difference. The point is, y'all use it to undermine them. What is so scary about lesbians anyway?"

Max pretended to be astonished. "You've only seen Oprah twice? Oprah rocks." He sipped his bourbon, and looked thoughtful. "Although, I admit it, I like Ellen, too."

Lacey put her hand on her hip and regarded him coolly.

"Okay." Max raised his hand in mock surrender. "I'll concede all that. It only matters, because in a national election you can't get elected if you're gay. So it's all very well if you don't care, and I don't care—but the bottom line is that a lot of people in Boise, in Scranton, in San Antonio— well, they really do care."

She looked at him skeptically, considering.

"So you think McCracken is losing because people think she's a lesbian?" she asked.

Max sipped his bourbon. “Well, why do *you* think she’s losing?”

“I think what *you* think, but you’re not saying—that McCracken is smarter, tougher, and a genuine leader, but she’s losing because she’s running a lousy campaign and Okono’s campaign is like a machine. I think the media loves its new shiny boy-toy Okono, but he’s an empty suit. I think the back-story—and the Okono people have been brilliant at exploiting this— is to paint Claire as a man-slaying bitch. And, of course I think the irony is that she’s probably a much warmer, nicer person than he is.”

Max fixed her with a level gaze. “Okay. So, fix it.”

He had obviously taken her by surprise. “Me?” Lacey replied. “How can I fix it? I don’t work for the campaign. I’m just a volunteer who’s organized a few bloggers.”

“Oh, Lacey...” Max started to laugh.

“What?” she asked defensively.

“You forget I know you. How many?’”

“How many what?”

“How many bloggers has ‘little you’ organized?”

“A few,” she replied

“Lacey, don’t be coy. Give me a number.”

“One hundred and ninety three,” she answered, staring hard into her drink.

Max chuckled. “And they blog...how often?”

Her voice was muffled by the glass. “Every day.”

“Lacey!” he shook his head at her, and laughed. She was laughing now, too, in spite of herself. “Some of them, I think, all day,” she admitted sheepishly.

He made a decision.

"Lacey—I'm going to call you tomorrow. What's the best number to reach you?"

CHAPTER THIRTEEN

Chicago, Illinois

HARRISON SAT AT HIS DESK and concentrated on his steepled fingers. The reports from the black & whites who'd canvassed the residential unit were sitting on his desk in front of him. Pieced together, they told a strange story. Antwone Green, 42, former teacher, former choirmaster of the Jehovah's Family Ministry, had no complicated business dealings, no suggestion of drug use or illegal activity of any kind. Both parents deceased, three siblings who worked professional jobs in the Illinois suburbs—no indication of financial dealings between them, saw each other occasionally and for holidays, calls from them were on Green's answering machine. No indication of bad blood or hard feelings. Airtight alibis for all three.

All said the same thing. Green was the baby and they'd all worried about the health implications of his lifestyle, urging him to settle down with one partner. The sister was on-record as saying the church was full of 'haters' and wished he'd chosen someplace else to invest his time, but none of the others were even regular churchgoers. They'd all heard of Kevin DuShane; the sister had met him once. Nice young man, she thought—if perhaps a little immature and over-dramatic. She thought her brother had a crush on DuShane, but doubted things had ever been physical between them.

For his part, DuShane had disappeared without a trace. The rent on his apartment was paid for the next four months—cash had been slipped through the landlord's mail slot with a note explaining he would be away for a while. They were still tracing him through Customs to see if or when he'd left the country. The Guard of Jehovah were seen regularly around Green's housing unit and at least three separate residents had seen them in Green's apartment complex that afternoon.

Jay Johnson stuck his head in the door. Harrison regarded him with a pained expression.

"Wait. I'll be right back," he said as he disappeared out the door. He reappeared five minutes later, closing the door behind him. With some fanfare, he deposited three bottles of pomegranate juice and three bottles of prune juice on Harrison's desk.

"Drink," he said with authority. As Harrison started to protest, he raised his hand.

"Don't think I don't know the signs. My wife is seven months pregnant. I know that look. Now, drink."

After Harrison finished the second bottle, Johnson made himself comfortable in one of Harrison's well-worn office chairs.

"Out of curiosity, how many days?" Johnson asked.

Harrison knew there was no point in dissembling. "Four, not counting today,"

Johnson started to laugh. He reached over and gave an unwilling Harrison a high five.

"You are the iron man!" he announced. "Five days?" Johnson shook his head in disbelief. "That deserves some kind of award."

Johnson paused, looking at his friend critically. "Man, haven't you ever heard of Metamucil?"

Harrison replied stoically. "It's for old people. I'd prefer not to discuss this, actually."

Johnson hooted. "It's not for *old people*. It's for people who got *old shit* stuck to their insides."

Harrison telegraphed a warning look. "It's not a big deal."

Johnson was enjoying his friend's discomfiture. "Five days? Five days? Who the hell goes five days without taking a dump?"

"Whatever," Harrison answered.

Johnson was now howling with laughter.

"You dumb-son-of-a-bitch, you're lucky you didn't explode!"

Harrison was starting to laugh in spite of himself. The thing about Johnson was, his good humor was contagious. They had started together on the neighborhood beat; Johnson had always had his back. Brash and irreverent, Johnson's sense of humor had gotten him in trouble with the top brass on more than one occasion. But Johnson was a great cop for all that, smart, industrious, and a very astute reader of human nature. He had become a good friend.

Johnson was probably the one cop with whom Harrison knew he could be honest. He shook his head wearily. "It's this case. I'm lucky I haven't developed hives."

Johnson looked sympathetic. "Pressure from the overhead?" he asked. Harrison knew Johnson thought most of the C.P.D. hierarchy was worthless.

Harrison rubbed his forehead. "Yeah, you could say." He threw Johnson a file across the desk

"Antwone Green. The original coroner's report concluded suicide."

He could tell Johnson was dismayed.

"You're shittin' me?"

Harrison shook his head impatiently. "I wish I was shitting you. I wish I was shitting at all."

Johnson was perplexed. "How could a gunshot wound to the back of the head be self-inflicted?"

"Good question," Harrison replied. "Here's another: this guy was a regular Joe. No priors. No complications. No drugs. No money."

Johnson was flipping through the file. "But somebody took out a professional hit on him..." Johnson concluded.

"Right. Why? And everybody at City Hall is apparently creaming themselves to get this thing resolved...yesterday. Why the interest?" Harrison wondered aloud.

Johnson considered the angles. "Well, there's always pressure to clean up high profile cases; it's been on the news. The chief takes an interest when the mayor takes an interest..."

"...when The Minister takes an interest..." Harrison left it hanging in the air.

"Jesus, not that creep?" Johnson was not a fan, apparently.

"The vic was the choirmaster at the Jehovah Ministry."

Johnson whistled, his eyes wide.

"Okay," Johnson conceded, "no wonder you're eating Rolaids like candy."

"It's a problem," said Harrison.

"It's a problem," Johnson agreed, nodding his head.

In addition to their incredible ability to put pressure on everyone from the governor on down, the Jehovah Ministry had tentacles everywhere—most officers would acknowledge—even within the Chicago Police Department. If the Ministry was involved—and that was looking increasingly likely—there was a real question of who in the department Harrison would be able to trust. And it wouldn't just be police officers whose integrity he would be forced to question, but everyone from the coroner's office to the D.A.

"So why am I calling Customs trying to track down some vacationer? What's his name?" Johnson asked.

"Kevin DuShane," Harrison reminded him, "friend of the vic. Apparently he was having an affair with somebody in the church and they thought he should be a little...quieter."

Johnson frowned. "I see. You getting calls?"

"Sure. Not threatening," Harrison laughed. "Nice, helpful calls. 'Tell us how we can help.' That kind of thing."

Johnson made a gagging noise in his throat.

"Anyone suggest taking over for you?"

Harrison chuckled at his friend's perspicacity.

"Roland, yesterday morning—said he had a light case load—said he was supposed to be on that night."

"And was he?" Johnson inquired.

"Not according to the duty roster," Harrison replied.

"He had to know you'd check..."

"Would *he* check?" Harrison asked. Roland was considered about the laziest detective on the force.

"Good point," conceded Johnson with a grin. "So what are we going to do?" Johnson wasn't giving up.

"Not 'we'. 'Me.' Frankly, this is probably a career killer either way it plays out. I don't want you to have any part in it."

Johnson looked aggrieved. "So that's why I haven't seen you in three days?"

"Something." Harrison looked at his partner sheepishly.

Johnson was annoyed. "You seem to be forgetting something." Harrison could tell Johnson was getting ready to lay into him.

"No," Harrison replied, eager to nip the conversation in the bud. "*You* are forgetting something. Like the three little kids—and the one on the way—you have at home. If someone ends up disgraced, or losing their job, or worse, you can't be part of that. I only answer to myself. If I go down, well, the damage ends there."

Johnson regarded him coolly. "Been thinking about this, I see?"

"Of course." Harrison didn't look at Johnson.

Johnson opted for another tack. "Look—did this guy off himself?"

"No, obviously not," Harrison replied.

Johnson continued his questioning. "Was he a bad dude—someone who deserved the wrong end of a .44?"

Harrison smiled. "Nice to little old ladies with cats."

Johnson persisted. "But I should walk away? Drop the investigation of a good guy that gets murdered by a bad guy?" He paused, giving Harrison time to absorb his argument. "Maybe I'm missing something, but isn't that sort of my job description? What I get paid for?" he asked plaintively.

Harrison sighed. "Look, we know how it works in this town.

Somebody at our pay grade that screws with the Ministry is not going to...well, let's just say—I'm not likely to end up riding a float wearing a medal."

Johnson looked Harrison straight in the eye, holding his gaze. "You're right. I know how it works in this town. And if I didn't want to be here, I would have made that decision a long time ago." Johnson picked up the file and starting leafing through it. "Anyway, we're getting ahead of ourselves here. We don't really know what went down, and until we do, I'm hanging tight. If you want me off this case, you can transfer me. Okay? We got that settled? Now, drink your prune juice."

Harrison smiled in spite of his concern. "Yes, sir."

CHAPTER FOURTEEN

Rockville, Maryland

THE PACKAGE ARRIVED IN A KINKO'S BOX by messenger, the gold foil address label in the upper left corner identified it as being from Max's office on 12th and F. Inside on top was a copy of a FOIA request in Lacey's name from the Federal Elections Committee. The request was backdated to four weeks ago. Attached was a copy of a document from the FEC sent to the Okono campaign alerting them to possible instances of suspicious (or in some cases clearly fraudulent) campaign contributions, and asking them to investigate and take immediate action.

The first document outlined individual instances of improper campaign contributions—contributors who had gone over the $2,300 individual limit. Many of these individuals had provided obviously phony names and addresses—and some were over the limit by thousands—in some cases tens of thousands—of dollars.

As Lacey started to read, she saw the names were listed alphabetically. The list went on for pages—nearly 300 pages.

Underneath the first bound copy was a second—this was a list of contributors the FEC had identified as problematic because they were apparently from overseas. There were 13,176 of these contributors.

Under U.S. federal law, only U.S. citizens are allowed to contribute to U.S. presidential campaigns. This is done to prevent foreign governments from using campaign dollars to woo U.S. candidates. Most presidential election campaigns (including McCracken's and the Republicans') had mechanisms in place to flag these contributions immediately and request further documentation, usually a copy of a valid U.S. passport. Confirmation was still difficult. The campaigns had no way to interface with the State Department to verify the documents provided were authentic. But the obligation was on the campaign to verify that the contributor was American. By law, foreign nationals were strictly prohibited from contributing—in any amount—to U.S. elections.

When a supporter wanted to make a contribution to a political candidate, the campaign was required by law to verify their name, address, and the name of their employer. For this reason, most political candidates utilized the services of a company in Arlington, Virginia, who had developed a software program called an "address verification system" or AVS. As soon as the contribution was logged, the candidate's system ran a check with the credit card company to verify that the address given was correct. This cost the campaign exactly twelve cents. If the address on the credit card matched the name and address on the donation form, the money was accepted. If not, it was rejected and flagged for someone in the campaign to follow up on. The campaign would then send a letter to the donor using the address provided and request more documentation. Under FEC rules, the campaign was required to make publicly available the name of anyone who had contributed $200 or more. Anything less than that was exempt from record-keeping requirements.

The easiest way to scam the system—whether you were a U.S. citizen or not—was to use pre-paid credit cards to make repeated contributions below the $200 reporting limit. Since using a pre-paid card meant that the systems had no way to match the donor's name to an address, the data processing/AVS systems utilized by the campaigns of McCracken and the Republican Joe Malloy immediately rejected these contributions. Not the Okono campaign. For whatever reason, the Okono campaign, despite repeated notices, and lots of hand wringing by the FEC, had declined to put a safety net in place to track these contributions. According to the report, two brothers from Palestine had apparently contributed more than $24,321 over six months by this mechanism.

In previous election cycles, these violations had been easily tracked and remedied before they had spun out of control. However, with Okono's emphasis on an internet strategy for raising and collecting previously unheard of sums—the FEC was literally months behind in tracking suspicious contributions—and those were just the itemized contributions. They had no handle at all on the majority of the contributions the Okono campaign received, those under the $200 reporting limit.

The Okono campaign claimed they were overwhelmed by the flood of contributions and could not police the system themselves—and their media supporters made sympathetic noises as they conveniently forgot, or forgot to report, that the campaign was legally obligated to do so. If a campaign couldn't track the money, they were obligated not to accept it, until they could process it according to election law. And the Okono campaign curiously had no trouble processing the money into its bank accounts.

Odd money amounts, or donations ending in odd cents–something like $42.89, for example—aroused suspicion because they suggested the very real possibility that the donation had been made in a foreign currency and then converted into dollars. For a candidate like Okono, who had made repeated calls to "limit the role of money in politics," Lacey knew the information provided in the FEC printouts was explosive stuff. She called Connor on his cell.

"Hey—I need your help. We need to get something to someone in the press."

CHAPTER FIFTEEN

Oglethorpe, Georgia

FROM PLANTING TO HARVEST, it would take almost five months, an eternity for a Georgia farmer used to the promiscuous fertility of the state's red soil. After much discussion and consideration, they'd planted Peruvian Runners—or simply 'runner beans' as the easiest to grow and the easiest to sell. The peanuts were planted after what (they hoped) was the last frost in late April. The first seedlings pushed through the soil in ten days. The plant that started to emerge, on which so many hopes now converged, was bushy and vigorous-looking with bright green oval leaves. In about forty days, yellow flowers appeared. Two months later the cylindrical green pegs that would become peanuts had formed and started to push themselves into the finely grained Georgia soil. If the soil remained at a consistent sixty-five to seventy degrees Fahrenheit, the shells and kernels inside would start to mature in the next month, about forty pods per plant.

The croppers inspected their fields every day to make sure the plants were developing according to the diagrams the land agent for the county had provided Miss Amalia. They watched the fields like overanxious parents, breathing a sigh of relief as the broad green nyctinastic leaves closed as the sun went down, like sleepy children closing their eyes at bedtime. So many worried men came to the big house, slapping their denim overalls free of dust at the front step, nervously rolling rumpled hats between callused hands, desperate to reassure themselves by looking again at the pictures, that Miss Amalia took to leaving them spread out on the hall table in numbered order. Miriam was given the awesome responsibility of keeping the pictures in order and making sure none disappeared. At night, Miss Amaila would find her silently sitting in the big armchair by the door. "Go on home now, Miss Miriam," she would say, giving her a few pennies. "Tell your parents you did a fine job today." Miriam was happy to help. With the money she received from Miss Amalia, and the pennies she earned for collecting pecans, she could earn the 9¢ admission to the Douglass movie theater in Macon.

Soon, there were signs that the nuts were starting to mature: changing color from a phosphorescent moony white to a warm reddish-brown. As if an alarm had sounded, everyone took to the fields. The children, the old people, no one waited to be told that every hand was needed. As Miss Amalia watched anxiously, the men worked down the rows, cutting the one and a half foot tall plants from their roots. The women followed, upending the root stalks, and exposing the goobers underneath to the drying sun. The county land agent had emphasized that once the harvest began, the most critical part of the process was to keep the peanuts away from the moist soil, as they were particularly susceptible to a lethal mold. So to ensure the soil was removed, the children followed last, sweeping the goobers with a stiff brush to remove the quickly baking soil from the drying nuts.

They were lucky and the sun shone for four days. The crunchy outer membrane turned a soft sand color as it baked in the yellow sun. Without a thresher to separate the nuts from the plants, the croppers did it by hand, row by row. The goobers were then packed in large wagons to go to the shelling plant where they would be inspected and graded. Most farms then simply sold to whoever was buying, but Miss Amalia had never particularly believed in the benefit of leaving to chance what industry and intellect could secure for certain.

In 1928, in Lancaster, Pennsylvania, a former dairyman for the Hershey Company decided to start a new candy company. When he sold his previous company in 1900 for the then unheard of price of $1 million dollars, it had made him a rich man. But Henry Burrett Reese was born to make candy. He loved to make chocolate, and he loved to eat peanut butter, and he was betting that most Americans would enjoy each flavor even more in combination. So, the H.B. Reese Candy Company was born, and within a few years was selling their chocolate and peanut butter 'penny cups' all over the United States. But all those penny cups required a lot of peanut butter, and all that peanut butter required an awful lot of peanuts (actually 540 peanuts to make 12 ounces of butter—to be exact).

After what came to be known as the "Goober Nut Party," Miss Amalia had written to the great man himself in her careful script and enquired if H. B. Reese Candy Company might be inclined to purchase one of the highest quality crops of peanuts in Georgia. As it turned out, they would, and they sent her a contract.

Macon County sits on the "Fall Line"–the geomorphic contact point between the Piedmont and the Coastal Plain, so called, transparently enough, because rivers flowing from Columbus to Augusta produce waterfalls. Less obvious was the fact that the Fall Line was the Mesozoic shoreline of the Atlantic Ocean. As such, it was one of the few places where the clay soil of the crystalline north combined with the sandy soil of the sedimentary south—creating a soil of almost perfect composition, rich in mineral deposits, fertile beyond belief—perfect for growing peanuts.

Of course, Miss Amalia had no way of *knowing* what quality of peanuts her land might producc, but she was a great believer in the power of positive thinking. She and her croppers needed the kind of break that Providence sometimes provides the righteously deserving or the white-knuckled desperate. Whatever the explanation, H.B. Reese Candy Company bought the Riverview peanuts and gave the croppers not only a fair price, but offered a contract for the following year. The peculiar upside-down plant had saved them.

Chapter Sixteen

February 2008
Chicago, Illinois

The Chicago Police Department was the second largest in the U.S.—responsible for the security of 2.8 million people. Its 15,000 employees were spread over twenty-five districts and five detective areas, each lead by a commander. Harrison belonged to BIS, or the Bureau of Investigative Services. All of them were under the control of the superintendent of police who in turn answered to the city council. It was the great irony of Chicago politics that the mayor—who had historically ruled the city like a feudal lord—actually held little power under the city's corporate charter.

Harrison had been assigned to Area 2 in the southern part of the city, known as Calumet, and a group called the Special Operations Section, or SOS. Area 2 had a nearly miraculous conviction rate and a bad reputation even then—it would eventually come out in the late 1990s that between 1971 and 1991, something like 200 suspects had been tortured to extract confessions. Internal affairs was ultimately able to document that at least 148 men—almost all of them African American—were consigned to death row as a result of confessions extracted by the "Midnight Crew from Area 2."

Because of the statute of limitations, the commander of the unit and the officers involved were not tried in criminal court, but many were facing civil cases estimated in the millions. Perhaps the worst part, or at least the part left untold, was that prosecutors had, for years, clearly ignored evidence that the suspects had been beaten. That part went untold, perhaps because the city's current mayor was then the chief prosecutor. The city council had quietly approved a settlement for the victims—$19.8 million.

When Harrison had first joined, the Special Operations Section was the most glamorous assignment in the force, but SOS's incredible successes came at a higher price than most people knew. Rumors that dirty cops were cooperating with (and stealing from) drug dealers, and participating in home invasions and kidnappings were rampant in the unit for years. The cops on the take kept a watchful eye on their honest brethren—too many contradictory reports or requests for transfer were a quick way to die in a hail of friendly fire. Good cops close to their pensions stayed silent, younger cops followed their lead. Internal Affairs was finally tipped off to what was going on by the many court appearances the cops missed. 'The Crew from Area 2' were intentionally allowing criminals with whom they were in cahoots to go free on technicalities and lack of evidence.

After allegations of widespread abuse within the department became public, the unit was disbanded. The good cops, like

Harrison, transferred to other units. Special Ops units like K-9, mounted patrol, helicopter and dignitary protection were made separate and distinct units. But a stigma remained for those who had been part of the unit. Harrison and Johnson were still feeling the vibes of unvoiced but deeply held suspicions. Questions clearly persisted on the part of some of their fellow detectives. If they hadn't been involved–why had they stayed?

It was true that for good cops, an assignment to Area 2 had been nothing short of purgatory. But the salary was a generous $43,104 to start, automatically increased to $58,896 after eighteen months on the job. By the time you added in overtime, duty availability bonus, and uniform allowance–plus vision, dental, and medical coverage, and paid sick leave, most detectives were making in the $80,000 range. Combine that with a guaranteed pension of not less than 75% of their highest salary—and it was a hard job to give up.

Harrison had also felt a sense of obligation. In spite of demographics in the city that matched black and white in almost perfect equality (38% vs. 35%), the police department remained 60% white. The C.P.D.'s history of race relations was, arguably, as flawed as that of many other big city police departments. African Americans were first hired on the force in the 1870s. But largely as a result of prejudice by the Irish majority, they were not permitted to wear uniforms or otherwise accorded any of the status so craved by those first recruits. For similar reasons, they were not allowed to patrol in white precincts, but strictly relegated to policing only black communities.

By 1968, the year Harrison was born, his father and others had founded what came to be known as the Afro-American

Patrolman's League, to document and deal with discrimination in hiring, assignments, and discipline. A legal review turned up the information that a disproportionate number of African Americans were being rejected for heart murmurs—murmurs curiously unsuspected and unheard by any other doctors.

Lawyers employed by the League continued to file lawsuits against the city until well into the 1980s. The litigation had two palpable effects. For the first time, the hiring practices of the Chicago P.D. were under the review of a federal judge, and with new scrutiny, the number of African American hires predictably shifted dramatically upward. The other effect, unfortunately, was not positive: a resentful, perennially beleaguered municipal department that felt under siege by the community it was sworn to protect. Community participation (guaranteed by federal oversight) created an antagonistic "us against them" dynamic that neither side had been able to resist.

However imperfect, securing a position as an officer of the Chicago Police Department represented a degree of achievement and respectability that was hard-won. Harrison's grandparents had moved to Chicago during what historians would later call the "Great Migration." Between 1916 and 1930, approximately seven million African Americans left their lives in the rural South and moved to the industrialized North and Midwest. His grandfather got a job at the Armour Meat Processing Plant and his grandmother went to work in one of the many subsidiaries created by the incredible diversity of by-products produced by the wholesale slaughter of animals—creating buttons from their horns and bones.

In the larger sense, his grandparents had left to escape the mummifying consequences of racism and to seek an education for their children, but the catalyst was the Great Flood of 1927, the most destructive river flood in U.S. history.

It began in the summer of 1926, when heavy rains battered the Mississippi's central basin. By September, the Mississippi's 2,320 miles of tributaries were gorged to capacity. On New Year's Day 1927, it happened. In Nashville, the Cumberland River broke through the 56-foot levees in 145 places and flooded 27,000 square miles. With no mechanism for spreading the word of the impending disaster, 246 people in seven states were killed.

The scope of the catastrophe was overwhelming. The floodwaters reached ten states directly: Arkansas, Illinois, Kentucky, Louisiana, Mississippi, Missouri, Tennessee, Texas, Oklahoma, and Kansas. Almost 20% of Arkansas was under water. By May, the Mississippi River below Memphis measured a whopping 60 miles wide.

Some communities did try to stave off disaster—for themselves. In New Orleans, the city council authorized the detonation of 30 tons of dynamite to re-route the approaching floodwaters away from the city and toward the rural and poor St. Bernard and Plaquemines Parishes.

Ultimately, more than 700,000 people were forced to flee their homes and seek temporary shelter. 330,000 African American refugees moved into one hundred and fifty-four refugee camps set up by then Secretary of Commerce Herbert Hoover.

What appeared to be his efficient handling of the crisis instantly catapulted Hoover into the national spotlight and the Republican Party's nomination for the presidency. But the truth was a more complicated affair. The conditions in the camps were deplorable, and it was only a matter of time before Hoover's inadequacies as a crisis manager were revealed. But Secretary Hoover was an ambitious man. Accordingly, he made a deal with Robert Rusa Moton of the Colored Advisory Commission. In exchange for Moton's agreement not to publicize the problems in the camps, Hoover promised he would, once elected, guarantee substantive reforms and improved living conditions for those who had lost their homes and livelihoods.

Behind the White House gates, however, Hoover must have considered himself and his political future safe. So, in a move that would change party politics in the United States, perhaps forever, he reneged on his deal with Moton. In frustration and anger over what they perceived as Hoover's betrayal, in the next election, Moton and the other African American leaders persuaded their followers to abandon the party of Lincoln—and vote for the Democrats. They did, in overwhelming numbers, and to Herbert Hoover's eternal dismay, elected Franklin Roosevelt president.

Despite this demonstration of electoral muscle, political gains were transitory. For most African Americans fleeing the dirty Mississippi floodwaters, the conditions they found in the rapidly industrializing Midwest were not appreciably more promising than what they'd left behind. Between 1910 and 1930, the African American population rose by about 20% in most northern states, and the population was almost entirely absorbed by the largest cities. In most cases, the sole consideration of where to relocate their families came down to basic economics: the cost of the train ticket.

In Chicago, African Americans and new immigrants were

utilized as strikebreakers. Fearful of the newcomers who were taking their jobs, ethnic and racial animosities frequently simmered over into violence in the seedy area known as "Back of the Yards," where the employees of the Union Stockyards made their putative homes.

Started in 1864 when a consortium of nine railroad companies purchased a 320-acre piece of land in southwest Chicago for $100,000, the meatpacking companies that comprised the Union Stockyards were the first truly global companies. The scope of their operations was staggering. The railroad cars loaded with cattle and pigs formed an unending stream in—and their meat and by-products—courtesy of the new technology of refrigeration—streamed out.

By 1870, the meat processing giants—Swift, Morris, Hammond, and Armour—were slaughtering two million animals a year and cleaning, cutting, and packaging their parts. By 1890, the figure had increased to nine million. The system was so efficient that the mechanized killing wheel and conveyors used in the meatpacking plants inspired not only the nascent automobile industry, but every factory assembly line in the world.

Within 30 years, "The Yards" were the largest factory complex in the world, employing 25,000 people and producing 82% of all the meat consumed in the United States. It is estimated that between 1865 and 1900, approximately 400,000,000 animals were butchered. So much animal waste drained into Chicago's South Fork River that it became known as "Bubbly Creek", due to the gaseous effects of decomposition. The yards closed in July, 1971, the river continues to bubble to this day.

Recognizing an opportunity, savvy entrepreneurs started

businesses nearby to take advantage of the by-products created by the slaughterhouses. Factories to process animal parts into leather, soap, fertilizer, glue, gelatin, shoe polish, buttons, perfume, and violin strings all sprang up in the neighborhood. Most women didn't have the physical strength for the heavy labor required in the stockyards. Many found employment in these 'affiliated' enterprises.

Eventually, with the development of the interstate highway system, access to rail became less important, and new roads made it cheaper to butcher animals where they were raised. After World War II, the meat companies saw their profits decline dramatically. Swift and Armour closed down their operations at the Union Stockyards in the 1950s, leaving thousands of workers without jobs.

Industry moved on, but one company adapted rather more skillfully than most. Armour had been making soap from tallow —the rendered fat from the butchered animals—for years. After the war, the company had the idea of adding a germicidal agent known as AT-7 to their product. By the 1950s, Dial was the best-selling deodorant soap in the United States. And ironically, one of the dirtiest industries in the world reinvented itself—packaged with a bright golden yellow wrapper— into the ambassador of clean (*"Aren't you glad you use Dial? Don't you wish everyone did?"*).

Harrison's grandparents spent their entire adult lives working in the Yards, his grandfather on the hazardous and perennially freezing killing floor, his grandmother in a factory whose working conditions were only slightly more humane (to the humans, if not the animals). But with factories closing everywhere, what had served one generation would not support the next. Harrison's father needed a job. He applied and was accepted by the Chicago Police Department. His parents almost swooned with joy. Most parents might worry about a child joining a big city police force. After all, being a police officer is a dangerous job. Except, of course, if you'd worked on the killing floor of the Union Stockyards—where the combination of cold-numbed hands, huge sharp knives, a floor slippery with blood and excreta, and the endless race to keep ahead of the giant swinging carcasses on the mechanized wheel—put you at risk every minute. No. Times were changing, this time for the better.

CHAPTER SEVENTEEN

Rockville, Maryland

THE KIDS WERE BICKERING IN THE BACKSEAT.

The cell phone rang. It was Connor in Chicago. She couldn't hear anything above the din.

"Sorry, Connor. What? What did you say?" She still couldn't hear him. Meanwhile, a disembodied voice rose above the ambient noise of warfare in the back seat.

"Mommy, I don't want this cheese." A quick glance in her rearview mirror showed her five year old holding a long flap of pasty cheese that he had carefully extracted from his sandwich.

She still couldn't hear Connor. "Sorry, can you repeat that...?" she said into the phone.

"I'm gonna drop it," her five year old said conversationally.

With thoughts of her husband's displeasure over ground-in cheese living on in perpetuity in the car's carpet fibers, Lacey sprang into action just as the cheese was languidly poised to drop on the carpet.

There was panic in her voice. "No!" she shouted, louder than she meant.

She put the cell phone back to her ear: "Connor, I've got to call you back, okay?"

The child paused mid-drop, recognizing instantly that he now had his mother's complete attention. He watched her watching him. His mother's focused scrutiny had suddenly raised the stakes.

He considered for a moment. "Well, can I put it out the window?" he asked.

She weighed all the options; none of them good. She sighed.

"Okay...but just *drop* it, don't *throw* it."

"Okay," he said.

Heedless of her instructions—and his promise—and with a wind-up worthy of a minor leaguer, he threw the cheese. The cheese arced smoothly past his elder brother's nose, out the opposite window, where it splayed itself in a perfect sheet on the roof of a passing Camaro.

The outrage from the nearly cheesed nose was palpable and predictably loud.

The elder child exploded. "Mommy, he threw his cheese at me!"

"I did not!" said the younger, eyes wide with innocence.

"You did so!" said the elder.

The two started wrestling in their car seats.

From the height of the SUV, Lacey looked down at the owner of a pavement-hugging Camaro. Sitting in the low-slung seat was a middle-aged Latino in a do-rag, who raised one eyebrow in a come-hither look that transcends all linguistic boundaries.

He was blissfully unaware that the sleazy black coolness of his conveyance was hopelessly neutralized by a dewlap of provolone starting to bead and sweat in the sun's heat on the car's roof. Lacey smiled back at him, over-brightly, overcome by guilt.

When she spoke to Connor later that afternoon, she learned that the reports filtering back from Super Tuesday were discouraging. As expected, McCracken had won the big state primaries, but the caucuses were a bloodbath. The McCracken supporters already knew that McCracken had lost all but one. They were now starting to learn how. Mostly, campaign observers reported, it had been chaos. Time after time, local organizers were reporting that they had been overwhelmed by the sheer volume of Okono supporters, who had turned out in numbers never before seen, and for which the local election boards were completely unprepared.

Because of the sheer volume of people (where had all these people come from?!), election officials weren't able to properly authenticate residency requirements—or much else. When people were challenged, things got ugly, with the veiled threat of lawsuits for racial discrimination. Urgent calls to hire last-minute poll workers had uniformly brought in obviously partisan Okono supporters in such a systematic way it was hard to believe it was coincidental.

Former Speaker of the House Tip O'Neill once said all politics are local. But nowhere is this more evident than in the way state boards of elections handle the voting process. What most people taking part in the process don't realize is that every state, every municipality, is terrified that some inadvertent mistake by one of the mostly elderly poll workers will lead to a lawsuit—for harassment, for discrimination, or infringement of civil rights.

This fear is not entirely unreasonable. Because of abuses in the South since Reconstruction, many African Americans and poor whites were villainously and illegally prevented from exercising their franchise due to the now infamous Jim Crow laws. As a result, every state official is all too aware that watchdogs for civil rights groups routinely inspect polling places. Mistakes, even inadvertent, may provide fodder for a costly publicity-generating lawsuit. Therefore, officials carefully instruct election judges and poll watchers—all of whom are volunteers— that they must be scrupulous in following the regulations exactly. But there is an undercurrent that any voter who complains about the process be assuaged in almost any way necessary.

The job of the poll worker seems relatively simple. In a primary, they are tasked with setting up the voting equipment, greeting voters, verifying the registrations, and providing voters with appropriate ballots. When voting concludes, they close the precinct (usually a school gymnasium, civic center, or church), tabulate and collect voting materials, and deliver them to the county elections office.

However, what might seem simple is complicated by a number of factors. In a general election, the United States has more than 200,000 polling places staffed by more than 1.4 million volunteers. At most, the volunteers attend training sessions for a few hours. Workers arrive at 5:30 a.m. and are required to stay in the building until polls close—usually around 7 p.m. They then start the process of putting away the tables and chairs, closing down the machines and tabulating the ballots. For a workday of approximately 16 hours they are typically paid $100.

But that was only the beginning of what was wrong with the process. The *median* age of most election workers is 72. And the potential pool of volunteers is mostly limited by circumstances to retired people and the unemployed—many of whom struggle with the new machines and procedures. The overwhelming percentage of volunteer poll workers are women.

The consequences of the lack of training were sometimes comical. In the state of Washington, long lines were reported as voters waited for hours after poll workers supposedly hid the electronic voting machines because they could not operate the touch-screen devices. In Chicago, poll workers inadvertently passed out computer styluses to use on paper ballots. When they didn't write, poll workers reportedly assured voters the pens were full of invisible ink.

Desperate for help, the states are constantly trolling for workers. Idaho and Wisconsin don't even require poll workers to be registered voters, others have minimal or no residency requirements. In Indiana, poll workers as young as sixteen are accepted. SEED, with its 120,000 dues-paying members, wasn't slow to seize the opportunity through various affiliates like Election Workers Now! Particularly in a caucus, where voters are required to provide minimal identification, if any, and with same-day registration states like Minnesota, Wisconsin, Iowa, and Maine, installing your supporters as poll workers provided a perfect opportunity to game the system.

McCracken supporters were prevented or discouraged from participating in the caucuses in every way possible. Controlling the process made it all rather easy. Phone lines at McCracken party headquarters rang off the hook as staffers heard the same specific allegations over and over, contest after contest. Letters from attorneys representing the McCracken campaign complained of "evidence of a premeditated and predesigned plan by the Okono campaign to engage in systematic corruption of the Party's caucus procedures."

In Arapahoe County, Colorado, caucus chairs asked all Okono supporters to step out of the long lines. When they did so, they were moved to the front of the line to register. McCracken supporters in line, but not registered by the deadline, were illegally turned away.

In Ramsey County, Minnesota, caucus chairs went down the long lines outside the polling places and informed McCracken supporters via bullhorn that that location was for Okono caucusing only, McCracken supporters should go to another high school across town. With so many McCracken supporters congregating at these other facilities—it took them a while to realize they'd been duped. By the time some of them returned to the original site, they were informed they were too late to be admitted. McCracken supporters later gave testimony that they stood and watched in frustration and fury as the poll worker manning the door continued to admit Okono supporters, even as he barred them from entering. Others, of course, never made it back to the polling place. After driving all over town trying to find the caucus site, many just gave up and went home.

In Elmore County, Idaho, Okono supporters not listed on voter rolls or from different precincts were registered without question. McCracken supporters were told they were ineligible and required to leave.

In Wyandotte County, Kansas, the preference cards on which the caucus-goers were supposed to record their vote were all pre-marked for Okono. At other caucus sites, Okono supporters were invited to step out of line to receive cards. McCracken supporters, even those at the front of the line were told there were no preference cards left.

In Cass County, North Dakota, caucus chairs deliberately miscounted votes to favor Okono, and counted unregistered people, people registered in other precincts, and small children in Okono's tally. In more than one precinct, caucus chairs 'counting' votes for Okono counted those in line, then patiently waited for them to reassemble—and then counted them again.

Precinct by precinct, county-by-county, state-by-state, the same allegations were made over and over about how the Okono campaign was contravening the process.

In Las Vegas, Nevada, unions supporting Okono refused to give McCracken supporters time off to caucus. Workers were offered lavish buffets, but attendance was conditional on registering for Okono. Other employees claimed their jobs were threatened if they caucused for McCracken.

Perhaps most disturbing, more than one mainstream media news outlet received reports from their own employees that large chartered interstate buses were dropping off hundreds of people at polling places on caucus days. The buses were all registered out-of-state. More than one of the "bus people" proudly told a network news reporter on-camera that he'd caucused more than five times for Okono—in different states—in addition to voting in his own primary. The network never aired it.

People later wondered why McCracken supporters had allowed the cheating to happen. The first, most obvious explanation was confusion. With so many people gathered in such relatively small spaces—caucusing frequently took place in multiple rooms of a building rather than all in one central location—it was hard to tell what was going on. For example, in multiple polling places when caucus chairs instructed the Okono supporters to move to the front of the line—there was some murmuring—but people hesitated to complain, since no explanation had been given. Many Okono supporters didn't even realize what was going on—they simply followed instructions.

At other polling places, when the McCracken supporters had specific problems with poll workers—who wouldn't give them preference cards or credential them, for example—they didn't realize ALL McCracken supporters were having these problems (how could they?) and they didn't realize the extent to which the poll workers were willing to shift things for Okono.

When McCracken supporters complained—particularly about the counting—the Okono people ignored them. They were in charge. There was no appeal.

The second explanation as to why the McCracken supporters allowed the Okono campaign to cheat may have been who they were. McCracken's biggest demographic support came from women and the elderly. Confronted at the caucuses with the aggressive in-your-face tactics and physical intimidation of the Okono organizers—McCracken supporters simply folded. Community organizer Saul Alinsky, whose foundation had trained Okono, was infamous for his cynical calculation as to how to secure an advantage over your opponents. One method he advocated was to put the opponent in an uncomfortable or unusual position. "Go outside the experience of the enemy. Cause confusion, fear, retreat." (Rule # 1) When the elderly white women raised questions about improper procedures and counting, they lacked the self-confidence to challenge the combative college-age African American and white males who called them names and brusquely told them they "didn't know what they were talking about."

Even as a pattern started to emerge of the tactics that were being used—it was too late for the McCracken campaign to mount a counter-offensive. The campaign seemed paralyzed by the bullyboy tactics—even as their hands were tied by supporters living in Happy Democratland—who constantly reminded everyone how lucky they were to have two such great candidates to choose from and warned the campaign *sotto voce* that they wouldn't countenance a strong pushback against Okono. Too many of them were still acting as if Okono's campaign was about positioning for a plum cabinet office—instead of what it was—war—total war— designed to win (as theirs should have been) the nomination.

With Claire McCracken's lifetime ties to the African American community, the campaign had built their coalition on the early presumption that Claire would receive significant African American support. Most assumed Okono's skimpy credentials —and stingy support in the past for issues affecting African Americans— essentially predicated against a strong run. But by not highlighting his inexperience and his changeable position on hot button social issues at the beginning, the McCracken campaign allowed Okono to gain traction that would not have been otherwise possible.

Curiously, the ambitious and carefully coiffed white men running in the Democratic primary had no problems piling on the one *woman* running—but they pulled their punches when it came to the black man. The Okono campaign wasn't foolish —or gentlemanly— enough to protest. In fact, the McCracken campaign suspected they encouraged a kind of locker-room camaraderie. "Bro's before Ho's," as one of the Okono campaign stickers read.

Okono's race operated as both sword and shield—allowing him to do and say things the others couldn't get away with, and protecting him from scrutiny on issues that would otherwise have been considered fair game. As his campaign made support for Okono a kind of racial litmus test of pure liberalism among Democrats, his African blood washed away the sin of his white family's slave owning past—with the strangely ironic result that the first viable African American candidate for president was not a descendent of slaves—but of slave owners.

CHAPTER EIGHTEEN

Medford, Oregon

CONNOR MURPHY LOVED THE PACIFIC NORTHWEST. He had lived most of his life on the East Coast, and still traveled there frequently. But when it came time to retire—he'd decided to choose for himself. To actually choose, in a Thoreau-ian way, where and how to live for the first time, to live intentionally. He was fifty-five, with a generous pension from the federal government. He had worked for the DEA for 30 years and had seen more layers of crookedness and infamy than most cops saw in a lifetime. A grown daughter had finished college as she had promised and had moved in with her boyfriend. His marriage had ended years before—at first with recriminations and anger over his long hours and dangerous profession—but then over the years, with acceptance and a kind of distant regard.

He'd taken a hiking trip to Crater Lake and decided that that's where he would settle. He bought himself a puppy—a purebred yellow lab with a thoughtful and easy disposition—and they'd arranged their lives around a cozy house outside Medford, and regular afternoon walks among the ancient conifers.

A Democrat all his life, he found himself strangely drawn to the candidacy of Claire McCracken. He acknowledged to himself that it was partly because after all those years of observing the basest impulses of human nature—he'd decided that women were actually better people than men were. Women were more apt to make decisions based on the core value—loyalty—that to him seemed most important.

Oh, they made bad choices—stayed with men that humiliated and abused them, did things for love or loyalty that their instincts for self-preservation should have made impossible. But maybe that was part of it, too. Women had much less instinct for self-preservation than men did—stories of mothers that starved themselves so their children had food, who denied themselves all kinds of things. Did men do that? Of course they did—honorable men—Connor thought. But still, he believed, women were more likely to make decisions based on their determination of the greater good, rather than on their own narrow self-interest. Of course, he'd never shared this belief with the hardened veterans of the DEA—but increasingly he'd come to believe it was true.

There was something about Claire McCracken, in particular, that inspired him. Obviously, she was a liberal Democrat, but one who seemed to have concern for traditional values—and he didn't mean that as code for gay-bashing or discrimination, as it was sometimes used. No, he meant it as respect for America, respect for a kind of can-do, frontier spirit that viewed every challenge as an opportunity and every opportunity as a blessing. He meant it as a sense of community—it was small town America with parades on July 4th and kids in camp uniforms paddling canoes, and blueberry cobbler set out on picnic tables draped with vinyl checked tablecloths. It was the sound of lawnmowers and the smell of sweet cut grass, and airplanes dragging banner advertisements over a crowded summer beach "skyvertising" half off margaritas to six-year-olds making sand castles.

If he'd ever thought about it, Connor might have noticed that it was always summer in his version of America. It was, reasonably enough, his own childhood. Cape May, New Jersey is populated less noticeably by its current year-'round residents or summer visitors, than by the famous Victorian mansions that line its leafy boulevards. Locals called them "painted ladies"—the curiously exuberant, architectural expressions that ironically now serve as a kind of memorial to some the area's very solid citizens of the last century. If their adornments—a little frivolous, a little garish, and over-colored—seem a strange choice for such conservative yeomanry, the sheer mass and volume of their arrangements speak to a very solid, very permanent temperament, much given to sense, masquerading as sensibility.

Off the fabled, tourist-attracting streets, were the smaller houses. The houses in these neighborhoods didn't have the fun-house dimensions and folly of the mansions on the main avenues, but they were appealingly trim and sturdy nonetheless. Connor had grown up amid a close-knit clan of Irishmen—an assortment of aunts, uncles, and older cousins that mostly came and went, as their own circumstances or inclinations dictated—without apparent discussion or discord.

There wasn't always a lot of money, but there was always enough to eat. And somehow everyone made a contribution. A cousin would leave a bundt cake on the breakfast table. An uncle had carved out a plot in the backyard where he planted enormous egg-shaped watermelons that grew with a kind of proud self-sufficiency in the brown dirt. Another relative had contributed the thicket of raspberry bushes lined up against the neighbor's fence like sentries; its tempting fruit half-hidden among bristling needles as fine as hair. His mother's tomato plants (bright red and green fruit—and in some years, yellow) grew against the lattice of an arbor in an inverted "V" on teepees of sticks. It was a world of community, order and sufficiency. In the 1950s, it was already old-fashioned.

Growing up, his father, a chief warrant officer with the Coast Guard, was Connor's model of rectitude and toughness, a distant figure, admired and mostly unknown. His mother, gentle and loving, was his paragon of womanliness and disinterested generosity. She was the exact personification of mothers on 1950s television: tidy, aproned, and in control.

But it was his brothers and cousins who were his childhood compatriots and co-conspirators. It was with them that he rode bikes to Sunset Beach to find the "Cape May Diamonds"—the clear quartz pebbles washed hundreds of miles down the Delaware River as it rushed for the Atlantic. It was with them that he dug up worms from the backyard and carried them in coffee cans to go fishing from the pier with their homemade poles. It was with them that he stole his father's binoculars to scout birds on the peninsula. And it was with them that he tried to get the younger kids to laugh by making faces during interminable Masses at the Star of the Sea Catholic Church.

When Connor was seven, he had a religious experience, only

it wasn't at the Star of the Sea. It was the day the Magnarama 24 television arrived on the delivery truck, courtesy of the Magnavox Company of Fort Wayne, Indiana. Every Saturday night at 9:30, he and his younger brother would sprawl on the living room rug in breathless anticipation of the newest installment of the adventures of the mysterious Paladin of *Have Gun Will Travel.* For 30 minutes, the Murphy boys would track the adventures of the craggy-faced, gun-slinging mercenary as he offered his services to anyone in need—for a cool $1,000. Except, of course, for widows and orphans, whom the kind-hearted Paladin exempted from payment.

Paladin, cool East Coast sophisticate that he was, lived a rather dandified (if rootless) existence at San Francisco's finest hotel. But to the consternation of the rough-talking Western roustabouts, he could spring into action at a moment's notice with his Colt .45 snug in its engraved holster, his faithful horse Rafter saddled and ready. Calls of "bed time" were ineffectual—neither of the boys would even twitch until the final stanza of the song that began:

Have gun will travel reads the card of the man
A knight without armor in a savage land
His fast gun for hire heeds the calling wind
A soldier of fortune is the man called Paladin.

Two hundred and twenty-six episodes later, Connor was a federal agent. He just didn't know it yet.

The television cost $249.50, an extravagance, when the average American salary was just over $3,000 a year. But the

Murphy family got by. In Connor's childhood, nobody was ever very rich or very poor. Except sometimes unaccountably after someone died, the family might find a mattress full of money that in her later years had apparently cushioned the old bones of a maiden aunt, or some savings bonds that no one had ever cashed in.

Of course, intellectually, Connor realized that things had changed a lot since his youth. Few people kept backyard chickens (although, apparently, Connor had heard, that was changing) or planted victory gardens. But Connor's vision of America persisted. Americans had gotten away from self-sufficiency in a way that was not healthy and not smart, he thought. So when he moved to Oregon, Connor had planted a little garden in his patch of loamy soil. Later, he'd added a little lean-to greenhouse.

Claire McCracken spoke to the vein in him that considered self-sufficiency and autarky a kind of a moral obligation. She talked about a commitment to children, to the poor, even to those who'd been discriminated against, less as a campaign slogan than as an animating principle of her life.

The other thing that attracted Connor to McCracken was her sheer unmistakable smarts. Sure, Okono had the same fancy degrees from the same fancy schools—and people routinely described him as "brilliant." But like many of her supporters, Connor saw in McCracken something noticeably lacking in Okono; a total command of the issues. She didn't grope for words when asked a difficult question—she practically bounded forward to answer it. There were no teleprompters, no stage show theatrics, so far her supporters had shown no signs of fainting as they did with Okono from the sheer Beatlemania of the guy.

It wasn't shtick, it wasn't hype. It wasn't even purely politics. McCracken just struck Connor as a real person, a real *smart* person—but a real person just the same.

It's an overused maxim that a federal agent learns to use his instincts. If he doesn't have good instincts, one way or another, he won't last long in the field. You had to be able to sense—in an almost chemical way—who was telling you the truth and who was shoveling shit. People made it out as if it were some sort of sixth sense—and maybe in a way it was—but it was no more or less scientific than a dog being able to detect explosives. Part of it was training, sure—but part of it—almost inarguably the larger part—was natural ability. Scientists had documented that nervous people, people who were lying—gave off different physiological cues or microexpressions. They blinked more frequently, their blood pressure rose. A DEA agent had to be able to listen to someone, hear him speak and watch him move and gesture, and decide quickly if the cues matched. If they didn't match—well, there was always a reason.

Okono's cues didn't match. He lowered his gaze when he should have been making eye contact. His mouth stretched in a big Hollywood smile. But the eyes didn't smile—they remained wary, considering. When challenged, his posture changed; defensive, stumbling, aggrieved. When people stretched out their hands—cameras captured the momentary irritation, resentment. Okono had to make a conscious effort of will not to shirk from the commoner's touch. What the reporters who covered him quickly discerned—but their editors never allowed them to report—Connor picked up long-distance, via videotape on the evening news. Okono was less cool than cold. Okono was selfish, hard-hearted, mercenary—and, for Connor, the coup de grâce—loyal only to himself.

Connor, like most of America, had heard that Chicago politics were notoriously corrupt. But he also knew what many Americans did not, that Chicago politicians had immeasurable influence. Due to gerrymandering, eight of Illinois' 19 congressional seats had some part of the city in their districts. When one considered how large a state Illinois was, and that Chicago only represented twenty five percent of the population, scoring three additional seats in Congress—for no good reason at all—should have been hard to justify.

So when Connor read in the Chicago papers that Okono had had a relationship with Joey Ali, a notorious political "fixer" in Chicago, his antennae were already raised. One thing Connor knew about was the psychology of criminals. He knew that someone like Joey Ali, who was a major bagman in Chicago politics, and shortly to be indicted on 24 counts of racketeering violations, did not have a close relationship with a politician unless there was a major pay-off. No one got out of those relationships for less than what they were given. It was kind of like using one of the check cashing places ubiquitous in poor neighborhoods; they'd give you your money immediately—but you paid for the convenience in the end. Curiously, a news media that had salivated at the prospect of financial malfeasance by the McCracken family—virtually ignored the Okono-Ali story. And something about the raw injustice of that decision infuriated Connor. He decided to investigate on his own.

First, it was just a couple of calls. He kept hearing the same thing. Okono had openly lobbied for tens of millions of state and federal tax credits, credits used principally by his developer buddies like Ali. And there was no doubt Joey Ali was dirty. Records documented that he had been awarded millions of those federal and states subsidies to build public housing that was now being condemned as substandard and abandoned all over the district and the state. Connor's sources confirmed that at least twenty of those projects—maybe more—were in Okono's own district, so the chances that Okono could have been unaware of what was going on was hard to believe. And there was mounting evidence that despite his denials, Okono had actually written letters in support of Joey Ali's development plans. It wasn't hard to connect the dots.

The newest rumors were that Okono and his pals were guaranteeing their own comfortable retirements by pushing to have Chicago—specifically the bombed out, still smoking embers of the mostly derelict *South Side* of Chicago—play host to the 2016 Olympics. Creating the infrastructure for an Olympics has historically been a losing economic proposition for the host city. The requirements of providing venues for the Olympic games were too huge and too varied to be easily absorbed and repurposed afterward into the public and private use facilities its advocates always promised. It was hard to imagine, for example, that the South Side of Chicago would develop, post-Olympics, a pressing need for archery or badminton facilities. More than the expense of the facilities themselves, were the exorbitant cost of the transportation networks required to bring spectators to the venues. After the excitement of the Olympic games, many cities found the light rail lines they'd installed at enormous expense barely used, the stations deserted.

However, for developers who owned land—frequently land in otherwise undesirable locations—it was a home run. City officials were being cagey, but the word on the street was that un-named developers had just been paid $86 million dollars by the city to purchase South Side property. Whether the city had included that in their Olympic cost estimate of $1.27 billion was unknown.

What's more, Joey Ali had strange—especially for those who thought he was Italian—Middle-Eastern ties. The press either never knew or never reported that Ali traveled more than twenty times to Pakistan between 2004 and 2006. Theoretically, regular visits to a country that was training most of the world's jihadists—alone—probably should have raised some red flags in the media. After all, it's a twenty-two hour plane trip and Islamabad is not exactly party town. Why all the visits? Connor wondered. Ali had never reported any overseas business interests in Pakistan or the Middle East on his business or personal tax filings.

For those who dismissed the trips as some sort of inconsequential "family business"—it might have been inconvenient to point out that all Joey Ali's immediate family were already in the U.S., and if he was sending money to relatives, that was easy enough to manage electronically. In any case, if Ali had been traveling to the Middle East on family business, he would have been traveling to *Syria*. Joey Ali was Syrian, not Pakistani.

There were lots of rumors. Former Okono volunteers told whispered tales of Joey Ali carrying black plastic garbage bags of cash to Okono's congressional campaign headquarters. Insiders at Ali's management firm hinted to investigators that properties bought by Okono had been flipped to buyers who paid a premium—properties the insiders claimed were never registered in Okono's name. Connor suspected none of it could be proved. But there were good reasons to wonder how Okono financed his increasingly expensive lifestyle. The salary of a state senator was notoriously meager and Okono had never had much of a law practice. True, he'd written a book that had made the bestseller list, but that seldom generated the kind of profits necessary to finance a lifestyle like Okono's. Yet he lived in a multimillion-dollar mansion, wore designer clothes, and sent his kids to an expensive private school. The money was coming from somewhere.

True or not, Joey Ali clearly believed he had connections in high places. When the special prosecutor handed out a 24-count indictment, Joey Ali was not unduly worried, apparently. Connor's FBI contact told him that one of Ali's employees would testify at trial that Ali had told her not to worry about the federal indictments—Joey Ali had been assured, he said, that the current special prosecutor was going to be replaced. No less a personage than the frozen-faced, helmet-haired U.S. Speaker of the House, Ali told his employee, would appoint a new prosecutor who would drop all the charges. At the time, the woman thought Joey Ali was crazy.

Chapter Nineteen

Chicago, Illinois

THEY STARTED WITH THE PEOPLE who had worked closely with Antwone Green.

The teachers and principal at the school at which he had worked insisted they simply didn't know much about him. He had rarely participated in after-school activities or socialized with the other teachers. They'd assumed he was too busy with his work at the church, they said.

When they started to interview church members, most of the members of the choir refused to discuss Antwone Green, Kevin DuShane, or the church, except in the most general terms. There was such uniformity to the witnesses' responses, it was impossible not to suspect that they'd been coached. "Yes, they'd worked with Antwone." "No, they couldn't imagine why anyone would harm him." "No, they'd never suspected he was gay." "No, he'd never had any relationships with members of the choir or church that they knew of." "No issues with drugs or money problems as far as they knew." He had a beautiful voice, they all agreed, a deep sonorous bass.

All suggested, unsolicited, that they thought he had been depressed or "down" lately, but stopped short of suggesting his death was a suicide. Apparently, The Minister had shown no such reticence. He had given a sermon immediately following Green's death about how they all needed to minister not just to the flock, but to the shepherds, which seemed to suggest Green had taken his own life. But when pressed by Harrison and Johnson, the choir members demurred. "They couldn't say" and "wouldn't want to speculate" they told the police.

Harrison and Johnson had one final stop. The church accompanist was a quiet man in his seventies who lived with his sister. Carl Barnes had worked with Green at the church for years, although it soon became apparent that he didn't altogether approve of gay men in general, and Antwone Green in particular. But Mr. Barnes was by nature a discreet man, and throughout the interview had remained closemouthed about any suspicions he may have harbored.

However, both Harrison and Johnson suspected that there was a story there, something that Barnes might not be willing to volunteer, but if pressed, might divulge. Just as they thought they were getting somewhere, the man's sister returned from shopping and, learning of the subject of their inquiry, had unceremoniously shooed them out. Barnes courteously escorted them to the door. As they were leaving, Harrison gave it one more try.

"Mr. Barnes. I appreciate your time, sir. I know you don't want to speculate about Antwone Green and Kevin DuShane..." Barnes nodded, solemnly. Harrison continued, "but you must have known Kevin DuShane was having a relationship with someone else in the church...?" Carl Barnes was an elderly man, but the gaze he directed at the detectives was sharp and unexpectedly defensive.

"I'm not saying anything against Congressman Okono," he told them and slammed the door. Harrison and Johnson walked down the house's crumbling cement stairs with carefully controlled expressions. Whatever the police detectives had expected from the interview, it wasn't that.

CHAPTER TWENTY

Chicago, Illinois

EVENTUALLY, THEY WOULD BE GIVEN the grandiose title of Office of Media Affairs, but to start with, everyone just called them "The Four Guys." Appelbaum chuckled to himself as he recalled how the whole thing had started almost accidentally with four pimply, whey-faced guys right out of college. They'd all had low-level crappy jobs: filling computer ink cartridges at the local office superstore, delivering pizzas, working at an auto-parts store—when they'd volunteered for Okono. Everyone started, of course, with the training. Any serious volunteer was schooled in the tactics outlined in The Professor's 280 page training manual. Those slated for leadership positions, either by dint of their eye-burning dedication or the accident of their geographic location (and its relative importance to the campaign apparatus), were sent to Okono Camp. Most new recruits for Okono returned completely indoctrinated, all but clicking their heels and snapping their elbows in salute.

First, Appelbaum had put The Four Guys to work simply

monitoring the various media internet sites and astro-turfing for Okono. When they'd demonstrated a badger-like viciousness in going after McCracken's mousey supporters online, Appelbaum had put them in charge of coordinating bloggers for Okono and decided to pay them. Why not? After all, there was plenty of money. When they'd recommended guys they knew who had network skills, and told Appelbaum they needed some techs and computer geeks who knew how to manipulate and work the system, he'd hired a few more. Appelbaum was amazed at how effective they were. McCracken websites claimed Okono had five hundred paid bloggers around the country. Appelbaum laughed to himself. What the penny-pinching McCracken campaign would be most appalled to learn was that he frankly had no idea how many of these guys were now working for the campaign.

They all looked alike, dressed alike, talked alike. Young, pasty, anonymous guys with brown hair, button-down shirts, khaki pants. They shlumped into the office throughout the morning wearing Chicago-weather-worthy parkas or thrift shop overcoats. Their features were indistinct, softly modeled, as if the clay hadn't been fired long enough. They lived in their parents' basements or low-rent walk-ups with one brick wall and intermittent heat. But it didn't matter what they looked like, or even who they were. Appelbaum chuckled to himself: these everyday shlemiels focused all their real-world angst and frustration (too short, too awkward, too ugly) and transformed themselves online into strike-force warriors; venom pouring from their fingertips with every keystroke, every salvo. A veteran of political campaigns, Appelbaum was a little bewildered to realize how personally invested they were: they didn't just want

Okono to win, they wanted to punish McCracken for daring to run against him. They didn't want to best McCracken supporters in an on-line dialogue, they wanted to annihilate them.

When the campaign organized the social networking sites, and the volunteers started pouring in, The Four Guys became the geeks in charge, by default. Pretty soon, they were arriving at the Okono campaign headquarters at 3:30 in the morning on weekdays and 5:30 on weekends to read the newspaper websites, political blogs, and monitor television and radio. Ted Mojasck was Appelbaum's key point guy. An unprepossessing guy with dark shadowed eyes, a too-short nose, and too-long upper lip, his pallid expression reflected the long hours he devoted to the Okono internet turf wars. Mojasck had sent him an email: The Four Guys needed a few minutes of his time. So he was here. As he walked into the room for their appointment, Appelbaum noticed The Four Guys and another guy he didn't recognize were already seated at the small conference table.

"Okay," Appelbaum said, with a glance at his watch, "What you got?"

Mojasck licked his lips a little nervously and began.

"David, as you know, I've been working on a project with Ranjiv..." he gestured to the other guy in the room, who nodded.

"...to disrupt the opposition's email chains, which has been pretty successful. But Ranjiv thinks we're missing some opportunities to really dominate the web."

"Okay, I'm listening."

Mojasck motioned for Ranjiv to take over.

"Well, it's pretty basic." Ranjiv looked almost embarrassed to have to explain.

"Right now, you know, we are, like, primarily focused on rapid response using Google alerts and other mechanisms."

Appelbaum nodded. He knew this.

Ranjiv continued. "But we haven't done anything yet, like, to really harness the capabilities of the new system—to, you know, basically, like, use the code built into every part of the internet to, you know, really take control."

Appelbaum was intrigued.

"Okay. So how do we do that?"

Mojasck interjected.

"We've already begun using spam filters against the opposition. But we could really take it to the next level. You know, like, flag their emails and websites and take them off-line."

"For how long?"

Mojasck and Ranjiv exchanged a glance. It was Mojasck who spoke.

"It kinda depends on how savvy they are. Could be, like... forever."

Appelbaum had a hard time concealing his glee.

"Anything else?"

The Four Guys looked at Ranjiv.

"Yes, well, like, it's theoretically possible to insert metadata, you know, into some of the websites to create really powerful negative affiliations."

The guys all nodded their heads enthusiastically.

"Meta-what?" asked Appelbaum.

"Metadata. Meta-tags. The embedded words or phrases in a web page that like, you know, help search engine bots index a page."

Appelbaum rubbed his forehead. "Am I following this? You're going to embed dirty words on their websites?"

Ranjiv chuckled goofily. "Unless the user opens up the html of the page, they're not, like, ever gonna see it. And, like, no administrators of these types of sites really have the, you know, sophistication to look at the code. No, no one sees the meta-data except, you know, the search engine. The amateurs hosting these sites will never suspect a thing."

Appelbaum paused. "I guess I'm missing something. So, what's the point?"

Ranjiv continued. "By embedding words that have nothing to do with the site—we make the websites harder to find. That's the first thing," Ranjiv paused. The Four Guys motioned for him to continue.

"And the second?" Appelbaum prompted.

Ranjiv dropped the bomb. "Like I said, we use really negative words."

"Like what?" Appelbaum noticed the Four Guys shifting a little uneasily in their seats. So this is big, he thought. Out loud he said: "Give me an example."

Ranjiv responded first. "Yes... well, so we were thinking... We might use the words: racist, white supremacist, KKK. So, like, when a user pulls up that page, all the other websites listed will be for those groups, so the supporter thinks the site is, like, insanely questionable. You know, like, guilt-by-association, big time."

"I should think so." Appelbaum looked at the young man over his glasses.

Ranjiv continued, obviously warming to their expanding options.

"Or...ummm... Like, perhaps something to do with child pornography and bondage and shit like that. Perhaps...even... ummm...we were thinking, you know...like kiddie snuff films?" he added, his voice crackling slightly with nervousness.

Appelbaum guffawed. This was even better than he'd imagined.

"You guys are going to link the McCracken supporters' websites to kiddie porn? All those suburban moms? You guys are *cold*."

The Four Guys laughed nervous geek laughter. Ranjiv snorted, then stopped abruptly when The Four Guys looked at him irritably.

Eyeing Ranjiv, Mojasck continued.

"And a reporter, who is, like, you know, looking for a credible person to interview is not going to consider profiling someone we affiliate with those websites."

"Right," Ranjiv added. "Also, if they go crying to the media, the media's gonna pull up the website, they're gonna see the same affiliations. And, man, they are like so discredited. You know, like, 'stick a fork in them'..."

"They're done!" the other four chorused to high fives.

Appelbaum forced himself to pause.

"What about us? Are we leaving any fingerprints when we do this?"

Again, The Four Guys deferred to Ranjiv. Ranjiv shook his head.

"No. You know, we run it over a large network using a masked IP address. There is, like, no evidence they can use against us."

Applebaum needed to be sure. "*Like* no evidence? Or no evidence?"

Ranjiv chortled. “No evidence.”

The Four Guys looked expectantly at Appelbaum. His metal chair scraped the floor as he rose.

“Well, gentlemen? What are you waiting for?”

CHAPTER TWENTY-ONE

Oglethorpe, Georgia

MIRIAM CARTER LOVED HER PARENTS in the careless way happy children do. Her mother was strict; conscientious about preparing Miriam for success in a broader world than Miz Tummy would ever know. But if Miz Tummy was demanding of her youngest child, she was endlessly giving, too. Miriam never questioned her absolute devotion to her brothers or herself. Childhood memories of her father were of him working—he and the older boys took scrupulous care of his twenty acres and managed Miss Amalia's farms for extra money, as well. Everyone in the community knew Big John and Miz Tummy—and knew them for what they were —honorable, savvy, bright, and strong. Her parents' reputation for sensible Christian neighborliness gave them real stature; and Miriam's awareness of her own enhanced status, due to her connection to them, was her greatest source of confidence and pride.

But she loved Miss Amalia, too. When she was little, she'd been fascinated by Miss Amalia's stylish store-bought clothes and soft hands. But as she grew, she began to appreciate Miss Amalia for her real quality; beyond the cultured voice and kind manner or her intelligent and thoughtful face. Her parents were the bass drum of her life: rhythmic, insistent, constant—the sound of her heart. Miss Amalia was the melody, high and sweet.

By common, if unspoken agreement, after Miriam finished her chores, she walked to the big house at Riverview. If Miss Amalia had some work for her, she'd sort correspondence or address envelopes to supplement her allowance. If there was nothing for her to do, Miriam was welcome to curl up in the library in the front of the elegant house and read until dinnertime. One night, Miss Amalia happened upon her, Cotton close on her heels as usual. She paused and looked at Miriam mischievously:

"Miriam, do you know what a 'Cracker' is?" Now, everybody in Georgia knew what a Cracker was: a Cracker was a low-down, no-account white person. By her nearest reckoning, she had called someone a Cracker that very morning. But Miriam wasn't sure that was an appropriate thing to say to Miss Amalia, who was after all, herself white.

Miss Amalia could see Miriam's native truthfulness struggle with her wish not to give offense. Unexpectedly, Miss Amalia laughed. She went to one of the high shelves, stepped on the little footstool kept handy for the purpose, and pulled out a leather-bound volume. Her eyes twinkled.

"Well, if you're going to call someone one, you ought to at least know what it means." Miss Amalia thumbed through the book quickly, coming to sit beside her. "Here it is: 'What cracker is this same that deafs our ears/ with this abundance of superfluous breath?' It's Shakespeare. *The Life and Death of King John*. I'm not sure you've read it yet?" Miriam shook her head 'no'. Miss Amalia continued:

"No? Well, you must read it. It's about the son of Eleanor of Aquitaine."

Miriam sat silently, knees pressed hard together.

"Do you know why I'm showing you this?" Miss Amalia asked kindly. Miriam was nervous.

"Because you don't want me criticizing white folks?"

Miss Amalia laughed. "Heavens, no," she said, "Criticize anyone you like." She smiled at Miriam. "In this context..." Miss Amalia tapped the beautifully bound book, "it refers to a story-teller, a court fool. But later the English used it as a pejorative term for the Irish and it came closer to its present meaning—shiftless, no-good, lazy." Miriam blurted out: "But you're Irish!" Miss Amalia had told Miriam something about her own heritage.

Miss Amalia smiled a rueful smile.

"Well, Irish descent, surely. But the English treated the Irish, my ancestors, very badly—in some ways as badly as the colored people are treated today. They had almost no rights and they were entirely at the mercy of the English aristocrats who owned the land they farmed." Miriam looked thoughtful.

"Sort of like croppers," she said slowly. Miss Amalia smiled and nodded.

"Sort of. But I'm telling you this for two reasons. Technically, I'm a Cracker, too, you see?" This was almost impossible to absorb. Beautiful Miss Amalia, with her expensive clothes and perfectly coiffed soft hair, sitting in her exquisite wood-paneled library like a model in a magazine ...a Cracker? But Miriam was starting to see her larger point, and nodded.

"So, first, I want to ask that when you criticize someone, you criticize them by describing their actions—not a group to which they belong." Miriam was embarrassed; she had offended Miss Amalia after all. She looked away. Miss Amalia, touched her shoulder softly, and looked at her with a kind smile, "And why else am I telling you this?" Miriam shrugged and shook her head.

"Well, I hoped you might understand that how people see you, the names they call you, it's not who you are. And, lastly, I suppose I wanted you to know...I want you to remember—" Miss Amalia seemed in a rush to get the words out, "...sometimes quickly, sometimes slowly, but *things change*. You have to believe they can change for you, too."

Miriam had remembered. In late July 1952, when Miriam was seven, Miss Amalia had purchased one of the first televisions in the county, and with special permission, Miriam watched the first broadcast of the Democratic National Convention with Miss Amalia and Cotton. Georgia's popular native son, Senator Richard "Dick" Russell was considered to have a chance against the favorite, Senator Estes Kefauver of Tennessee. No one wanted to miss it. A firm supporter of Roosevelt's New Deal, rural electrification, and farm loans, Dick Russell had also sponsored the National School Lunch Act in 1946 that achieved the double goal of providing poor children with a healthy midday meal and subsidizing agriculture. Personable and courtly, Russell had a brilliant, encyclopedic mind and he was always thinking. As political mentor Bobby Baker would later advise Lyndon Johnson, "All Senators are equal; but Russell is most equal."

It would be hard to create more drama for a viewing audience. Miriam sat transfixed, staring at the small skittery picture as

Miss Amalia absentmindedly fed almonds from a porcelain dish to an appreciative Cotton. As the delegates voted by state, the tension from the Chicago convention hall was palpable. On the first two ballots, Kefauver had a clear lead. But Kefauver—who had created a sensation in New Hampshire by campaigning via dogsled in a coonskin cap, and by roundly defeating an incumbent president—had made an enemy. Beating him in the primaries was one thing, but what President Harry Truman truly resented was Kefauver's Senate investigations into senior Truman administration officials. The corruption was penny-ante, a few undeclared fur coats and similar political gifts. But it included the embarrassing revelation that Bess, the ever-practical First Lady, had received a coveted "deep freezer" from a political crony.

Kefauver was out. There was another possibility: Truman had great respect for Russell. But there was one problem. Russell would need to renounce segregation to have a chance in the North, Truman believed. Would Russell do it? As Senator from Georgia, could he do it? He would not. Accordingly, Truman manhandled a compliant Averell Harriman of New York to drop out and throw his support to the political flirt, Illinois Governor Adlai Stevenson. On the third ballot, Stevenson, the choice of the political bosses, trumped Kefauver to take the nomination. Kefauver had racked up an impressive 3,100,000 votes in the primary; Stevenson a modest 78,000. It didn't matter. The people had spoken. Just not the people who voted.

The drama, the excitement, the sheer spectacle and pageantry of that experience stayed with Miriam forever. When she later ran for political office, she always made it sound as if the idea had come coincidental to her work for civil rights, and in a way it had. But the desire to participate on a larger stage, to be smack dab in the center of pivotal events—was born right at that moment.

Every night at dinnertime, Miz Tummy said a modest grace: "Lord, let our crops and children grow." And Miriam had grown until she was taller than all the girls and plenty of the boys. She ended up a formidable five foot ten inches tall. When Miz Tummy would see her slumped over, bowing her head, she would take Miriam's chin in her hand "Hold yourself proudly, Miriam, the way God made you.

As a practical matter, her parents had always made their children's education a priority; it was, they believed, the surest way for them to get ahead. Miss Amalia fostered something else—her imagination and curiosity. She taught Miriam to love books the way she herself loved them, as if they were alive. When Miriam graduated from high school in 1962, her parents would have been satisfied. Eight years earlier, the process of integration of the schools was a huge step forward for civil rights, but it had created a considerable backlash as well. Dr. Thomas Brewer of Columbus, Georgia, was well known all over the state for his relentless quest for racial integration in the schools and other public places. Shortly after the new legislation passed, he was shot dead in a warning missed by no one. But it was for their children that most southern African Americans feared most. Shy and sweet Autherine Lucy was beset by an egg and epithet-hurling mob when she tried to enroll at the University of Alabama. Many African American parents willing to wage the battle for civil rights themselves were dismayed by circumstances that still in the 1960s put their children on the front lines.

It was Miss Amalia who'd seen a wider world, who insisted Miriam attend college up north. She'd helped Miriam with her applications and she'd helped Big John with the money. By the time Miriam graduated from law school, Miss Amalia was already dying, but as incandescent and mischievous as ever. The disease didn't change her, it just stripped her down to her essential elegance. Her body stayed straight and tall, her back and spirit unbowed, her large eyes bright and clear. Her belief in Miriam never dimmed: "You can change the world, Miriam," she told her.

One morning, Miss Amalia never woke up. A big-city lawyer from Atlanta came out with the paperwork. Big John wanted to buy his farm; everything was all mechanized now. In the 1930s, it had taken a team of four horses 55 hours to plow a 40-acre field. Now a modern tractor pulling a 25-foot disc harrow could do it in an hour. But as it turned out, Big John didn't need to buy it. Miss Amalia had left it to him in her will, as well as the farms he'd managed and the house itself.

In her will, she'd declined to give away Cotton's grandson. Known to everyone as 'Junior', she'd left the ancient dog money "so he can settle where he will." Some distant relatives considered using this provision to challenge the will, alleging incompetence. But after the first salvo, it hadn't gone anywhere. Miss Amalia's request might have appeared eccentric—but nobody in town—even the most pragmatic and hard-hearted—would agree that Cotton's descendant should be treated like an ordinary dog. For herself, she'd requested an unadorned stone marker in the graveyard without name or date—inscribed with nothing but a mis-transcription of one of the psalms. Of course, they'd ignored that, and put her name on the large granite slab, anyway, but they'd used the curious translation of the psalm, just as she wrote it out.

"I said to myself, 'I will confess my rebellion to the Lord.'
And you forgave me. And all my guilt is gone."

Psalm 32.5

In later years, Miriam would return from the city to visit her parents and find her father sitting on the porch of the beautiful antebellum house. An elderly man, still tall and handsome, but bone-sore and weary, thoughtfully keeping company with a stately curly-haired old dog. A snow-white dog just like his grandpa, dignified and circumspect as a judge.

When Miriam first started campaigning, she thought she needed to wear red to stand out in the crowd. As it turned out, Miriam stood out plenty in any color, but she liked red, so she just kept wearing it. People responded to her energy, enthusiasm, and endemic integrity. Of course, she was also notorious for providing all who crossed her path—famous and sundry alike—with a list of suggestions. Improving yourself ought to be everyone's lifelong goal, thought Miriam. Impressed with her accomplishments as a civil rights attorney, the good citizens of Atlanta made her the first African American woman to be elected to Congress from Georgia.

In her late thirties, she married a good and wise man, a fellow attorney. He liked to tease that he'd mostly kept up with her for twenty-five years. That they'd never had children was a sorrow to them both. Her husband's public joking that he could never hold her still long enough hid the private pain of many years of disappointment. But the experience that broke so many couples had made them stronger. They'd had a wonderful and full life. They'd enjoyed a rare marriage of passion and regard that had changed over the years, but never diminished. In her personal life, Miriam always considered herself blessed.

But, although few would agree with her, she considered her professional life less of a success. Entrenched special interests made effecting change difficult. With real regret, Miriam had come to believe that most politicians didn't really care about the constituents they served. After almost twenty years in politics, she simply hadn't seen many candidates that weren't animated by self-interest. But Claire McCracken was different. When Miriam met Claire McCracken, she was the first candidate for national office—black or white—who really seemed worth a damn.

Chapter Twenty-Two

March 2008
Medford, Oregon

Connor Murphy was sitting on his deck, sipping an overpriced coffee from the local yuppie emporium, investigating criminals. How times had changed, he thought. When he'd started his career as a federal investigator, every lead had been gained by painstaking legwork. If you wanted to check records, you inevitably presented your badge to a suspicious older woman in a dusty, under-heated county clerk's office, who grudgingly pointed you to rows and rows of files in vertical hanging stacks and advised you in humorless tones not to make a mess. You then began the tedious process of sorting papers and reading files. It was like shifting sand.

Now everything was on the internet. That's how Connor found Okono's early campaign finance documents. All the reports claimed that Okono had—virtually since his first contest—been rolling in money—but the numbers didn't bear that out. If anything, Okono seemed strangely under-funded.

What seemed odd was that despite the constant re-telling of the Okono mythology that his success was based on grassroots community activism, campaign finance records told a different story. It had not been individuals making small-sum contributions that had financed the early campaigns, but PAC's and lobbyists—at a rate of almost 10 to 1 to individual contributions.

Regardless of its source, Connor found it hard to believe that Okono had run successful campaigns with so little money. In 1997, he collected $12,000 from PACs and $4,000 from individuals. In 1998, $13,500 came from PACs and a measly $1,500 came from individual contributions. Curiously, in all the years from which data was available on the Federal Elections Commission website, virtually half of the contributions designated as being "from individuals" were from one person—Joey Ali.

The Feds were going after Ali, and presumably the governor, but there was strangely little interest among the press corps in unraveling Ali's links to Okono. *Newsweek* had sent a reporter to cover Joey Ali's upcoming trial, but most media outlets seemed to have accepted the Okono campaign's explanation of their relationship as a kind of benign acquaintance, without investigating further. But Connor felt certain that there was some way that Ali was transferring money to Okono, he just didn't know how—yet.

Connor picked up the phone and left a message. Lacey called him back with the information he'd requested within the hour. Neither mentioned the name of her contact.

She paraphrased their conversation from her scribbled notes:

"He says $16,000 would have been low for a state senate seat. But Chicago is a one party town, so once you win the primary, you're home free. So maybe for the first year, but after that it would go up a lot—to about $50-$60,000, as contributors start to want to jump on the bandwagon."

Connor rubbed his chin. "But it doesn't, it goes down," he told her.

Lacey continued: "I asked about that. His guess is, it's not on the level. Okono had to be taking in and spending more money than that. Running a campaign in a densely populated city is expensive. You've got to have storefronts, the media buys are more expensive. It adds up."

Connor was puzzled. He asked: "Okay, so why hide the money? Why not report the income if he's gotta spend the money anyway?"

Lacey paused, considering. "Hmmmmm."

"What?" Connor asked. He could almost hear the wheels turning.

"Well, I was just thinking..." Lacey replied "What if he didn't need to pay for it?'

"But you just said—"

She continued: "I know. Someone had to pay for it. What if it wasn't Okono?"

It was late. Connor was tired. "What? I'm not following."

Lacey asked: "Did Joey Ali make any charitable donations?"

"Sure," Connor replied.

She continued: "To foundations? The Driver or James Hunt Foundations, for example?

"Yeah. Both of them," said Connor.

"You said Okono was sitting on the boards of those foundations, right?" Lacey questioned.

"Yeah," said Connor slowly.

"And those foundations gave millions of dollars to groups like SEED, right?" asked Lacey.

"Yeah," Connor said.

Lacey continued: "Well, does SEED have a big 'get-out-the-vote' operation in Chicago?"

Connor laughed. "The biggest. It's huge."

Lacey laughed. "Well, there's your missing money."

CHAPTER TWENTY-THREE

Chicago, Illinois

At first, when Harrison had gotten the call, he'd thought the guy was putting him on. The stranger on the other end of the line wanted to talk about Joey Ali. Harrison had assumed the guy was a reporter on a fishing expedition—there'd been lots of news in the local papers about Joey Ali and his cozy relationship with Okono—but hardly anyone in the national media was really pursuing it. Harrison had tried to persuade the guy that he was wasting his time, but when the man insisted that he needed to talk to Harrison, Harrison had grudgingly agreed to a meeting. Harrison was more than a little surprised when the guy's credentials checked out. Connor Murphy, former federal agent. Good guy, people said. Trustworthy. Serious. Murphy explained that he was recently retired, claimed he was pursuing this on his own. Harrison was skeptical—figuring that Murphy was more likely to be one of those guys with a comfortable retirement that started work as a PI to avoid the golf games and boredom. Harrison had asked his

Bureau contact point blank: “Is this guy an adrenaline junkie?” To be honest most of the good ones were. You either thrived on that kind of stress or it destroyed you. The response came with a cynical laugh, “No more than anyone else.”

He’d agreed to meet the guy at a bar close to the airport. Murphy said he was in town for a few days. Harrison hated to take time away from the Antwone Green investigation, but they’d reached a kind of impasse. No witnesses. Superiors claiming —despite the evidence— no obvious signs of foul play. New paperwork for other cases was already starting to pile up on his desk.

Kevin DuShane, the boyfriend, had disappeared. If he was hiding out in the Caribbean, they hadn’t been able to find him. No credit card receipts, no ATM use. It was theoretically possible, of course. But in our cashless society, it was harder and harder to hide from authorities. Even if you were able to pay for your hotel in cash, most still insisted on a credit card imprint. It was unusual for someone innocently on holiday to carry that much cash—especially when it was now so easy to hit an ATM when necessary.

Of course, the authorities loved ATM transactions. Not only did they leave an electronic trail of exactly where a ‘person of interest’ had been, but once flagged, investigators could then pull up the ATM’s video for information on all kinds of things that would make tracking the suspect easier: their appearance, whether or not they were injured, or if they were with someone. Better still, many Caribbean countries had video cameras on major thoroughfares. So if authorities traced a suspect to a nearby ATM with the handy time stamp, they could sometimes pick him up on street surveillance cameras, as well. If Kevin

DuShane had been in the Caribbean on a straightforward vacation for a few weeks, it was incredibly unlikely that there would be no trace of him.

People shoved and jostled as the bar started to fill up with the happy-hour crowd. Murphy was waiting for him in a booth at the back. Trim, handsome, bright blue eyes, only his grey hair identified Murphy as a man in his fifties. Strong handshake, looked Harrison right in the eyes. Harrison thought: so far so good. Murphy had been waiting, already had a beer. Harrison gestured to the waitress who, he noticed with amusement, was being particularly attentive to the good-looking Murphy. Harrison ordered a draft.

"So what can I do for you?" he asked.

Murphy was not the type to waste time, he saw. He pulled out a small leather satchel.

"Actually, I think I can help you."

Harrison started to feel like he was being set-up, but was too smart, and too cautious, to betray any impatience.

"Great...what with?" Harrison asked.

"The Bureau has been tracing Joey Ali's money," Connor said simply.

"I figured." Harrison wasn't surprised. The Feds were trying to build a case against Ali and a number of his political cronies. There were rumors that the ties went as high as the governor's office.

Connor continued: "Some of the money went to the Jehovah Ministry."

"I'm not surprised. There's a cost to doing business around here," Harrison said, shrugging his shoulders.

Connor continued, "...and some of the money went to a landlord of a derelict building on the South Side," he said.

"Again, I'm not surprised...there are lots of political favors being paid back, here," Harrison replied.

"For four months rent," Murphy continued.

"O—kay..." said Harrison, cautiously.

"For a tenant by the name of Kevin DuShane," Connor said. Harrison paused, stunned in spite of himself. Connor continued, pulling more copies from the satchel. "I understand that Mr. DuShane is a person of interest in a murder case you're investigating?"

"He is."

"And Mr. DuShane is currently on vacation in the Caribbean?"

"So they say," Harrison replied evenly.

Murphy looked at Harrison steadily. "So, Detective Harrison, can you explain to me why Joey Ali is paying some rent-boy's rent?

Harrison smiled at Murphy. This might turn into an investigation after all.

After Harrison's brief explanation of what he and Johnson had discovered in the Antwone Green case, Murphy slid copies of statements showing wire transfers across the table to Harrison. The most important thing was the cash. The Feds had used marked bills, but so subtly, Harrison was unable to distinguish the marks they'd used. Connor showed him the list of serial numbers and then a photograph showing the same serial numbers deposited in cash one week later in the landlord's LLC account. The time stamps told the story—if the lag had been longer, the money might just (arguably) have entered circulation, and it would be tough to prove a link with Joey Ali. The fact that the transaction happened so quickly—considering that four of the seven days would have been accounted for by the bank's internal record-keeping (surprisingly, banks were less efficient at moving cash than processing checks) —an experienced investigator would consider it an open and shut case.

"Can I use this?" Harrison had to be careful; whatever capacity Murphy was working in, it wasn't official.

"Sure. These are just copies. You'd have to put in a formal request. But all the evidence was gathered using Bureau protocol. Connor looked at Harrison closely: "*Will* you use it?" he asked quietly.

"Why wouldn't I?" Harrison felt defensive under Murphy's steady gaze. Was this a reference to him having worked Area 2, Harrison wondered?

Connor smiled slightly, trying to defuse the situation. His question had clearly offended Harrison. "Well, you must be wondering why you're seeing this from me and not through official channels?" he offered.

"Yeah, well, I guess I am wondering that," Harrison replied.

Connor raised his eyebrows slightly, resigned. "Apparently, there's been a decision made not to pursue this."

"I see," said Harrison

Connor continued: "Just like there's been a decision made not to implicate Okono in any of the 'pay to play' case against Joey Ali."

Harrison was surprised but said nothing. Of all the politicians in Illinois, it was well known that Ali had the closest ties with Okono. If Joey Ali was dirty—and few in law enforcement doubted Ali was dirty—Okono was up to his sparkling white smile in it.

"Look. I have a bias, here, I won't deny it," said Murphy.

Harrison looked up: "You're working for the McCracken campaign?" he asked.

Connor responded: "No, not in any official capacity. I'm a supporter, that's it. But because of my background, I guess my nose just kind of leads me around when I sense something's not on the level. And Joey Ali is about as far out of plumb as you can get."

Harrison laughed. "Yeah, I've got a nose like that. It's gotten me in no end of trouble, sometimes."

Connor was suddenly serious: "Maybe so, but it's what makes you a good cop, an honest cop." He paused, as if slightly embarrassed.

"Anyway, I just thought if this were my investigation–I'd want the information." Harrison nodded. He had a good feeling about Murphy. He'd provided answers to all the questions a good investigator would ask, and as far as Harrison could tell, he had been completely straightforward. The murder of Antwone Green, on the other hand, was getting more complicated by the minute. Harrison paused, testing the water.

"You could have told me all this on the phone. Why come all this way?"

Murphy nodded, as if he'd expected the question.

Harrison looked at him thoughtfully, suddenly knew the answer: "You suspected Antwone Green's murder was linked to Okono, didn't you?" Harrison said slowly, carefully.

Connor Murphy's expression never changed, but his voice dropped an octave.

"You can put it together as well as I can. Better probably,

since you're a homicide dick. Joey Ali is a shyster, but he's not a murderer, and Antwone Green was a professional hit. Personally, I like the Guard for it. Ali and The Minister? Maybe they have business dealings... In this town, who knows?" Connor shrugged his shoulders.

"But you said it yourself." Murphy looked at Harrison. "The only link between Joey Ali and Kevin DuShane is Congressman Okono. "And frankly..." Murphy looked nervously around the crowded bar "that scares the shit out of me."

Connor Murphy took a long sip of his draft, wiping the foam off his mouth with his sleeve.

Murphy paused. "Although knowing it, and proving it are two different things. I don't expect the Guard leaves many loose ends."

Harrison smiled. "Not usually, no. But we might get lucky."

Connor Murphy shook his head and looked at Harrison doubtfully. On a purely theoretical level, Harrison conceded that Murphy was probably right. But another part of Harrison, even in spite of the increasingly long odds, still couldn't accept it—had to believe there might be justice—someday—for Antwone Green.

"Agent Murphy, you really don't think we're ever going to find Kevin DuShane, do you?"

Well, I dunno," said Murphy thoughtfully. He then paused for dramatic effect.

"Do you fish?"

Harrison laughed in spite of himself.

CHAPTER TWENTY-FOUR

Chicago, Illinois

HARRISON TOLD JAY JOHNSON about his meeting with Murphy the following day. He spread out the copies of the wire transfers and the time stamped photographs of the money. Johnson whistled.

"They had tracers on Ali's money?" Johnson asked.

Harrison replied: "Yeah, I mean it figures. It's no secret they've been watching Joey Ali for months, maybe even years. I mean, the guy's facing, like, 24 charges of racketeering."

Johnson was flipping through the pile of pictures. "So Joey Ali pays off a landlord for a tenant that's a material witness to a capital crime...after the guy disappears...?" he asked.

Harrison sighed. "Well, to be honest, the guy disappeared before the murder, so at this point we don't really know what information he has."

Johnson looked up from the pictures. "But he was having an affair with Okono." It was a statement, not a question.

Harrison rubbed his forehead: “We don’t know that either. We have a witness that might know something...”

“Dendra Jones...?” Johnson supplied. Harrison nodded. Johnson continued, “Who has mysteriously disappeared into thin air?”

“Yup,” agreed Harrison

“A little old lady who can’t make it to the grocery store by herself,” prompted Johnson.

“Right,” Harrison concurred.

Johnson continued, “Is gone. Overnight.”

“Right,” Harrison replied, adding: “Leaving no one to care for the cat she’s been giving insulin shots to for the last six months.”

“Right,” said Johnson.

Johnson flipped the file closed and looked up at his partner expectantly, “So which angle are we working first–the church or Joey Ali’s business?” he asked.

“I don’t know,” Harrison responded with a shrug. “Any preference?” he asked.

“Sure,” Johnson replied, a mischievous gleam in his eye. “The church. I like a little religion now and then.” They made an appointment with The Minister.

He welcomed them in his effusive way and invited them into a large, comfortable office. But before they’d even had time to sit down, he was all business.

“Gentlemen: what can I do for you?” he asked, obviously not interested in exchanging pleasantries.

“Well, sir, as you know, we’re investigating the death of Antwone Green.”

The Minister nodded without speaking.

Harrison and Johnson ran through the litany of what had now become the standard questions. The Minister answered "no" to each. When they got to the question about drugs or money problems, The Minister stopped them, obviously irritated. "Why would you ask that?" he challenged them. Johnson was nonplussed.

"Well, in a situation where it looks like a professional—" They were startled by the fury of The Minister's response.

"Who is suggesting such a thing?" his big voice reverberated around the room. Harrison looked at Johnson, plainly not offering to intercede on his behalf. "You go right ahead, big guy," his look seemed to say.

Johnson did his best to maintain his composure, but he was clearly intimidated. The Minister's barrel chest and powerful build bristled with indignation.

"Well, sir, Mr. Green died of a gunshot wound to the back of the head." He paused. Johnson was floundering, surprised at the vehemence of The Minister's denial of something he assumed was obvious.

The Minister appeared to calm down. He took a deep, windy breath, rattling his diaphragm.

The Minister regarded the detectives with a supercilious smile. "It was burglary, correct? Things were taken from the apartment?"

Johnson looked at Harrison for help. Harrison merely smirked. He was clearly enjoying his partner's discomfiture.

Johnson responded to The Minister: "Well, yes, sir, a few things were taken, but the consensus of all the officers on the scene was that the burglary was staged as a cover for the murder."

"MURDER!?" roared The Minister. Harrison speculated idly on The Minister's ability to project his voice to the back row. It was an amazing demonstration of vocal gymnastics.

"Antwone Green wasn't murdered!"

Now, Johnson was getting angry. Harrison could see the vein pulsing under the skin of Johnson's forehead as he kept himself tightly under control.

"With all due respect, sir, most suicides are not dexterous enough to shoot themselves in the *back* of the head."

The Minister was ready with an explanation: "Antwone surprised them!" The Minister intoned, determined. "He obviously came home unexpectedly while they were robbing his apartment!"

Johnson swallowed. "Again, with all due respect, sir, if that were the case, the perp would have shot him as he entered...in the front...and it would have been unusual to aim for his head."

The Minister was having none of it. "Obviously, the person was hiding and Antwone had his back to them."

Johnson was prepared: "Okay, in that scenario—why shoot at all? Why not just run? In that scenario, the victim hadn't seen the perp yet and wouldn't be able to I.D. him."

"Detective," said The Minister, his voice dripping with scorn, "these are all very rational, well-considered rebuttals, but they hardly reflect real life, do they? Some person, high on *something...*" The Minister waved his arms to indicate an entire universe of illegal substances, "decides to rob an apartment. They are not necessarily acting rationally."

The Minister had mentioned the one point that was tough to argue. A professional burglar wouldn't have trashed the apartment and he wouldn't have shot Green in the head (particularly not in the back of the head). But a crazed druggie? Both Harrison and Johnson had seen how completely irrational drugs made people, particularly people who became criminals to get more drugs.

The Minister was already congratulating himself, sure that his argument was a winner. Johnson regarded him steadily, keeping his voice carefully neutral.

"And, sir, that would be a good point..." The Minister all but bowed, so certain was he of his argument.

"Except for the fact, that the perp navigated three deadbolts and a security system without a scratch on any of them." The Minister looked surprised, his eyes narrowing. Johnson continued,

"And Green's security code had ten digits, which I'm told, would be statistically almost impossible to crack without knowing the combination...except by someone who knew exactly what they were doing."

The Minister, so confident moments before, was now sullen, uncooperative—sulking after Johnson's smackdown like a bratty kid that's just been deprived of a sweet. The two cops rose to leave. Harrison spoke: "Uhhh, sorry. One more thing, Minister?" The Minister inclined his head.

"Sir, do you know Kevin DuShane?"

The Minister looked surprised at the question.

"And what relevance would that have to your investigation?" he asked imperiously.

Harrison's tone was measured. "Perhaps none. But we'd very much like to speak with Mr. DuShane."

The Minister barely looked at him, but raised his hands dramatically in a gesture of helplessness. "I'm sorry I can't help you."

"You don't know where he is?" pressed Johnson.

"I'm sorry, detective," replied The Minister.

Harrison continued: "Do you know Kevin DuShane well, sir?"

Again, the imperious look. "Not well," said The Minister.

Harrison persisted, "But didn't you plan his vacation?"

The Minister raised his brows in surprise, but his eyes were steady, unsmiling.

"I?" he said haughtily. "Plan his… vacation? No, of course not. Why would I plan someone's vacation?" His air was disdainful, petulant.

There was a slight pause. The Minister acted as if he was amused by the question, but his eyes were hard and cold.

"Gentlemen—I don't even plan my own vacations," he said with a barely disguised sneer.

Harrison nodded to Johnson. They both stood up. Time to go.

"If it's all right, sir, we'd like to leave a statement for you to sign."

The Minister raised an eyebrow.

"It's just a formality. Please check it over carefully and make sure we've recorded your comments correctly."

The Minister nodded his assent. Harrison and Johnson courteously proffered their hands. The Minister ignored them and remained behind his desk. He nodded briefly without speaking, as they made their departure past the two burly Guards of Jehovah posted in The Minister's outer office.

As Harrison and Johnson were pulling out of the enormous church parking lot, Johnson turned to Harrison.

"Hey, thanks for helping me out back there. Jerk."

Harrison chuckled. "You were doing fine."

"Hmmmm..." Johnson replied, unconvinced.

Johnson lifted his shirt and looked over his shoulder. Surprised, Harrison asked: "What on earth are you doing?"

"Checking myself for poison darts," Johnson replied with a straight face.

Harrison laughed out loud. Johnson continued: "All I can say is...good thing we didn't drink the dude's coffee."

"So, do you think he's as bad as his reputation? Harrison was interested. For all his joking around, Johnson had an amazing intuition about people. Johnson shrugged.

"C'mon, Jay," Harrison pressed his partner. "Anything strike you?"

Johnson was eating an old donut, flicking desiccated confectioners' sugar onto the upholstery. "You mean aside from the fact that virtually every member of the choir claims as common knowledge that The Minister paid for Kevin DuShane's vacation?"

"Yeah, aside from that..." Harrison pressed.

"Well, I guess..." Johnson considered his answer.

"Yes?" Harrison prompted.

Johnson looked at the stale donut dejectedly, then threw it out the window. He turned to his partner, brushing sugar off his hands.

"For one of the toughest guys in Chicago, he's a huge baby."

Chapter Twenty-Five

New York, New York

Tolero Star Securities had always had a scrappy, street-fighting culture that made the patrician nabobs of investment banking a little nervous, a little disapproving. It was the brainiacs at Balthuzar Brothers who had pioneered the securitization of residential mortgages. They were the ones who came up with the idea of grouping a bunch of mortgages together and selling, essentially, the lender's risk. The less risk on his books, the more loans the lender could make, the more interest he could earn; everybody was happy. But Balthazar Brothers had been too cautious to jump into the mortgage rip tide with both feet, the way Tolero Star Securities had. That was understandable. Balthazar Brothers was already the most formidable investment bank on Wall Street. They had nothing to prove. Tolero Star was different. After all, they reasoned, small securities firms don't get to be big investment banks by being reticent about risk. And Tolero Star wanted to be big.

It seemed as if their strategy was paying off. In 2006, Tolero Star reported a banner year with a mind-boggling $9.2 billion in revenue. Investors eager to leverage the benefits of Tolero Star's acumen in their own returns, had flocked to their doors, making them the seventh largest securities firm in terms of capital—with assets under management of approximately $350 billion. Approximately 15,500 employees worldwide kept everything percolating along.

But gamblers and stock jobbers know they're only as good as their last trade. And the company that had never posted a loss since its founding in 1923, had made a bad trade. Tolero Star's huge returns were accomplished as a result of leverage—and while that is the universal maxim of most of Wall Street's most successful investing—Tolero Star had made two mistakes that can't be made together. They'd leveraged too much—accountants now estimated their ratio of leverage to assets at thirty-five to one— and they'd invested in assets that, as a result of the economic downturn and foreclosures, were completely illiquid. They had based their forecasting on the presumption that the underlying asset—the house—wouldn't lose its cash value. In the event of foreclosure, theoretically, they still owned something they could sell. But in down markets, houses sell slowly and stocks sell fast. Caught somewhere in the middle of the economic cyclone was Tolero Star.

CHAPTER TWENTY-SIX

Rockville, Maryland

IT WAS THE BEATING AFRICAN DRUMS, pulsing through her computer speakers as she opened the link to the church website, that made Lacey fairly certain that Okono's church and his close 20 year relationship with its minister might become a campaign issue. A quick review of the church website—which touted the congregation's "non-negotiable commitment to Africa" and allegiance to a "Black Value System" (which exhorted its parishoners to only patronize black-owned and run businesses and celebrate only the black experience)—confirmed that this was a church on the loose, untied fringes of the mainstream fabric. The church's bedrock philosophy was something called "Black Liberation Theology," a radical Afro-centric doctrine first credited to William H. Cone. Supporters argued it was a means of social and spiritual empowerment. Critics accused it of being a Marxist doctrine of wealth redistribution that incited hatred and violence, and whose aim was to manipulate black anger and white guilt to achieve anarchy. Whatever it was to its critics or supporters, it was pretty obviously controversial. More to the point, however, it put paid to the idea that Okono was a uniter, not a divider. For a biracial candidate who was continually trying to emphasize his "foot in both camps" impartiality—it was a pretty strong indication that Okono's feet had voted, and they had voted black.

The story had been circulating on the internet for months. There was even the seemingly outlandish claim that The Minister had traveled to Libya to meet Muammar Gaddafi (*Gaddafi!*) in the early 1980s. Usually, when there are allegations that an organization's funding is tied to a foreign state sponsor of terror, one might expect some sort of journalistic inquiry. All the major networks and news organizations knew of the story. And, most at least, had heard examples of The Minister's fiery anti-American diatribes—lashing out at Jews, the U.S. government, and white people, generally, for the planned extermination of African Americans. Extermination, The Minister warned, even now being delivered by the various mechanisms of legislation, incarceration, and drug addiction. Nobody ran it.

Lacey and her bloggers had been posting links to the church website for weeks, encouraging Okono supporters to check it out themselves and come to their own conclusions. Many of the McCracken supporters had written or called media contacts, or simply used the emails provided for popular news programs to ask why the networks weren't covering the story. Others systematically contacted all the major news media—even the McCracken campaign. Silence. When week after week went by, and nothing about Okono's church was mentioned, they began to worry. After all, this had happened before with Okono.

At the beginning of February, the McCracken bloggers had started seeing references in the online comments sections of major news outlets alleging that some of Okono's most successful taglines had, in fact, been borrowed without attribution from other sources. They started investigating and sent the information, unsolicited, to the McCracken campaign. For a candidate who had made his reputation on his uplifting rhetoric, it seemed like a blockbuster.

When the McCracken campaign finally raised the issue at the end of February, the press downplayed it, and blunted the edge of the accusation by equating McCracken's limited use of one or two lines from others, with Okono's extensive borrowing—as a kind of plagiaristic equivalency. But the evidence of Okono's plagiarism went far beyond borrowing an elegant speech from a Boston politician and friend.

Okono had borrowed punch lines, phrases, and ideas without attribution, time after time; including his first national speech. Virtually his entire economic plan was lifted wholesale from McCracken's. The scope of the plagiarism was compelling to anyone who'd witnessed the epic self-immolation of a presidential candidate years before, who'd been savaged by the media after he strayed from originality on a single, regrettable occasion. Equally illuminating should have been the media response this time—which essentially amounted to a collective yawn. "So what's the big deal?" they said. McCracken supporters marveled. Okono seemed to have some Antaean ability to emerge unscathed, a Teflon candidate.

Equally tepid was the media's response to investigations (again largely done in the blogosphere) that a significant number of events and descriptions in Okono's "autobiography" were demonstrably untrue. The media had largely cheered when one of the afternoon talk show queens exposed a best-selling writer who had fictionalized aspects of the story he promoted as his "memoir." But there was no censure of Okono's fabrications, perhaps because there was no reporting of it. Claire McCracken's every statement was scrutinized *ad nauseum* for its strict adherence to the facts. When she strayed, she was branded a "congenital liar" with a "complicated relationship to the truth." Okono's far more extensive literary enhancements and fabrications remained like the man: masked, concealed.

As weeks passed, it became increasingly clear that the McCracken campaign wouldn't touch the story of The Minister. Mostly they were afraid. They were still doing a delicate soft-shoe to hold on to the African American super delegates who had pledged (or *almost* pledged—fingers crossed!!) their support. McCracken needed the "supers" far more than the supers needed McCracken. A McCracken win had always been predicated on the support of African Americans. At this point, they held the whip hand, and they knew it.

But, in fairness, many of McCracken's white supporters represented even more of a problem. The liberal elite of the Democratic Party had made it clear that they were not going to countenance attacks on Okono—no matter how justified. Some of her closest advisors—African American themselves—urged the McCracken campaign to make The Minister and his church an issue. The campaign wouldn't do it, they were too afraid of the backlash.

When Okono became a serious contender, and it became clear he would make a serious dent in their primacy with African

Americans, the McCracken campaign should have made some cold calculations as to what a winning coalition could look like if it didn't include the black vote. They didn't do it. They didn't do it for the same reason they spent $30 million in Iowa, a state they always knew they were almost guaranteed to lose: they couldn't cut their losses.

Finally, someone got tired of pussyfooting around and ordered the tapes of The Minister's sermons from the church website. $19.95 bought candidate Okono a whole heap of trouble. Viewing the tapes provided the immutable evidence that for 20 years, Congressman Okono had worshipped in what most people would consider a racist church. He'd been married, and his children had been baptized, by what many would conclude was a racist minister. The ties between The Minister and Okono were close and long-standing. The title of Okono's second autobiography was taken from the title of one of The Minister's sermons.

The Okono campaign went into frenzied spin control, but they knew how bad it was. Realistically, it was unrecoverable. First, The Minister was a "crazy uncle" who was retiring anyway—Okono downplayed the extent to which The Minister had been his mentor since he listened to his sermons on tape at Harvard. As it appeared to snowball, Okono had no political choice but to repudiate him entirely. To do so, the Okono illusionists positioned Okono in front of a phalanx of American flags, lined up like soldiers behind their general. If the flags had been animate, one suspects they wouldn't have stayed. Because Okono—who had had every opportunity in his privileged life—spoke not about the good of America, but of the bad, and he admitted maybe he wasn't so post-racial after all. Never had bald political necessity been garbed in so much convenient self-righteousness. Predictably, the media loved him for it.

CHAPTER TWENTY-SEVEN

Menlo Park, California

APPELBAUM LOVED SILICON VALLEY. His wife teased him that it was the proximity to all that cash, and he admitted that between the money from the tech companies and the venture capital firms, it was close to a Democratic fundraiser's paradise. The weather was nice, too—if a little banal. Today he had appointments with the money guys. It bored him, but there was no way around it. He'd meet them, sometimes arrange a photo-op with O. and the guy's wife and kids. Talk to them a little about strategy—how the race was going so far—next objectives—maybe do a little damage control on The Minister thing—shit like that. Then he'd turn them back over to Kim Matheson and she'd get the dollar commitment.

He looked at the list of appointments in front of him. He'd met this guy before. Paul Johannsen. One of the titans of Sand Hill Road. Harvard Business School. Right out of school, started a venture capital firm with a couple of classmates and invested in some dot-coms. Thing exploded. Appelbaum didn't know if the guy was lucky or smart—he supposed when you were making that kind of money, it didn't matter. Johannsen was completely idealistic, a real boy scout—he'd told Appelbaum at their first meeting that he wanted to use his money to do good in the world. What a yutz. Appelbaum smirked at the memory.

A friend had introduced Johannsen to Okono at a fundraiser he'd lined up for his HBS buddies—and they were all sold. Liberty! (yay!) Justice for all! (yay!) Clean Air! (yay!) Clean water (yay!) And here's this fresh, young, handsome black guy—untainted by the same old "politics as usual" as represented by the McCrackens (this was an easier sell, since none of them were from Chicago and knew about Okono's questionable tactics in his own races). And he went to Harvard! And he was about their age! And he had young children! Why, really, he was just like them (okay, maybe not so nebbishy)! Only *black*! Awesome.

If they'd sort of sold out their idealistic principles by just making money hand over fist, (but not *really*, not in their hearts) Okono had been out working in the "hoods" (wow. They felt more authentic just getting the jargon down. Should they throw in a "brother?" Just kind of casually? Could that work? Too much?). They were enthralled. They left with certifiable man-crushes and went out to proselytize. He was black; "they was *bad*." Appelbaum got a headache thinking about all the liberal shemendricks in New York and California suddenly channeling their "inner" black power.

The narrative was set. McCracken was hard, not likeable. Jesus, even her husband was afraid of her—a real ball-buster and, really, who needs that? Too much like the humorless women in business school: too pushy, too eager, too mean. The subtle subtext, that they would never admit, was that they didn't want a woman president any more than they would welcome a woman employer. It would be weird...and kind of threatening. What they said out loud was that they were happy to support a woman—just not this woman. Of course, it was almost impossible to conceive of a female candidate on the national scene with more policy credentials than McCracken, but no matter... they loved this guy, Okono!

Now of course, Appelbaum knew, none of these guys would buy a stock without investigating the company. And they certainly wouldn't recommend it to a potential investor without due diligence—but they gleefully passed around misinformation about Okono. Worried that he has no legislative track record? Why, here's a list thoughtfully pulled together by a 'reporter' for the *Daily Kos* that profiles 900 (Yup. You heard that right, Bub. Nine. Zero. Zero.) pieces of legislation Okono passed in the Congress. More than McCracken!

Now, Appelbaum wondered, would these guys pass around numbers they hadn't checked, about a company they wanted people to invest in? Earnings of 3,000%? More earnings than any other company!!? Some crazy shit like that? No. *No.* That would be *illegal.* But these guys, these fat cats of finance—who theoretically lived and died by the quality of their research of potential investments—they sold Okono as carelessly as boiler room pitchmen sell a hot stock. And they knew nothing about him.

So one might think the numbers might be close? Maybe not 900 *exactly* (nine hundred was a lot!), but 850? That wouldn't be too bad, would it? Appelbaum smiled to himself. Well, what if it were... 2? How bad would that be? Would these guys still be good with that? Appelbaum wondered, chuckling.

Of course, McCracken had a few bills herself, so the Okono supporters were quick to make the point that Okono's work represented real legislative accomplishments—real substantive stuff. So what were they? Did they know? Because Appelbaum did. The two pieces of legislation Okono had passed in Congress were to name a post office and to honor an African country.

Appelbaum thought about P.T. Barnum and the wire-haired Harvard psychology professor advising the campaign. It was true that they were separated by more than a hundred years, yet they both understood...well...sales. It was all right-brain psychology. All emotion. All delirium. Appelbaum chuckled. Okono was the South Sea Bubble and tulipmania all over again.

But Appelbaum cautioned himself. He ought not to be so sanguine. He must remember to be careful. In this case, the truth would be... inconvenient. If some of these...discrepancies... between the facts and the version the Okono campaign was promoting were pointed out to the money mandarins, it might cramp their ardor a bit. It was lucky, then, that it was rarely pointed out to them, because all the deferential liberals who were nabobs of capital wanted to believe in Okono. And believe they did. At least for now, thought Appelbaum. How they achieved it, Appelbaum was less sure. After all, truth be told, Okono had missed 46% of the votes in this, his first session in Congress. Honestly, how could the guy pass 900 pieces of legislation when he wasn't even there? Jesus! Appelbaum thought, his mouth in a crooked smile. If Okono had *actually* passed 900 pieces of legislation, he might have had to consider voting for him himself.

CHAPTER TWENTY-EIGHT

Washington, DC

THE THREATS WERE MAKING HER STAFFERS NERVOUS. At first, they were from constituents—or people who claimed to be constituents. But the bullying and hate that Congresswoman Miriam Carter was attracting as an African American—who refused to switch her support from McCracken to Okono—had become frightening.

Some—both black and white—called her a traitor to her race, an Uncle Tom, an ingrate. Others would no longer speak to her at all. To them, she was apostate. Her only answer, she told them, was the testimony of her life. Their anger pained her deeply, but it seemed to her misplaced. Like many of the African American leaders, she had pledged her support to McCracken long before Okono had even officially declared he was going to run. McCracken had a record of working on issues that were important to the African American constituency. Okono didn't have a record of working on much of anything except getting elected. As to veiled threats or implied insults, Miriam Carter had long since developed a tough skin. And she had never been easily swayed—particularly when she believed her decision was a matter of principle.

Dozens of other prominent African Americans had folded under the pressure. Other members of the Congressional Black Caucus had spoken out about the death threats they were receiving: prominent leaders, lions of civil rights. Their complaints received scant attention from the media. Some were sincerely torn about not supporting the first viable African American candidate for national office. Others had no such scruples. To their minds, Okono wasn't ready. Worse, as long-time advocates of civil rights, many of them saw him more as an interloper than a fellow traveler.

But in the end, it didn't matter—the Okono supporters' back door machinations and efforts to intimidate would ultimately triumph with almost all of them in the end, because it wasn't about race, it was about money. The threat of the almost unlimited war chest the Okono campaign could offer a future opponent to defeat them in their next contest was, they knew, not idle. No one had ever seen the kind of money the Okono campaign was able to command—according to FEC filings, the Okono campaign was spending a staggering $293,000 an *hour*.

So what difference did it make if what the African American patriarchs said about Okono in private was different than the fulsome support they offered in public? In fairness, a few didn't care about Okono's money machine. They were nearer the end of their lives than the beginning—and they were looking to their legacies—hopeful to be remembered wisely and well. They became increasingly fearful that the Okono movement was sweeping beyond them, past them. If they didn't climb aboard the bandwagon now, they feared their own accomplishments would be consigned to the sidelines forever: irrelevant, un-memorialized, un-remembered.

But there was more to it than that for the African American matriarchs. This contest—that pitted the constituencies of a white woman against a black man—was nothing new, only the venue was different. The presidential campaign actually represented the apotheosis or "perfect storm" of a grudge match that had brewing since female abolitionists (of both races) had fought for civil rights, but were themselves denied the franchise until fifty years after it was granted to African American males. For more than a century, civil rights for African Americans males butted up against civil rights for women, and mostly, the African American males prevailed.

Even in 1964, after the Civil Rights Act outlawed discrimination, discrimination against women (particularly in employment) was greeted with a wink and a nod. Contrary to the law, the Equal Employment Opportunity Commission expressly condoned "help wanted ads" that differentiated by sex. Educated, professional women (black and white) who wanted to rent an apartment or apply for a credit card were forced to find a willing male to co-sign their applications.

And then there was the civil rights struggle itself. There was an increasing historical awareness that African American women had been thrown on the front lines—as intentional victims, not leaders. Women like Rosa Parks, Autherine Lucy, Elizabeth Eckford were all heroes, but they were silent heroes. In the rallies called to protest their ill-treatment, the mighty male ministers spoke to the crowds on their behalf. The women were not allowed to speak.

So, too, the organizers—women like JoAnn Robinson, and Daisy Bates, Fannie Lou Hamer and Ella Baker—who led the voter registration drives, organized the boycotts—their work and words went largely unrewarded, unrecorded. They did the organizing, a man took the credit. Many of them believed they had had the worst of it: insulted, beaten, and imprisoned by white supremacists, then ignored and disregarded by the black men whose purposes they'd served.

But if Miriam Carter suffered privately from divided loyalties or ancient feuds, she never said so. As she traveled the country with McCracken, Miriam Carter told the crowds in public the same thing she told her staffers in private...that she had been behind Claire McCracken from the beginning for the only reason that mattered. She thought she would make the best president. Actually, she thought she would make a *great* president, one for the history books. She'd known her a lot of years. She'd seen her buffeted and tempered by all the exigencies and humiliations of modern political life and, in her opinion, it hadn't just made her a better politician, it had made her a better person.

Miriam was fond of telling people that if her life had taught her anything, it was the relevance of Martin Luther King, Jr's exhortation to judge people not by the color of their skin, but by the content of their character. At one point, McCracken had spoken to her about it directly. Claire had told her she appreciated everything Miriam had done, but she understood the kind of pressure Miriam was under—and for her own good, she should leave the campaign. Carter wouldn't do it. "This isn't about race," she said, "it's about experience and personal history. I gave you my word that I would fight for you to the end, and that's exactly what I'm going to do."

CHAPTER TWENTY-NINE

April 2008
Rockville, Maryland

WITH THE PENNSYLVANIA PRIMARY only weeks away, McCracken's campaign had started to regain some of its momentum. With nothing to lose, Claire McCracken broke out of the chrysalis created by her staff and put it all on the line. She started connecting with people directly in a way that felt less constrained, more authentic. The popular infatuation with Okono was dimming slightly, as the strange reality dawned on many Democrats that they really knew very little about this man who was running for president. To some of them, that didn't seem quite right somehow.

One of the most persistent criticisms of Okono was his lack of foreign policy expertise. As a congressman only nine months into his first term when he started running for president, he simply hadn't had the time on the national stage to develop personal relationships with world leaders.

So it should have made some in the press wonder, why Okono and his omnificent and savvy team of media handlers—as adept as Rumpulstiltskin at spinning gold from chaff—didn't emphasize the one foreign leader with whom Okono *did* have a close relationship—Obongo Malinga of Nigeria. Malinga! The name sounded more like a Parker Brothers board game you might play on a rainy afternoon at the beach than a corrupt would-be African potentate. But from the McCracken supporters' point of view, Malinga was McCracken's get-out-of-jail-free card.

In August 2006, Okono had made a trip to Nigeria as a delegation of one. No doubt this was viewed as what it was—a victory lap. African American politicians were accorded great respect in Africa. But while there, at rallies and events, Okono appeared constantly at the side of the opposition party candidate—Obongo Malinga; who was running for president. This, in and of itself, might qualify as a violation of the Logan Act (which prevents American politicians from taking a foreign policy position contrary to the U.S. government). But standing alongside Malinga, Okono criticized the Nigerian government and its current president for corruption—a fair, if undiplomatic, criticism. However, the censure seemed oddly misplaced. Nigeria's government had a better record than most, and Malinga was widely reported to have his own corruption issues, having inexplicably accumulated a billion dollar fortune during a two-year term as oil minister. The rumors were prolific that Malinga had been set up in the oil business by Gaddafi.

Moreover, Malinga was running on a seriously—some said virulently—anti-American platform. The current Nigerian government had been extremely cooperative in extraditing suspected Al-Qaeda terrorists involved in the embassy bombings in Dar es Salaam and Nairobi, and was working with the U.S. to neutralize local Al-Qaeda organizations in the country. Malinga promised the Nigerians if he became president, the cooperation with the Americans would end. In language that would be difficult to misinterpret, Malinga promised his supporters: "Our government will not be held at ransom to extradite Muslims to foreign lands." No mention was made of refusing the $496 million Nigeria was receiving in U.S. aid.

All of this would have been controversial enough, but in the aftermath of the election only a few months before, things had gone from bad to worse. Most observers conceded the election was probably rigged (although which party was more responsible remained unclear). When the government was returned by a slender margin, opposition leader Malinga called on his followers to take to the streets, where they initiated a program of what the U.S. envoy called "ethnic cleansing" against the majority Nibuyu tribe. Eventually the U.N. stepped in and brokered a power-sharing arrangement to end the violence, but not before more than 1,000 people were killed and 600,000 were displaced.

Killing people of any religion ought to be considered a bad thing. However, in the context of a U.S. election, supporting a Muslim leader who is exterminating Christians—is probably not on most strategists' recommended list. When Malinga's followers (who called themselves "the Taliban") torched a Christian church with fifty women and children inside, Okono's ties to Malinga became a public relations problem that was hard to overestimate.

When Lacey first started to read about Malinga in the

blogosphere, she was frankly skeptical. But the story was fascinating, so she did more research. And as she did research, she documented everything. But since all of this information was in the public domain and from mainstream U.S. news sources, it wasn't hard to start pulling it all together.

The picture that started to emerge was damning. Whether Okono encouraged Obongo Malinga and they were good friends (as Malinga claimed) or Malinga had simply traded on the enormous appeal and naiveté of the American—was hard to know, but in one sense it didn't matter. The relationship was sufficiently controversial that Okono could not fail to be damaged by it. Either Okono was manipulated by Malinga, or Okono was complicit in Malinga's misdeeds—neither augured well for making a case to the American people that as commander-in-chief, Okono would be "ready on day one."

Lastly, belying the claim that Okono had little real relationship to Malinga—were the amazing similarities between the two campaigns—or at least amazing if they were coincidental. Malinga's campaign in Nigeria emphasized the use of social networking, small cash donations and even utilized the same campaign slogan—"Change We Need"—all months before Okono's campaign got started in the United States.

At first, no one believed Lacey. She wasn't offended. The claims were outrageous; if she hadn't done the research herself she wouldn't have believed it either. Muddying the water was the fact that TruthChecker.org had supposedly investigated the story and found it untrue. The problem was that they had only investigated one aspect of the allegations—that the Okono campaign had made a $1 million campaign contribution to

Malinga. There was no verifiable evidence for that claim, as TruthChecker.org pointed out.

However, the underlying and more important issues about Okono's relationship to the African strongman were demonstrably true.

So with assiduous care, Lacey wrote a four-page synopsis appended to thirteen pages of footnotes from reputable news sources (and not blogs, either: print media, the big boys). She sent it to a big media guy; a "friend of a friend," thinking he'd want the scoop. He read it, thanked her, but identifying Okono's relationship with the strongman as "too tangential," declined to print it. With urging from Connor and her bloggers, Lacey identified 35 of the most prominent journalists in the U.S. At her own expense, she sent the report to them FedEx—figuring that at least they wouldn't think she was living in D.C.'s Lafayette Square with tin foil on her head. And the bloggers all waited, feeling sure that *someone* would cover it. But there was no response. No story. No coverage of Okono's only foreign policy experience, or his close ties to the man who had fomented the epic violence that had been in the news for weeks— the new President of Nigeria, Obongo Malinga.

Chapter Thirty

Chicago, Illinois

As Harrison and Johnson approached, they passed two truculent Guards of Jehovah seated in the outer office. Entering The Minister's office, the first thing Harrison noticed was that The Minister's recent media trials had aged him. The second thing he noticed were the packing boxes. Harrison had heard that when the tapes became a *cause célèbre*, The Minister had been pressured to step into retirement more quickly than originally planned in an effort to contain the fallout for Okono. But for a man as notoriously thin-skinned as The Minister, a magnificent house on the edge of a golf course in a gated, mostly white community, and an enormous pension from the church, had obviously not lessened the sting of Okono's repudiation. He appeared crumpled, aggrieved, bitter. He did not rise to greet them or ask them to sit. They informed him they were still trying to establish if there was any connection between the church and Antwone Green's murder.

"Gentlemen." He waved his arms theatrically in front of them like a magician—only to twist his wrist and open his hand, to reveal his empty palm.

"There's nothing there."

Harrison and Johnson looked at each other, perplexed. The Minister continued: "Sometimes the simplest explanation is the best. Antwone lived in a—" he passed his hand over his forehead as if the idea pained him, "neighborhood in transition. The police...you.." he pointed at the two detectives accusingly, "ignore the area. The Ministry tries to provide the residents with some security, of course—" he paused modestly, "and yet...sometimes there is crime. Random crime."

Harrison spoke.

"And you're convinced that that's what this was?"

"What else?" There was no mistaking the hostility in The Minister's voice. It wasn't a rhetorical question. It was a direct challenge; a threat: What have you got? his eyes said. Make your accusation or get out of my face.

But they didn't have anything, and The Minister knew it. Lots of guesses, lots of circumstantial pieces of information that might, with the most phenomenal luck, make a case; but nothing substantive enough to challenge one of the most powerful men in Chicago.

In one sense, Harrison and Johnson's experience working in Area 2 was the defining aspect of the case for two reasons. First, if they hadn't worked in Area 2, they might still have been idealistic (or naïve) enough to be tempted to try to make a case with what they had—phone records showing Kevin DuShane's last calls were to The Minister's unpublished cell phone number.

Witnesses who claimed The Minister told them first-hand he'd arranged DuShane's 'vacation'. Witnesses who claimed to have overheard Green pressing The Minister about DuShane and his relationship to another man they both referred to as "our friend." But both knew: knew first-hand what went on, how evidence disappears when it becomes inconvenient, and frightened witnesses change their stories. With no hard evidence of a motive or connection, and The Minister denying everything, none of it was enough. In fact, it wasn't anything, and all three of them knew it.

If the first problem was the difficulty of making the circumstantial case against a powerful and influential figure, the second problem was making it stick. Anyone taking on The Minister would have to have unimpeachable credibility. Through no fault of their own, Harrison and Johnson were linked to the most discredited, most corrupt cops in Chicago—maybe even in the United States— cops who had become notorious for framing African American defendants.

All The Minister had to do was to mention that the cops bringing charges against him had been members of the infamous "Midnight Crew from Area 2"—and even people within the department would question their integrity. The fact that they'd both worked with internal affairs to bring the bad guys down, that they'd never accepted as much as a free beer, that they were African American themselves—none of that would matter. No one would hear it above the PR din of allegations of racism and corruption The Minister would create to protect himself.

Harrison and Johnson talked softly as they walked to the car.

"Je-sus," Johnson almost spat the word. "What was that Jedi mind-control shit?" he asked Harrison.

Harrison smiled, but didn't answer. He wasn't surprised that Johnson was pissed off at The Minister's patronizing high-handedness.

Johnson continued, "I hate that shit." Johnson again waved his arms, imitating The Minister.

"Does that shit work for that motherfucker? he demanded. "That's what I want to know. Does that shit work on *anybody*? Jesus—he must think we're all feebleminded." Johnson continued his pantomime:

"Gen-tle-men," Johnson intoned—mimicking The Minister's stentorian tones, and waving his arms around in the air like a ninja master in a Jackie Chan movie. "There...is...NOTHING... THERE." Johnson paused. "I'd like to tell that calypso-singing motherfucker—We're the police. We decide what's there."

Harrison started to laugh. "What? What did you call him?"

Johnson looked slightly abashed. "Motherfucker?"

"No. The singing thing? What was that? Did you make that up?"

Johnson hooted, "You didn't know?"

"Know what?"

"Our minister, there..." Johnson hooked his thumb behind him to indicate where the Guards of Jehovah were still watching, "was a Baptist preacher before he converted to his whacked-out version of Islamo-Christianity."

"I knew that," Harrison replied.

"But before he was a minister, he made his money as a Calypso singer."

"*No*!" Harrison couldn't hide his surprise.

"Truth. Also, do you know that the Guard of Jehovah believe

some crazy black scientist named Yakub created white people six thousand years ago by breeding them in the Aegean ocean?"

"Why the Aegean, particularly?" asked Harrison, curiously.

Johnson looked at him steadily, frowning.

"Don't know. Don't care. But it explains one thing."

"What's that?"

"If you believe shit about aliens, maybe thinking you can do some freaky Yoda mind-control thing wouldn't seem that crazy to you."

Harrison unlocked their car. Johnson leaned against the door, obviously taking some satisfaction from the fact that their continued presence in the parking lot was causing consternation to the two members (now four members!) of the Guard, who had them under surveillance from across the parking lot.

"I got one question," Johnson asked.

"Okay," Harrison said, still laughing.

"Who gets the Ferrari?"

Harrison immediately stopped laughing. "What?"

Johnson continued by way of explanation. "Guy got axed, right?"

Harrison replied evenly. "I guess...took early retirement."

Johnson shrugged.

"Whatever." He wasn't interested in the semantics. He continued.

"So. My question is, who gets the Ferrari?" he demanded.

"What Ferrari are you talking about?" Harrison asked.

Johnson pointed across the parking lot. "*That* Ferrari."

Parked near the rectory door was a gorgeous, bright red, late-model Ferrari. Harrison shrugged his shoulders. He still wasn't following. Johnson was practically hopping with irritation.

"Brah, that's The *Minister's* Ferrari."

Harrison couldn't believe it. His mouth dropped open.

Johnson nodded, pleased with his partner's stunned reaction. "So I'd like to know how a guy who's got it so bad in America comes to be driving a $300,000 car."

"Fair point," Harrison conceded.

"I mean," Johnson continued, "that *car* sure could buy a whole lot of religion for somebody. In fact, for some people that *car* might be its *own* kind of religion."

Harrison laughed and rolled his eyes.

"Jay?" he said to his partner.

"Yeah?"

"Get in the car."

Chapter Thirty-One

May 2008
Menlo Park, California

THE CALLS FROM THE OKONO CAMPAIGN for fundraising help were weekly, now, but Paul Johannsen was happy to help. Campaigns were expensive, people had to put their money where their mouths were. Johannsen joked to his friends that raising money for the Okono campaign had almost become a full-time job. Who cared? He loved it! Democracy in action! And he was really getting the kids involved, taking them to rallies, buying the Okono gear: hats, shirts, the whole thing. Even his preternaturally skeptical wife Joan was on board. She'd even condescended to allow him to put an Okono bumper sticker on the Mercedes station wagon. Livin' large!

So, when it came time for the primary in his home state of Nebraska on Tuesday, May 13th—he decided to take the kids. Why not? See the grandparents and get a little civics lesson. They'd love it! Joan worried about their schoolwork. But the teachers at the kids' private school in Palo Alto were all for Okono, too. They loved the idea!

Now, of course, Nebraska was one of those complicated states where the primary didn't actually count. The caucus in February had already allocated the delegates for the national convention. But tell that to Nebraskans! This was the most exciting primary contest in decades, and suddenly it seemed like everyone who was anyone on cable TV was coming to Nebraska. And in Nebraska, they watch plenty of cable TV. For a modest, well-meaning state not used to the national spotlight, it was all a little intoxicating.

Kids being kids, Johannsen would have hesitated to get their hopes up unless he was pretty sure Okono was going to win. But he knew a little secret. Okono had trounced McCracken 68% to 32% in the caucus! Well, you don't get more decisive than that! Woo-hoo! What a blow-out!

Now, of course, the polls in February had shown the race as dead-even, even then, which made a bunch of sour-grapes McCracken people start hollering about fraud in the caucuses. So Johannsen was looking forward to a re-match! The polls were still showing the race almost too close to call, but Okono had picked up momentum since February. Johannsen expected an even bigger Nebraska primary win than the caucus rout.

Inexplicably, his parents were supporting McCracken. Well, you know, Johannsen reminded himself, they *were* elderly. Whatever. Her demographic. But he had to admit his mother's opinion of Okono concerned him. Both his parents had participated in the caucuses—along with 38,000 residents of the state. Of course, they'd participated, Johannsen mused. His parents were both from good Swedish farming stock, and they took their civic responsibilities seriously.

Johannsen's great great grandparents had immigrated separately to the U.S. around 1865, which according to family lore coincided with the first year there was a dramatic drop in the cost of the transatlantic fare. Both families were peasants, literate, but desperately poor—trying to eke out a living, farming tiny plots of lands in an unforgiving climate on hardscrabble soil.

Johannsen knew the story: peasants in Sweden were virtual serfs—with no civil rights. Sweden's stratified class system made it almost impossible for the lower classes to improve either their social or financial circumstances. Until the 1830s, it was illegal for them to leave, the upper class wasn't simply going to allow its agricultural workers to wander off in search of a better opportunity elsewhere. However, after a number of crop failures coincided with a population boom, the ruling class started to suspect the Malthusian model might be right after all. All those hungry mouths might be better off in America.

Peasants like Johannsen's great great grandparents were eager to go. The U.S. Homestead Act of 1862 granted each immigrant/applicant title to 160 acres, providing the applicant agreed to improve the land. Swedish pioneers collected their supplies in Chicago, and went off to do just that.

Johannsen's family had settled in Nebraska, where there was a growing Swedish community, but life had not been easy. Carving farms from the wilderness was backbreaking physical labor. And with so little civilization nearby, if they wanted something, they either made it themselves or did without. But the fates, or the weather, favored them. For almost sixty years, the high plains of the 100th meridian had record rainfall. With enough rain, the uberous soil yielded copious harvests, the kind of bounty the new immigrants had only dreamed of in Scandinavia. But as more and more farmers came west to till the soil (eventually the government privatized 270,000,000 acres), the native prairie grasses were plowed under. When the first serious drought occurred in 1930, there was nothing to hold the soil. Over the next few years, the farmers watched as the soil and their prosperity blew away in a great black cloud, heading east. It stopped on its way to drop dirt pellets like snow on some East Coast cities—and then it was lost, useless to anyone—drowned in the Atlantic.

The drought and the dust storms lingered for six years. With no way to make the land pay, the farmers piled up debt. The banks foreclosed. The plight of the "Okies" was perhaps the most famous, but the devastation ranged across six states: North Dakota, South Dakota, Nebraska, Kansas, Oklahoma, and Texas. Nobody knows how many died from malnutrition and dust pneumonia from the "Black Rollers" — the choking, all-enveloping dust storms that infiltrated and obscured everything in their paths. The storms were so catastrophic, more than 2.5 million people had left the plains states by 1940. Johannsen's grandparents were not among them. His grandfather had obtained his teaching license and sold insurance on the side. His grandmother somehow scraped enough food from a little garden to feed the family and raise a few hogs. Johannsen's parents both remembered a childhood of poverty and want. They both remembered going to bed quietly hungry, so as not to increase their parents' anguish over something they couldn't change.

Before the primary season, his mother had taken the unusual step of asking him to help McCracken. He wasn't really interested in the election, which at the time, looked like a foregone conclusion for McCracken, anyway. By the time he'd been recruited by a business school buddy to help Okono, he'd frankly forgotten all about her request. Oh, well, he figured. She'd get over it.

Anyway, he thought Okono's story would appeal to his parents, and, at first it had. His mother always proudly told the tale of how she had been in the audience in November of 1958 when Reverend Martin Luther King, Jr. preached at the Salem Baptist Church in North Omaha. Both of Johannsen's parents participated in multiple civil rights demonstrations–including the protest to end segregation at Omaha's Peony Park amusement park in 1963. Early on, when he told them about his fundraising for Okono, both had told him that they were supporting McCracken, but if Okono were the nominee they'd happily support him. Privately Johannsen suspected that his mother was supporting McCracken, and his father was supporting his mother.

But something had happened at the caucuses to change their minds. Neither of his parents was exactly voluble. As a general rule, he knew that Swedes (notoriously and proudly tightfisted) approach speaking as if it costs you something. But his mother, always so kindly and measured, had taken to referring to Okono as a 'thug' and a 'cheat.' Johannsen was appalled.

Oh, well, he figured, nobody likes to lose. Perhaps they were more invested in the primaries than he'd suspected. With the kids playing out back, he figured he'd work on his dad a little about Okono while his mother was making dinner. His father was a big deal in the local Kiwanis and Lions Clubs; his opinion carried weight. Johannsen extolled the virtues of Okono and his incredible personal story. But to Johannsen's surprise, his father appeared completely uninterested. He barely looked at his son, but continued watching the television as if his life depended on it, stone-faced and unbending. With her super-acute maternal hearing, his mother must have overheard his pitch. All of a sudden Paul realized his considerate, temperate, unflappable mother was... furious. He could tell by the way she was slapping the mashed potatoes on the kids' plates as they sat down to eat at the large farm table. Oh, brother! What was this? His mother was making Johannsen really uncomfortable.

Okay, he did feel a little guilty when his mother told him how disappointed she was that he wasn't supporting McCracken, a woman. When he launched into his usual spiel about Okono's great story fulfilling dreams for a better America, she held up her hand.

"There is more than one way to make a better America," she said, looking pointedly at his daughter.

Johannsen shifted uncomfortably in the hard rush seat, but said nothing. What was going on? His mother was always so nice!

She continued, "Electing a woman president is something *I* always dreamed about." His twelve-year-old daughter looked confused.

"Wait," she interrupted: "Grandma: Are you saying there's never been a *woman* president—of any color?"

His mother remained silent, looking at Paul as if inviting him to answer. Johannsen paused, scratched his head and looked uncomfortable. His daughter looked at him thoughtfully. He knew he was always harping on what a historic election this was. Should he have told her? Didn't she know? His mother and daughter exchanged a silent look, as the older woman shook her head 'no.' Now his son piped up; full of the confidence of a precocious ten- year-old.

"That can't be right, Grandma. Girls make up like half the population. African Americans are only like 14%."

The uncomfortable discussion continued throughout dinner. Perhaps, his mother had said to him pointedly, placing a large roast on the table, he owed a little more to white women than to black men.

"C'mon, Mom," Johannsen, said, feeling like he was getting the worst of the exchange. This was all rather unfair. She was making it sound like he was a bad guy, here.

"You're not suggesting I support a candidate because she's white?"

His mother bristled at the suggestion. "Certainly not." She regarded him steadily: "I'm suggesting you should be supporting McCracken because both candidates would make history, and she's more qualified." His father, whose head was bowed as he said a silent blessing, now said, perhaps coincidentally, a loud "Amen."

Wow. For the first time in his life, Johannsen thought about his incredibly capable mother in the context of *her* life, not of his. Frankly, it had never occurred to him before that she might have wanted a different life. Moms had dreams? *What was that all about*? Was his mother, God forbid, a feminist? Probably she was spending too much time volunteering at the Women's Crisis

Center again, or something. Stuff like that always got them a little antsy. He remembered when Joan was answering some domestic- abuse hotline. He finally told her she had to stop. She had been coming home brimming with anger and furious about injustice. Worse yet, she wanted to tell Paul all about it. Ugggh. *No.* Who wants to hear stories like that? Thank heaven she'd given it up.

But, Johannsen conceded, maybe his mother did have a point. Women *had* basically fed, clothed and educated him—well, to the present day. Of course, he supposed he was grateful and all. But was that enough reason to vote for one?

As he entered the Okono headquarters the next day, Johannsen decided it was not. He understood women voting by gender just as African Americans were voting overwhelmingly by race. However, since he was neither a woman nor an African American, that left him in the clear, he posited. Was he *not* voting for McCracken because she was a woman? That was a tough one, because in the back of his mind there was a niggling voice that told him maybe that was part of it. Perhaps it was paranoia, but he felt like his daughter was looking at him with a more appraising eye. Oh, well, Johannsen thought, she was a teenager. When they got home Joan would explain things, take her to the mall and buy her some tank tops or something, smooth things over.

When he was talking to his father this morning, he'd talked about Okono's overwhelming support in the state. Why, he wondered, were the morning broadcasters still claiming it was a statistical dead heat? His father hated controversy of any kind, and clearly did not want to engage. Finally, he looked at his son with sympathy. "Son," he said, "I wouldn't take those caucus results to the bank, if I was you," and that was all. Johannsen looked after him, gaping.

Johannsen was surprised to see that the Okono campaign wasn't projecting a big win either. "It's going to be a squeaker!" someone doing phone push-polling called out from the back of the room. Everyone was rushing around. One group was calling out reporting numbers from various precincts which another volunteer wrote on a huge dry-erase board in an indecipherable scrawl. Other volunteers busily made calls to get people to the polls. Johannsen and the kids had volunteered to drive a mini-van to ferry people back and forth to the precinct. Eventually, the polls closed. It had been a long day. 92,000 people had participated, two-and-a-half-times the number that had participated in the caucus. And, most importantly, Okono won. But for some reason that was inexplicable to Johannsen, the margin of victory was far different than in the caucus. In the caucuses, a whopping 36 point spread favored Okono. In the primary, Okono won 49% to 46%, the point-spread a measly... three.

Driving to Eppley Airfield in Omaha to catch a flight home the next day with his kids, Johannsen started talking to the limo driver. Traveling as much as he did, Johannsen had developed an enormous respect and appreciation for limo drivers. "What had happened?" he asked the driver. "What had changed, to collapse Okono's margin of victory from the caucus blowout in February?" The limo driver looked at Johannsen curiously, and shrugged. "It didn't count," he said simply, as if it were obvious. "They didn't need to cheat."

Chapter Thirty-Two

Chicago, Illinois

Everyone likes a story. Or at least that was The Professor's first premise. The second premise was that all good stories have three elements: an exciting plot, an interesting protagonist and finally, of course, a moral. The first story was the leadership story, or the story of self. And if anyone ever had an interesting story of self, Appelbaum mused, it was the aging, disheveled, but oddly luminous man seated across from him at the Formica conference table. In a campaign that prided itself on being cutting-edge, The Professor was clearly a throwback to an earlier time. Balding, bespectacled, with a walrus mustache and an irreverent grin, from the top of his unkempt head to the rainbow socks he wore with his Birkenstocks, The Professor exuded a kind of enthusiastic readiness for civic misadventure. It had always been so. Right from the beginning, The Professor seemed to have been destined for a life of contradiction: the son of a suburban rabbi devoted to the rights of rural farm workers, a privileged Caucasian who temporarily dropped out of Harvard to work for civil rights for poor blacks, a male American Jew who was teaching himself Arabic to work for social justice for Muslim women in the Middle East. Determinedly idealistic about his goals and yet ruthlessly cynical about the means necessary to achieve them. Raised in a community for whom the displacement of the dustbowl was a recent memory, The Professor had internalized the inequalities of life until the core of his being thrummed with a profound and personal commitment to social justice. Appelbaum knew enough of The Professor's history with the Farm Workers to have taken the recommendation of one of the campaign's Harvard policy wonks seriously, that this man was probably the world's leading expert on 'movement building.'

In April 2007, with the sounds of an aria that the opera-obsessed Professor played constantly trilling in the background, Appelbaum and Okono had met with The Professor at his Victorian clapboard home on a tree-lined Cambridge street. All that had been required of them was to listen and marvel at the plan The Professor laid out for them. The plan was a result of a two-year study The Professor had undertaken at the request of one of the nation's leading environmental groups. The Wilderness Project had been working to raise public awareness of conservation and ecology since the 1890s, but by their hundredth anniversary they appeared to have run out of steam, seldom able to mobilize their 800,000 members to communal action. After evaluating the performance of the group's 63 chapters and 360 local organizations, The Professor had pinpointed the problem. The Wilderness Project's volunteers were operating as 'lone wolves,' and the group was doing nothing to get them to network or cooperate with others. The solution: encourage the volunteers to build relationships among themselves. Relationships, which in the long run, would create a sense of obligation, when it was a question of whether or not to roll out of bed on a Saturday morning to meet up at a protest, or take action to support the group's goals. The other issue was the appeal that The Wilderness Project made to supporters—which was rational, and issue-based, left-brain. It wasn't motivating supporters to action, The Professor argued. To hook them, the appeal needed to be more manipulative, emotional, right-brain.

The first area of the Okono campaign to draw on The Professor's expertise was the internet operation. The Professor's plan focused on pop-up ads on political websites, which invited potential supporters to sign up for social events; gave them the names of people most active in their area and encouraged them to contact them by email and attend a 'meet-and-greet.' From the psychological point of view (The Professor was, after all, a trained psychologist) it emphasized the primacy of relationships—to the group leader, to the other volunteers and most importantly to the candidate—over platforms or issues. Media pundits noted the brilliance of the strategy to create a relationship with the voter before the campaign asked for contributions—so refreshingly dignified after the McCracken campaign's almost embarrassingly relentless begging for small dollar contributions. But the pundits didn't bother to notice, Appelbaum thought to himself, that only a well-funded campaign could afford such a luxury.

By June, the Professor had set up the field organizer and volunteer training systems, and the Okono Camps—week-long camps devoted to giving thousands of 'leadership teams' and local organizers crash courses in the take-no-prisoners Alinsky-based principles of community organizing. But the Professor brought more to organization building than the sometimes controversial tactics utilized by Alinsky. Because under The Professor's direction, after the volunteers absorbed Okono's mythologized personal story—"The Story of I," there was a second story almost equally as powerful— "The Story of Us." For Democrats discouraged by the ham-fisted policies of the current Republican administration, it was an irresistible invitation to join with other disaffected souls.

Finally, there was "The Story of Now," which included an explanation of the 'skills of action' identified by Alinsky. If some aspects of it seemed a little cynical, a little manipulative—there was nothing less at stake than the future of the country! How could they scruple over minor irregularities? The brilliance of the plan was that to the participants, the whole experience felt incredibly organic and personal—as if they were spontaneously and independently fomenting their own tidy revolution within the echo-y confines of an elementary school gymnasium. Unbeknownst to them, the whole process was orchestrated by a genius psychology professor, who had discovered that the personal storytelling during workshops created precisely the right kind of right brain appeal necessary to fully engage the volunteer.

Of course, Appelbaum recalled, O. had at first resisted the reliance on emotions, uncomfortable that they might be creating something they couldn't control. So, they'd given The Professor's plan a road test. For the first primary in New Hampshire, they'd used a conventional organizing and marketing strategy. They lost. In Iowa and South Carolina, they'd instituted The Professor's model, and won big. Okono was initially a little put-off by the "Mein Führer"-like mania that seemed to overtake his supporters as they started referring to him with quasi-religious zeal as "The One," but he was quick to sense the power it gave him. After a disagreement with Appelbaum on the way to a campaign stop, his cold eyes bored into Appelbaum's as he prepared to exit the limo. "Watch this," he said simply as he exited the car to the roar of the waiting crowd's adulation. It was a none-too-subtle reminder that the puppet could turn puppeteer.

By June, The Professor had written a closely-held 280 page brass-knuckle instruction manual on every aspect of running the campaign, and more than 23,000 volunteers had participated in at least eight or more hours of what The Professor called 'leadership training' and what the McCracken camp called 'obedience training.' Rather than focusing on Okono's record, or position on hot-button issues, volunteers were instructed to focus voter and media attention on Okono's inspirational story and their own personal stories—the more hard-luck and tribulation-filled the better. The student taking the semester off, the single mother of four working as a waitress, the taxidriver working his way through night school, the university professors and champagne liberals passing out flyers and getting their hands dirty—the high-low involvement of these people, the campaign argued, was evidence of the 'new politics' of hope and inspiration, of respect and empowerment that the Okono campaign was all about. Of course, the voters and the media weren't allowed to read The Professor's 280 page training manual—that, after all, might have told a different story.

CHAPTER THIRTY-THREE

Rockville, Maryland

WITH OKONO CONTINUING TO POWER through the caucus states, and McCracken prevailing in the big state primaries, it was clear that the Democratic National Committee was going to be forced to come to a decision about how to handle the delegates of the states that had moved the date of their primaries. The tickets to watch the deliberations of the Democratic Party elders were supposed to be available online on a first-come, first-served basis. Under its own charter (the Democratic National Committee is a private corporation, after all, despite its public role) the meetings of the 30-member Rules and By-laws Committee (RBC) were required to be held in public. Requests for tickets were to be made online or by fax—and the DNC provided a date and time: Tuesday, May 22nd at 10:00 a.m. Trying to pre-subscribe earlier would be useless, the DNC warned. Tickets would only be available at 10:00:00 exactly.

However, when McCracken supporters logged on at the hour stroke to request tickets, most were diverted to a mandatory

'Party Builder' volunteer sign-up page. When they completed the form, and re-loaded the ticket request form, the tickets were gone. The rumor was that Okono supporters had been told in advance to pre-register. When they logged on, the cookies on their computers took them directly to the ticket request page.

The DNC had also insisted that tickets would ONLY be available by fax or over the Internet. However when hundreds of Okono supporters showed up in person at 9:00 a.m. at the DNC's 4th Street, S.W, D.C. headquarters, tickets were distributed to them first, the number then subtracted from the pool of those available online. The McCracken supporters were outraged—considering it one more example of the Okono campaign scamming the system with the willful assistance of the people running the Democratic Party. Perhaps it was not a hopeful sign that the page on the DNC website devoted to providing instructions on the ticketing process to both sides, had a link to "Join Team Okono."

Despite what they considered willful cheating and attempts at misdirection, the McCracken supporters doggedly held to the belief that there was still a chance. Largely unreported by the mainstream media (who kept insisting that McCracken wanted to "change the rules")—many of her supporters knew that the DNC had quietly broken its own rules—in favor of Okono. Five states had broken the proscriptions on timing and changed their primary dates: Iowa, New Hampshire, South Carolina, Florida, and Michigan. As Floridians pointed out, they were the least culpable; the date of their primary had been willfully changed by the Republican-controlled Florida legislature to create exactly this kind of chaos.

The Okono campaign kept to their careful script. The Rules and By-laws Committee's by-laws, they said, set out with great specificity what punishments would be accorded. They were exactly right. The problem arose, because the punishments specified under the rules, were not the ones that the DNC had applied. Under the RBC by-laws, every state that moved the date of its primary, without prior permission, should have lost half of their delegates—and that was what the McCracken and Okono campaigns had agreed to in January.

However, for some reason never publicly explained, the DNC decided that Iowa, New Hampshire, and South Carolina would be accorded *all* of their delegates, and Florida and Michigan, *none*. As a McCracken supporter it was hard to ignore the fact that the states that were not punished under the rules were states where Okono had won (New Hampshire, although technically a McCracken win, accorded each the same number of delegates). And the states that McCracken had won, were stripped of all their delegates. The fact that this would now be publicly debated for the first time, by both sides, gave the McCracken supporters hope that the DNC would be forced to stop playing fast and loose with the rules.

Complicating the issue was the fact that Okono had voluntarily withdrawn his name from the Michigan ballot. McCracken supporters pointed out that there was no requirement for him to do so. Instead, they argued, it was nothing less than a calculated choice made by his campaign not to have his name appear on a ballot in a state where all the polls indicated he wouldn't win.

If his goal was to honor a commitment to the DNC not to campaign in order to punish states that had moved their primaries forward without permission, they pointed out, then why hadn't Okono removed his name in Florida where he was considered to have a chance? And why did his campaign run television ads in the Florida market prior to the January 29th primary?

In response to criticism for this double-dealing by the McCracken campaign, the Okono campaign acknowledged the ads, but contended they were overflow from their ads targeted for the South Carolina primary on the 26th. However, there were two problems with this claim that should have been immediately apparent to anyone in the media. Television coverage in South Carolina was the *Atlanta* market, not the Florida markets. And the South Carolina primary took place on January 26th; the ads were still running in Florida on January 29th. Curiously, her supporters pointed out somewhat acidly, there was no bleeding of McCracken's South Carolina ads into the Florida market.

The McCracken supporters were livid, not only about the DNC's chicanery, and the Okono campaign's willful misrepresentation, but the obtuseness and persistent misstatements of the press. Personally, Lacey was filled with guilt. Without knowing the date, she had promised to be the Maryland coordinator for the rally planned in support of recognizing the McCracken delegates (and victories) in Michigan and Florida. Now scheduled, as luck would have it, for the same date as her son's sixth birthday.

With great trepidation, Lacey had asked her son if he'd consider postponing his party. This was not something she took lightly: Lacey considered her children's birthdays sacrosanct. In past years, she'd spent many a night pre-party up until the weeest hours—decorating and cooking and filling super-hero-themed goodie bags. And she knew her son had spent weeks trying to decide on a theme (Power Rangers? Bakugan? Pokemon?); deliberating with enormous care among the kid birthday themes that dominated an entire aisle amid the tiki torches and the silver- anniversary paraphernalia in the party superstore. The crayon- colored moon bounce had been ordered a month ago.

Her sons had been troopers for Claire McCracken. At first, before Lacey became active, she'd brought them to a rally for the candidate most Democrats then believed would be the first woman president of the United States. They'd patiently stood in an interminable line, and then clapped and cheered at all the right places.

Then when Lacey had volunteered to help the campaign before the Maryland primary, the children accompanied her a few times to the Metro station to wave signs, bundled against the freezing cold in every red and blue piece of outerwear they owned. But soon, Lacey discovered she couldn't bring them anymore. As she stood there one day with her children and another woman at the Rockville Metro—a well-dressed young white male had walked by them and said loudly "Cunts for McCracken." Another young man said loudly, "There'll never be a woman president in *my* America." Lacey was too astounded to speak. This was Rockville, Maryland! Progressive! Educated! *Really* DEMOCRATIC! Who on earth were these people? The other Metro riders, who clearly heard the exchange, rushed by the McCracken volunteers, eyes averted, and said nothing.

Lacey worried about exposing her sons to that kind of hostility. Despite their protests, when she next went to wave signs of support at the Metro station, she left them home. It was just as well. As the primary date drew near, Okono supporters became aggressive, repeatedly crossing the sidewalk outside the station to stand in front of the McCracken supporters, purposely stepping backward to block them from distributing buttons, pins, or literature. When the McCracken supporters, trying to avoid a confrontation, re-crossed to the opposite side—the Okono supporters moved in front of them again, over and over. The grandmotherly woman partnered with Lacey gave up and went home. She profusely apologized to Lacey with tears in her eyes—she just couldn't handle the stress of confrontation with the Okono people, she said.

So Lacey hesitated to ask either of her children to do more. She was surprised when her little guy acquiesced without complaint. He had become as invested as she was. In fact, he wanted to come to the rally!

The moon-bounce guy was irritated when she called to reschedule, but they both knew he still had plenty of time to rent it out. With all the end-of-school-year activities, it was doubtful a moon bounce in the shape of a Hot Wheels racecar would languish in the warehouse. Lacey ordered the cake, picked up and addressed the invitations, sent an email reminder to all the parents, and the birthday was set for the following week.

With the birthday emergency resolved, she turned her attention to the logistics for the event. Connor Murphy was flying in from Portland, and she was looking forward to meeting him face-to-face for the first time. Connor had been one of the most conscientious and active bloggers in the network, and they'd struck up a long-distance friendship. Connor was staying in D.C.

with friends. Lacey was incredibly grateful when he'd volunteered to help with the Maryland delegation. Because of their proximity to D.C., the group from Maryland was expected to be one of the largest.

Lacey had booked a hotel room for her friend Jackie and herself in the city. It was going to be a long day: Lacey and her helpers needed to be up at 5:00 a.m. to distribute the state signs, coordinate the donations of water from volunteers in Maryland, D.C. and Virginia, and hand out noisemakers to the Marylanders.

Lacey was meeting both Jackie and Connor at the state coordinators' meeting that night. Lacey was a few minutes late, but easily found Jackie and Connor in the crowded hotel suite. The state reps were given clear instructions. The organizers were very definite: they didn't want any problem with the hotel or D.C. police. Only ticket holders and hotel guests were to be on hotel property. As the meeting broke up, many of the coordinators crowded around the small hotel TV as one of the organizers, a professor at American University, was interviewed about the upcoming rally on local television.

Afterward, there was a dinner organized at the hotel—and that's when all the trouble started.

McCracken supporters had come from all 50 states. Lacey knew this first-hand since she and Connor and Jackie were painting the signs for all 50 state delegations. The hotel dining room, rented for the dinner, was filled with McCracken activists from all around the country. The room was buzzing with excitement—protesting was not something these professionally dressed, middle-aged women did. If they had done, it had been 20 years before and in somewhat different attire. But here they all were, introducing themselves to each other. In some cases they'd already met online—others—especially those active in the primaries and caucuses—warmly exchanged hugs and greetings with 'old friends' they'd canvassed or volunteered with in other states.

After dinner, the organizers gave last-minute instructions to the large group. The strategy they had decided to adopt was to emphasize that they were protesting not the rulers, but the rules. Or, more particularly, how those rules had been selectively applied. Some insisted the participants refer to it as a rally, not even a protest—so concerned were they that the event not appear coercive or critical of the Democratic establishment. Certainly, no one should criticize the fellow Democratic candidate Okono, they insisted. They would impress the Democratic Party elders with how law-abiding they were, how respectful of the process—how mutually committed they were to Big D democratic ideals.

But history is littered with examples of a naïve and respectful yeomanry petitioning a perfidious king or lord for redress—only to be tortured or executed as it became clear the authority whose intervention they were seeking was in league with their persecutors.

It was a large group of mostly women, and as is often the case, there was a lot of discussion. Finally, a tall woman in a black pantsuit stood up in the back of the room. In a lanyard around her neck she wore RBC credentials. She was visibly angry.

"You don't get it!" she yelled at the organizers standing in the front. Everyone strained to see what was going on.

"You don't get it!" she yelled again, more loudly this time. There was no microphone, but her voice carried, even in the large room.

"They're *laughing* at us!" she yelled, her voice pulsing with anger.

Everyone looked at each other perplexed. Who? *Who* was laughing?—the room started to hum as everyone asked their neighbor. The organizers made repeated calls for quiet, which the audience, being mostly women, respectfully listened to, and completely ignored.

"I just came from a meeting of the committee," the woman said.

"They're laughing at us with our little peaceful...rally." She spat out the words. The room was agog. A number of people rose to shout her down; unsuccessfully. They were promptly quashed. The McCracken supporters wanted to hear this. The room resonated with cries of: "Let her speak."

An area around the woman had cleared.

"You want to make a difference? Forget being nice! You need to break the doors down!" There were shouts of "No!" from the audience—but she held the floor and their attention.

"You don't understand," she said, more softly now.

"It's all decided," she said her voice laced with sarcasm. "Whether you carefully stay off hotel property (she motioned to one of the organizers, who minutes before had presented a painstakingly produced color-coded map of the hotel grounds to show which areas were off-limits)—"and follow all the rules. It doesn't matter—because tomorrow they're going to give this thing to Okono. They're even giving him some of McCracken's delegates."

This was, apparently, too much. The room erupted. All of the McCracken supporters sitting carefully at the white-clothed tables looked at each other in horror. Could it be true? How did the woman know? *Who was she?* What was going on?"

The organizers moved quickly to calm the group. The woman, obviously upset, left the room with some friends, and the meeting gradually returned to order. But the dining room was full of urgent whispers. How could it all be decided? Who was she? Where did she get her information? No. No. *No.* She couldn't be right. What was going on? The news was too disturbing to absorb. The one thing all the McCracken supporters agreed on was that it couldn't be true. The campaign had twelve sure votes on the committee, didn't they? *Didn't they?* They had twelve votes...they had twelve votes. McCracken supporters were walking around the various groups breathlessly muttering the vote tally–*Twelve votes. Twelve votes.* Like an incantation that could ward off evil.

In the end, it didn't matter that McCracken had twelve votes. In retrospect, McCracken's supporters should have focused on how many votes Okono had. Okono had eighteen, and thanks to the duplicity of the DNC in allocating tickets–he owned the room. McCracken supporters who became unruly (people who, in other situations, the media might describe as "little old ladies") were unceremoniously manhandled like professional criminals by the cyclopean 'security' men–while carefully coordinated outbursts from Okono supporters were studiously ignored.

The question of whether or not South Carolina and Iowa should be punished was not revisited by the Committee. The settlement on Florida came fairly swiftly. The McCracken campaign argued that under the RBC's own rules, Florida should have been penalized by 50%, not 100%, as was done. This time everybody was watching. The Okono campaign had no room to maneuver.

However, Michigan was another matter entirely. Okono had voluntarily removed his name from the ballot. Correspondingly, he had received only a few write-in votes. In any contest, if a participant voluntarily abstains from competing, the game is automatically considered forfeit. According to the RBC's rules, Michigan's delegates, like Florida's, should have been reduced by half, netting Claire McCracken 33 delegates and Okono none.

However, added to her nineteen "halved-votes" from Florida, McCracken would end the day with 52 additional delegates. For all the Okono supporters and pundits who claimed the numbers for McCracken "didn't add up;" they added up just fine—within 55 points of Okono. Too close. Therefore, the 30 unelected members of the Democratic National Committee's Rules and By-Laws Committee decided to award all the delegates elected by voters who had pulled the presidential lever for 'undecided' in Michigan to Okono—plus all the votes from the other three Democratic candidates who had since dropped out. Then, for good measure—they gave Okono four of McCracken's delegates, as well. When asked by confused reporters for the scientific method the Rules and By-laws Committee had used to reapportion the delegates—the RBC chair admitted there was none.

"It just felt right," he said, shrugging.

Chapter Thirty-Four

June 2008
Rockville, Maryland

In the aftermath of the DNC's Rules and By-Laws Committee meeting, it would be hard to overestimate how angry the McCracken supporters felt. Certainly, there was a curious psychology at work. Many of her supporters self-identified as "good girls." So, it was easy to understand their affinity to Claire McCracken, who was, after all, the ultimate good girl, the apogee of correct womanliness to a whole generation raised on the premise that working hard and being "nice" was more important than being anything else.

Certainly, being smart or beautiful, or rich or powerful might be praiseworthy in the abstract. It might be well to be any one of those things (or if you dared brave your sisters' envy, a few of them all at once)—but you better be a card-carrying member of Nice, or you could expect not just the full opprobrium of the male establishment, but the strident disapproval of most women, as well.

But it wasn't just female psychology that was affected. Phylogeny, or perhaps a less abstract form of Darwinism, had long since determined that super-competent woman like Claire McCracken were *ipso facto* ball breakers, and a society that valued survival could not be in the business of busting balls. Whether that accounted for the blistering and unremitting philippics she received was hard to say. What one could be sure of is that they didn't have that much to do with Claire McCracken. After all, she was no "bra burner," no "libber."

The honest, irrefutable truth was that Claire McCracken had made remarkably traditional choices in life. When it had been a question of following her own career prospects or supporting her husband—she'd supported her husband. When her involvement in touchy social or political issues became a sticking point for her husband's political enemies—she'd quietly stepped aside. Everything she'd done for most of her career spoke powerfully to the fact that she considered her husband's career, her husband's life—more important than her own.

Traditionally, people who are powerless in a society and want more are exhorted to improve their chances in life through education. So she had. At a time when a girl from a lower-middle-class family might have reasonably skipped college, she'd attended one of the best. And when her fellow students and professors, animated by her prodigious talents, had encouraged her, she'd gone to one of the best law schools, as well.

But as it turned out, for women, education was only half the answer. Did it improve their socio-economic prospects? Absolutely. But did it raise them proportionally to their professional accomplishments? Not hardly. Skeptics of a gender wage gap liked to point out that women chose traditionally less well-paid professions and more often worked part-time to care for children. All true. But comparing men and women with the same credentials working the same hours, women still earned less than their male counterparts—and they didn't just earn less than white men—but black men and Asian men, as well.

Many women of Claire McCracken's generation were the first women in their family to work outside the home. They had experienced discrimination first-hand, watching as a less-qualified, perhaps younger man was promoted above them. They had had years to internalize its meaning. Promoting a man was the safe choice. The women who were passed over could be depended on to smooth his path (it wasn't *his* fault!). In contrast, men who were passed over became querulous and disruptive.

What McCracken crystallized for these women was that society's expectations for women were incredibly complicated. Careful and committed mother, supportive and attractive wife, conscientious and helpful employee—these were the standards most reasonable women sought to meet. Every day! So many obligations to so many people! If anyone wondered if women had achieved a valued voice in society, they had only to observe how woman acted—seeking approval, subject to another's decision-making, constantly worrying about how to make themselves as skinny, *as small,* as possible.

McCracken was not small, physically or otherwise. She had the kind of physiology that didn't respond obligingly to caloric restrictions or sweaty workouts. And she had tried to appear quiet and submissive, but it just never really came off. She wisely gave it up at about the time in a woman's life that she was allowed to be a little more out-spoken. Claire McCracken was permitted to be in her sixties, the woman she'd pretended she wasn't in her forties—smart, self-assured, remarkable.

And women got it. Not at first, but little by little, until they *really* got it. They got it *hugely*—and it filled them up with pride in spaces they never knew before were empty. At the beginning, the press in its constant forecasting (which in retrospect is always so completely wrong they reasonably ought to just self-censor themselves and not engage in it at all) had declared "President Claire" inevitable. Foolishly, McCracken's supporters thought in retrospect, they had believed the contest would be fair. But they could see now, or believed they saw (which amounted to much the same thing), that someone's thumb had been on the scale the entire time—that their votes were subject to a kind of censitary suffrage—not fully counted because of their lower status.

Suddenly it became apparent that a whole lot of women—maybe even a generation of women—women with jobs and families, living apparently comfortable, middle-class lives—women who'd never thought of themselves as disadvantaged, realized for the first time that they were second-class citizens. When doctors and lawyers had reported what went on in the primaries and caucuses, no one believed them. No one cared, except other women. They had thought their professional or academic accomplishments had earned them respect. But they heard the way the pundits referred to McCracken (sly, ambitious, mercenary, calculating, bitchy). Now, those same pundits were attacking *them* (those progressive, conscientious card-carrying women of Nice!) as losers, dead-enders, even racists—because they refused to fall in line behind the bully Okono.

And they got pissed. All of a sudden, they weren't buying the whole "stand aside for the greater good" bit anymore. Not interested in being loyal to a party machinery that promoted its bright, shiny male toy over the more experienced and harder working woman. No way. Not this time!

What rankled with all of them was the cheating. How could you support someone as chief executive, someone responsible for upholding the laws—when he seemed to have a pretty cavalier approach to "one person/one vote?"

For Lacey, there was another consideration. A group had gathered the night before the rally to paint signs. By 2 a.m., only three of them were still at it. Connor, Jackie, and Lacey were mostly just talking to keep themselves awake. Inevitably, they had spoken of the most recent defection. In a surprise move, Democratic candidate Chet Williams, who had recently dropped out of the race, had just endorsed Okono. There was widespread wonder at what had prompted his sudden support for Okono. They knew that privately Williams had repeatedly criticized Okono for his lack of experience, his hubris. He'd even accused him of intellectual laziness in not providing concrete plans to back up his rhetoric. On a personal level, it was no secret Chet Williams considered Okono a huge asshole. On the other hand, Williams might be willing to go after Claire McCracken hammer and tongs under the klieg lights, but in private conversations it was obvious he respected her, even liked her. It was a stumper.

Sitting cross-legged on the carpet, paintbrush in hand, Lacey speculated aloud that Okono had promised Williams the vice presidential slot.

"Oh, no..." Jackie said calmly. "He can't accept." She said it simply, a statement of fact. Lacey and Connor were completely surprised.

"Why not?" Connor asked.

Jackie never pulled any punches. "Because he has a love child with one of his staffers and everybody in the press knows about it," she said simply.

Lacey and Connor's eyes popped like over-heated corn, their mouths wide O's of wonder, their chins on their chests. Jackie had connections, she was an unimpeachable source. If she said it—said it as fact—it was true.

What they all knew was that Williams had been bleeding votes from McCracken since Iowa. So why was the press pretending he was a viable candidate all that time, if they had information that was so explosive—so completely dispositive? Williams' whole shtick was that he was a good guy, an honorable guy. And his wife was no political spouse/Kewpie doll, either. She gave Williams enough gravitas to offset his personal-injury-lawyer pomade hair and porcelain veneers. Jackie seemed unfazed by the revelation. But Lacey and Connor were naïve enough to be shocked. If the press wasn't reporting a story this huge, this salacious, they had to want to keep Williams in the race. From the point of view of a McCracken supporter, the only reason to keep Williams in, was to help Okono.

A consensus had been steadily growing among the McCracken supporters that they didn't owe the Democratic Party anything; they thought Okono was little better than a crook. Voting for him had become anathema to them. As the primary calendar started to wind down, Okono supporters had been given instructions to woo the McCracken supporters online—and good foot soldiers that they were, they accepted their orders without hesitation or demur. What they didn't realize was that it was too late, they'd burned all their bridges. These efforts at conciliation all had a discernible sameness. They would start out making noises about party unity, but when it became clear that the McCracken supporters weren't planning to obediently get right behind Okono—the vitriol came tripping off their tongues. The Okono disciples were furious that these froward, recalcitrant, contrary women wouldn't simply buckle under to their demands. No, their *obligation* to support Okono!

So Lacey made a fateful decision. After the rally, when it became clear that the fix was in, she called the national campaign headquarters for the presumptive Republican nominee, Governor Joe Malloy, in Arlington, Virginia. Since Lacey didn't know anyone on the campaign, she just called the general number. She explained she'd organized a large group of McCracken supporters who were disgusted with the Okono campaign. They weren't Republicans, but Governor Malloy, the Republican nominee, was known for his moderate views on social issues. Could they meet with someone in the campaign?

The response was immediate. How many McCracken supporters might be involved? Lacey had no idea. The suggestion was made for a conference call. Malloy's campaign explained that an almost unlimited number of people could be accommodated, with perhaps eighty or so able to meet the candidate in person at the Republican's glass-walled Crystal City headquarters. There was no commitment given or required. This was an exploratory meeting for the McCracken supporters to get a sense of Malloy. There was less than a week to make the arrangements.

Immediately, Lacey and the other McCracken supporters started having problems with their email. Messages were suddenly returned as undeliverable. Other messages were inexplicably delayed for 36 hours. Leaders of the McCracken groups, reading their email over their morning coffee, received messages from their ISP providers informing them that their email accounts were in lock-down—that they'd already exceeded their daily maximum—before they'd even sent one email. Whether it was the volume of messages, user error or faulty equipment, no one knew. Some suggested darkly that it was the Okono campaign, but this was laughed at as improbable in the extreme. Why would the Okono campaign trouble themselves about them? And how would they do it anyway? Ridiculous.

At last, the day arrived. The eighty people present on Saturday afternoon went through a brief security check before being admitted to the downstairs meeting room. Many of the long-time Democrats admitted to being nonplussed by the professionalism of the Republican offices on a lazy summer afternoon. At Malloy's headquarters, clean-shaven twenty-year-old volunteers wore navy blazers and ties. By contrast, at McCracken's headquarters, weekend volunteers were scruffy forty-year-olds wearing jeans and message T's. It was definitely a cultural shift.

Governor Joe Malloy was just as he appeared on television. Bright, straightforward, sincere, not one to dissemble or parse words. He told them frankly that they would disagree on abortion—he was pro-life, but he promised to appoint justices based on qualifications not ideology. Physically, he was very stiff, but he overcame it with a kind of puppy-like eagerness to shake everyone's hands and make a connection. Lacey, who expected perhaps a hundred people on the conference call, was staggered when she was told almost 6,000 McCracken supporters had called in.

On Monday morning, she'd just finished getting the kids breakfast when the phone rang. It was Bill Flowers. He ran one of the other McCracken groups and they'd become friendly, although they'd met for the first time at the Malloy event over the weekend. Very good guy.

"Lacey—I just got an email from Josh Stein from the *Political Insider*," he said.

She'd gotten an email from Stein herself. After he'd written in his column that no serious McCracken supporters were in attendance at the meeting with Malloy, she'd sent him a polite email letting him know that three delegates and four major fundraisers were in attendance, in addition to one of McCracken's national campaign reps. Anyone could see that the fact that these people—Democratic stalwarts—had attended an event for the Republican Malloy was a huge story. Stein had asked Lacey her name, which she verified, but that had been his only question.

Flowers continued, his voice stressed. "He wouldn't tell me what it was about—but he says it's going to be in his column in twenty minutes."

Lacey was only half paying attention, trying to minimize the incredible adhesive ability of breakfast cereal by quickly scraping and rinsing the kids' breakfast bowls.

"Uh, huh," Lacey said

Flowers spoke quickly, obviously sorry to be the bearer of bad news:

"Lacey, he's going to say you're not supporting Okono because you're a racist."

"Oh my God."

CHAPTER THIRTY-FIVE

Washington, DC

TO OUTSIDERS, THE NATIONAL PRESS CLUB existed as a kind of sanctum sanctorum—an ivory tower of journalistic rectitude and professionalism smack in the middle of downtown D.C. As such, it was assumed to be dominated by the *eminence grises* of the journalistic establishment—the tanned and gorgeous news anchors, the quick-with-a-quip pundits, the Jack Russell-like investigators, and wordsmiths otherwise favored by nature or society. But most low-level journalists were not so favored, and for them, the Press Club had an even more potent allure. In the most basic terms, the idea of belonging to a social club was outside the ken of the lowly average reporter. Their high-flying TV counterparts dismissed them as didactic and humorless, and joked to each other that most beat reporters' clothes hadn't matched since their mothers stopped color coordinating their Garanimals. And, of course, unlike their spray-tanned and veneered colleagues on television, print reporters were famously underpaid; none of them had any money. So the Press Club—*their* club, assumed an importance somewhat out of proportion to its facilities or benefits, precisely because for many of its members, it was probably the only club they would ever be invited to join.

But still, the Press Club's aura of linguistic gravitas was unmistakable and carried immeasurable cachet for credibility and integrity. It was for precisely this reason that Fairfax Custis had arranged the press conference in the Holeman Lounge. The backdrop of its elegant dark wood paneling lent dignity to even the most incredible of stories, and Lenny Sinkowski had an incredible story.

Lenny Sinkowski wouldn't be anyone's idea of a credible witness. Convicted of forgery and fraud in multiple states, he had used at least thirteen aliases—that he admitted to. An acknowledged drug user and criminal, he'd lived an itinerant life of small-time cons, and was now receiving a social security check based on a somewhat dubious claim that an on-the-job spinal injury had left him permanently disabled. If you were going to choose someone to make allegations against a popular presidential candidate, no one would choose Lenny Sinkowski.

Of course, if you were going to choose a lawyer to represent Sinkowski, you wouldn't choose the mercurial and eccentric Fairfax Custis. Custis was a notorious Don Quixote drawn to improbable (or at least unwinnable) social justice cases. His reputation had been further damaged when courts in North Carolina had censured him as a "vexatious litigant" during a messy and acrimonious divorce, for filing complaints against everyone from his own lawyer to the state supreme court. He had also been (briefly) charged with assault for nearly throttling his wife's process server—an exigency that's been known to happen in lawyerly circles, but is still generally considered poor form.

The substance of Sinkowski's allegations against Okono were these: Sinkowski claimed that in November of 1997, he and then State Senator Okono had done drugs together—specifically crack cocaine. The purpose of Sinkowski coming forward, he claimed, was to dispute Okono's claim that he had never done drugs after high school. Sinkowski claimed not to have realized who Okono was until he saw now-Congressman Okono via satellite (Sinkowski was hiding out in Mexico at the time—presumably to escape prosecution) making a nationally televised speech.

The salacious part of the allegation was that Sinkowski, who was gay, and was visiting Chicago for a family wedding, claimed to have given Okono a blow job in the backseat of a chauffeured limousine, and then again the following day in his hotel room. He reported that when he had originally contacted the Okono campaign, he had spoken to a Mr. Antwone Green, who identified himself as a friend of Congressman Okono. Mr. Sinkowski claimed that Mr. Green had himself acknowledged a homosexual relationship with Okono. According to Sinkowski, Antwone Green later died under suspicious circumstances. His death was still being investigated by the Chicago Police Department, Sinkowski said.

Without any documentary evidence, no major news organizations gave any space to Sinkowski's allegations, but they persisted on the internet—partly because Sinkowski made no attempt to hide his unsavoury past (which under the circumstances seemed sort of impressive)—and partly because there was just something about the story that had that strange element of truthiness, or weirdness, that gave it a longer than usual half-life.

The reporters attending the press conference expected to find Sinkowski laughable, ridiculous—a fey little man with a high-pitched voice—and in a certain way he was. The reporters reminded themselves not to be taken in. The appearance of sincerity was the con man's stock-in-trade, after all. But despite the reporters' obvious skepticism, Sinkowski persisted in making his case. He ended the press conference by noting that he didn't expect the reporters to believe him, but he hoped they would investigate the story and establish the truth for themselves.

In spite of themselves, the reporters found themselves strangely impressed. If Sinkowski was getting anything out of subjecting himself to this level of public exposure and ridicule, it wasn't clear what it was. Those who had dismissed him as a grifter involved in a new scam, who pointed to his tessellated career of forgery and petty crime—were suddenly less sure. There was...something...

And that's when something truly strange happened. Two U.S. marshals accompanied by two D.C. police officers showed up to arrest Sinkowski on what they claimed was an outstanding warrant from Delaware. To anyone familiar with the D.C. criminal justice system—many of whose convicted criminals unconcernedly wander the streets for years before D.C. issues a warrant for his or her arrest—this would be curious enough. In fact, Sinkowski's arrest was completely inexplicable—except for the fact that the mayor of D.C. was a well-known supporter of Okono.

Held for four days at D.C.'s First District Station on 4th Street, S.W., without being charged, Sinkowski was then extradited to Delaware—a state in which he denied ever having had dealings. After a further few days in custody, he was quietly released, no warrant for his arrest ever having been produced. Of course, the fact that the attorney general of Delaware was the son of Okono's choice for vice president, might have been considered germane to any reporters who followed the story of how a political critic of a U.S. presidential candidate had been silenced and arrested in the nation's capitol, but it wasn't. None did.

CHAPTER THIRTY-SIX

Washington, DC

THE *POLITICAL INSIDER*'S JOSH STEIN was not managing editor John Tweed's favorite reporter. Partly it was the issue of personal hygiene—or really the lack thereof. For the fastidious Tweed, it started with Stein's yellow fingernails, which he habitually gnawed almost to the cuticle. His clothes were wrinkled, even stained. He rarely shaved, or washed his greasy hair. Reporters sharing a cubicle with him complained that he left his dirty, smelly laundry near his desk.

Foulmouthed and suspicious, even by newsroom standards, he prided himself on his rudeness—and wore his New York City roots like a badge of honor. At 35, he had developed a soft, womanly roundness, and was so out of shape, he habitually panted when he walked. It all combined to give him the look of a malevolent rabbit, fattened for the stew.

The other reporters referred to Stein as a "DFK" or Dork Face Killa—according to the urban dictionary, an "extremely unattractive person married to an attractive person." The other reporters noted that, in truth, he wasn't much of a writer, his popular posts seldom longer than a paragraph or two.

What Stein did have, and this was kind of a miracle, was access. Somehow, perhaps because he was in New York, and they were all in Washington, Stein was the IM buddy of most of the up-and-coming Democratic power brokers. Whether Stein checked the information they fed him before publishing his column was an issue Tweed had raised in more than one executive session.

Tweed was upset. "Jesus, Josh—tell me this woman's a racist."

As usual, Stein was eating something loudly into the mouthpiece. "Who gives a shit? She's just some little fucking housewife from Connecticut."

"Maryland...who went to Smith..." said Tweed.

"Whatever. Who gives a fuck?" replied Stein. Tweed tried not to let his irritation show.

"Smith is, like...I don't know... one of the most liberal colleges on the East Coast. Tell me Josh, what's a racist doing at Smith?" asked Tweed.

Stein was uninterested: "How the fuck should I know. Look, I took it from an AP article."

"AP's not what they used to be," said Harrison.

"Whatever. Your opinion. Thanks for sharing," Stein replied caustically.

"And the AP didn't accuse her of anything more than a sort of prank. You were corresponding with her. You had her email, her phone number. You specifically did not ask her to comment. Do you get that it looks bad?" Tweed asked.

"Whatever. The husband's whole family are racists." Tweed

struggled to keep his composure.

"Josh—you ever heard of the Morris Trust?"

"No. Who fucking cares?"

"The husband's family started it."

"So. Big deal. I'm happy for them."

"You know what the Morris Trust does, Josh? The *only thing* the Morris Trust does?"

"Obviously, you're going to tell me."

"They give money for programs...programs for little black kids, Josh."

"And I care about this...why?" said Stein rudely.

"Because if her lawyer gets your lily-white ass on the stand, she's going to ask you how much money *you* give to little black kids, Josh."

"This conversation is pointless."

"You purposely mis-portrayed the event to downplay it. That's going to look like bias. You said there were 50—basically—dead-enders there."

"So—what the fuck's your point?" replied Stein.

"Jesus. Josh. There were 6,000 McCracken supporters... diehard Democrats... on a fucking conference call with the REPUBLICAN candidate—didn't *that* strike you as the story?" asked Tweed.

"Whatever." Stein was still uninterested.

"And then less than 20 minutes after you post it directly on the internet—without passing it through editorial or legal, I might add— the *Oceanic* and all your JournoList list-serv buddies have it. That looks like collusion," added Tweed.

"Cooperation," said Stein.

"Not if it's not true," replied Tweed.

"Who's going to know?" responded Stein.

"Her lawyer told me the only person that applied to the club was white," Tweed answered.

"So?" Stein's voice was muffled by his sandwich.

"If it's true, and she'd be an idiot to lie...where's the racism? White people discriminating against other white people?" asked Tweed.

Stein was petulant, aggrieved: "I don't see why you're making such a big fucking deal about this..." he said.

Tweed was getting exasperated: "Do you have anything—anything—that says this woman's a racist?"

Stein became defensive.

"Look. She's a fucking cunt who impersonated a black woman on a chat room," he said.

Tweed replied: "I looked. She impersonated an old lady. She never specified any race in her profile. Jesus, Josh. She used a pseudonym to hide her identity on the internet. Millions of people have done that."

Stein was unimpressed: "Whatever. If she was so fucking proud of what she was doing, she would have used her own name."

"Like you use your own name when you comment on your own pieces?" asked Tweed.

Stein paused; he hadn't realized Tweed knew he was praising himself in print. "Don't be an asshole. All the reporters comment on their own stuff."

Tweed was prepared to concede the point: "Right. Under pseudonyms. Jesus, Josh—a lawyer could tear you apart."

There was silence.

Tweed spoke: "Josh—you got this from Appelbaum, didn't you?"

There was a pause.

"So what if I did?" Stein answered.

"She's got malice."

"What the fuck are you talking about?" Stein was sensitive about his lack of education.

"You can't win a lawsuit for libel unless the person can prove that the smear was intentional. The AP article, okay—but your article was a leap—and the stuff going up on your buddies blogs is even worse. You purposely smeared this woman, Josh. Worst of all—you did it at the direction of the Okono campaign because she and some of these other McCracken people are saying stuff that Okono doesn't want people to hear. Not exactly a Murrow moment."

"Screw you."

Tweed continued. "And you did it intentionally, with pre-meditation, with no effort to check the facts, or even speak to her...and she's a private citizen—as you so aptly said, 'a fucking housewife.' The lawyers are telling me that's considered–bad faith, malice—maybe even 'extreme malice,' said Tweed.

Stein was skeptical. "Some fucking cunt from Connecticut is going to sue me?"

"Maryland, and she probably has a case," replied Tweed.

Silence.

"Stein?" Tweed wasn't sure the reporter was still on the line.

Stein was thinking out loud:

"No way she does it. She's too scared."

Tweed could feel the vein in his temple throbbing. Stein didn't seem to realize the exposure he'd created for himself or the paper.

"Why do you think so?" he asked acidly.

Stein blurted it out:

"Because the link I used had her address and phone number. She's getting death threats."

Tweed was horrified.

"*Jesus*. Is that true? How do you know that?" he asked.

The swagger returned to Stein's voice.

"Let's just say I have my sources. This is hardball. She's just some mom. She's got little kids. No way she wants more of what I can dish out."

Tweed closed his eyes. He was a decent man. Stein had crossed so many journalistic and ethical boundaries, it made his head spin. The internet could get ugly and out of control very quickly...and there were a lot of nuts out there. His reporter was essentially inciting violence against a soccer mom with little kids because she wasn't supporting Okono. He said, slowly, considering.

"Josh—don't *you* have little kids?"

"Yeah. Two. One on the way. What's your fucking point?"

Tweed took off his glasses and rubbed his eyes. He should fire him on the spot...for being a bad reporter and an asshole. Worse than that, Tweed had seen his soul, Stein was the devil.

"Never mind," was what he said.

Chapter Thirty-Seven

Rockville, Maryland

THE PHONE RANG. Lacey, dreading it, picked it up anyway.

"Get out of bed." It was Max.

"I'm not in bed."

"Under the bed?" he demanded.

"No," she replied.

"Closet?"

"No." Lacey laughed. "I was thinking of a long trip to the Hebrides, though."

"Where the hell is that?"

"Islands off Scotland. Very Remote. Many sheep. No internet."

"Lacey." Max's tone was scolding, but kind.

"Did you talk to a lawyer?" he asked.

"Sure. Everyone in our family is a lawyer," she replied.

"And?" he asked.

"Well, naturally, there are lots of different opinions. But, in a nutshell: it's hard to prosecute, expensive, and even in the unlikely event we win, there's not usually a big reward...And, of course, the publicity from the trial just keeps the allegations on replay."

There was silence as Max absorbed her words.

"How expensive?" he asked

"Couple hundred grand," she replied, "The paper will have lawyers and they'll drag it out as long as possible to make it as financially painful for us as they can. Their insurance will pay all the costs on their side, so they don't care."

"So do it," Max said.

"Max," she said patiently. "I don't have a couple of hundred grand lying around. What do you suggest? I take my kids' college money?" said Lacey.

"But you'll win," he said confidently. "The guy was totally out of line."

There was a bitterness in Lacey's voice Max had never heard before.

"Knowing something and proving it are two very separate things. Anyway, you're a lawyer, it's not as if the party that's in the right necessarily wins," she reminded him.

Max considered:

"This really pisses me off. Stein is such a fatuous turd; a completely insufferable little fink," Max said.

"So they say," replied Lacey. The fact that Stein was a huge jerk didn't make her feel better.

Max continued: "Listen, you have to defend yourself."

"Max," Lacey paused. "I don't know *what* to do. Some people say answer every allegation you can—wherever it appears. Other people tell me not to say anything. They think the more I deny it, the more they'll go after me. I've basically felt like I was going to vomit from the moment I read it. And, I'm scared, Max. We've been getting calls at the house, threats...people saying things like I'm a racist bitch who deserves to die and they know where I live...that they know I have little kids." Her voice broke. Max could hear it through the phone line. Lacey was right on the edge.

"You need to go on TV," he said.

"What?" Lacey was horrified. "And say what? I'm a really nice person?"

Max laughed. "Well, you *are* a nice person, Lacey."

Lacey was amused in spite of herself. "Max, that's not helpful. Besides, I said really nice."

Max continued, "*Really* nice, okay? Look. People have to see you, get a sense of who you are. Lacey, I'm telling you... it's the only way," he said.

"Oh, shit," she said, unpersuaded. "I feel nauseated just thinking about it. I'd be terrible."

"Well, then that's not so bad," Max said teasingly. "You just told me you've been ready to vomit for days."

Lacey ignored him. "Max. Honestly. I don't know anything about television," she said.

"True. But you know plenty about public speaking. You'll be fine. You don't have to dazzle them with your intellect. People just have to see you as a real person."

"Ugggghhhh. No, Max, no. I don't want to..." Lacey was pleading.

"Lacey, I'm going to set it up. You have to do it, okay? You can't let them get away with this," he replied.

"But, you—! You can't set it up. Okono's your guy."

"First, of all, let me just be frank: there's some weird shit going on with this guy. We're supporting this guy in spite of who he is, not because of who he is. That never really works out. Second—" Max paused, as if considering how much he wanted to say "... let's just say I develop a conscience where my friends are concerned."

Lacey sighed.

"Max, you're a good man," she said.

"Yeah, whatever. Don't tell anyone, you'll ruin my reputation."

CHAPTER THIRTY-EIGHT

New York, New York

ON THE LAST DAY OF JUNE, a curious article ran in the "Bits" section of the *New York Times* Technology page. Entitled *"Google and the Anti-Okono Bloggers"* The veteran reporter queried:

> *Did Google use its network of online services to silence critics of Okono? That was the question buzzing on a corner of the blogosphere over the last few days, after several anti-Okono bloggers were unable to update their sites. The bloggers in question, most of them supporters of Claire McCracken and all opposed to Congressman Okono, received a notice from Google last week saying that their sites had been identified as potential 'spam' and Google had removed their websites until further notice."*

After their initial stonewalling, Google reluctantly admitted to the *Times* reporter that apparently "mass spam emails" (presumably generated by Okono supporters) had "flagged" the sites to Google as spam or as containing "inappropriate content," resulting in their automatic suspension. When asked how many messages Google would have needed to receive to trigger the automatic suspension, the Google spokesman at first declined to name a number. When alerted by the reporter that the McCracken supporters believed Google *themselves* might have been involved in the chicanery, he became more forthcoming. "Well, not less than 100,000, probably," he said thoughtfully. "But frankly," he said, sounding harassed, "we can't figure out why the system flagged these sites as having inappropriate content. As to designating them as spam, this isn't something your average user could do. I mean, we still can't figure out how they did it, and we're, you know...geeks."

Chapter Thirty-Nine

July 2008
Columbus, Ohio

MAX WAS RIGHT. Or at least partially right, Lacey thought. Although she still couldn't watch the YouTube videos of her appearances on the national news shows without cringeing, almost immediately Lacey received thousands of sympathetic emails. Mostly they were from other McCracken supporters who felt manhandled—either by the Okono campaign directly or by what they considered the media's unflattering and unfair depiction of their candidate. They poured out their stories of skullduggery and malfeasance in emails that went on for pages. She also heard from people with whom she'd volunteered locally. One or two told her she'd become too controversial to lead the local group. But many more, in fact the overwhelming majority called and sent emails offering their unqualified support. Lacey had been through enough and was more than willing to step aside. They refused to consider it. "Don't you dare," they told her. They were not giving in to bullies and thugs, they said, and they weren't letting Lacey give in either. And something about this unexpected but ultimately overwhelming evidence that she was not alone gave her the courage to keep going. Within a week, she had a plan.

News anchors and pundits pontificate about swing states and swing voters. But to anyone analyzing voting records in the United States, an unmistakeable pattern emerged. As it turned out, it wasn't so much a question, for example, of how Ohioans voted. Every four years most areas in the state swung predictably into the red or blue column. The breakdown—the true predictor of an election's outcome—was by county, specifically the few swing counties in the battleground states. Looking at historical data, pollsters had figured out which counties those were—and although the information wasn't exactly secret—it wasn't utilized by either the campaigns or the media to the degree you might expect. Lacey thought that was a mistake. Since time was short and their resources were limited, this narrow focus on a few counties in a few states gave the plan a kind of elegant simplicity that made it seem, well, possible.

Lacey laid it all out, then sent her plan out in an email to the leaders of some of the other McCracken groups. Within 20 minutes her phone rang. The voice was ladylike, but rushed; a woman who liked to get things done quickly.

"Lacey, I'm Betty Jo Overton. I lead a large group of McCracken supporters in Ohio." The woman paused. "I like your plan." Lacey was silent, surprised. The voice on the phone continued. "In fact, I love your plan. I have to tell you—" she paused chuckling, "over the years I've worked on a lot of Democratic campaigns and I've seen a lot of strategy plans..."

"Uh...huh," Lacey replied.

The woman continued. "And mostly I just think they've got their heads stuck up their asses." There was something sort of compelling about the juxtaposition of the woman's cultivated tone and tough talk

Lacey laughed, relieved.

"And I don't?"

"No," Betty Jo laughed. "I think your plan might actually work. I'm calling to offer my help. But I think there's someone you ought to meet."

—∾—

His looks did not inspire confidence. Nor did the chain smoking. Or the ponytail. He spoke in the "dese and dose" vernacular of the rust belt, and his tales from the campaign trail with the McCracken campaign sounded more like braggadocio or invention than experience. But he talked about how poorly the campaign had been managed, spending $30 million dollars in Iowa—only to come in a humiliating third. Not to mention how few voters in Iowa were even Democrats. The campaign, he pointed out, could have put each one of them on a plane to Disney World for what the campaign had spent per Democratic head—and Lacey and Betty Jo knew that was true. And like millions of people, before and after, who judge a person's veracity on how nearly his views coincide with their own, they believed him.

Lacey and Betty Jo were not hard-nosed political operatives—and so, they reasoned, perhaps understandably, that maybe Danny Englund was the kind of 'real deal' back-room pol one imagined died out with LBJ. Who knew? Maybe he had some sort of native political genius—like a later-day Kenny O'Donnell. They were flattered that he was reaching out to them to help. It was all very hush-hush, of course. Englund reported that the McCracken team had real reservations about whether Okono should be president. There were things they knew—things that as Democrats it was impossible for them to reveal—about the presumptive nominee of their party. Nobody spelled it out, but, of course, most in the room had read enough to give them suspicions.

Lacey, it turned out, had a hidden talent for opposition research. With what they now knew from the information Max had provided about the suspicious Okono donations, not to mention Okono's weird ties to The Minister and Connor's investigation of Joey Ali, Okono seemed stranger and stranger as a candidate for national office. Whole years in his résumé appeared to be missing. Okono's campaign had rejected the request of a *New York Times* reporter, who was doing a fawning profile, to give the name of even one friend from college the reporter could interview. The fact that all of this was ignored by the press—that people who actually tried to press the point were mocked and ridiculed—made it all start to feel a little conspiratorial. Surely, the McCracken supporters thought—literally week after week—*someone* in the press was going to start doing a little investigating, start asking some questions.

According to the scuttlebutt, some did. Supposedly, a *New York Times* reporter received verification from an insider that the Okono campaign had extensive contact with—were essentially directing the efforts of—a massive 'get-out-the-vote' operation notorious for registering fraudulent voters. Others claimed a *Wall Street Journal* reporter was investigating the allegations of caucus fraud. Still other reputable reports surfaced of a prize-winning journalist who claimed to have seen a tape of a damaging speech given by Okono. These stories fueled the internet rumor mill for months, but nothing seemed to come of these inquiries.

Lacey herself had mailed a summary of her op-research on Malinga to veteran journalists she knew through friends. They all thanked her very politely—but never used any of it.

Democrats who weren't gung-ho for Okono started to feel like adherents of some outlawed religion. McCracken supporters who hadn't fallen in line with the party rhetoric were derided and ridiculed as dead-enders. Their complaints about Okono fell on willfully deaf ears. It all felt very rabbit-hole-ish. The candidate they knew to be remorselessly corrupt—was almost universally heralded as Mr. Clean.

So when Danny Englund told Lacey and Betty Jo that Okono's nomination was a kind of coup engineered by the party elite—he was preaching to a ready-to-be-converted choir. Disgusted with the Democrats, Lacey and Betty Jo started organizing McCracken volunteers for Republican Governor Joe Malloy.

Before the meeting, Lacey had raised the issue of the recent allegations of racism. She and Betty Jo had spent a lot of time on the phone firming up the details of their plan, and Lacey already liked her enormously. But more than that, Lacey wanted to be fair to her. "Controversial" is, after all, seldom a good thing in politics. And, although everyone assured her it would all eventually blow over, Lacey was constantly aware that at least for now, she was wearing a label that couldn't help but make her a liability in the political trenches. Was Betty Jo sure she wanted to be connected to her?

Betty Jo laughed.

"You think I didn't check you out?" When Lacey looked stricken, Betty Jo took Lacey by her shoulders and looked into her eyes. Lacey noticed for the first time that Betty Jo's eyes were the color of expensive single malt.

"Lacey, are you a child molester?"

Lacey's eyes opened wide with shock. She shook her head, quietly, 'no'

"A racist?"

Lacey still looked stunned. "No," she whispered.

"Cheat on your taxes? Piggyback on your neighbor's internet? Steal towels from hotels?"

Lacey shook her head. "No. No. No."

"Take extra condiments from fast food restaurants?"

Lacey was still shaking her head.

"Okay," Betty Jo said. "I now know everything I need to know about you, okay?" She looked at Lacey, her eyes twinkling. "I knew who you were the first time I met you. And I know enough about the Okono campaign to know they lie about everyone, including their own candidate. You're not a racist. You're a nice suburban mom who collects coats for poor kids in the winter and volunteers for the PTA—am I right?"

Lacey nodded.

Betty Jo continued: "But you happen to have an ability for organizing that is kind of exceptional, kiddo. So, that's what I know about you. And, one more thing I forgot to mention?"

Lacey looked up expectantly. Betty Jo shook her slightly.

"I know you're my friend." Lacey gave her a hug, her eyes filled with tears.

—m—

One month and 20 days after the last primary, on a hot Wednesday afternoon at the end of July, the mainstream media reported for the first time that former Democratic candidate for president, Chet Williams, had a love child with a web designer on his payroll. One of the tabloid press had trailed him to an upscale hotel where he met with her and her newborn in a hotel room for 14 hours. As he came out, the reporter attempted to question Williams about the woman and child. Former presidential candidate Williams then barricaded himself in the men's bathroom. He was rescued 40 minutes later by hotel security.

Chapter Forty

August 2008
Atlanta, Georgia

Miriam Carter walked to her Chrysler Crossfire SRT-6 coupe. She'd spent the last two hours with a group, mostly women, of long-time Democrats, the party faithful. What most people who saw the male figurehead in charge of the DNC didn't realize was that women ran the DNC. Not just the Washington D.C. offices—which were largely dominated by an outspoken group of African American women—but the day-to-day volunteers: the people stuffing the envelopes, manning the call centers, making the donations. They were women, predominantly (although not entirely) middle class, middle-aged white women. And, as Miriam Carter had come to learn, they were mad as hell at the way their party had treated Claire McCracken.

Most obviously, they were infuriated at how they believed the Democratic Party was twisting its own rules to hand Okono the nomination. Why, they asked, had it taken the Democratic

National Committee until the last week in May to honor the votes cast in Florida and Michigan? The Republican National Committee, they pointed out, had resolved the same issue in February. Why was the DNC allowing the gross violations of voter registrations by organizations like SEED, who were widely believed by McCracken supporters to have been transporting Okono supporters from polling place to polling place in North Carolina and other states? Where was the DNC in Lake County, Indiana when the Mayor of Gary (and state chair for the Okono campaign) held back the results of his county until midnight—in a move that flabbergasted even CNN's usually unflappable Wolf Blitzer?

Why had the DNC never addressed the issue of caucus fraud? Despite repeated legal challenges filed by the McCracken campaign, and hundreds of eyewitness accounts from their own workers, why had they never investigated the allegations of cheating? Why weren't they monitoring Okono's donations? Why were they allowing McCracken supporters—superdelegates—even members of the Congressional Black Caucus—to be harassed and threatened?

Largely unseen except by insiders, the state conventions were an embarrassment to a supposedly democratic process. In Nevada, where McCracken won by a 51%-45% majority—she ended up with three *fewer* delegates to the national convention because of intimidation and skullduggery at the district caucuses.

In Washington state, many Democrats who went to the polls February 19th didn't realize their votes didn't advance the cause of their candidate. Delegates had been chosen at the caucus ten days earlier. If the primary, for which voter I.D. was required, had counted, Okono would have been ahead by six points. By contrast, Okono's lead in the caucus, for which no I.D. was required, was a whopping 37 points. In virtually every state that had a caucus and a primary, the same results played out, over and over. In the system used by the Democrats, in which delegates were allocated proportionally, this made a huge difference.

Delegates in Florida, no longer considered sufficiently faithful to Okono (young and idealistic, they'd foolishly assumed he'd favor a new contest and lobbied for a new primary) were summarily replaced with handpicked successors—their new credentials rubber-stamped by an obliging DNC.

Rumors abounded that the DNC headquarters would be moved to Chicago—to the same building as Okono's headquarters, in fact. These rumors were vehemently denied by the pugnacious DNC chair who, in school marm-ish tones, chastised middle-aged McCracken supporters like toddlers for being taken-in by ridiculous internet rumors. Until, of course, it happened. Almost overnight, the Democratic Party had become the Party of Okono—and the historic aggregation and consolidation of power where the party of many became the party of "the one" occurred as smoothly and with as little outcry as the Anschluss. How could this be happening in an American election?

At some point, the consensus of McCracken supporters changed from a concern that the DNC wasn't doing its job to mediate between the two candidates, to a conviction that they were actively working to assist the other side. But when the DNC did nothing to address their concerns, longtime party workers turned would-be whistleblowers were amazed and disturbed to find the media was completely uninterested.

To the reported aggravation of Okono personally, so far McCracken and her supporters had demonstrated a marked disinclination to fall in line. Despite the pundits' constant refrain that 'the numbers' were against McCracken—saying it did not make it so. The margin that separated the two candidates was razor thin—one way or the other, the superdelegates (party stalwarts and elected officials gifted with a delegate's vote at the national convention) would decide the contest—and, although a majority had now expressed their support for Okono—they were not committed until they cast their ballot on the floor of the convention.

A new rumor began to percolate through the McCracken-supporting ether that the Okono campaign was planning to block a roll call of the states. Even to the conspiracy-minded among them, this seemed impossible—there had been a public roll call at Democratic National Conventions every year since 1852. It was one of the most exciting and memorable parts of convention history. But it was also the one least subject to manipulation and control. The DNC chair denied it—he was shocked—*shocked*—at how quickly these rumors started and spread on the internet, he said. Until the Okono campaign confirmed it to no less an authority than the *New York Times*.

Now that the Okono apologists had their marching orders, the consensus flipped—well, why *would* there be a roll call? McCracken and her dead-enders were just trying to be disruptive (subtext "bitchy") to demand one. Of course, missing from this leitmotif was the simple truth that there was no issue of anyone making a demand. The fact that the public roll call was a universally acknowledged Democratic tradition whose discontinuance had occasioned horror only days before—was completely forgotten.

Well, so what? Okono had *won*, his supporters insisted. Making him "prove it" at the convention harkened back to Jim Crow-era Southerners who asked African American voters to demonstrate their literacy by reading—Chinese. It was, Okono supporters whispered, 'racist' to put Okono through the same kind of floor fight white politicians had weathered for 75 years. the *Political Insider's* Josh Stein wrote an article suggesting that not just McCracken's political future, but her personal legacy, was at risk unless she quickly got in line and was seen to be working as hard as she possibly could for Okono.

To Miriam, trying to eliminate the roll call was just more Okono-style politics. Not many people outside Chicago knew Clarice Setter. But Miriam did. Okono had been Setter's protégée—until he decided to run for her city council seat. It was his first election. Setter was a longtime civil-rights activist and well loved in the community. It would be a cakewalk for Setter, the polls predicted. But, at the last moment, Okono had hired attorneys to challenge all the nominating petitions of his opponents. With Appelbaum's help, he had managed to disqualify every one of his opponents, including Setter –the woman who had given him his start. Okono ran for the seat unopposed, and won. Yes, indeed. Miriam knew Clarice Setter. She had met her when Setter was campaigning for Claire McCracken.

Okono had reason to fear a floor fight at the convention, Miriam believed. Every poll showed Claire McCracken doing better in the general election against Republican Governor Malloy than Okono. Democratic strategists wondered and worried that the polls were so close between Malloy and Okono, a virtual dead heat. If Okono couldn't beat an old, stiff, white guy—who continued to support an unpopular war, nominated by a party that was in power when a recession appeared on the horizon like a blimp at the Thanksgiving Day parade—well, what was wrong?

A large part of the problem was among women and independents, like the folks Miriam Carter had spent time with tonight. Pew Research polls were showing that only 43% of white women had a favorable view of Okono, down from 56% in February. Among independents it was the same story, from a 62% favorable rating in February, Okono had recently slid to a discouraging 49%. Most telling were the reasons given. If voters didn't like Malloy, 73% said it had to do with his politics. However only 54% of those who had an unfavorable view of Okono disliked his politics. His toxic personal connections were what were bringing his numbers down. Miriam had heard the buzz for weeks now: people in the party were saying Okono couldn't win in the general election.

Miriam unlocked the car doors from 20 feet away. Her good friend, Will Gault, the chair of the Kentucky DNC and a close friend of the McCrackens', had been insisting on a roll call. Gault was the quintessential small-town southern politician—literally a used car salesman, who had expanded one small franchise in Louisville into three lucrative car dealerships. Before receiving the appointment as state DNC chair, he'd served his time as a state senator for ten years. Not only was Gault popular among the Democratic elite, but he knew where all the bodies were buried in a one-party state where the Democratic controlled legislature buried plenty of political bodies.

Six days before, a man—the proverbial 'lone gunman'—had entered the Kentucky DNC offices and claimed he wanted to volunteer. He asked for Gault by name, which later struck lots of people as very odd, since neither state senators nor state DNC chairs have what might be termed a high profile. When the receptionist in the outer office tried to deflect him, he pushed his way past her, pulled out a hand gun and emptied his magazine into Gault's chest—killing him instantly. There was never an opportunity to question the man the police later identified as Raymond T. Watson. After a brief car chase, Watson drove his car into a ditch. According to police at the scene, he emerged from his vehicle (pronounced with suspended consonants) firing at the officers. Understandably, it would seem, they returned fire. Watson died at the scene. All very tidy.

Watson was not known to have ever had any personal or business dealings with Gault or his family. In fact, police were at a loss to identify any motive for the shooting whatsoever. The media briefly covered the horrifying developments. After all, Gault was a longtime friend and stalwart supporter of McCracken. The fact that he had pledged to deliver all of Kentucky's 37 votes to her at the roll call—though well-known, was curiously uninteresting to the media. They all treated the murder as a freakish accident of fate, which by sheer coincidence took place a week before the Democratic National Convention.

Miriam Carter considered it something else entirely—a none-too-subtle warning of what could happen to people that refused to fall in with the Okono line. Privately, Gault had been insisting to other state chairs that Okono couldn't win—that the McCracken supporters should take the fight for the nomination to the convention floor. Perhaps, Miriam thought to herself, she was getting paranoid. But she knew that like herself, Gault had been receiving threats—frightening late night telephone calls—on private lines only a restricted few knew. And Gault was famously stubborn about resisting pressure and intimidation. The fact that the reporters who covered the story of Gault's assassination never mentioned these threats (which the FBI, at least, took seriously enough to investigate), amounted to journalistic malfeasance.

Miriam Carter didn't want to believe in evil. She knew politics, and politics demanded accommodation. She'd even practiced it herself sometimes. But the idea that there was a sinister force at work to compel support, or silence the opposition? In America? That she found a little far-fetched. But not since her early days working as a civil rights attorney had she experienced this kind of fear. The people around her were genuinely *afraid.* She saw it in their faces, heard it in their voices. They talked about a "Chicago Machine" that "disappeared people." All too often, conversations with colleagues had ended abruptly, sadly, when she reiterated her refusal to desert McCracken. "You don't know these people," they told her, all but begging her to reconsider. To Miriam Carter, who had always considered politics, and to some extent, life—a game—it was hard to believe.

The inside of the car smelled strangely, sort of like sneakers left out in the rain. As she got behind the wheel, she noticed her hands felt sticky. She wiped them off, but as she turned into traffic, she noticed they were starting to tickle, like she was having an allergic reaction. Strangely, it didn't hurt. Just as suddenly, she all at once felt dizzy, nauseated, as if there were a great weight on her chest—which she recognized in a strangely clinical way was her lungs filling with fluid. "I'm dying," she thought. "No," she thought, ever precise: "They're killing me."

Chapter Forty-One

Detroit, Michigan

The African American host of the Detroit public access station was putting in his time. He'd already sent his tapes to the big networks and was hoping for a call. Of course, he'd been hoping for about four years. But, he figured, you never know. The show interviewed local newsmakers mostly about regional issues, but he was a big, good-looking guy, affable to his guests, and deferential enough to get some of the more prominent local celebrities. He introduced his guest of the evening as his long-time hero. But in truth, growing up, he'd cared about basketball, not politics, and he barely knew the man's name. Of course, he hadn't grown up in the projects, but in a comfortable Detroit suburb, the son of a dentist.

If he'd come of age in meaner streets, he might have known of Archie Newton, or at least heard his name. At 86, Newton still spoke with the soft cadences of his southwestern Texas childhood, where he'd grown up as the youngest of 14. It might seem surprising to some, perhaps, but if you were an African

American born in the 1920s, San Antonio was one of the best places to live. The proximity of the Mexican border and a still visible Native-American population largely made racial discrimination moot. Part of the frontier mentality was that everyone minded his own business—and what a man chose to do on his own property, or could accomplish by his own industry, was his own affair.

Of course, each ethnic group still self-segregated. Latinos, whites, and African Americans all had their own stores and businesses, stores that catered almost exclusively to their own community. Archie Newton's family had been successful farmers and somehow (no one quite remembered how) ended up owning a funeral home. And then, because it made sense, the Newtons started to supply the caskets, flowers, and clothes for the deceased. Then, because they already had one (and, like any business, there were certain economies of scale), his father had bought another funeral home, and then another, all over southwestern Texas—until the Newton family had become mini-moguls of death.

His parents put a premium on education, and every one of their children finished college, most, like himself, going on to law or graduate school. By the 1950s, Newton had become a famous lawyer handling civil rights cases for such luminaries as Malcolm X and the Black Panthers. He never stopped exercising the entrepreneurial muscle he learned from his parents, however. He bought a radio station catering to Detroit's African American community and renovated and refurbished a landmark theatre, where he produced shows with African American headliners.

He ran for city council and, to no one's surprise, won handily—for the next 20 years. Like many black activists of his generation, he converted to Islam. But unlike many of them, he had retained his Christian name. When asked, he replied he thought he owed it to his Baptist mother.

The host read the prepared questions, nodding his head at appropriate moments. He had a date tonight and he'd be psyched if the taping finished a little early. His big wind-up was a question about candidate Okono. It was a no-brainer, an uncomplicated question designed to tease out an endorsement Newton had already given publicly.

"I was introduced to Okono by a friend who was raising money for him." Then, without any prompting from the host, Newton said,

"I was contacted by my good friend Muhsin al-Nasih. He asked me to write a letter in support of Okono's application to Harvard Law School." As the host blinked uncertainly, Newton sought to explain

"Mr. al-Nasih is the principal advisor to Prince Abdul-Wahid bin Khair al Din, one of the richest men in the world."

Whatever the producers had expected, this was not it. The host was off his prepared cue cards now, so he just asked the most obvious question:

"And did you?" he asked

"Yes, I did," said Newton.

"I said, there's a young man who has passed all the requirements necessary to become president of the Law Review and I hoped they would treat him kindly."

The program had never had a particularly large audience, but seemingly within hours, the story had exploded on the internet. First was the tie with the highly controversial Muhsin al-Nasih, a black nationalist and outspoken critic of Israel (and by extension U.S. Mideast policy), who had served as OPEC's principal American lawyer for 20 years. The idea that al-Nasih had raised money to pay for Okono's law school would raise Jewish hackles everywhere. And the questions would start. How would such a radical international high-roller even know a then-29-year-old community organizer from the South Side of Chicago?

But, weirder still, for a candidate who was constantly harping on his Christian credentials, was the additional link that Newton provided (without any prompting) between Okono and one of the richest, most proactive Muslims in the world (a man his critics called an Islamic Supremacist!). A man who was not only a member of the Saudi Royal Family but close advisor to the King? Well, it wasn't clear what to make of *that*. What was clear, however, was that it probably wouldn't play that well on Main Street.

The Okono campaign immediately went on the offensive. Press Secretary Jim Latchky insisted that Newton was mistaken—calling the story a "fabrication." Okono did not know al-Nasih, Latchky insisted petulantly. Al-Nasih had never raised money for Okono, and never solicited a recommendation for Okono from Archie Newton. Of course, the obvious question went unasked: how could Latchky be certain of any of this, if, as Okono claimed, he did not know al-Nasih?

The Okono campaign recognized within hours that they had a major problem on their hands. Okono was already on thin ice because of his relationship with The Minister and other black activists who the Israeli-lobby considered rabidly pro-Palestine.

Reporters were on the phone in minutes to the Harvard law professor Newton had mentioned writing.

"Would he comment on Newton's statement: Had Newton written to him on behalf of Okono?" they asked.

The law professor sounded paralyzed, like a groundhog just realizing it had broken cover too early. "Let me call you back," came the response. Reached a few hours later, he was better prepared. He said simply:

"No comment."

Next reporters contacted al-Nasih. He confirmed that he had known Okono for years, but refused to address Newton's statement. He politely said he must decline further comment "out of respect for Congressman Okono."

Just as the story was picking up steam, Josh Stein ran a piece in the *Political Insider* that a spokesperson for the Newton family was, essentially, issuing a retraction. The spokesman Stein cited claimed Archie Newton (whose age he misstated by 2 years) had mis-remembered the event and had a failing memory. Stein ended his column authoritatively: "This should put the Okono/al-Nasih story to bed for good." In other words: show's over, folks. Move along.

But there was one problem. Contacted by a lone journalist to confirm Stein and Latchky's joint story; Newton's family insisted they didn't even know the man who claimed to be their family spokesperson. Archie Newton had an exceptional memory, they insisted. They had *never* retracted Newton's comments; never been contacted by, or confirmed *anything* with Josh Stein. Said

Archie Newton's longtime assistant of the "family spokesperson" quoted by Stein: "Who *is* that guy?" They'd never heard of him. Newton, and his family, stood by his original statement about helping Okono, he insisted.

Chapter Forty-Two

Quantico, Virginia

TWO MEN IN LAB COATS HUDDLED OVER A MICROSCOPE.

"See what I mean?" said one.

"Well, I guess that confirms it. It's hard to think of another explanation for how or why sodium cyanide is in a congresswoman's car."

The younger one asked: "The guys on the scene didn't report any odor. Is that curious?"

"Not necessarily," the older man replied. "It was probably in a powder form. Sodium cyanide releases hydrogen cyanide gas when exposed to the air but a lot of people can't detect any smell...and it's completely odorless when dry. So the smell might not have been that strong. Probably strongest when she first opened the car door. But by the time she was found unconscious, they've got all the doors open—the chances of it being detected by the emergency rescue people was pretty remote. Also, keep in mind, we're evaluating this from the point of view that it's a crime scene. When the EMT's arrive, she's still alive, the rescue guys are thinking heart attack or stroke. She's...what?... late 50's? Early 60's? You can't blame them for not suspecting poison. Holy shit." He paused, stunned. "I can hardly believe it myself."

The younger man was still looking at the slide. "So, what was the mechanism for dissemination? They just left some in the car expecting the fumes to overwhelm her?" he asked.

"Maybe," said the older man, "But remember the coroner's report? There was dermatitis on the hands. I would guess they put it on something they expected her to touch."

"What? You think they just scattered it on the seat?"

The older man considered. "Well, they found some residual traces on the seats, but probably not enough to kill her. And you couldn't be certain someone would touch the seat."

"So, what? Gear shift? Steering wheel?" the younger man asked.

"That would be my guess," replied his colleague.

"But how would they get it to stick? It's a granular powder."

"Not sure," the older man replied. He looked at the slide again, obviously thinking. There was a long pause and he considered the options. Finally he said, "Ask the techs to test all the surfaces for DMSO."

"DMSO?"

The older man nodded. "And tell them as a precaution to wear heavy rubber gloves—not the usual nitrile. Protective suits, the whole thing."

The younger man started taking quick notes in an illegible scrawl. "Okay. Anything else?"

"Yeah," the older man replied. "Two things—call the coroner in Atlanta: ask them, did they notice a garlic smell on the deceased?"

"Okay." The younger man wrote it down. "What else?"

"Have the techs bring a UV light when they're testing the car."

"Why a UV light?" asked the younger man

"Para-benzoquinone in DMSO reacts with cyanide to form cyanophenol," said the older man.

The young man, smiled, pleased. "Which is fluorescent."

"Right," said the older man. "They're looking for a blue-green glow."

Chapter Forty-Three

**August 2008,
Arlington, VA**

THEY HAD BEEN INVITED FOR A POW-WOW with the former McCracken-pol, Danny Englund. Curiously enough this was to take place at the headquarters of the Republican candidate for president, Joe Malloy. Englund greeted them warmly as they shuffled back into his tiny cubicle. Certainly working for the Republicans had improved his wardrobe—but the stale cigarette smoke that clung to him tighter than a shadow and the constant snapping of his Nicorette gum seemed to indicate he hadn't abandoned all his bad habits. As they perched on folding chairs, Englund had handed them each a copy of what he grandly called his 'white paper'. As they started to read he began.

"Obviously, as youse can see, I'm workin' for the Malloy campaign. My, ya know, purpose or whatever, is to organize the McCracken supporters, youse guys, and to do that, I've like developed a strategy of like lasering in on key counties in battleground states." New to suit-wearing, he shot his cuffs importantly and smiled smugly. "I don't mind telling youse, the folks around here have been pret-ty impressed."

Betty Jo quickly flipped through the pages of Englund's paper and exchanged a long look with Lacey. Danny Englund smiled expectantly, obviously anticipating their congratulations and praise.

Betty Jo locked onto Danny Englund with a piercing stare.

"Your plan?" she questioned sweetly.

"Yeah, my plan," he bristled, then just as suddenly he relaxed. "Brilliant, ain't it? See us old Democratic dogs aren't about half dumb—"

Betty Jo cut him off. "Danny, this is bullshit. This is Lacey's plan. Our plan." Betty Jo kept a careful watch on Lacey from the corner of her eye—afraid of her friend's reaction.

Englund objected: "No, I—"

Betty Jo continued, her voice still polite, but with a hard edge now.

"We brought you this plan. When *we* introduced *you* to the Malloy campaign guys. And we don't need you to organize us. We're already organized. We have 14,000 volunteers. You said you were going to help us do some fundraising, get some money for flyers and stuff...from Democrats."

Englund snapped his gum, irritated. "Jay-sus, Betty Jo! Don't be such a bitch. We're all the same team, youse and me right?

Lacey addressed Englund coldly, calmly, her voice soft. "Tell me, Danny, how many volunteers have you signed up?"

Englund brightened. "Well, that's the beauty of my plan, right?" He caught Lacey's eye.

"Okay, *your* plan, whatever. McCracken's supporters aren't

going to sign up with a Republican, right? So you bring your volunteers and I'll direct youse."

Lacey regarded him steadily. "I see. So, it's our plan and our volunteers, but you're going to be in charge, is that right? And the Republicans are providing the funds—and, of course, your salary?"

Englund frowned. The meeting obviously wasn't going as he had anticipated. Drawn by the undercurrent of tension, Malloy staffers were curiously sticking their heads around the thin partition.

"Right," he said carefully. All at once, he brightened once more, remembering. "Did I mention they'll be prizes, ladies?"

Betty Jo was so appalled she couldn't help herself, "Prizes? Prizes for what?"

Englund treated her to his best game-show-host smile. "Well, I thought, ya know, a little friendly competition between the McCracken groups—ya know to see which of youse gets the most volunteers. And the winner gets an all-expenses paid trip to go with me to the—wait for it—Republican National Convention! How's that for great, girls, huh?"

Lacey couldn't stand it anymore. She stood up. "Betty Jo, we need to go."

But part of Betty Jo resisted, shocked that all their plans had unraveled so quickly and completely. She wanted to believe that they still might salvage something—but then she saw the look on Lacey's face and she saw...cold, epic *wrath*. Polite, smilely Lacey looked like Zeus about to unleash a thunderbolt. Betty Jo quickly ushered her out of the office as Englund followed, wringing his hands and looking even more confused than usual.

As they emerged into the summer sunshine, Englund's remonstrances to return and "work things out" still ringing hollowly in their ears, Lacey took a deep breath.

"Betty Jo, I'm sorry. I hope you understand. I can't do that to my volunteers," she said apologetically. "Even if I could hold my nose, they wouldn't stand for it, and they'd be right. Danny Englund promised to set us up with McCracken donors. That's never happened. Now he's glomming off the Republicans we introduced him to—passing off our plans, our volunteers, our hard work—as his own. Frankly, and I'm sorry if this sounds mean, but the guy is as dumb as a rock. And, I could excuse that if it weren't so obvious he thinks he's smarter than we are. For me, this is about restoring power to people who feel they were crushed by the process. I'm sorry—but I don't see how putting them under the thumb of someone like Danny Englund accomplishes that."

Betty Jo considered. Typically, she made her decision quickly.

"You're right, Lacey. We do our own thing. Raise our own money. It won't be easy—but hey!" she said with a laugh "Who said that truth, justice and the American way was supposed to be easy?"

Lacey laughed. "Gosh, Betty Jo, I think I got you out of there just in time," Lacey said with a wink.

"Why do you say that? Betty Jo asked curiously.

Lacey laughed, "You're already starting to sound like a Republican."

Chapter Forty-Four

September 2008
Riyadh, Saudi Arabia

PRINCE ABDUL-WAHID BIN KHAIR AL DIN was not a handsome man. Of middling height, his male-pattern baldness was almost disguised by his copious use of hair spray and blow dryer. It wasn't so much that people didn't notice he was balding, as that they were so distracted by the implied engineering required to achieve the sculpted erection of hair he had left. He had small dark eyes, a small dark mustache and a very large dark mole to the left of his mouth. It was often said that he looked like a man from a different time, specifically a Lebanese rug salesman from the 1970s. The closely fitting dark turtleneck, the large-patterned suit, the rimless tinted glasses—all conspired to create a look more at home in the era of disco balls and male falsetti.

However, as he contemplated his life as the 29th richest person in the world, it is doubtful that any of that concerned him. What did annoy him, he claimed, were the financial magazines that consistently under-reported his $25 billion fortune. For a private man, he'd taken the unexpected step of inviting one of its reporters to spend a week with him. Of course, it was hard for any reporter to get beyond the Prince's 317 room palace, conspicuously adorned with 1,500 tons of Italian marble. Or the two indoor pools (one designed to look like an African watering hole with 25 taxidermied animals in natural poses (which the reporter considered vaguely wonderful and disturbing at the same time. Should you splash?).

There were 250 television sets—mostly tuned to CNBC's business news—Prince Abdul's obsession— and four kitchens devoted to Lebanese, Arabic, Continental, and Asian cuisines, respectively. It was like eating in a different restaurant every night; especially as the prince insisted on eating in a different part of his palace, as well. Ah, the foibles of princes!

His jewelry collection was valued at over $700,000,000, but seldom worn by his 24-year-old fourth wife. The children from his first marriage had made him a grandfather, and he famously doted on his two grandchildren. He followed a predictable, if unusual, routine that seemed more appropriate to a rock star than a businessman. After dinner, he read the papers from the U.S. and U.K. and then stayed up until four or five in the morning, frequently texting friends and business associates nonstop. He claimed to require only four hours of sleep. True or not, official business hours for Crown Holdings began at a very civilized 12:00 p.m. and ended at 6:00.

Three hundred cars—one Mercedes was supposedly encrusted with diamonds—ferried the prince and his retinue to Crown Holdings' various offices and construction sites. When he wanted to visit one of the five-star hotels that he owned in London or Paris, he had an Airbus A380 (the world's largest passenger aircraft), designed to look like the interior of a house, to fly him there in style and comfort.

If it irked him that the western press persisted in claiming he served as a front for monied Saudi interests—perhaps for the House of al-Saud itself, or that the size of his investments could not be accounted for by the size and value of his holdings; it didn't appear to trouble him. Prince Abdul claimed he was used to people underestimating him.

If in some ways, the prince was a caricature of an oil-rich Arab, in others he was distinctly unique. He had frequently criticized Saudi traditionalism and urged the sand kingdom to embrace not just election reforms, but a platform for women's rights. He was proud of the fact that he had hired the first female pilot in Saudi Arabia, and that more than 65% of the staff in his palace and investment company were women. To further her education, Abdul had made a very large donation to the University of New Haven, in exchange for having professors available to teach his wife in the palace.

He had met Muhsin-al-Nasih (then Donald Cleaver of Detroit) when he was in college in California in the early 1970s. It wasn't a particularly good college, but that hardly mattered. Prince Abdul was there to make friends. Donald Cleaver was a radical, a mentor and confidante to Black Panther leaders advocating revolution. Somewhat prosaically for the time, Cleaver claimed to be the reincarnation of a legendary African poet-warrior from the third century. Still, risible as it may have seemed to some, Prince Abdul was intrigued. The Saudis were interested in investing in

Africa, and forming friendships with black nationalists in the U.S. would help the Saudis establish immediate *bone fides.*

In 1977, Prince Abdul returned the favor by introducing Donald Cleaver (now styling himself Muhsin-al-Nasih) to the Saudi king. Notoriously decisive, the king decided then and there to make the newly-minted lawyer OPEC's lead U.S. counsel. Many years had since passed, but Muhsin-al-Nasih had remained a close advisor and friend.

But in spite of the high-priced public relations firms in London and New York recommended by al-Nasih, Prince Abdul remained controversial. Supporters pointed to his generous support of educational initiatives to support Islamic Studies—$20 million to Harvard; $20 million to Georgetown, $20 million to the Louvre (whose new wing would be dedicated to Islamic art). Critics (particularly supporters of Israel), claimed he'd given millions to controversial organizations like the Foundation for American Islamic Studies and the American Islamic Partnership. Organizations whose leaders had, they claimed, been indicted "on terrorism related charges in federal courts," according to one news release.

And it was true that not all Prince Abdul's efforts were well received. His humanitarian contributions to one U.S. city devastated by a rogue tornado had been ignominiously refused after he made statements questioning the fairness of U.S. policy toward Palestine. So, when Archie Newton's comments about his friend al-Nasih and fundraising to cover the cost of Okono's Harvard's law school tuition hit the airwaves, Prince Abdul expected to get some calls from reporters. Perhaps not the Americans, but surely the Brits or the Germans would cover the story? Nothing. Ah, well, all to the good.

Prince Abdul had long since recognized that the key to acceptance was understanding, and the key to achieving understanding was providing the other guy with a financial incentive to keep an open mind. Muhsin al-Nasih had advised him well. As it turned out, Prince Abdul had some very open-minded friends in America, who understood him very well indeed.

Chapter Forty-Five

Washington, DC

Adelita Bouchard always meant to pay the money back. So much money flowed so freely through SEED's national headquarters, with so little accountability, it hadn't really seemed as if it would be a big deal to use her company debit card to give herself a loan. When they found out, of course, it turned out, it *was* kind of a big deal. She had been completely humiliated, but they'd been mostly pretty nice about it. The Washington D.C. metro area was an expensive city in which to live. As a single mother, it was not easy paying for day care and making ends meet on her modest salary. Most of the money had gone for basics for the baby, charges to CVS for formula and diapers. One month she couldn't make rent. Another month, her sorority sisters from the University of Alabama had come to town and she'd been forced to act as hostess, in a way that, even at the time, she knew she couldn't afford and would live to regret.

After speaking with her boss, she'd gone for credit counseling, and they'd worked out a payment schedule to repay the money she'd borrowed using the company card, deducting the money automatically from her bank account. Everything seemed fine, everyone happy. At least until the point when she started asking questions about SEED's extralegal relationship with the Okono campaign.

Adelita Bouchard was an idealist. As a native of Alabama, her parents had experienced segregation and discrimination in a way African Americans in the north would never know. For generations, her people had been the victims of Jim Crow laws that kept them from voting, kept them from having a voice in the system, kept them from real property ownership. She wanted to change that.

But for all its noble aspirations, it was hard not to become disillusioned with SEED. Adelita was good at her job: efficient, well organized, and smart. Within two years, she had moved up to become assistant to the director. But what had become apparent to her in those two years was that founder Ford Rauschenberg ran the organization as his personal fiefdom. And perhaps more disquieting, was her growing belief that SEED was less about advocacy, enfranchisement, and home ownership for the underprivileged, than it was a cold-blooded, soul-less super-corporation, whose sole purpose was to consolidate power and money. What few of its idealistic volunteers realized was that SEED now operated as a thoroughly corrupt multi-headed hydra—using the least privileged in society as a kind of human shield for their mercenary operations.

Most disturbing to Adelita was the 'Muscle for Money' program used to extort money or extract concessions from corporations and political enemies. Successful campaigns had been waged against Sherwin Williams, H&R Block, Jackson Hewitt, and Money Mart among others. SEED was in the business of providing mercenaries —to anyone that could pay. Unions paid them to send three hundred people to protest and wave signs. Corporations paid them to stay home. One way or another, SEED got its money.

At first, Adelita thought every successful campaign was a win for the little guy. But more and more, it came to look less like SEED holding corporations responsible to change unfair practices, than protection money paid to keep them quiet. The corporations, having paid, simply maintained the status quo. In other cases, there was no real grievance against a company—just a shrewd calculation that the company was sufficiently publicity averse and asset rich, to make the payoff worthwhile.

Trade unions, like Service Workers International, paid SEED to intimidate those it perceived as hostile, or with whom they were engaged in negotiations. In one case, they'd hired SEED to send a crowd outfitted in union garb to harass the FairIsle Group and its CEO Davis Shubenstein. The mob—because that's what they were—had broken up a banquet and staged an angry and noisy protest outside of Shubenstein's house. If anyone had polled the crowd, few in the group even knew what the union acronym imprinted on their shirts stood for. Why would they? They weren't members! In the end, the FairIsle Group paid. They all paid.

Attorneys general in 15 states, both Republican and Democratic, were investigating SEED for voter registration fraud. The allegations were serious: election board supervisors in Franklin County, Ohio, had received more than 23,000 voter registrations from SEED—for people who didn't exist. A Houston newspaper had investigated and found 40% of the 27,000 registrations submitted by SEED in Harris County were phony.

Part of it, Adelita knew, could be explained by circumstances. SEED specifically and cynically targeted as recruiters people with little to lose: felons on work-release programs, the indigent, the homeless, addicts. These were people holding onto the bottom rung of desperation. For many, the few dollars a day SEED promised for new registrations meant the difference between eating or getting their fix. New registrants were essentially bribed with pre-paid gas cards or fast food restaurant gift certificates. There was no downside for them. Why not register again? Who would know? Who would care? For SEED recruiters, there was no incentive to play it straight, either. In fact, the opposite was true; if the SEED recruiter didn't make their quota, they were fired.

Did SEED know what the recruiters were doing? Adelita had concluded they did. It was hard to imagine why else SEED would insist that recruiters sign an affidavit before they began recruiting, holding SEED harmless and stipulating that the recruiter alone was responsible for any of his or her actions. When they were caught, SEED had chosen their scapegoats well. "It wasn't SEED!" its well-paid national directors protested. *They* would never countenance such a thing, they assured their Big-Foot friends in Congress. The recruiters were 'bad apples,' they said. Anyone who looked into his or her background would conclude as much.

SEED's defenders claimed that the media attention given

to these incidents was a red herring used by Republicans to disenfranchise the poor and underprivileged. Certainly, they acknowledged, some of their workers may have been a little overzealous and under-scrupulous about securing new registrations (one man claimed he'd been registered 75 times by SEED—under different names). But these were largely administrative or bookkeeping issues, they argued. Multiple registrations did not prove multiple votes. In fact, they pointed out, there was no proof that any of the phony registrants had ever cast a vote.

Of course, there was lots of *anecdotal evidence* that they had. Its critics alleged that SEED routinely hired buses to pick-up prospective voters and carry them from precinct to precinct on election day. These civic-minded citizens (on the theory that if one vote is good, more is better) were rewarded with the ubiquitous gift cards for their hard day's work. There was also evidence that for as many registrations that were flagged as fraudulent, an unknowable number escaped scrutiny by overworked and under-staffed county election workers. SEED's policy of holding thousands of registrations—sometimes for months—and then dumping them all at once on the registration deadline, compounded the difficulty of detection.

Phony voter registrations made for easy headlines. Less attention, Adelita knew, was paid to some of SEED's even more controversial practices. The Okono campaign had been caught by the FEC claiming an $800,000 payment to one of SEED's subsidiaries during the Democratic primaries was for "event staging." Adelita had to smile at the person who'd thought of that subtle euphemism. It was 'staging' all right: 'staging' a win for

Okono in the caucuses in Texas and elsewhere. Eventually, the Okono campaign had been forced to concede the payment was for "volunteer recruitment" and similar services.

Adelita even suspected, as did many Claire McCracken supporters, that the Okono campaign had hired agitators to heckle McCracken at her campaign events. Even McCracken fundraising events (with tables costing $5,000 a pop), were consistently disrupted by protestors. Wearing flip-flops and T-shirts—it seemed unlikely that these putative 'protestors' were paying their own way to the expensive events.

What most of America didn't realize about SEED was that, in many ways, it was as much of a conglomerate as any of the corporate giants it kept in its crosshairs. Headquarters in New York and Washington provided support and resources to more than 750 chapters in 53 cities. SEED ran its own housing corporation, law office, and at least two radio stations. SEED was fond of claiming to its partisans that its' volunteers had registered more than one million low- and moderate-income citizens to vote—in 2004 alone.

It wasn't as if there wasn't important work to do, Adelita thought. 12% of the United States population lived in poverty; in the cities the figure was even higher. As many as 25% of U.S. city residents were poor—figures that were among the highest in the world among industrialized nations. SEED paid lip service to their concern, but, Adelita thought, their objective was elsewhere.

In July, she'd been contacted at home by Suzanne Saturnino of the *New York Times*. She never knew where Saturnino had gotten her name. The Okono campaign had finally been outed by the FEC on the $800,000 payment to the SEED subsidiary, and the

Republicans were doing their best to make it an issue. Saturnino offered to tell SEED's side of the story, and had promised her that anything she said would be considered background only. They met at La Madeleine—an upscale eatery in McLean catering to a heavy lunch crowd (proving that at least in northern Virginia—real men *do* eat quiche and crepes and tangy Caesar salad).

She hadn't meant to say anything incriminating. Adelita had long since become sanguine about most of what was going on. However, as she began answering Saturnino's questions, she could tell by Saturnino's reaction that much of what Adelita was telling her was a complete surprise. Later, when people asked her why she had even agreed to meet with the veteran reporter, she was never really sure. Possibly, Adelita conceded, looking back, she was lonely, feeling more and more disaffected with what was going on in the office.

Although technically non-partisan, SEED had been an unofficial arm of the Democratic Party for years. By hiding behind multiple subsidiaries (something approaching 160 at last count), they had managed to shield most of their more controversial activities. However, taking the field for Okono, they either got reckless or careless. Reporters who noted with satisfaction that the Okono campaign didn't appear to provide local politicians with 'walking around money' to sway constituents—a standard practice within both parties—missed the 'volunteers' for Okono canvassing in Philadelphia being handed $50 Target gift cards as they re-boarded the SEED bus.

But, soon enough, another aspect of SEED's operations seemed destined to attract scrutiny. At the beginning of September, the U.S. Treasury had announced it would bail out Fannie Mae and Freddie Mac. As Government Sponsored Enterprises (or GSE's), most of Fannie Mae and Freddie Mac's bank creditors had done business with them on the assumption that their investment was backed by the full faith and credit of the United States government. With U.S. credit at stake, defaulting on the loans was unthinkable. But the sub-prime mortgage lending-spree was officially over, and the process by which it had inflicted so much damage on the U.S. economy was going to start to receive scrutiny. It was easy enough to blame everything on the greed of Wall Street bankers—on the first round—but sooner or later, people were going to start putting the numbers together, and the numbers told the story.

SEED had become infamous for its tactics in extorting loans from banks for would-be homeowners with risky credit. Loans that were made by Fannie Mae and Freddie Mac were then bundled into securities sold by Wall Street. And, Saturnino knew, the biggest beneficiary of Fannie Mae's campaign largesse was Okono. Right then and there, Saturnino knew, even if she got nothing else, she had her story. But there was more.

Republicans were starting to scream about the so-called "liar loans" or "no-doc" loans where lenders gave loans up to 95% of a home's purchase price and required nothing more than the borrower's name, address, date of birth, and social security number. No information about employment, income, or assets was required. And none of the information that was required was ever verified—hence the name.

But Adelita completely rejected the notion that it was the so-called "greedy poor" who were at fault. A number of unscrupulous banks, Sunset West primary among them, lured unsophisticated mortgage applicants with artificially low 'teaser' rates. Once the interest rate adjusted, an index plus formula applied. If the rate was capped so the lender could only charge a certain incremental increase on the mortgage's interest payments, under the terms of the loan, the additional interest in excess of the cap was deducted from the principal. The strange result: a borrower could be making all their payments and watch their debt increase. There was virtually no way for the borrower to avoid foreclosure or financial ruin. Sunset West didn't care; they'd already sold the mortgages to someone else.

SEED screamed about the predatory lending practices of other banks—but said nothing about Sunset West, the most infamous of them all. To Adelita, this was no surprise. After all, Sunset West, it turned out, was one of SEED's biggest customers. Why was this shocking? Because SEED received 40% of its annual income from the U.S. government to help poor people become homeowners. SEED was ensnaring the very people it was promising to help in Sunset West's perfidious pyramid scheme, coolly receiving a percentage on every transaction—at taxpayer expense. It was so ballsy that it took Saturnino's breath away.

But there was more. Adelita told Suzanne Saturnino not only about SEED's 'Muscle for Money' program, but also that the Okono campaign had illegally shared its list of maxed-out donors with SEED, so that they could approach them for more contributions. According to Adelita, the communication was direct and from the very top. The head of the Washington D.C. office claimed to be speaking directly to Okono.

Of course, telling Saturnino wasn't enough. With allegations like these—tying the presumptive Democratic nominee to an organization perpetrating fraud on a massive scale, there had to be proof. Saturnino knew it had to be ironclad before her bosses would risk running the story. She hated pushing it, knowing she was probably putting Bouchard in peril—at least of losing her job if nothing more—but she had to see documentation. Or Adelita had to give her enough information so that she could track down the documentation herself.

If it were true, not only would Okono's career be finished; he and some of his top lieutenants were probably looking at jail time. The breadth of the fraud was staggering. Adelita claimed to have proof that SEED had used underhanded tactics in all fourteen caucuses, thirteen of which were won by Okono. Bouchard, who never paid much attention to politics, didn't seem to fully grasp the implications of these revelations, but Saturnino did. The caucuses represented the statistical difference in delegates that had decided the Democratic nomination.

CHAPTER FORTY-SIX

New York, New York

THE ARTICLE WAS PRINTED in the June 1968 issue of a left-leaning political magazine. It became so popular, and so iconic, that eventually tens of thousands of reprints were requested. It was the work of two PhDs, then teaching at Columbia. And, in some ways, it might have seemed a strange choice of subject matter for academics. But, the times were strange. Both were unabashed socialists. They believed in complete redistribution of wealth in America. They were preaching nothing less than revolution and anarchy.

The article took as its working hypothesis that the economic elite used welfare as a mechanism of social control. By providing a safety net, they argued, the elite lulled the economically disenfranchised into complacency. Therefore, they posited, society would never change until the social nets were destroyed, and the poor were forced by necessity to rebel against their economic overlords. To help the poor, they needed to sabotage the very systems on which the poor had come to rely. Only when the system was destroyed, they argued, could a new, more equitable system emerge.

Their plan was brilliantly simple. The authors pointed out that the eight million people currently receiving welfare were seriously fewer (perhaps by as much as half) than the number of people legally entitled to receive it. If they signed up those additional people, they reasoned, the system could not sustain the level of payments. The system would, they argued, catastrophically, and inevitably, crash. The article posited that "cadres of aggressive organizers" could organize violent demonstrations to bring the political establishment to its knees. Sympathetic, well-placed journalists would then start to publicly suggest "a federal program of income re-distribution"—that would share out the spoils evenly—both to those who could work, and those who could not.

As their manifesto made clear, the strategists never pretended that the poor who would be manipulated into turning up at their demonstrations were anything but tools. The poor must be led to believe they were protesting about their specific concerns, concerns that were irrelevant to the academics. The academics didn't care about affordable housing, better and cleaner mass transit, or even universal healthcare—those were throwaways. They needed chaos, disorder, dislocation. They needed people to bleed. Better yet, and more specifically, they needed poor people to bleed. On television.

They got it. Pippen and Clothard founded Welfare Now! and by 1969 claimed 25,000 active members. At their behest, members staged mass demonstrations, sit-ins, and boycotts. They stormed welfare offices where they shattered glass doors, overturned furniture, filing cabinets, and desks. They smashed electronics and ripped phones from the walls, disabling for weeks the social services offices they attacked. They weren't choosy, they didn't need to be. The intention was to create chaos. Protestors disrupted meetings of everyone from congressional committees to city and town councils, and threw rocks and tear gas at police—all the while demanding money to which they claimed to be entitled.

For the academics, it all worked beyond their wildest expectations. Clothard was quoted in the New York newspapers as saying "The prospects for the poor will only improve when the rest of society is afraid of them." In 1970, the Supreme Court considered the case of *Goldberg v. Kelly*, where twenty individuals suspected of welfare fraud had been denied benefits by their New York City caseworkers. The court ruled that, henceforth, no welfare recipient could be denied benefits without an evidentiary hearing. Perhaps predictably, the welfare rolls swelled. In ten years, the number of people receiving assistance from the federal government more than doubled. By 1975, the city of New York declared bankruptcy. In the 'city that never sleeps', there was one person on welfare for every two people who were working.

Denied federal bailout money, but buoyed by a loan from the teacher's pension fund, almost inexplicably, New York City—being New York City— inverted itself and was saved. There were no riots, no calls for a socialist state. In fact, rather to the contrary, there was a backlash against a system that was obviously no longer working the way it was intended.

Disappointed, the academics moved on. There would be other

ways, other opportunities, to overwhelm the social system, they reminded their followers. By 1982, Ford Rauschenberg who had worked for the academics on Welfare Now!, refocused his energies on their voting rights initiative called Power Vote (Rauschenberg would later become famous as the founder of SEED). Perhaps cynically, they found themselves a militant African American to be its spokesperson. Years later, before he ran for the state senate, Okono would run Power Vote's Chicago subsidiary. Clothard, Pippen, and Rauschenberg lobbied energetically for what came to be known as the "motor-voter" system, whereby people could register to vote when they received their licenses from the Division of Motor Vehicles, or signed up for social services. On its face, there was nothing sinister about the legislation—far from it—a democracy has the obligation to make sure its citizens can freely and fairly cast their vote. But critics alleged that the organization was always intended as a front...for bigger things.

Critics categorized the academics' plan as "a Trojan horse movement." The ostensible reason for most of the community organizations they founded was to provide greater access to social services for the poor, a laudable goal. But, critics charged, their manifesto revealed that their actual intention was to dismantle those services, so the poor would revolt and create a socialist state. As one critic noted: "...their real objective is to lure the poor into service as revolutionary foot soldiers, to mobilize poor people *en masse* to overwhelm government agencies with a flood of demands calculated to break the budget, jam the bureaucratic gears into gridlock and bring the whole system crashing down. Fear, turmoil, violence and economic collapse would accompany such a breakdown—providing perfect conditions for fostering radical change. Carefully orchestrated media campaigns would float the idea of 'a federal program of income redistribution' in the form of a guaranteed living income for all—working and non-working people alike."

In time, the plan came to be known as the Clothard-Pippen strategy, with their names listed alphabetically, his first. But Pippen was the real brains behind the operation. Born in Canada, she grew up in the Bronx, the only child of Russian immigrants who never fully acclimated to their new country. At fifteen, she left home to attend the University of Chicago and immediately established her *bona fides* as an intellectual heavyweight.

Brilliant, reserved, intentional, Pippen combined a tireless belligerence and steely-eyed pragmatism. She only cared about results. She became an accomplished writer and a powerful, compelling public speaker. If some of her colleagues kept their distance—wary of her advocacy and involvement in engineered confrontation, controversy, and chaos, her graduate students huddled around her in Socratic fashion, adoringly eating Chinese take-out at her feet. Her trim figure, large eyes, and pixie-like hairstyle were a source of admiration, as well. She carefully maintained her Main Street appeal.

She learned to tailor her arguments to the audience. She sucked in the perennially naïve feminists to whom she argued that the "poorest of the poor" were women. To already defensive African Americans, she argued that the current economic system was merely a new form of slavery. With each interest group, she fine-tuned her arguments with an entirely cynical calculation as to what would win them over; like a barber honing the blade of his razor on a strop.

Of course, voter registration efforts could change the political system, but it couldn't cause the sort of social and financial breakdown Clothard and Pippen were seeking. They needed a new issue behind which to mobilize the poor—an issue that could—by engineered massive public participation—cause economic collapse.

It may have seemed curious to some Washington insiders that the voter registration groups, like Power Vote and SEED, began to lobby Congress and multiple administrations for less-restrictive lending requirements for would-be homeowners with poor credit. But their change in focus went unchallenged, if not unnoticed. After all, weren't members of both parties always touting home ownership as the surest way to create a responsible and stable citizenry? The Republicans were as enthusiastic as the Democrats. After forty years of spectacular successes and devastating reverses, Pippen had finally found the means to an end, the perfect Trojan horse. It would be worth the wait.

Chapter Forty-Seven

Chicago, Illinois

Without much hope of finding anything, but annoyed at the prospect of simply giving in to his superior's now pressing demands that he move on, Harrison had obtained a search warrant for Kevin DuShane's apartment. Black and whites had already been through the entire complex asking the residents if anyone had seen Kevin DuShane. They all heard the same story—DuShane was on a vacation paid for by the Jehovah Ministry Church. The apartment was Harrison's last hope.

When Johnson found out where Harrison was headed, he insisted on accompanying him to the South Side apartment complex.

"Have you ever been to Orchard Park?" Johnson asked Harrison—eyeing him curiously as they walked.

"Not sure," said Harrison. Johnson stopped walking abruptly.

"If you'd been to Orchard Park, you'd remember," he said, shaking his head.

Immediately, Johnson was on his cell phone, asking someone on the other end if they could meet there. Harrison was not sure why they needed a guide, but said nothing. He'd learned to respect Johnson's instincts. Johnson's ties to the local communities were unparalleled, and had helped crack more than one case in the past. Johnson snapped his phone shut.

"Got a guy meeting us there, let's go."

The name Chicago comes from the Potawatomois word "skikaakwa" meaning 'skunk'—a reference, it has long been assumed, to the acrid, pungent-smelling skunk grass that grew along the river. By the late 1770s, the first non-Indian settlers were calling it "Eschikago." One of the first was a Haitian, Jean Baptiste Pointe du Sable, officially named in 1968 as the city's founder.

Du Sable had a fascinating story. The son of a Caribbean slave and French pirate, he had studied at a Catholic school in France. When he immigrated to America, to ensure his freedom, he'd traveled north and west, finally establishing himself on the swampy western shore of Lake Michigan. The mosquito-plagued marsh might not have seemed to have much to recommend it to other settlers, particularly those looking for arable land. But du Sable quickly realized the one commodity the adjacent old-growth forest did have in munificent supply—animals. More specifically, small, furry animals whose sheer numbers made them easy to catch. He established the first trading post in the area and became rich trading fur.

Undoubtedly, one of the reasons for his commercial success was the area's remarkable access. Eschikago possessed a unique geography on the continental divide. The so-called "Chicago

Portage" connects two of the most important waterways in the world. On one side of the divide, the water drains from Lake Michigan to the St. Lawrence and into the Atlantic. On the other side, water drains from the Des Plaines, Kankakee, Illinois, and Mississippi rivers into the Gulf of Mexico. The city of Chicago sits like a colossus, straddling the two.

The city had grown immensely from its humble beginnings. Present day Chicago was divided into four main sections. The Loop was the nexus of most of Chicago's commercial, civic, and financial activities, and was named for the circuit of cable cars that originally surrounded what came to be considered downtown like an embrace. The North Side, with its beaches and parks along Lake Michigan, was the most densely populated, famous for its art galleries and trendy eateries. The demolition of the notorious Cabrini-Green housing project in 2003, had paved the way for upscale townhouses and general revitalization of the area. Lakeview, Andersonville, and Boystown were known for their large and sophisticated yuppie and gay populations. The West Side was dominated by Garfield Park Conservatory, the South Side by the University of Chicago.

All four quadrants of the city were unusually mixed. Multi-million dollar condos in converted warehouses stood check-by- jowl with impoverished neighborhoods of 'unimproved' buildings. If real estate in the North Side was generally considered the most attractive, there were plenty of poor—and expensive— neighborhoods scattered throughout the city. But the South Side was an exception. With only a small oasis around the university, the rest of the area looked like a war-zone.

Orchard Park was one example. It stood close by an affluent

neighborhood of mansions and manicured lawns populated by professionals —including members of the University of Chicago faculty. But if the geography was contiguous, Orchard Park shared little else with its glamorous neighbors up the street.

As they drove up to the development, Johnson answered his phone. As Harrison pulled into the first available parking space, Johnson waved out the car window, and spoke into the phone,

"Okay. I see you." They got out of the car. Waiting for them was an African American man in his mid-thirties. He carried a clipboard. Harrison made a quick survey of his attire: crisp, plaid, button down, short-sleeved shirt, creased khakis, pocket protector. Harrison's quick guess was high school math teacher or exterminator.

Johnson was introducing them. They shook hands.

"John Williams," the man said simply.

"Reverend John is a pastor at my church," Johnson said by way of explanation. Johnson attended his neighborhood church in a nice, working class suburb on the North Side. Harrison thought to himself, Well, I read that wrong.

"Part-time pastor. I'm still studying," Williams said somewhat sheepishly.

Johnson was never put off by false modesty:

"Reverend John's an expert on most of the projects around here. He's spear-headed a lot of the church outreach efforts."

Harrison was impressed.

"And, if I may ask...?"

Williams laughed and finished his thought.

"What was the connection?"

"Right."

"I used to do pest control for the city."

Harrison smiled to himself, pleased. He still had it. They all looked somberly at a nearby trashcan, overflowing with detritus, swarming with cockroaches. As they stood in the project's main entry, rats skittered across the pathways.

"Reverend John spent a lot of time here," Johnson said, thoughtfully.

Reverend John gave them a quick overview. In 1990, Orchard Park had opened as a redevelopment, run by a non-profit group called Forestlawn. Federal money paid for the property's complete renovation as part of one of the earliest public-private partnerships sponsored by the city's mayor and Okono.

The development had 504 apartments. By Reverend John's estimate, a hundred or more were now vacant, their doors and windows covered with grafitti'd plywood boards. The tenants who remained had nowhere else to go. The living conditions should have been unimaginable: sewage that backed up into sinks, rat and cockroach infestations so intense that pets and children were at risk, rotted garbage stacked up in clogged trash chutes. And basic utilities: water, electricity, heat— that constantly malfunctioned, Reverend John said. Harrison noticed the unmistakable stench of urine in the hallways, the broken electrical fixtures, the collapsed walls, and the black scar of fire damage on many of the units. Reverend John told them federal inspectors had recently rated the development an 11—on a 100-point scale. The development now faced demolition.

"The city basically outsourced public housing to a few chosen private developers," said Reverend John. On Reverend John's list, in addition to Joey Ali, Harrison noticed some of Okono's biggest supporters and members of his inner circle. "They received hundreds of millions of dollars in city, state, and federal subsidies. But because these units are subsidized housing—they're rent controlled. So the developer who got all his money up-front had no financial incentive to maintain the property—with the inevitable result." Reverend John shook his head.

"Many of these loans are only available to owners who qualify as minority-owned or disadvantaged. They're meant to help the community," Reverend John continued.

"Then guys like Joey Ali find people willing to front for them for a percentage of the booty...and they screw their own people."

Harrison kicked some of the debris out of the way with his foot.

"I take it you're not a fan of Okono's?"

Reverend John gave him a level look.

"When Okono ran for the Congress, a group of residents here held a protest *against* him. In the statehouse and Congress he was always lobbying for tax credits and federal subsidies for his developer buddies. Ali alone collected almost $87 million to renovate 30 buildings, and there was no maintenance. Problems with electricity, heat, you name it. I mean, most of these walls aren't even insulated."

Johnson shrugged. "Maybe he didn't know."

"There are at least eleven of these projects in Okono's own district that I know of," Reverend John added. "And I forgot to mention one more thing..." Both Harrison and Johnson looked at Reverend John.

"Yeah?" Johnson asked

Reverend John continued. "In the middle of winter...it was

maybe two degrees... the residents of this development finally got the city to sue ForestLawn to turn on the heat...so that people wouldn't die."

Johnson nodded. "Yeah. Okay."

"Guess who represented them?" Reverend John asked.

"Okono?" Harrison guessed. Reverend John nodded.

"The residents? asked Johnson.

"Well, that's good, right? People can't live without heat in Chicago."

Reverend John looked at him sympathetically.

"Okono didn't represent the *residents*. He represented the developers. His buddies. Okono was the attorney for Forest-Lawn."

Harrison whistled. Reverend John paused to shake the hand of an elderly woman he recognized coming out of her apartment. After a few minutes, she left, pushing a hand-held cart. Reverend John continued.

"You know why they turned off the heat?"

"No, why?" Johnson asked.

"It came out during discovery for the court case," said Reverend John, by way of explanation.

"Their accountants had run the numbers, and advised them it wasn't cost-effective to heat uninsulated units in the middle of a Chicago winter. So ForestLawn just turned off the heat and left people to freeze. They figured, even if the city made them turn it back on eventually, they had saved a few bucks." Harrison and Johnson were silent. By any measure, it was a damning indictment.

Harrison consulted the apartment directory, hanging by one

forlorn metal hinge. DuShane's apartment was to the right, about halfway down the row.

Johnson was thoughtful. "Look," he said, finally "Most politicians are pretty corrupt, but Okono's really bringing people a lot of hope, don't you think?"

Reverend John regarded them both. "You know what I say about Okono?"

Harrison was silent.

"No, what?" Johnson replied.

Reverend John continued. "All these people who believe he's going to do all those great things for America?"

"Yeah?" said Johnson.

"He's spent his entire professional life representing one district–this district–the South Side." Carter gestured at the ruined development.

"And what has he done to change the conditions *here*? What has he done for *these* people? That's what I say about Okono."

Johnson was defensive. "Hey, man–look–maybe he didn't know, okay? The dude's in Washington most the time...I mean, how does he know about all the shit with the garbage and all?"

John Williams appraised him calmly: "He couldn't know because he lives in Washington–is that what you're saying?"

"Yeah, right," answered Johnson.

"Where does his family live?"

"Jesus, man, I don't know," Johnson answered dismissively.

"With him, right? In D.C.?"

Reverend John pointed down the ravaged block of projects with his index finger. "His family lives in a big, fancy house about eight blocks from here. His kids get driven to their private school 'cause, as you can imagine, nobody that has a choice is going to send their kids to the neighborhood *public school* with all the hoodlums and drug dealers...and you wouldn't make little kids walk past this place, right?"

Finally, they reached Kevin DuShane's apartment. Reverend John offered to stay outside and keep a watch–for, what, exactly–Harrison was afraid to inquire. The apartment had obviously been uninhabited for months. There was a hole in the sheetrock of the living room wall, and in a couple of places Harrison was disgusted to see wires exposed. The complex was literally falling apart. Harrison had seen jail cells that looked more inviting

Johnson looked around. "Well, at least it explains one thing."

Harrison looked at him inquisitively. "What's that?" he asked his partner.

Johnson continued, "If you live in a shit-hole like this, a Caribbean holiday sounds pretty good, no matter who makes the offer."

Harrison nodded, disappointed. He'd known it was a remote chance, but he'd been hoping to find something. From the remaining dust on the cheap plywood cabinet in the living room, Harrison could see that someone had recently helped himself to DuShane's large television. All that remained were some mismatched thrift store furniture and a few snack boxes in the kitchen, already ravaged by vermin. That was it: no books, no computers, no pictures. Nothing.

If DuShane had ever had a personal life, there was no longer any evidence of it. Harrison had sent the techs over this morning to see if they could lift some prints. He'd been hopeful, but now that he had seen the apartment in person, Harrison was starting to doubt they'd find anything. He and Johnson had already been through all the state and federal databases, no official records came up to match Kevin DuShane, and, apparently, nobody around Chicago ever knew him as anything else. With no birth certificate, medical records, tax returns, or license, the inescapable conclusion was that DuShane had been an assumed name. Dendra Jones had most likely been right that DuShane came to Chicago as a runaway. The most likely explanation seemed to be that he had simply assumed a new name with his new life. Harrison was forced to admit that after months of digging, they still had absolutely no idea who the guy was. Or where he had gone.

The results came a few hours later. The techs had found no prints in the apartment. Not one.

CHAPTER FORTY-EIGHT

New York, New York

THE PREMISE OF THE U.S. INVESTMENT BANKING SYSTEM is that if a portfolio is sufficiently diverse, almost any level of risk can be amortized. The odds of all companies or all economies experiencing downturns at the same time are considered statistically impossible. The fatal flaw in this argument is that it presupposes your risk stays where you left it. Or, put another way, that the Vietnamese rice company whose stock you buy only invests in Vietnam, the Swedish bicycle company is safely invested solely in Scandinavia, and your Argentine vintner restricts itself to investments in South America. However, when the Vietnamese company holds mortgages on the homes of firefighters in Queens (NY) and stock in a Brazilian coffee company in *their* portfolio, then there is no such thing as diversification—or rather there's so much diversification—it cancels itself out. Everyone shares the same inter-related, interdependent risk.

Historically, people involved in large enterprises have put

a lot of faith in the idea that some things are determined by someone, somewhere, to be too big to fail. The idea is always that the dislocation that would theoretically attend their passing is potentially so disruptive, it will rend the fabric of society. Of course, seldom is this actually the case. But when investment banks that had happily (no, gleefully!) solved the problem of high risk mortgage debt by packaging them all together, and selling them to someone else—found to their dismay that they themselves carried an enormous, staggering number of those investments on their own books, they were singularly unprepared for what happened next. They had simply never considered the possibility that some failures might be too big to save.

Middle-class people who lose their jobs stop spending money. At first, catastrophe just skims along the top. They cut back on all the obvious 'fun-to-haves'—a long weekend at the beach, the impulse buys at the big-box stores, the great (cheap) stuff from China. (After all, they're okay, they have some money in investments). As unemployment stretches on, they mentally adjust their belts a little tighter, and out go all the extracurriculars: karate lessons for the kids, date-night, a new winter coat. Eventually, however, people with no money stop paying their bills—and finally (perhaps) through a combination of hard luck and bad decisions, they lose their house, especially if they had been tempted by easy loans to buy more house than they could really afford.

Much of the U.S. system is based on the idea that real estate is the safest investment, fed by mostly-true tales of all the fortunes that are created in real estate. But savvy real estate investors recognize two things that homeowners seldom do. First, never become emotionally attached to a property you invest in—i.e., don't live in it. Living in a house you buy as an investment is like naming the chicken you might need to eat—hard on the kids. Second, never buy at the top of the market. Even people who theoretically understood that the central tenet of ANY investing is buy low, sell high—had lost their heads in bidding wars for houses that were already overpriced by any metric. They would pay for their mistake.

But, of course Main Street is very far from Wall Street—two worlds that really, mostly, occupy separate universes. After all, how common is a $50 million bonus in Boise, Idaho? Predictably, there had been tremors when the big banks started writing off billions in mortgage debt. Tremors turned to shock waves when Tolero Star faltered and was sold at a Fed-officiated fire sale. But there was still a widespread belief that the system was fundamentally strong.

Pundits would later decry Wall Street's lack of foresight. When Tolero Star had vanished beneath the surface with only a few bubbles, did the bankers not see the financial crisis looming, they thundered? Well, actually, no. To many astute observers on Wall Street, the collapse of Tolero Star raised more questions than it answered. Did Tolero Star have exposure to risky investments? Beyond a doubt. But the circumstances that triggered their collapse were based on (unfounded) rumors that Tolero Star had liquidity problems. At the time the rumors began, on that fateful Monday morning in March, Tolero Star had a healthy $18 billion in cash reserves—but somebody was already shorting their stock.

What happened to Tolero Star was neither more nor less complicated than an old-fashioned run on a bank. As the rumors swirled, more and more lenders demanded more collateral to lend less money. Increasingly, their bank customers wouldn't lend Tolero Star money at all—and at that point the managers at Tolero Star knew it was over.

Whether or not the short selling was orchestrated by three hedge fund managers (reputed to have celebrated Tolero Star's demise over a champagne breakfast where they pledged to make Helman Brothers their next target)—there was more speculation than answers. Whether some opportunistic bottom feeders got lucky—or illegally manipulated the markets to make their own luck—was unknown. What *was* clear was that some hedge fund managers had made a lot of money betting against Tolero Star.

Tolero Star's managers claimed that three of Tolero Star's biggest trading partners were intentionally targeted with requests that they become a third party to Tolero Star's trades with their customers. Normally, they would have granted these 'novation' requests without question. But as the three banks were flooded with requests by customers who wanted to get out of trades with Tolero Star, the banks started to worry about their own exposure. And they did what sensible, well-run investment banks do—two of the three pulled credit—within 12 hours.

To what extent the crisis that led to the demise of Tolero Star was engineered was unknown, perhaps would never be known. But lots of people had their suspicions and the "champagne breakfast" hedge fund managers were on the top of most people's list of suspects.

But if the rumors were true and the speculators and short-sellers were eyeing Helman Brothers in March as their next victim, to outsiders it looked like Wall Street was simply following the law of the savannah and culling the herd. After all, Helman Brothers —like Tolero Star— was never really part of the club.

In the first six months of 2008, Helman Brothers' stock was down 73% on news that it had reported losses of $2.8 billion and been forced to sell almost $6 billion in assets. Of course, this was small potatoes compared to what some of the largest securities firms had written off, but confidence in Helman Brothers had been shaky for a while.

In August, they announced layoffs of 1,500 people, a little under 10% of the work force. On September 10th, they had announced a further loss of $3.9 billion dollars, and that they were looking to sell-off a majority stake in their investment management business. At about the same time, mugs, hats, and umbrellas emblazoned with the Helman Brothers corporate logo started appearing on eBay, as cynical employees looked to cash-in one more time. At that point, Helman Brothers was a rampike, still standing, but dead. On the 15th of the month, after begging for assistance from their unsympathetic Wall Street brethren, the SEC, and even the Fed—it was over. Helman Brothers filed for Chapter 11 bankruptcy protection and became the largest bankruptcy in U.S. history.

Started in 1844 by a Jewish cotton broker from Alabama who'd emigrated from Germany, Helman Brothers had taken some of the most iconic companies in America public—companies like Sears Roebuck, F.W. Woolworth, Mays Department Stores, Macys, Gimbels, and B.F. Goodrich. Of course, as one unsentimental wag put it, most of those companies weren't around to shed any tears, either.

Reading the *Wall Street Journal*, Paul Johannsen had a different reaction—the reaction you have when someone you know becomes a little famous for a while. It was kind of exciting. He called his wife after reading the story on the internet. As it turned out, they knew the three hedge fund guys of 'champagne breakfast fame'! In fact, all three had hosted the first moneyman 'meet-and greet' they'd attended for Okono. His wife remembered, with more than a little pleasure, that one of them—the little bald guy— had complimented her on her dress.

CHAPTER FORTY-NINE

Manassas, Virginia

THEY HAD DECIDED TO MEET at the usual place in Old Town, a cute little Portuguese restaurant on Nokesville Road near the train station. It was a beautiful, warm autumn evening, the sun just beginning to set. Connor had gladly accepted the hostess' offer of an outside table under a stylish teak and tan umbrella. It was a cute place, not inexpensive, but frequented by a quiet, professional crowd who enjoyed its faux Tuscan décor and light Italian and Portuguese cuisine. Connor was waiting for a friend. Joel Samuels had been the deputy assistant director of the FBI crime lab at Quantico for the last five years. He'd been Connor Murphy's friend for twenty.

Samuels sat down. His shoulders sagged. He had scoliosis. Probably all those years bent over a microscope, Connor thought.

"Long day?" Connor asked. He gestured to the waitress for another beer.

"You could say that," Samuels replied.

"I appreciate you taking the time to see me."

Samuels looked at him skeptically. He didn't believe in bullshit.

"I'd see you any time. You appreciate me taking the time to talk to you confidentially about an ongoing Bureau investigation," he said.

"Okay." Murphy smiled and shrugged. Samuels wasn't exactly known for his interpersonal skills, but Connor wasn't offended. Samuels looked off into the distance. Some teenagers were testing their skateboarding prowess in the little square opposite.

"Somebody murdered her."

Connor choked on the foam of his beer. He wiped his face with the back of his hand. Samuels handed him an extra napkin without looking at him.

"Seriously?" he asked.

Samuels spoke quietly: "No other conclusion is possible. The car tested positive for traces of DMSO and sodium cyanide."

"Wait a second," Connor interrupted. "Remember, I'm not a scientist. Back up here—what is DMSO?"

Samuels regarded him critically. "You need to take notes." He pulled out a lined yellow legal pad from his briefcase.

"Here." He handed it to him.

"Government issue?" Connor asked. Connor knew how Samuels felt about "company" property.

Samuels replied, "I bought it at a CVS on the way."

"Okay." Connor started to take notes. "Shoot."

Samuels' beer arrived. He took a long sip. "DMSO is Dimethyl sulfoxide"—Samuels spelled it out. "It's a by-product of the wood industry. Truly a wonder drug—like aspirin—used to treat inflammation for rheumatoid arthritis, intracranial pressure after severe head trauma—but it has fallen into ill repute in recent years after a death was tied to its use. It's available commercially, at health food stores—a lot of horse people use it."

"Okay." None of this was really making sense, but Connor knew better than to rush Samuels. He knew by long experience that Samuels was telling him what he needed to know.

The waiter came to take their order. When they'd handed back the menus, Samuels continued. "It's colorless, and at least until it's ingested—odorless."

Connor interrupted: "What about after it's ingested?"

"It produces a strong garlic odor people frequently find offensive," Samuels replied.

"Okay," said Connor, taking notes.

Samuels continued, "Most relevant to this case, though, are not its independent uses, but the fact that it's a polar a-proctic solvent."

"A... what?" Connor asked.

"From a chemist's point of view..." Samuels explained, "it contains a dissociable hydrogen atom—essentially a hydrogen atom bound to an oxygen atom."

"Okay. I'll take your word for it. So?" Connor wasn't seeing the tie-in.

"As a solvent, it can donate a hydrogen proton." Samuels paused, sipping his beer, still watching the skateboarders.

"And that means...?" Connor prompted.

"I guess you would say it mixes well." Samuels laughed at his own joke.

"Okay." Connor looked bewildered. Samuels was clearly bemused by Connor's still-confused expression.

He continued. "In layman's terms—It dissolves things...and it penetrates the skin..."

"Whoa. Now we're getting somewhere." He had Connor's full attention.

"So if you wanted to inject someone with something...?"

Samuels patiently corrected him. "Not *inject*. It's topical. It penetrates into the bloodstream through the skin, carrying whatever it's mixed with...in this case sodium cyanide."

Connor was too astonished to speak.

Samuels continued.

"I spoke to the coroner in Atlanta. They all noticed a pungent smell of garlic from the deceased."

"Maybe she ate Italian?" suggested Connor.

"Coffee and cookies were in her stomach," Samuels corrected him.

"I read that the family didn't want an autopsy," said Connor.

"One reads a lot of things." Samuels paused, as if unsure he wanted to say more. "The family had no choice. As you probably know..." he looked at Connor significantly, while Connor tried hard to look innocent, "she had received death threats that were the subject of an on-going Bureau investigation."

Two large platters of food arrived. Samuels, consulting the impressive wine list, ordered a bottle. Connor waited for the waiter to leave.

"Okay, so what about the cyanide?"

"Sodium cyanide." Samuels was always precise.

"Readily available?" Connor asked. Samuels sipped the remnants of his beer and nodded.

Connor probed further. "As what?...rat poison?" he asked.

Samuels replied. "It used to be available commercially as ant killer. But now it's more regulated, mostly confined to industrial uses. In addition to the danger from topical exposure, it also produces a highly toxic, extremely flammable gas that's liberated by carbon dioxide, called hydrogen cyanide or HCN."

"So somebody in an air-conditioned car in August..?" asked Connor

"Their breathing would release the gas, yes," responded Samuels.

"And cyanide does what, exactly?" Connor asked.

Samuels considered. "In the most basic terms..." he looked significantly at Connor, "it prevents the body's cells from synthesizing oxygen and they explode."

"Ugggh." Connor was disgusted.

"It's not pretty," agreed Samuels. He continued. "Initial symptoms would be nausea, dizziness, rapid breathing, diaphoresis."

Connor was writing as fast as he could. "Dia-phor—what?"

"Excessive sweating," replied Samuels. He continued, "Within minutes there might be vomiting, unconsciousness, convulsions, and fluid would start to accumulate in the lungs."

Connor was confused. "But it took her a day to die...right?" he asked.

Samuels weighed his words carefully. "I think it might be more correct to say that in deference to the feelings of her loved ones, she remained on total life support for nine hours."

"I see."

Samuels continued in a lower voice. "By most reports, her systems were fully shut down and she had little or no brain function by the time she arrived at the hospital—perhaps even before."

The waiter brought the wine, uncorked it, and after a quick sampling by Samuels, poured two glasses. They both patiently watched the waiter move out of earshot before resuming their conversation. Samuels paused, thoughtfully. He went on to explain. "People don't really survive sodium cyanide poisoning. Even with a full course of amyl nitrate, sodium nitrate, and sodium thiosulphate administered almost immediately, there's usually irreparable brain damage." Samuels paused again.

"So to be accurate, she wasn't dying at the hospital—she was really, already clinically dead."

Connor considered. "But the press reports said that she died of a brain hemorrhage after a burst aneurysm."

"Maybe she did," Samuels shrugged. "It would be nice to think the press sometimes reports things accurately." As Connor looked puzzled, he continued.

"But that's the biological explanation of what happened, not the proximate cause. The proximate cause was cyanide poisoning."

"So why didn't it show up in the autopsy?" Connor paused to sip his wine. It was delicious with the Lasagna Bolognese, the house specialty.

Samuels explained. "Cyanide naturally occurs as a bacterial by-product as tissues decompose." Samuels continued. "It's notoriously difficult to stabilize in tissue samples—particularly if blood is only taken from one site, or unless organ samples are stored in containers with a 2% sodium fluoride additive."

"And were they?" Connor asked hopefully.

"Were they what?" replied Samuels.

"Stored with the additive?" Connor replied.

"No," said Samuels.

"What about the body? Any tell-tale signs?" asked Connor.

"Sure. Victims turn bright-pink, like a bad sunburn."

"Ahh...What does that look like on an African American?" asked Connor quizzically.

"Like an African American with a sunburn," said Samuels.

"I mean," Samuels paused to consider. "I suppose their mother might notice, not a Caucasian coroner."

"Anything else?" Connor said.

"There's sometimes dark vomit around the lips. Internal tissues might be bright-pink due to oxyhaemoglobin. The mucosa on the lower third of the esophagus may be damaged, and depending on how dilute the solution, the stomach might show some damage where the rugae have eroded, or petechial hemorrhage occurred," Samuels concluded.

"Okay. Whatever that means. Any of that show up?" inquired Connor.

"Yup," said Samuels.

"Which?" questioned Connor.

"All of it," replied Samuels.

The waiter appeared to ask how everything was. They both waved him away with thanks. Connor said quietly. "Well, that's proof, right?"

"Not necessarily," Samuels replied. "There was damage to the esophagus—but the victim was on a ventilator for nine hours—there's no way to prove when the damage occurred. The stomach and stomach contents revealed high levels of cyanide—so much so that the examiner became ill as the gas left the body cavity. But the assistant who took over stored the samples in a formalin preservative..." Samuels trailed off.

"Okay..." Connor answered, waiting.

Samuels continued, "Rendering the samples useless."

"But you said the M.E. got sick from the fumes," Connor protested.

"Or handling the viscera," Samuels agreed. "No doubt about it. But without the samples, it wouldn't hold up as evidence. A defense attorney could just claim the M.E. had the flu and didn't know it." Samuels considered a moment. "You know, there's a good reason bad guys use sodium cyanide to poison people."

Connor nodded, aggrieved. "Yeah, because it's virtually undetectable and impossible to prosecute."

"Well, that..." Samuels laughed a mirthless laugh, "and its highly effective. It kills something like 95% of people exposed to even small amounts."

They both sipped their wine soberly. Their food was growing cold. Something was tugging at Connor.

"Wait. Where have I heard about HCN?"

Samuels looked thoughtful. "Ever investigate any arsons?"

Connor shook his head. "No. Why?"

Samuels explained. "Most lay people describe it as smoke inhalation–but it's actually inhalation of HCN that causes most deaths in structural fires."

Connor considered–he knew he had heard about it–and, recently. He just couldn't place it. "No, that's not it, but somewhere..."

Samuels considered for a moment. "Ever been to the Holocaust Museum?"

Connor nodded his head. "Sure. Last time I was in D.C."

"Well, HCN was the Nazis' weapon of choice for murdering the Jews and undesirables in the concentration camps."

"What?" asked Connor, not sure he'd heard correctly.

"Sure," Samuels replied. "HCN is the chemical composition of the gas marketed in the 1940s as Zyklon B."

Chapter Fifty

Oxford, Mississippi

THE FIRST PRESIDENTIAL DEBATE between the two political parties' nominees was scheduled for the last week in September. If there was nothing remarkable about the timing—the choice of location was laden with symbolism. Mississippi was the scene of some of the most contentious, even violent episodes in the civil rights movement. And, the state university known as "Ole Miss," in Oxford, Mississippi, had been at its epicenter.

In 1962, a handsome U.S. Air Force veteran with an unblemished nine-year service record named James Meredith had attempted to enroll at the University of Mississippi. He applied one day after the inauguration of John F. Kennedy, inspired, he said, by Kennedy's belief that things could change. Of course, previous attempts to register African Americans had been made, so far with disastrous consequences. In 1958, the state had committed an African American teacher named Clennon King to a mental institution after he attempted to attend summer school at the university.

But James Meredith had a powerful ally that Clennon King did not have. The United States Supreme Court had ruled in his favor—agreeing with his contention that he had been denied admission to the University of Mississippi solely on the basis of his race. Three times that September, Meredith was turned away by an ugly mob. Finally, on September 30th, surrounded by federal troops and U.S. marshals, Meredith was able to enroll and take his seat in a Colonial American History class.

Even then, his admission was not achieved without violence—two people died in the angry clashes prior to his admission, and over 28 U.S. marshals were wounded by gunfire. Meredith and his guards had been assaulted by a mob hurling bricks, Molotov cocktails, and glass bottles. Many in the crowd carried (and discharged) weapons. The crowd was only finally dispersed by tear gas.

That first hurdle overcome, life at the university still wasn't easy for Meredith. If he sat down at a table in the cafeteria, the other students would leave. In the classroom, if the students weren't able to leave, they turned their backs. At all hours of the day and night, Meredith was harassed by students bouncing basketballs on the floor above his room. Racial slurs and threats were left in Meredith's mailbox or slipped under his dorm room door. Compounding all of these challenges, he had no privacy. For Meredith's protection, he was escorted everywhere by U.S. marshals, who were with him 24 hours a day until he graduated.

From a purely tactical point of view, Republican strategists thought the Malloy campaign was out of its mind. Holding the debate on a campus so fraught with reminders about toxic race relations in the past could, they believed, only benefit Okono—

the first African American in U.S. history to win a major party's nomination for president.

The strategists argued that the media and attendees at the Gertrude Ford Center could hardly miss (directly across campus, west of the Lyceum above the campus' center point known as "the circle") the life-size, bronze-cast statue of the diminutive Meredith striding towards a limestone portico with the words: courage, opportunity, perseverance, knowledge—one word emblazoned on each of the four architraves—a testament to Meredith's fortitude and achievement.

But, whatever the reason, the Malloy campaign accepted the Okono campaign's choice. Perhaps at that point they were just eager to make sure the debate took place. The Okono camp had been making noises about no debates at all.

The debate was supposed to cover foreign policy and national security, but the recent bank failures had pushed the U.S.'s overseas entanglements out of the news. The economy was on everyone's mind—including that of the moderator—the sad-eyed *eminence gris* of public television.

Throughout the debate, in a move that was purposely respectful, Republican candidate Malloy referred to his opponent as Congressman Okono. Okono, by contrast referred to Governor Malloy as "Joe." Commentators were struck by the fact that Malloy never looked at Okono directly, but consistently addressed his answers to the moderator. Insiders speculated that the truth-telling Malloy couldn't pretend to respect a man he had come to despise. Malloy made it a point to emphasize Okono's naiveté and lack of preparation. But if Malloy's answers were more knowledgeable and assured, the way Joe Malloy looked—

very old, very stiff, and very, very white—was a hard sell to a generation who grew up on the youthful, multi-cultural, waxed and buffed perfection of television performers.

Okono, on the other hand, looked the part of a hero: whip-slim and elegant. But for all his physical advantages, Okono, the barker of "new politics," was no debater. He seemed uncomfortable, disengaged. He stammered. He stuttered. The great rhetorician whose soaring words of hope had inflamed the hearts of students at college campuses all over America, did not perform well without a teleprompter, a fact that (for the most part) the media obligingly failed to point out.

In early strategy sessions, one staffer had suggested Okono wear a wireless electronic receiver, whereby a coach could feed him the answers to tough questions. Appelbaum regretfully rejected the idea as too risky. A previous presidential candidate had been busted when the network chosen to provide the pool video had—contrary to an agreement between the campaigns—unwittingly set up cameras behind the candidates. Minute 23 of the C-SPAN video had clearly showed a rectangular object placed between the Republican candidate's shoulder blades, and what appeared to be a wire snaking around his upper arm and neck.

The media had mostly ignored the story, even as a NASA scientist, expert in analyzing digital photos, had confirmed it. But the moderator of that debate was also the moderator of tonight's contest. Without ever acknowledging that he believed the reports, he'd made it clear to both sides that he was not going to be embarrassed again by flagrant flouting of the rules. Besides, one of the tech guys pointed out, someone with a spectrum analyzer could detect the frequency and tune in—even record the coaching as it was broadcast to Okono! No, it was too risky.

If his staff didn't have much confidence in his debating skills or broad knowledge, what Okono did have was resources. Most political campaigns ration campaign buttons and paraphernalia. Not Okono's—his lawn signs and stickers were free and everywhere. But a larger indication of the truly gargantuan, limitless money the Okono campaign had amassed was the profligate way they spent it. And there was no better example of that than what happened at Ole Miss.

When Malloy came out on the stage, he was seeing it all for the first time. A veteran of political campaigns, the Republican governor prided himself on his rugged adaptability. Okono, by contrast was like a delicate hothouse bloom. Appelbaum and Okono's other handlers knew that to perform even adequately, Okono would have to be relentlessly prepared and rehearsed. What should have concerned people was the level of preparation that the Okono campaign staffers thought was necessary for a man who declared himself ready to lead the free world. Because Okono's team did the unheard of in campaign spending—they paid their set people to create an exact replica of the stage at the Ford Center—down to the curtains and the cup holders—so Okono could practice.

The calculated gamble paid off. The debate may not have changed many minds. But the Okono campaign considered it a huge win, simply because it wasn't a devastating loss. Okono had held on and by doing so, had exceeded expectations. That was enough. More to the point, they all congratulated themselves, Okono looked great, so straight and handsome—compared to the aging-before-our-eyes Malloy.

As the Republican pols had predicted, the network commentators couldn't resist the historical significance of the debate with the first African American presidential candidate taking place at the site of one of the most significant —and hardest won— battles in the civil rights movement. And why would they? It made for a great angle. What they did not mention was the strange later career of James Meredith.

After his graduation, Meredith kept himself aloof from the civil rights ministers, claiming they had corrupted the movement in exchange for money and favors. In 1968, after receiving a law degree from Columbia, he famously declared that he thought East Coast liberals (like Columbia professors Clothard and Pippen), not Southern conservatives, were the greatest enemies of African Americans. Meredith's claim, derided by his fellow civil rights activists, was that a segment of the white liberal elite were merely using African Americans as pawns in pursuit of their own socialist agenda. His fellow activists turned on him with a fury. After working briefly for a conservative Republican senator (he claimed no Democrat would hire him), Meredith had largely flitted from job to job, selling insurance one year, used cars the next. Meredith's increasingly conservative views and grandiosity had become an embarrassment to the civil rights establishment.

Previous to the event, commentators had waxed rhapsodic on-air about the wonderful symbolism if James Meredith himself were present as a witness to the great achievement of another African American. Curiously, the only two who seemed uninterested in creating the historic parallel were James Meredith and Okono's team. For whatever reason, Meredith did not attend the debate. When asked directly, the Okono campaign refused to comment on whether or not he had been invited.

Chapter Fifty-One

October, 2008
Washington, DC

On the first Sunday in October, the Malloy campaign sent an email to the reporters covering the presidential race that they were convening an emergency conference call. The announcement was not unexpected given the revelations in recent weeks. An intrepid journalist from one of the national weekly magazines had started tracking some of the donations to Okono the FEC had identified as problematic. A preliminary investigation revealed donors with obviously made-up names contributing tens of thousands of dollars to the Okono campaign.

During the conference call, the Malloy campaign announced that the Republican National Committee was filing a complaint Monday morning with the Federal Elections Commission, asking them to examine all contributions received by the Okono campaign, both itemized and un-itemized. Tellingly, the problems the RNC identified were in the itemized filings, which represented less than half of the total contributions received.

Okono had now raised more than $460 million dollars—more than any campaign in history. At least $250 million of that amount was from so-called 'small dollar donors' and no information about their identity—who they were or where they came from—was provided at all.

By contrast, the Malloy campaign pointed out, Governor Malloy had kept his promise to accept only public financing (a point on which his campaign was continually reminding people) and was limited to a measly $85 million. Most importantly, his campaign manager hastened to point out, the donors of all contributions Malloy received—of any dollar amount—were available online to anyone who cared to look. They concluded: "We believe that, in violation of the law, the Okono campaign has accepted contributions from foreign nationals and has knowingly done so, through at least its failure to reasonably investigate where all the money is coming from."

Coming this late in the game, it seemed obvious that the Malloy campaign didn't really expect to get any legal redress. Even in the highly unlikely event the banks froze the Okono campaign's assets (a campaign could wish, after all), nobody was going to be able to sort through a presidential campaign's muddled books in time to make a fair appraisal. However, it was a way of generating —they hoped— some media attention to the Okono campaign's profligate spending, and even more staggering fundraising. People, the Republicans reasoned amongst themselves, would have to start asking where all the money was coming from, wouldn't they?

That Monday, there was another news item pulled off the wire services. Without explanation, the judge responsible for sentencing Joey Ali after his 14-charge conviction for RICOH violations announced that Ali's sentencing date would be delayed— again. This time, the sentencing date was postponed—until December...after the election. When pressed by reporters, the judge declined to give a reason.

CHAPTER FIFTY-TWO

Erie, Pennsylvania

IT WAS ON THE SCHEDULE—that immutable, unchanging plan for the day that might literally have been carved in stone, so strictly did the Okono campaign adhere to it—as just a quick 10-minute stop. The preternaturally calm Appelbaum would later be almost apoplectic on the subject, but in fairness to Okono's handlers that day, it didn't take much more. Okono was just supposed to do what the British royalty called a "walkabout"—a simple, waving, hand-shaking, baby-holding walk among the common folk. In this case, the common folk of a very important swing state that by every calculation Okono needed to win.

The questioner was just a guy. An everyman. Nothing particularly good, or particularly bad, had ever happened to him. He was throwing a baseball to his son in the backyard of his modest one-story ranch when Okono came down the street, surrounded by a few dozen spectators and a buzzing drone of press people, reporters dragging heavy recorders in black microfiber messenger bags and sound guys waving unwieldy hanging microphones like little boys waving too-large fishing poles.

Invited by the candidate, the guy asked a question—a pretty simple question. And Okono, who had been warned repeatedly about his propensity to become professorial, demonstrated why they never let him off the teleprompter, and why he'd never really actively practiced law. Because both successful politicians and expensive lawyers know to parse the question, to break it down to the elements they want to answer—and never to offer more information than necessary.

"If you're elected, will my taxes go up?" is what the guy really wanted to know. The guy was making about $30,000 a year as an electrician's assistant. The easy answer would have been "No." But, nobody wants to be seen living a small life. So because there were a lot of big press and big people around, the guy's question got bigger, too. What the guy actually asked (stripped of all its frippery) was "When I'm really successful, will my taxes go up?" No way could Okono win with that one.

What Okono should have said, was "Let's not deal in hypotheticals—what are you earning right now?" Instead, he ended up explaining his worldview: that compensation should be determined not by work quality (skills or education required or market demand) but by quantity (how hard you worked). There was, said Okono, a moral equivalency between the waitress that was working hard and a lawyer working hard, and "I think when you spread the wealth around it's good for everybody."

Rushing to get the tape back to New York, some reporters were, at first, not entirely sure they had heard Okono right. Okono was rarely off-message, never unscripted. His handlers seldom, if ever, allowed un-vetted questions from reporters, never mind the general public. "He said *WHAT*?" their producers barked in their cell phones. But soon enough, the network producers all had the videotape, and the tape recorded the exchange plainly enough. Still, no major networks ran the story. Only a New York daily picked it up. But, somehow, somewhere, someone posted the video on YouTube and it went viral. And then *everybody* saw it.

The Okono supporters rushed to discredit the guy. An Okono-supporting state official was eventually reprimanded for routing around in government computers looking for the guy's personal information. As usual, they did a great job—helped by a willing media. In subsequent weeks the media would make it about the guy. They would make much of the facts that the single father owed taxes (a modest $1,000), that he hadn't completed his apprenticeship to be licensed as an electrician, that he refused to really endorse either candidate, and that he'd instructed his gay friends that he wouldn't allow them around his kids. All of which might have been interesting to know, but was pretty irrelevant to the discussion. Okono supporters rushed in to explain that the guy would actually do better under Okono's tax plan. It didn't matter, because it wasn't about the guy or his question—it was about the answer. Okono didn't believe in capitalism.

Chapter Fifty-Three

Rockville, Maryland

Everyone was feeling the after-shocks of the recession. Everyone Lacey knew was worried about losing his or her job. People who'd over-invested in houses when it appeared the real estate market could never peak, were now trying to sell for less than they'd paid. Her husband's internet business was no exception. At one time, he could barely keep the high tech computer toys that were his company's staple in stock. Now they languished in his warehouse, as he was forced to cut prices again and again for just a few sales. Investments they had thought would provide a cushion in an emergency were themselves devalued to nothing. Beachfront property they owned languished in the real estate listings. No one was buying. They'd cut back on everything: piano lessons for the kids, the housecleaning service, even date night was forfeit. It wasn't enough. Lacey had sent a résumé to a friend that was a corporate recruiter. He'd called her with the bad news.

"Shit, Lacey. Have you ever Googled yourself?" he said by way of greeting.

"No," she answered, surprised.

"There are all these crazy stories that you're a racist."

"But it's not true!" she protested.

He sounded exasperated. "Of course, I know it's not true. It doesn't matter if it's true. You're controversial. No company is going to hire you for the type of position you're qualified for. Actually, no company is going to hire you at all, for any position. The first thing people do these days is look people up on the internet."

Lacey was speechless, near tears.

"It gets worse."

"How could it get worse?" she asked. She didn't really want to know.

"Your husband's not going to be able to get a job, either. You guys cross-reference on a lot of these stories. He's screwed, too."

"Oh, God," she replied. It came out like a moan.

"But everyone said it would blow over..." her voice was pleading.

He replied with an ironic laugh: "Today's headline is tomorrow's birdcage liner, or whatever?"

"Something," said Lacey, the strain in her voice obvious.

"Well," he said matter-of-factly, "that was before the internet. Now, everything–even the most outrageous stuff some college-dropout posts from his parent's basement–with no effort at verification– lives forever."

"I can't believe this," Lacey said. "Tell me. What do I do?"

"Lacey, I'm sorry. I know this is really unfair. I don't know what to tell you. I just don't know."

Chapter Fifty-Four

Medford, Oregon

LATE AS IT WAS, HE ANSWERED ON THE FIRST RING.

"Hey, it's Connor. I need some help."

"Sure."

"You guys were looking into the threats against members of the Congressional Black Caucus a few months ago?"

"Some of them."

"Were you checking out Miriam Carter?" Connor asked. There was a pause.

"Yes."

"Did you pull phone records?"

"Connor, c'mon," the voice was amused, exasperated.

"Any line on the threats?"

"Sure."

"Who were they?"

"Well, some college kids..."

"Okono's?"

"Some of them worked for the campaign...just goofy kids."

"Anything else?" Connor pressed.

"Yes." There was a long pause.

"You gonna tell me?" Connor asked. Again, the man paused, then seemed to make a decision.

"Why not? Re-routed calls. Untraceable. Professional."

"You guys take them seriously?"

There was a dry laugh on the other end of the line.

"Since she's dead, that's a bit of a loaded question, wouldn't you say, Connor?"

"Just trying to get your read on things."

"Yeah, we took them seriously."

"What was she doing?"

"Who?"

"Miriam Carter. You must have been keeping tabs on her," Connor replied.

"Maybe."

"So what was she doing?"

The man on the phone sounded almost amused for a moment. "Well, the night she died, she was meeting with a group of McCracken supporters."

"Yeah, I know," said Connor "Tea and cookies were in her stomach."

The man laughed, "Well, I wouldn't describe it as a tea party exactly..."

"No?" Connor was surprised.

"No, more like the overthrow of the Democratic Party complete with embarrassing press revelations of the opposition."

"No shit?" Connor said. There was a pause. "You know the M.E. thinks she was murdered?" Connor asked softly.

"Of course, she was."

The line was silent for a few seconds as Connor mentally composed himself.

"You guys have a bead on who?" asked Connor.

The voice was dismissive. "You never did homicide, did you?"

"Not really, no," Connor said.

"Well, you look at who benefits."

"Okay." Connor paused, waiting.

"So, if a feisty middle-aged lady who appears in generally good health—"

"Great health, actually."

"Right, okay...and who is known for her determination...and ah...let's say... powers of persuasion, is planning to lead a floor fight for her candidate on the floor of the Democratic National Convention. On live TV..."

"Yeah?"

"Well, who benefits if she dies rather suddenly?"

"The other candidate?"

There was a chuckle on the other end of the line.

"Good night, Connor."

CHAPTER FIFTY-FIVE

Columbus, Ohio

LACEY STEPPED OUT OF THE GATE at the Columbus airport and was immediately spotted by Betty Jo. It was a happy reunion. The two women had become close friends in the process of coordinating thousands of McCracken supporters for Joe Malloy. Hundreds of those volunteers were now converging on Ohio and Pennsylvania from across the country in the weeks before the general election to pass out flyers and electioneer for Joe Malloy.

By any measure, Betty Jo would be hard not to like. But Lacey now knew that her carefully coiffed hair, high-heeled boots and impeccable grooming hid a secret; Betty Jo was no Barbie Doll. Beneath the hairspray and nail varnish lay the fearless heart of a warrior, and Betty Jo wasn't just brave, she was smart. You never had to explain things twice to Betty Jo—she got it. It was like she had a switch—if she was 'on', then she was passionately committed; if she was 'off', then she was completely uninterested. The Republicans in Ohio didn't know what hit them.

If they'd expected someone to sit politely by as they explained their strategy to woo McCracken supporters, they didn't know Betty Jo. She'd been volunteering in political campaigns a long time, long enough to know that Malloy's 28 year old volunteers didn't know what they were doing. But, more to the point, the Malloy campaign needed to re-calibrate their skill set to a Democratic audience.

If Governor Malloy wanted to broaden his appeal —and voting base—his campaign needed to emphasize those aspects of his character and record that would appeal to Democrats and independents. It should have been easy to do. Malloy was an essentially moderate guy, but the Republican experts in marketing on Malloy's staff were used to selling a different kind of candidate to a different audience. Their earliest efforts merely superimposed the new candidate onto the old strategy. Betty Jo could see right away it wouldn't work. To their credit, they mostly listened to her.

But it didn't really matter. What most people following the election in those last weeks didn't realize was that, for the Republicans, the situation in Ohio was dire. And the likely electoral result would have more to do with lawsuits wending their way through state and District courts than whether Malloy could expand his base with women or Latinos.

Ohio had a tessellated electoral history. If the vote counting controversies in Florida were perhaps better known nationally, citizens of Ohio had witnessed more than their share of double-dealing, fraud and down-right cheating in previous elections by Republican state officials. So much so, that polls showed a majority of the state's residents questioned the fairness of the previous presidential election's results and voted out the Republican incumbent responsible. Unfortunately, for those looking for balance, his Democratic replacement was no less partisan.

Previously, the state had followed a protocol for new registrations in accordance with the 2002 *Help America Vote Act*. After a voter registered, a postcard would be mailed to verify their mailing address and correct information. When the prospective voter returned the postcard, they would be formally registered.

If the card was returned to the board of elections "return to sender" –a notation would be made on the voter rolls that further authentication was required and the registration would be forwarded to the secretary of state's office where they would try to match it against drivers licenses registered with the Ohio Bureau of Motor Vehicles. If there was a match, the voter was registered.

If there was no match in the state database, the registration would be sent to the Social Security Administration to see if they could verify the applicant's social security number. If the Social Security Administration made a match, the voter was registered.

If, however, after all these steps, no one in the system could verify the information provided, the voter's registration was suspended, pending documentation. Even most voter advocacy groups considered the process fair.

But the new Democratic Secretary of State, Gwendolyn Brown, had decided to institute a new policy to allow for early voting. Under the new rules, a voter could register by showing a copy of any utility bill and providing the last four digits of their social security number and then immediately cast an absentee ballot.

In the middle of August, Brown had ordered county election officials to immediately give all new voters who registered an absentee ballot, so that they could *simultaneously* register and vote.

County election officials cried foul. Under Brown's instructions, a cell phone registered to a post office box address would meet the requirement for a utility bill, and applicants could provide any four digit combination of numbers they wanted—they were allowed to cast a ballot before the numbers could be verified with the system.

In early September, Monroe County officials point blank refused the secretary of state's directive as illegal. Under Ohio state law, they pointed out, a voter is required to be registered for 30 days before they are eligible to cast an absentee ballot. Further, they argued, because Brown refused to keep these ballots separate from voters whose information was already verified —there was no possibility of further scrutiny or checking of these ballots.

But Gwendolyn Brown had powerful friends. Brown's former campaign manager was now director of the Ohio arm of SEED. So, perhaps not coincidentally, Power Vote sued the Monroe County Board of Elections on behalf of a homeless coalition.

Meanwhile, the Republicans demanded more scrutiny of the process. If the early voting were to take place, they insisted they be allowed to have election observers present to witness the process. When Brown refused, they filed suit and further requested that Brown be required to turn over names of registrants with mismatched records to county election officials so the names could be authenticated.

Complicating the situation further was the economic crisis. As of October 2008, more than 5% of mortgages in Ohio were delinquent or in foreclosure. From January to June, that number was topping out at a staggering 67,658 foreclosures. Brown and the Okono campaign claimed that the Republicans were perfidiously trying to use foreclosure lists to block qualified voters from participating in the election. Moreover, voter participation had always been a half-full/half-empty partisan issue. Democrats were always inveighing against voter suppression and Republicans always howling about voter fraud.

So, even Democrats who disagreed with Brown and were privately shocked by her blatant partisanship and banana republic tactics—couldn't find it in their hearts to speak out. In their view it was a moral issue: fraud was preferable to suppression. Many were also concerned about the Okono campaign's allegations of "caging"—a vile practice previously utilized by the GOP to cherry pick certain 'undesirable' zip codes with election mailings and disqualify ethnic voters who did not verify their addresses. But the allegations had no merit here—not only was the secretary of state's office controlled by a Democrat, but a law passed in 2005 required election officials to mail election materials to all registered voters.

In the Power Vote case, the lower court judge ruled that Ohio counties were prohibited from requiring potential voters to provide a mailing address—the court ruled that applicants must be allowed to list "non-building locations such as park benches as their address"—essentially making it impossible to verify if the person was even a resident of the state.

However, on October 14th, the U.S. Sixth Circuit Court of Appeals reversed the lower court and ruled that Ohio Secretary of State Brown had to take additional steps to authenticate the new voters. But just as the Malloy campaign breathed a sigh of relief, three days later, that decision was overturned by the U.S. Supreme Court on purely technical grounds. The Republican National Committee, who had filed the suit, was not a qualified party, the Supreme Court ruled. Not only was Gwendolyn Brown not required to provide the names of the suspicious registrants to the county officials, she instructed the 88 county boards to ignore public records requests for the information, as well.

2008 became the first Ohio election to permit voters to vote absentee without demonstrating need. But most observers didn't realize either the scope of the numbers or the consequences of the decisions being made by the courts. And the press did little to clarify the stakes involved, either in Ohio, or nationally. But the facts were straightforward enough. Between January and October, more than 666,000 Ohioans registered to vote for the first time or with changes to their registrations. More than 200,000 of those registrants could not be confirmed as residents of Ohio, having provided either a drivers license or social security number that did not match what was in the system.

Adding to the confusion, out of Ohio's 88 counties, a statistically improbable 20% of the suspicious registrations came from one county–Cuyahoga—alone. Cuyahoga had long been considered a Democratic stronghold ruled by ward heelers. Perhaps not surprisingly, it was the site of some of SEED's greatest get-out-the-vote activities. It was also where SEED was currently under investigation for submitting phony registrations in the names of esteemed local county residents: Jive Turkey, Sr., Dick Tracy, Mary Poppins, and Michael Jordan.

Would the 200,000 unverified votes make a difference? Someone thought so. In 2004, for comparison, the vote differential for the two presidential candidates in Ohio was a modest 118,599 votes.

Chapter Fifty-Six

Washington, DC

It was Tuesday, October 21st. The election was fourteen days away. Even knowing what she knew, Adelita was still supporting Okono. As an African American and a Democrat, she felt she had no other choice. But she also knew that the information she had provided would be damaging, potentially ruinous, to him as a candidate. And she couldn't help but be hopelessly conflicted about her obligations to her race versus what she considered her obligation to her country and a democratic process. Should she have said nothing? What if she spoke out after the election? The Republicans, after all, were famous for dirty tricks. Democrats had long justified their own tactics as defensive and imitative. Maybe they were right? She worried. Maybe there *was* no other way to win? She'd weighed the pros and cons of her decision a million times on many sleepless nights over the last months.

She had already seen the anger and hate directed at African Americans who had supported McCracken. If she knew any

African Americans supporting Malloy, she didn't know any brave or foolish enough to say so. It was easy enough, Adelita thought, for the white women supporting McCracken—they were voting for Malloy as a protest vote, easily changing their allegiances (albeit temporarily) from the Democrats to the Republicans. But it was a lot easier to change the name of your party than the color of your skin, and she couldn't help but realize that vilified as the McCracken 'dead-enders' were in the press, her actions would be viewed through an even more critical locus.

Suzanne Saturnino had promised to protect her identity, but Adelita knew she had to be realistic. Did the director know she'd spoken to the *Times*? The way she had looked at her when Adelita told her she was quitting to take another job, made Adelita wonder. Of course, that might have been paranoia on her part. But they'd figure it out soon enough. There were only a certain number of people who had access to the information she had provided. Conventional wisdom was that giving a whistleblower a high profile was actually a better way to provide for their safety than changing their name and moving them to a new neighborhood. But it also meant standing up to a lot of abuse. Adelita felt she had reason to worry. African American leaders were not so subtly threatening violence if African Americans thought Okono was 'denied' through Republican skullduggery. There was a tension in the air she'd never felt before. What would their response be to betrayal by one of their own: an African American who tarnished the golden crown of their presumptive prince?

On June 9th, Saturnino and the the *New York Times* broke the story that Rauschenberg, SEED's founder, had withheld information from its board of directors *for eight years*, that his brother Donald had embezzled more than $1 million dollars from the organization in 2000. Tipped off by friends in the media, Ford Rauschenberg had quietly stepped down as CEO a week before. His brother Donald —who inexplicably was still employed by the organization eight years after the discovery of his crime—left the same day.

Outraged board members demanded a forensic audit. Rauschenberg's chosen successor as CEO, Yolanda Jones, refused. Rauschenberg's influence persisted. When eight SEED board members insisted on the audit, Rauschenberg engineered their removal. In August, the former board members filed suit to obtain access to SEED's financials. SEED counter-sued. To defuse the matter publicly, the press was told that in future, Rauschenberg would run SEED's international operations. But since no one really knew what SEED's international operations were, his role remained a mystery. One thing was clear—he was raising lots of overseas money for something.

Not that Rauschenberg really needed to, Adelita thought. If the money SEED was raising overseas was for Okono, Rauschenberg had already more than done his part, and not just through SEED and its hundreds of affiliates. Less well-known than Rauschenberg's involvement with SEED was his founding of the largest and fastest growing union in the country, Service Workers International—with members ranging from janitors to doctors. SWI had contributed more than $33 million outright to Okono. The Republicans were floored. To put it in perspective: fully 38% of the money the Republican Joe Malloy received *in total* by agreeing to accept public funding had been contributed to Okono by a single donor.

Adelita's cell phone rang. She was so anxious that she nearly dropped it. Suzanne Saturnino had told her the story about SEED was about to run. The individual state cases against SEED were starting to heat up, the evidence becoming so overwhelming that even the mainstream press was beginning to cover it. The *Times* had been investigating for a month, and Saturnino was certain her editors wouldn't risk being scooped on a such a big story. Typically, the Okono campaign had gone on the offensive claiming on a section on their website entitled "Fight the Smears" that Okono had never worked for SEED. His community organizing had been with an organization called Power Vote, they claimed—but, apparently, the communication between SEED and the Okono campaign had suffered a breakdown from their formerly free and easy exchanges, because a quick web search of SEED's website pulled up a link to their affiliate, Power Vote.

Moreover, the states' attorneys general had now been gathering evidence for months—they had a complete list of SEED's various names: Power Vote chief among them. Embarrassingly (although not for the Okono campaign, who refused to acknowledge its existence, even petulantly chiding reporters with the temerity to insist) there emerged a photograph of Okono at the blackboard teaching a "Power Training" course for SEED. The woman listening to him eagerly in the foreground was wearing a SEED T-shirt. Internet sleuths soon found an article posted on a SEED subsidiary website where the director of the Chicago SEED talked glowingly about the annual courses Okono had taught for SEED since 1994. Putting one more nail in the coffin, she proudly noted the get-out-the-vote assistance the supposedly non-partisan group had provided Okono in all of his campaigns.

"Hello?"

It was the daycare run by a woman from her church. Oh, shit, literally. The baby had had the proverbial scatological "accident." Adelita needed to bring an extra set of clothes with her when she came to pick her up.

"There's nothing in the diaper bag?" Adelita asked. "No, they'd used those last week," they said. Now Adelita remembered, she'd meant to replace the extra clothes. With so much else on her mind, she'd been distracted. Damn. She'd have to run home early and get the baby's clothes if she wanted to get to the daycare before she started wracking up overtime charges—a usurious $10 a minute that ensured parents took their responsibility to be on-time very seriously —or paid the consequences.

"Okay, no problem."

Except with rush hour in D.C., that assurance was more hopeful than real. But, Adelita thought, there was a chance. She found her manager and quickly explained the situation. He was a good guy, with young children of his own. "Go," he said, laughing.

Rush hour in D.C. is never pretty, but she was lucky and made good time. She darted up the stairs to her apartment, grabbed a onesie, a few diapers, and a light jacket for the baby and was back in the car in less than five minutes. Traffic was blessedly moving. She got to the daycare with two minutes to spare.

In all the confusion of other parents arriving to pick up their kids, Adelita spoke briefly to the daycare operator, who gestured her over to the corner with a smile. This was the moment Adelita looked forward to all day, the moment that made all the juggling and the uncertainty and the exhaustion worthwhile. The baby sat on the carpet in her diaper playing with some brilliantly colored plastic blocks. Teesha's beautiful face lit up when she saw her mother. I am so lucky, Adelita thought, not for the first time, picking up her delighted daughter. Adelita took her over to the changing table and from long practice had her in the onesie and out the door in minutes. As she was strapping Teesha into the car seat, her phone rang again.

"Adelita?"

The baby was babbling happily in the background.

"Yes?" Distracted by the baby, for a second, Adelita couldn't place the voice

"It's Suzanne. Suzanne Saturnino." Her voice sounded grave, unlike her usual business-like friendliness.

"Oh. Hey. Hi, Suzanne."

There was a pause.

"Are you calling to prepare me? Is it coming out tomorrow?"

"No...ah...not tomorrow."

"Okay." Adelita waited. Suzanne sounded stressed, unhappy.

"I guess they can't wait much longer though, right?"

"They're not going to run it," Suzanne blurted out.

Adelita was stunned, unbelieving. "What? You mean, not ever?"

"I don't know." Suzanne's voice was quiet, depressed.

"They killed the story. They're reassigning me."

"What?" Adelita was in shock. "I can't believe this is happening."

She paused: "I mean, I thought you said you got all the corroboration you needed. You said it was ironclad..."

"I know," Suzanne replied, "I know what I said. It was, it is. They just decided not to run it."

"But why? I mean this is significant! This is subversion of our democracy! This is a huge story!"

"I know," Suzanne answered, "I guess..." Saturnino paused, "too huge. It's not just the caucus fraud and voter registration fraud—it's the economic angle."

"Because of SEED's links to Fannie Mae?" asked Adelita.

"Right," Suzanne replied "It totally ties Okono to the collapse of the banks, everything."

There was silence on both ends. Finally, Suzanne spoke.

"They're afraid it's a game changer."

"What?" Adelita wasn't sure she'd heard her correctly. The baby was still gurgling happily in the background. Adelita could hear Suzanne swallowing hard.

"That's what they said. A game changer. They're afraid if they run the story, Okono will lose."

Chapter Fifty-Seven

November, 2008
Chicago, Illinois

As Harrison surveyed the crowd, patiently waiting at security checkpoints to be admitted to McClellan Park, he was struck by the atmosphere. The crowd was jubilant, celebratory—they'd backed a winner and they knew it. Chicago Transit Authority and Metra had announced that extra buses and trains would be available to bring people to and from the event. No one would be stranded on this night. Stations would remain open and trains would continue to run past the usual 1:00 a.m. closing, for as long as they were needed.

Organizers announced people would start to be admitted through the Park's Congressional Parkway and Michigan Avenue entrance at 8:30 p.m. Central time. Ticket holders, advised by an email from the Okono campaign, were instructed to bring their ticket and a photo I.D. No chairs, strollers, coolers, or large bags were allowed. Alcohol was strictly prohibited. Ticket-holding parents could bring children if they could carry them. But the era of equality had not yet arrived in McClellan Park. Those with a ticket would see Okono appear, in person—the architectural splendor of the Greco-Roman Field Museum his Olympian backdrop. There were more practical advantages as well: ticket holders could warm themselves by buying hot dogs, pizza, and hot chocolate on the freezing cold night. In contrast, people without tickets (the overwhelming majority) could only watch the broadcast on the Jumbotron at Butler Field. Only half-frozen bottled water was available for their purchase.

Whatever the inequalities, Harrison surveyed the set-up with approval. Security was tight. The stage was shaped like a rounded T. Along the back were rows upon rows of American flags (exactly as they had been arranged when Okono "separated" from The Minister, he reflected). Protective bulletproof glass surrounded the podium and the Chicago P.D. was prepared for any contingency. If the worst happened (carefully undefined by the chief, but widely assumed to be violence or terrorist attack) all exits to the park would be immediately opened. There had been generic talk of 'backlash' by the Okono campaign if Okono didn't win. Perhaps prophylactically, the C.P.D. put out a press release that they were prepared for crowd control—and, in the event Okono lost, dealing with tens of thousand of disappointed, potentially angry, supporters.

Harrison noticed the crowd was not dissimilar from the average population downtown: students, young professionals and African Americans of every age—except perhaps for a higher percentage of nose piercings. The crowd was enormous—estimates put it as high as 250,000, more in the overflow areas. Everyone was standing shoulder-to-shoulder. A huge portrait of

Okono dominated the overflow area, towering 24 feet tall. Some joked that the uniform for the night was an American flag, an Okono pin, and a cell phone. Many proudly displayed "Okono-art"—cut-outs, pins, buttons, T-shirts and hats. A man, walking arm in arm with a friend and wearing a sweatshirt supporting gay rights, sported a red, white, and blue feather boa and a tinsel Statue of Liberty crown. A poor, middle-aged woman wore one of hundreds of pairs of Okono sunglasses—the candidate's name spelled out in plastic directly in front of her iris. Apparently, it didn't matter that she couldn't see; after all, she wasn't going anywhere. They all somehow negotiated miles of yellow police barricades and row upon row of porta potties lined up like bright blue soldiers. There was literally a city of white tents. Vendors hawked Okono paraphernalia of every description—most with a proud inscription "I was there/Okono Victory Night."

Experiencing first-hand the crowd's euphoria, Harrison recognized that this was no run-of-the-mill political rally. They idolized this man, Harrison realized. Over the last few months, Harrison had kept in touch with Connor Murphy. Murphy had been filling him in on his own investigations regarding Congresswoman Carter and Joey Ali. But, Harrison thought ruefully to himself, it wasn't as if Murphy needed to tell him. He'd been a cop a long time. He could fit together pieces of a puzzle as well as any cop out there. When someone threatened someone powerful and he or she died—all of a sudden—violently, out of the blue? Well, let's just say—maybe Okono got lucky or maybe he made his own luck. But, for Harrison, the tipping point had been Orchard Park. Orchard Park had made him ill. Because Okono wasn't just gaming the system, he was taking advantage of people he was obligated to protect. Reverend John was right: those tax credits were made available primarily to minority-owned businesses, not just to give some black people a leg up, but because it was assumed they'd have the most sense of responsibility to their own community. What Okono had done was worse than a sham, it was a violation—it was rape.

The news organization's trailers were corralled along Columbus Drive like steers in a kill-pen, a nice, orderly, straight line; their enormous satellite dishes open to the sky like white flowers from a land of giants—stamens facing the sun.

As promised, the gates opened at 8:30 p.m. Central time. As the crowds waited to hear the election returns, thousands of windows in skyscrapers behind them glowed with light. One building's lights created a pattern: "USA," it said. People were prepared for a long night; the networks were predicting a nail-biter. The Okono campaign was calm, cool, not worried, they said.

At 8:54 p.m. the first returns started coming in, flashed on the huge screens tuned to MSNBC. Okono won Pennsylvania, not totally unexpected, but a hard loss for Malloy. When a few minutes later, the networks called Ohio for Okono (surprising, given the Okono campaign's own polling in the state, which showed Malloy with a slight lead), the race was effectively over. When Virginia swung into the blue column 20 minutes later, any suspense was over. By 10:00 p.m., the networks all simultaneously proclaimed Okono the winner: president-elect.

The crowd was ecstatic. Tears coursed down many faces. People jumped up and down and hugged each other in happiness and relief. There would be no violence, no demonstrations.

The Republicans, who over the past eight years had shamed themselves by their convulsive, vise-like grip on power, seemed resigned, this time, to let it go.

At 11:00 p.m., Malloy made the obligatory call to congratulate his opponent and concede the election. Whether there were irregularities in the voting in Ohio as rumored, Malloy gave no hint of any hesitation. What discussions he had with his senior staff about the role of SEED or others could only be guessed at.

For Harrison, the moment was bittersweet. He could hardly remain unmoved by the other African Americans around him, some quite elderly. Physically, they'd already sacrificed something to be here tonight. With no chairs, many stood for hours. The press of the crowd made actually getting to a porta-potty extremely unlikely. The night was freezing, the wind whipping off a gray and choppy Lake Michigan. By any standard, it was uncomfortable. But, of course, they would see this night; this historic night —a night many of the elderly people in the crowd never believed they would see in their lifetime, never see in America. To them, Okono was an outsider who'd been lifted up by the American dream. By stint of hard work and natural ability, this man, this proud African American man, now took his place with the gods of the world, first among many. It had once seemed impossible, unthinkable. Now it was accomplished fact, history. An African American man had just become the most powerful person in the world, and part of Harrison couldn't help but feel grateful and happy that this should be so. He cried because it was Okono.

CHAPTER FIFTY-EIGHT

February, 2009
Menlo Park, California

OUT FOR HIS DAILY JOG in the unchanging California sunshine, Paul Johannsen paused to consider the events of the past few weeks. Well, they all sure were happy. WHO-HOO! A Harvard man back in the White House (how sweet was that?). Well, of course, technically the last guy was a Harvard man, as well (Business School, in fact), but how exactly that came about wasn't totally clear. In fact, most elections were not that much different than an enormous, national Harvard-Yale game —if the public but knew! But Okono!!! That was news! The kids had been excited for weeks, felt like they were really involved in the election. God, what a great country! For the first few weeks after the inaugural, they had all been walking on air.

The first tiny prick in the balloon came at dinner with a friend from Harvard, Tom Marshall. Tom was one of those masochists who'd done a combined business/law degree and his tenure had overlapped with Okono's. Tom had supported Okono, he told Johannsen. But not everything the campaign was saying about Okono's career at Harvard was totally accurate, he'd told Johannsen in confidential tones.

"Like what?" Johannsen had pressed him. He could tell his friend was uncomfortable, but Johannsen had now raised more than $350,000 for Okono. He'd *invested* in the guy. He wanted an answer.

Marshall was uncharacteristically indirect, almost apologetic.

"Well, you know, you look at his career." Marshall shrugged. Johannsen regarded his old friend a little coldly.

"Go on," he said simply. Marshall might be uncomfortable, but he wouldn't walk away from a challenge. Marshall squared his shoulders.

"Okay. Well, for example, he was president of the Law Review. That's pretty much a guaranteed Supreme Court clerkship, but Okono didn't even get one of the circuit courts. That's pretty unusual." Johannsen rushed to interrupt. Tom raised his hand.

"And let's be fair—it wasn't discrimination—you've got some very good judges who would love to promote a black guy."

"So? Maybe it was a lean year for Harvard?" Johannsen suggested combatively.

Marshall shrugged. "Seven students from our graduating class ended up with Supreme Court clerkships...at least two of them were executive editors on the Law Review—*under* Okono."

Both sipped their drinks in silence. Johannsen pressed the point.

"Okay, so why not Okono?" Johannsen was practically radiating hostility. Marshall looked him in the eye. "Look, I'm not saying this to piss you off. Maybe we should just drop it, okay? Hooray, Okono won, and leave it at that, okay?"

Johannsen couldn't leave it. "No, I need to know. Tell me."

Marshall shrugged. "Look, I don't know. But I know he never wrote any articles for the Law Review, and that was considered sort of strange."

"What, none?" Johannsen was appalled.

"None that were printed," Marshall replied.

Johannsen persisted: "But didn't he graduate magna cum laude?"

Marshall laughed. "Yeah, well...we're talking Harvard," he said with a smirk "What are the statistics I read? Something like 96% of our class graduated; 82% with honors."

"Yeah, but how did he get elected president of the Law Review—there had to be some reason?" Johannsen had insisted.

Marshall shrugged, noncommittally. "Well, he's a likeable guy, charming. People thought he was cool. You know, we had all these blowhards—just dying to show off how smart they were all the time. Okono just kind of...listened. And he was a little older than the average student. But it definitely wasn't his grades. I mean, I know he wasn't in the top 10%—probably not in the top 30%, just going by what people said at the time. And, you know, the election was sort of complicated..." Marshall left the sentence hanging.

Johannsen didn't know. "No, what do you mean?"

Marshall continued. "Well, first of all, I think 19 people put their names in, but it was really between these two guys—both brilliant— battling it out—I think there was something like fifteen votes called without a clear winner."

"Yeah. So? Is that so unusual?"

Marshall shrugged. "Actually, it is. Four or five votes would generally be considered normal. As I understood it, Okono was chosen as a compromise candidate, and with everything that was going on on campus, people latched on to the idea and went with it." Marshall sipped his drink.

"Wait. What do you mean 'everything going on on campus'?"

"Oh, man, you remember?" Marshall continued, shaking his head. "Roderick Drumm was calling for all those sit-ins on campus to protest that there were no tenured African American women on the law school faculty. People were carrying signs 'Homogeneity breeds hate'–shit like that. There was definitely some major consciousness raising on the whole race thing."

Johannsen considered. "Yeah, I guess I do kind of remember that. But that was a good thing, I thought?"

Marshall rushed to reassure his friend. "Hell, yeah. I mean there ought to be African American women on the law school faculty. I don't believe in quotas exactly—but everyone needs to get the same consideration—the same shot. Personally, my memory was that the women didn't get tenure because they were shitty teachers—but the real issue was that there were few women generally and no African American women, so people reasonably assumed maybe there was discrimination. Obviously, diversity's always a good thing."

Marshall continued. "Look, I'm not saying Okono's not a bright guy. I think he probably is. And who ever really knows why someone gets chosen for some of these things? Maybe I'm just jealous—here's this guy from my class elected President of the United States, right?" Marshall laughed at himself, shaking his head.

"Right," said Johannsen unconvinced.

"I'm just saying..." Marshall looked around the room as if he didn't want to be overheard, "from my, maybe limited, perspective, Okono's Harvard career was not the home run the campaign makes it out to be. This idea that people were just knocked out by the guy's brilliance. That wasn't really the case. That's all. And it wasn't a discrimination thing. The people, at the time, who were most disappointed in him were the other black students. You know, they felt like he had this historic opportunity, and he basically wouldn't bestir himself to do anything with it."

Afterward, Johannsen admitted to himself that Marshall's revelations had been a minor disappointment. But Johannsen reminded himself to be realistic. Who didn't re-cast their résumé to show themselves in the best possible light? The last president had also gone to Harvard, and they *knew* his grades—no way he got in without a few high-placed calls being made. Of course, the situation had been slightly different. Okono's predecessor had no intellectual pretensions—in fact rather to the contrary—he seemed to relish being a dope. But a replay of the last administration was precisely what Johannsen had been committed to avoiding.

No, Johannsen decided, Okono's Harvard career shouldn't be an issue (although Johannsen was surprised the press hadn't made more hay out of it). But, there were other issues; things that mattered. Some of the choices to fill key posts weren't exactly the kind of "change" Okono supporters had hoped to see. But, Johannsen, reflected, he was a businessman, and he wanted to be fair. He understood that sometimes pragmatic decisions had to be made that trumped, for a time, at least, one's ideals.

He confessed that he wasn't exactly clear why Claire McCracken had been selected for a position in the new administration. Throwing a former opponent a bone as a sop to their supporters he understood. But they weren't talking about some do-nothing, well-paid sinecure. As one of his partners pointed out, she was being chosen for the toughest job there was, the position in which you put the smartest, most intellectually agile person you can find—the very face of the Okono administration abroad. The meme throughout the campaign had been that McCracken was a gorgon coasting on her husband's coattails, and was so divisive, so corrupt and so untrustworthy, her candidacy was anathema to the pure-hearted, new politics Okono-ites. But, if all that were true, why would they choose her as Secretary of State? What was the real story?

Paul Johannsen wanted all the right things: he wanted clean air and good education, and ecologically responsible fuel alternatives, and affordable healthcare, and civil rights for gays and an end to mountaintop mining. He wanted the U.S. to be strong, but act with honor. He wanted a responsive, transparent democracy and an end to the 'imperial' powers assumed by the executive branch in the last administration. Essentially, he wanted Utopia and he wanted it wrapped in a bow and delivered to his multi-million dollar Eichler-designed glass walled, light-filled house in Palo Alto (or, alternately, the summer house on the Vineyard). For $350,000, he thought that's what he was getting with Okono.

The transparency, at least, hadn't happened. Johannsen had heard from friends in the media that reporters who had been covering the White House for years were crying foul about the secrecy and lack of access. Johannsen had watched Okono's perennially tongue-tied Press Secretary Don Phipps' daily briefings on C-SPAN on a few occasions, and been less than impressed. The guy was arrogant to the point of being supercilious, he thought. Press Secretary Phipps seemed aggravated just having to talk to the peon reporters. And it wasn't just Phipps. The Okono-ites were all a bit regal, as if the reporters and public had not yet fully grasped the degree to which the Okonos expected them to be grateful for taking on such an onerous job on their behalf. Antoinette was widely quoted as saying her husband was "...one of the smartest people you will ever encounter who will deign to enter this messy thing called politics." Ayiyiyiyi! Johannsen thought. Not good! In Johannsen's view, even if it were true, well, it just set the wrong tone. Wasn't this administration supposed to be dedicated to serving the interests of the American people for a change?

Worse, facts began to emerge that the fleshy-faced press secretary had spearheaded a 527 political PAC whose television spots attacking a fellow Democrat in 2007 had become a by-word of smear and innuendo. Perhaps worst of all, Phipps' attack ad had argued that the other Democrat's lack of military and foreign policy experience made him unqualified for high public office—the same charge which could be reasonably leveled at Okono. That political operatives were a pretty cynical bunch who used whatever argument best suited their purpose at the time, was not exactly news. However, it was not exactly the "new politics" Okono's supporters had been promised. As the editor of an Okono internet fanzine commented dispiritedly: "Every time I see Don Phipps as the campaign's voice, I get further and further from seeing Okono as a transformative figure."

Johannsen sighed. It was like all the nuttiness about Okono's birth certificate and whether Okono had been born in the U.S. and was eligible to be president. Of course, it was ridiculous, Johannsen thought. Hollywood actresses aside, why would Okono's mother, an American citizen, opt to travel to the third world to give birth? It made no sense. But to some extent, Johannsen thought, it was the campaign's own fault. Because, however nutty some of these "birther" people appeared, they hadn't made the story up. The whole controversy began when Okono's African relatives claimed in the media that he was born in Nigeria.

Now, of course, Johannsen thought, people say lots of things—particularly people wanting to claim a world leader as a native son. But critics pointed out that the Okono campaign had now spent more than $800,000 in legal fees to resist providing an original birth certificate—something most people are required to hand over to obtain a driver's license. It seemed a reasonable question. Anyone could see the document the Okono campaign was flashing on all these news programs was not going to satisfy their critics. And, in fairness, Johannsen thought, where was the signature of the doctor and the name of the hospital? Anyone could produce the document they were showing in PhotoShop. Hell, Johannsen thought, he could do it himself.

And why were the Democrats fighting legislation that required future candidates to provide all documents currently required under the Constitution to the FEC before their names were placed on the ballot? Surely, that eliminated any future question?

Shouldn't the Democrats favor that kind of transparency? What was the big deal? Cable news pundits spent so much time trying to ridicule and mock these "birther" people—why not address the issues they raised, and put an end to it?

Proud, over-eager relatives aside, Johannsen didn't believe Okono was born outside the United States. More likely, he thought, Okono was sensitive about something else, his parent's marital status or a funky middle name, perhaps. But, Johannsen was still idealistic enough to believe that no democracy was ever served by secrecy. If the campaign hadn't tried so hard to restrict the public's access to Okono's school and health records (and everything else for that matter), in all likelihood, he thought, this movement wouldn't have gained the traction it had.

Worse, the Okono-ites persisted in pretending that any criticism of the Okono Administration's policy initiatives was part of a vast, right wing racist conspiracy. The allegations grabbed some headlines. But, in the end, Johannsen thought, it wouldn't wash. As far as policy disagreements, Johannsen didn't think it should come as a surprise to the Okono Administration that not everybody in the country was a Democrat. In fairness, Republicans had opposed healthcare reform since the 1970s (under, you know, *white* presidents), how was it suddenly a racial issue? As for criticism of Okono and his ties to SEED recently making headlines, Johannsen knew for certain, now, that most of the opposition research on Okono had been done by liberal Democrats. McCracken supporters were the *fons et origo* of much of the resistance to Okono. And Johannsen was forced to concede: McCracken supporters had their own, legitimate reasons to distrust Okono.

There were lots of ways to defuse the anger, Johannsen thought. But, in his opinion, the Okono team were handling it all backwards. Instead of trying to engage their opponents, as Okono had promised to do, the Administration simply used one of its press organs to go after its critics and smear them into silence. One of his best friends, a McCracken supporter, a person Johannsen respected, had started to refer in Orwellian fashion to the Okono Administration as "The Ministry of Truth."

Johannsen was also concerned that a lot of issues on which Okono the candidate had campaigned no longer seemed to be priorities for Okono the president. Environmental activists, women's groups, advocates for gay rights—had all been disappointed in the first months of his administration. Not simply because the administration wasn't pushing more aggressively, but because the Okono administration was pushing in the opposite direction.

The Okono guys were so skilled at crafting their message, it covered up the surprising amount of inaction. Lots of photo-ops covered by White House photographers and thoughtfully provided after the event to Okono fanzines like the *Huffington Post* and *Daily Kos*—but no access by real reporters to the event itself. But perhaps that was to be expected from an administration that had assembled the largest press team, and smallest policy team in U.S. history.

Social issues were complicated. Johannsen got that. It wasn't going to be possible for Okono to make everyone happy. Incremental progress was better than no progress at all. But Johannsen was becoming more and more concerned about the administration's handling of the economy. They'd invited him to sit in on a few round table discussions with other money guys (he recognized a number of them as major contributors). After all, Johannsen reflected, Okono certainly had the connections to Wall Street. But most of the meetings had been bullshit.

The Okono decision makers were all academics; what they knew about how markets worked, was what they had read in a book. When the Wall Street guys weighed in with an opinion (usually diametrically opposed to the academic's own), the Okono economists cocked their heads in a patronizing and surprised way as if they considered it some kind of marvelous trick that the bankers had learned to speak. Worse (and this still shocked Johannsen), it was rapidly becoming apparent, that none of the Okono people actually believed in free market capitalism.

When the Republicans had accused Okono of being a socialist during the campaign—Appelbaum had laughed it off, a suggestion as outlandish as believing the government was keeping alien cadavers at a remote government facility in Nevada. "What will these crazy Republicans think of next?" Appelbaum had reassured him with a wink and a chuckle. And it *was* nutty, right? After all, nobody believed in communism or socialism any more, right? It was a failed system. And all the European countries that had embraced socialism were retrenching after they essentially bankrupted much of their tax base. South American countries that nationalized industries had learned the hard way that you had to incentivize risk and hard work, and you couldn't do either if the government was providing everyone with the same paycheck.

But, Johannsen told his partners after returning from a meeting in D.C., it was like all the Okono policy wonks had missed the last thirty years. The whole "Mr. Gorbachev, take down this wall" thing about a free economy—apparently, they hadn't been there, missed it. Johannsen believed in safety nets, he even believed in proactive interest rate manipulation by the Fed (although his faith had been shaken in its efficacy in recent months), but he wasn't really sure what the Okono people were talking about any more. Much of the stimulus money allocated by Congress was still unspent. By the laws of Keynesian economics, that money needed to be in the system already. Nobody had as yet given him an explanation as to why it wasn't. Even an armchair economist could figure out that with the debt the U.S. government was amassing; there were only two long-term possibilities: default or inflation.

But Johannsen believed that rushing forward on some of the important social programs—programs Johannsen himself supported—might be problematic when the economy was in free-fall *and* the government had piled up huge deficits. After all, social programs aren't funded by the government, they're funded by the taxes the government collects from its working citizens. After all the euphoria of the campaign, Johannsen found himself in the unlikely position of being delighted that a candidate he'd supported had actually won (finally), but no longer sure who or what he had voted for.

He'd been a willing votary, he acknowledged that. Right before the election, a friend had cautioned him about sending the *Daily Kos* article on Okono's legislative accomplishments. It wasn't true, she said. She was a McCracken supporter, so he didn't entirely believe her, maybe didn't want to believe her. Right before the election, he'd finally checked it out. He'd had an intern sift through everything for two days. He was genuinely horrified to discover his friend was right. Okono had virtually no legislative accomplishments in the Congress. Most of the 900 bills on the list were introduced when he was in the Illinois state house, and even then, he'd had nothing to do with most of them. Some, Johannsen was chagrined to find out, Okono had actually voted against. Johannsen was embarrassed thinking about it. He couldn't even remember how many hundreds of classmates, business associates, and friends he'd sent it to. But he knew where he'd gotten it: Appelbaum had forwarded it to him. Appelbaum— who had to have known it wasn't true.

He'd also finally gotten some insight into Appelbaum and his astro-turfing business. He was now prepared to admit what his wife had suspected long ago. Underneath his pretensions of altruistic idealism, Appelbaum was a beguiler, a charlatan, a shyster. The effulgent glow that Okono had cast had prevented him for seeing Appelbaum for what and who he was. And Johannsen was beginning to question: what else had it prevented him from seeing about Okono?

CHAPTER FIFTY-NINE

April, 2009
London, England

When Prince Abdul-Wahid bin Khair al Din entered his London hotel, he was trying to be low-key. Therefore, as he passed through the limestone portals, past the priceless seventeenth century tapestries and ormolu clocks, under the magnificent crystal chandelier, past the four foot high glass vases filled with long-stemmed exotic flowers (*a la moderne*), Prince Abdul-Wahid had only two security guys instead of the usual half-dozen. Hotel guests having afternoon tea, listening to the tinkling keys of the atrium's piano, craned to identify the source of the commotion (fame and wealth create a powerful magnet). Catching just a quick glimpse of the prince, they excitedly whispered to each other that it was that famous magician—you know, the one that dated the supermodel! Nobody could think of his name right away.

Of course, what they didn't know, was that when Prince Abdul-Wahid entered his hotel, the world famous Hotel Edward

VII—it was really that, *his* hotel. The magician, for all his proximity to supermodels, probably didn't own one of the world's most sumptuous hotels or, if in the unlikely event he did, he probably didn't own three.

But Abdul wasn't moved by the exquisite *objet d'art* or crystal or gilt, he got enough of that at home. No, Abdul loved London at any time of the year, but he especially loved it in the spring—all that cool, moist, greenery made a welcome change from hot, dry beige sand. Sadly, he wouldn't have much time to enjoy it. As usual, Abdul was there on business, only this time, it wasn't his business. He was here as an unofficial member of the Saudi delegation to the Group of 20, or more simply: G20, and he was there to make sure that his king was happy.

The G20 was (normally) a meeting of finance ministers and governors of the central banks of 19 of the top 31 economies in the world. Heads of state didn't usually attend the G20. In fact, this was only the second such meeting. But with burgeoning social unrest as the result of the growing global recession (everyone had watched as millions of Frenchman had protested their government's failure to act more aggressively in recent weeks), there was a consensus among world leaders that being seen getting out in front of the issue was politically expedient.

The Saudi king had already had a private meeting with the new U.S. president. Prince Abdul had read the report of their conversation on the plane. Considering the gravity of the economic situation, most of the press remained strangely uninterested in the conversations between the world's most powerful bankers. Most spent their time attending receptions and gossiping amongst themselves about the stylish first lady's weirdly droopy right eye—apparently the result of a botox injection gone wrong and part of the "prettying-up" she'd received after the election.

As the meeting was drawing to a close, American journalists were pressuring the President about what the G20 had achieved that would be tangible to Americans. Of course, the question demonstrated a profound misunderstanding of what Okono was trying to do. Securing more money for the International Monetary Fund, while physically located in the U.S., offered no direct economic benefit to the U.S. The IMF was essentially an aid organization lending money to poor countries.

Both the French and the Germans were resisting Okono's calls for more aid to the IMF. France and Germany were more interested in encouraging cash infusions into their own shaky economies than contributing towards the $1.1 trillion Okono wanted for what they considered "global welfare" in Africa and Asia. After all, they argued petulantly, let China do it. China had become the unofficial ATM of the third world during the last eight years. So be it, they agreed.

But the Americans and Saudis were not nearly so sanguine about Chinese influence, or the French president's posturing. Abdul knew first-hand that the Saudi king detested the French president, referring to him on more than one occasion as "that obstreperous monkey." "Let him go," the king had said privately. But Prince Abdul had cautioned the king, if France's tempestuous president walked out of the meeting, as he was threatening to do, it would reflect poorly on Okono's leadership at this, his first international diplomatic test.

There were other concerns, Prince Abdul reminded the king. Aside from the pressing humanitarian considerations of securing the aid for the IMF, there were other aspects as well. Abdul reminded the Saudi king (whose official style included "Custodian of the Two Holy Mosques") that virtually all of the poorest countries that would receive aid had exploding Muslim populations. The king was obligated to the brothers of his faith. Happily, thought Abdul with a smile, Okono was now obligated to the king.

Hours later, when the members of the G20 assembled for the official picture, reporters were astonished to see Okono bow from the waist upon greeting the Saudi king. The White House immediately began the farcical process of trying to persuade reporters who saw it that they hadn't seen it, or that they'd seen something else, or better still, that there was nothing to see.

Okono spokesperson Jim Latchky, peremptorily claimed it wasn't a bow, that Okono was just "tall." When reporters showed a disinclination to let the matter drop after these first unsatisfactory explanations, the Okono press people showed their irritation with the reporters—*there was no bow*. Josh Stein helpfully repeated the party line with a headline that must have strained even his own credulity: "No Bow from Okono," but the video told a different story. Journalists who conceded that the White House was lying were quick to point out "it didn't really matter" and dismissed it—after all, it had only been established protocol that American leaders not bow to kings for 200 years. Left on the table, was that in a room full of kings, Okono had bowed to only one.

Chapter Sixty

Rockville, Maryland

THE PHONE RANG. It was Max.

"So are you ready to run a campaign?"

"What?" she asked with a laugh, surprised.

"How about as a candidate?" Max asked.

Lacey laughed, in spite of herself.

"Max, don't you know? I'm controversial...and besides, as should be abundantly obvious by now, I know absolutely nothing about getting into politics," she said.

"Jesus, Lacey. Dirty tricks, death threats—You're already *in* politics."

They both laughed.

"Lacey, you may not realize this, but you guys kicked some ass. With no resources, that's pretty impressive. How many volunteers did you end up with?" he asked.

"A little over 14,000," she replied.

"Are you shittin' me?" Max was completely taken aback.

Lacey was offended. "No, of course not." She continued,

"Anyway, why not Betty Jo? I think she'd be an amazing candidate."

"I agree. I'd still like to meet her." Max was hard to distract. "But, right now, we're talking about you. So how about it?"

Lacey was dismissive. "Honestly, Max. I couldn't. For one thing, I'm not qualified."

The line went dead for a minute.

"Hello?" Lacey said.

"Why do women always do that?" asked Max.

Lacey was surprised. "Do what?" she asked.

"Lacey, I've got guys barely out of diapers who ran the college Democratic club with, like, 20 members—they think they're qualified. But women, no matter what their accomplishments or skills— never think they're qualified. You tell me, why is that?"

"Dunno," Lacey said.

"Why not let the voters decide?" he asked.

Lacey laughed. "Max—Why? Why the sudden interest? Are you a secret lobbyist for some industry that needs to escape regulation?"

Max sighed. "Lacey. Don't be tiresome. You're re-running the last campaign. Okono already screwed those hedge fund guys." They both laughed.

Lacey considered. "So much for avoiding regulation. The angry Transylvanian townsfolk are after them now; and after they gave Okono so much money. Sad for them."

"Luckily, I'm not easily moved to tears," replied Max. "Lacey, I want you to think about it."

"Max, you don't want me—I'd be a liability. This racist tag is going to follow me like a tin can the rest of my days."

"Lacey, listen to me. People will meet you, they'll get to know you, it will go away. Politics is all chance. I've been doing this a long time and I know how to hedge a bet. Listen to me when I say this, because I don't say it often. I'll gamble on you anytime."

Chapter Sixty-one

May 2009
Stromsburg, Nebraska

The first thing his father told him was that she'd miss the fair. The town put on a Swedish Midsommer Festival every year at the end of June with costumed local children dancing around a maypole. His father always helped out with the Swedish pancake breakfast on Sunday morning, but it was his mother who'd always organized the hundreds of dirndl-wearing, blonde-braided volunteers.

The doctors said it happened suddenly, in her sleep. His father hadn't noticed until his breakfast didn't appear, and then he'd gone up to check. Johannsen hadn't realized his parents had been sleeping in separate rooms. It was nothing, his father said, just that his snoring kept his mother awake. They still had date nights his father said, waggling his brows, in a way that seemed unseemly to Paul under the circumstances.

The wake was at the large Queen Anne style, white clapboard and black-awninged funeral parlor on Main Street in nearby

Osceola. His father insisted his mother wouldn't have wanted a fuss, nothing fancy. Standing in the carpeted entryway greeting the mourners, Joan was, as always, perfect. She made all the right noises, said all the right things. His powerhouse lawyer wife had nothing in common with his housewife mother except maybe nerves of steel, but they'd held each other in high esteem, nevertheless. When Joan spoke of the respect she'd had for his mother, Paul knew she was speaking from her heart.

His father looked lost, as if he'd shrunk two sizes in as many days. They said when a couple had a long and happy marriage, the husband didn't long outlive the spouse. Johannsen would have to step in—get somebody in to take care of his father, pay the bills. Maybe he could persuade him to move to California? The kids would love it, but he doubted his father would agree to leave his home and friends.

Johannsen was amazed at the number of people that turned up at the wake. Of course, he knew his mother had always been active in the community. When he was in high school, he remembered the mayor telling him his mother ran everything in town. At the time, he'd been aggravated, wishing she were more available for him. Apparently, not much had changed. For three days, the room was packed with a line out the door. People from all her volunteer activities: from the church, from the library, from the hospital, even from the animal shelter. All the people in the town: waitresses, doctors, lawyers, dentists, policemen, merchants—they all came to pay their respects to his mother. He'd never thought to ask his parents what they did with the money he sent them. But now he could see, they'd helped almost every charitable organization in town.

But it was more than that. For the first time in his life, Paul Johannsen realized that his mother had *been* someone. He'd always seen her as a wife and a mother. After all, she'd never held a job. What he suddenly realized was that she'd held hundreds of jobs—and she'd been really good at all of them. Everyone was saying how lost they felt without her. She'd been so smart, so focused, so energetic. How had he misunderstood who she was so completely?

People were incredibly kind, had so many wonderful things to say. He wished he could remember them all, to tell his children and maybe someday his grandchildren. "This was who my mother was," he'd say. But he realized he needed these people to tell him. He'd never really known. Over and over, he heard people memorialize all the things she'd done, all the ways she'd helped them, and it ended the same way, over and over "...and she never asked for anything for herself."

And Paul Johannsen thought back over his 45 years and remembered all the things she'd done for him. From the complicated yucky things, like finding salamanders under rocks for science projects, or learning algebra, to the mundane minutiae of mothering. All the beds and dinners made, and cuts cleaned, and homework helped, suitcases packed, even balls pitched. The den mothering and classroom parenting, and sickroom tending, and they were right, Johannsen realized. Paul Johannsen couldn't remember a single time his mother had asked him for anything for herself.

Except once.

CHAPTER SIXTY-TWO

July 2009
Washington, DC

IT OFFICIALLY STARTED TO UNRAVEL ON THE 20TH OF JULY, but of course, like so much else in Washington, the leaks had been coming for months. The names of the organizations involved were staggering: the *New York Times, Washington Post, Newsweek, Time, The New Republic, The Nation, The New Yorker, Los Angeles Times, Baltimore Sun, Salon, The Guardian, The Atlantic,* *CNN, CBS, MSNBC, NBC, National Public Radio, Politico, Huffington Post, Bloomberg News*, among others. Its defenders and aficionados called it simply the J-List, a group of 400 self-described left-leaning journalists, bloggers, newscasters, pundits and policy wonks who had created an invitation-only online enclave on google groups. Its stated intention was to allow its members to share information and opinions in a supportive setting, but at some point, some of its members at least, had crossed a line. To its critics, JournoList was nothing short of a nefarious organization to control the public's access to information and shape public opinion—and they claimed to have the email-exchanges to prove it. Of course, as it turned out it wasn't just public opinion in general. No.

What the J-List members were accused of was a startling pattern of consistently shaping news stories to benefit one man: Okono. As one investigative journalist who examined the cache of email exchanges beginning in 2007 explained: "Again and again we discovered members of JournoList working to coordinate talking points on behalf of then-Congressman Okono." Another headline described the email evidence more starkly. In an article entitled, "The Vast Left-Wing Media Conspiracy" published in the *Wall Street Journal*, the author noted "Everyone knew most of the press corps was hoping for Okono in 2008. Newly released emails show that hundreds of them were actively working to promote him." The most damning emails showed JournoList members working to stifle news stories about Okono and The Minister, with one JournoList member going so far as to advocate false accusations and other Alinsky-style tactics to silence the conservative opposition: "Take one of them—Fred Barnes, Karl Rove, who cares—and call them racists." Another advocated burying The Minister story by putting those who raised the issue on the defensive. "Refuse to discuss The Minister. Turn it around on them. Ask: 'Why do you have such a deep-seated problem with a black politician who unites the country?"

As the story broke, the more prominent members of the J-List said nothing publicly and waited for the storm to pass. A few less well-known members waded in with fiery denunciations of the conservative journalists who had exposed the group, claiming that publishing the email exchanges was an assault on both the freedom of the press and their freedom of speech. How exactly that squared with the J-List members' public support for revealing (and printing) private diplomatic emails from the U.S. State Department obtained by an on-line guerilla watch-dog group, or emails exchanged between scientists promoting an anthropogenic theory of global warming, oil executives, tobacco executives and financial services companies—all of whose emails or private correspondence had become fodder for major news stories in recent years—was not exactly clear. Apparently, ferreting around in people's 'sent messages' was somehow different when it was the journalists themselves being exposed.

A self-identified conservative with a popular syndicated column claimed not to understand what all the blather was about. After all, she pointed out, most of the discussions were pretty banal. She argued that the journalists were engaged in private conversation and deserved not to be "outed." Commentators on the left praised her for her practical impartiality, while commentators on the right remembered that she had been one of McCracken's most virulent critics during the primaries—at one point devoting almost an entire article to describing McCracken as a "soul-less cyborg." Both sides politely refrained from mentioning that her defense of her colleagues was not entirely selfless: she was, herself, a member of JournoList.

As the furor raged and the ethics of the group were argued (at least inside the Beltway), the founder of JournoList publicly pulled the plug on the google group. But not before many of its members had found a new home on google groups, which they named (in what must have been intended as a poke-in-the-eye of their critics) "Cabalist." By July, they had 197 members.

Chapter Sixty-Three

June 2009
Washington, DC

Adelita Bouchard struggled with the baby on one hip and a bag of groceries on the other. It had been a discouraging few weeks. She had given her information to Congressional investigators, but despite promises to the contrary, the leading Democratic member had just announced there was simply not enough evidence of wrongdoing on the part of SEED to justify the expense of Congressional hearings. Meanwhile, she'd been pilloried all over the internet by idolatrous Okono supporters, who claimed (without any evidence) that she was a front for some revanchist Republican plot to de-legitimize Okono. A few months ago, she would still have been sufficiently idealistic to be shocked by this. Now she wasn't even surprised. After she strapped the baby into her car seat, she opened the rear hatch and put the rest of the grocery bags in the back. She noticed a rumpled looking white guy approaching her from across the parking lot.

"Adelita Bouchard?"

"Yes?"

The man handed her an envelope. "You've been served," he said, and he walked away. With real trepidation, she opened the envelope. Power Vote was suing her for $5 million.

Five days later, her lawyer informed her that SEED had quietly filed the papers to legally change its name to Neighborhoods International for Community Empowerment or 'NICE'. Hardly anyone in the media reported it.

"Nice, indeed," thought Adelita with disgust.

Chapter Sixty-Four

September, 2010
Medford, Oregon

It was wonderful to see Connor again. Lacey had called him when she'd found out she was coming to town. While it was a long drive from his house bordering the state park, he was used to making the trip, and he'd happily agreed to meet her. She was in town for a book signing of her children's book, which was rapidly becoming a bestseller. When Lacey spotted Connor across the store, she rushed up and gave him a big hug. Same old Lacey Connor thought, pleased. She excused herself from the hatchet-faced agent from the publishing house and grabbed her handbag.

"I'm allowed an hour," she said under her breath, with a friendly wave to the sullen agent waiting at the book-signing table, who was obviously displeased at her break for freedom. "Is there someplace we can go and grab some lunch? I'm starving." He steered her to a cute eatery down the street where they grabbed one of the tables outside. As they waited for their salads, they sipped iced tea.

Connor couldn't resist teasing her. "So, it seems like they keep you on a pretty short leash." Lacey laughed with a big smile:

"They do. He does," she said "But in fairness to him, it's his responsibility to keep the schedule, and he's the one that gets yelled at if we're late to the next appearance. I, on the other hand, have no responsibilities whatsoever."

"Sure," Connor said, teasingly. "You're just the talent."

Lacey snurfed her drink. "Well, I guess I've been called worse."

"So, you enjoy it...the traveling and all?" he asked skeptically. Connor enjoyed his freedom too much to relish having a sour-faced handler. Lacey shrugged and smiled.

"Sure. Honestly, it's not much. After all, it's just a little book." Lacey put her fingers together an inch a part. "I'm grateful they're promoting it. My agent says they don't really do many book tours any more. I know I got really lucky. Did I tell you that I got a silent auction donation request for a signed book from some yeshiva in Brooklyn?"

"No."

"Signed by the chair of the auction," Lacey paused for dramatic effect, "Mrs. Josh Stein." Lacey laughed.

"You're kidding me," said Connor, shaking his head, disgusted. "That was ballsy. I hope you sent her away with a flea in her ear." Lacey looked sheepish.

Connor looked up quickly. "Lacey! You didn't? You didn't send that little shit a book?"

Lacey covered her face with her hand, ashamed. "I did. I sent it. I know. I know. I'm just no good at being mean to people, Connor," Lacey finished apologetically.

"Lacey. That's so lame. The guy tried to destroy you."

"I know. I know. But the kids at the school looked so nice."

Connor started to laugh, shaking his head. Lacey started laughing, too.

Lacey continued. "It still seems strange how it all happened. I mean, I'm not sure if I would have tried writing if I weren't really out of employment options. But it's really worked out."

It was a beautiful autumn day. Downtown bustled around them, people rushed by. Lacey looked around the crowded outdoor mall. "This is a great town. I didn't know you got this much sun in Oregon."

"This is Rogue Valley, it's the driest and sunniest part of the state."

Lacey eyed him, kiddingly. "I guess I should have known you'd need that for your greenhouse." Connor was always trying to persuade Lacey she needed to grow her own vegetables. Connor started to his defense when she held up both hands in mock surrender.

"Connor, it will please you to know, that following your suggestion, we have added a greenhouse lean-to to the new house."

"You need to get a few chickens, too," Connor said earnestly. He never gave up. Lacey laughed. "Let's see if I can keep the tomatoes alive, first."

The waiter came by and refilled their iced teas.

Lacey looked at Connor appraisingly. He looked just the same. "So how are you?" she asked.

'I'm great. I told you, I think, I met a nice gal..."

"Sue, right?"

"You've got a good memory. And we enjoy the same kind of things. It's an easy trip to wine country for a long weekend. And of course, Crater Lake's really close and we like to get out there and hike."

"And you just got back from Italy?" Lacey asked. Connor smiled.

"Great trip. Have you ever been?" Lacey nodded.

"It was my first time. I loved it. I can't wait to go back."

Lacey smiled, pleased."So, you're doing alright?" she asked.

Connor made a face and shrugged. "Naw. I mean, my stocks still aren't worth shit, but I left them in, like you told me..."

"Good man," said Lacey. They both laughed.

Connor continued. "And I've got my pension. But this economy is tough. But, you know, like everybody else these days, I keep it simple, don't spend much."

"How about you guys? How's Daniel doing?" Daniel was Lacey's husband.

Lacey paused. "Actually, he's renovating houses. It turned out he couldn't get a real job, either..." Lacey laughed. "But he really enjoys choosing the properties. He's been pretty successful."

Connor shook is head. "I never understood how people do that."

Lacey shrugged. "Well, he's still an accountant at heart, so he approaches it like a math problem. You buy the property for x–the neighborhood median is y, so you can spend z. Of course, in this economy, not much is selling, so the margins are a lot tighter...but he's making it work, renting the places he can't sell." She paused, as if considering whether she should say more. She added thoughtfully.

"The IRS are going after Daniel for some work he did for his old company..."

Connor looked appalled. "Oh, shit."

Lacey smiled tightly, grateful for his concern.

"I'm sure it's nothing. You know, Daniel's a straight arrow..."

"The straightest," Connor interjected.

"I'm sure it'll get resolved before long." She smiled brightly, determined to put him at ease. "Please don't worry about us. Everything's going well."

Connor was happy for her, happy for them both. He knew she'd end up on her feet. Lacey was tougher than she looked.

"I'm glad, Lacey. I'm really glad."

The waiter served their salads. "Do you keep in touch with the McCracken people?" Connor asked.

"Sure," she replied. "All of them. Betty Jo's revolutionizing the Ohio real estate market." They both laughed.

"I love Betty Jo," Connor said.

"Yeah, she's pretty unstoppable," agreed Lacey. "I'm not sure those Republicans in Ohio have recovered yet." She smiled ruefully. "But maybe if they'd listened to her, Malloy might have won Ohio."

"Did you ever figure out how to email each other?" Connor asked. When the email networks were disrupted, he'd served as a go between to Betty Jo and Lacey.

"Wow." Lacey put down her fork. "Did I never tell you this?"

Connor, munching his salad, shook his head, "No, what?"

"Have you ever heard of ICANN?"

Connor shook his head 'no.'

Lacey continued. “My husband told me about them.” Lacey’s husband Daniel was a computer guy.

“Basically they’re a non-profit, under contract to the Department of Commerce. They monitor ISP addresses—all the big ones — .net, .com, .org. and they actively work to prevent spam.”

“Okay. Sounds good. I hate spam. I like all my anatomical parts just as they are,” Connor answered.

Lacey sipped her iced tea. “Good to know. Anyway, under ICANN’s direction, various different servers started ‘Blacklists’ called DNSBL’s that list the IP addresses of known spammers and share them with all the major mail servers to reject their messages.”

Connor wiped his mouth. “So far so good.”

Lacey continued. “But there’s almost no verification. If the DNSBL receives notice that someone received spam from an email—they immediately block it. Some of the blocks automatically expire after 30 days. Some of them never expire until they receive a complaint. And, of course, they never notify the sender that they’ve been placed on the list.”

“So, how does someone find out if their email is on the list of suspected spammers?”

“I had a friend send an inquiry about my email address to about 25 of the biggest DNSBL’s”

“And...?”

“I was blocked, of course.”

Connor exploded. “No!”

“Yup. Know *when* I was blocked?”

“When?”

"Three days before the conference call with Malloy."

Connor supposed he shouldn't be surprised at the perfidiousness of the Okono-ites. Somehow he still was. But there had been a few rats in the McCracken camp, as well. They were both silent for a few minutes, concentrating on their salads. Finally he asked:

"So what do you think, was Danny Englund for real?"

Lacey looked sad. "I wish I knew. He was a pretty dopey guy. Was he smart enough to come to us on his own? Were they stupid enough to send him? I don't know. Maybe. The word is that he was a total flake, a freelancer. But that's what the McCracken campaign would sort of have to say now anyway."

They both paused to eat their salads. "You know, Max asked me to run a campaign?"

"Yeah? I'm not surprised. You'd be great, Lacey."

"I thought about it," she shrugged, embarrassed. Then she laughed. "...for about ten minutes. But then I realized it would never work."

"Why not?"

"Hard to explain. But I guess...for me, everything's changed now. How can I stand shoulder-to-shoulder with SEED and the Service Workers Union when I saw what they did during the campaign? I mean before—" she shrugged, "greedy corporations, Republicans..." she laughed. "Well, good Democrats are conditioned to think it's okay to go after them with somewhat questionable tactics because they're bad people."

"Sure. Eat or be eaten," Connor said with asperity.

"Well, all I know is, it suddenly looked a lot different when fellow Democrats were on the receiving end...When *I* was on the receiving end, I guess," she admitted sheepishly.

"And it wasn't just the Okono brown shirts, it was the press, too. I grew up revering the *New York Times*. I really believed if the *Times* printed it, it was true. I thought if there was fraud or wrongdoing, and they found out about it, they had real integrity, they'd take it to the mat. Truth to power, and all that. But we gave it to them—the illegal campaign contributions, the ties to the Nigerian warlord, the Joey Ali stuff. God knows what else...And they *buried* it."

"Maybe they thought it was bad info?" Connor suggested.

"They could have looked into it themselves. We didn't expect them to take our word for it. But it was more that that..."

"Yeah, what?"

"You know, when I was doing opposition research on Okono I came across this *Newsweek* article "Inside Okono's Dream Machine" all about the "respectful tone" he took toward his opponents and his high-minded themes of hope and change, and how maybe he was too earnest and naïve to survive presidential politics."

Connor laughed. "So what? That was like mother's milk to most of the press during the election."

"But they talked about his early campaigns. They claimed his refusal to go negative went way back...to running for president of the law review and working with Republicans in the state senate."

"So?"

"But they left out the *actual campaigns* which Okono ran by getting everyone else disqualified on his first run—and in his later runs by giving the press salacious details about his opponent's divorce records. Does that sound like 'refusing to get personal' or 'kneecap' anyone?"

Connor laughed. "No, that pretty much sounds like the definition of getting personal and kneecapping someone."

Lacey continued. Her voice rising slightly as she explained.

"You're supposedly writing an article about how he conducts himself in an election—but you don't cover the election? How does that work? They jumped the timeline from Harvard to working in the state senate. Obviously, they knew about the elections and purposely left it out. And there's hundreds of examples like that: an early *Vanity Fair* article that talks about Okono's early influences but never mentions his ties to The Minister or the crazy church. Even Nicholas Kirov—"

"Wait. I know that name...?"

"Right. Big reporter for the *New York Times*, travels all over the world doing exposés on corruption and malfeasance, especially about the treatment of women and girls."

Connor nodded, "Yeah, so, stand-up guy."

"Right, stand-up guy. But he conducted an interview early on with Okono where Okono recited the Muslim call to prayer..."

"Yeah, so—he lived in a Muslim country as a kid."

"In perfect Arabic...and Okono talked about going to Muslim classes where he got in trouble for making faces instead of studying."

Connor laughed. "C'mon Lacey. So, you're saying Okono's a Muslim?"

"I don't know and I don't care. The Black Liberation Theology they practice at his church is a kind of hybrid of religions. Maybe that's what he believes. Maybe he's a Christian. Maybe he doesn't believe anything. Personally, I don't give a shit what religion someone practices, or if they practice any at all. But that's not my point."

Connor smiled. "Okay, so what's your point?"

"Okono's comments were part of the public record. People who *do* care had a right to know. That article got buried, and the audio was taken off the *New York Times* website."

"Who did that?"

"Who knows? Maybe hackers, maybe the *Times* itself. But Kirov knew about it, and certainly his editors knew about it, and when the hoopla erupted, they kept to the party line that anyone who doubted Okono's strict adherence to Christianity was either a racist or a nut."

Connor rubbed his forehead. "I'm not sure I'm following."

Lacey sighed. "Suggesting that someone is Muslim because he has a different skin color is a lot different than suggesting he's Muslim because he tells you himself that he made faces at the other kids when he was studying in Muslim school."

"I see your point."

Lacey continued. "They didn't just fail to investigate. They actively covered up any information they thought might be damaging. That feels worse, somehow."

Connor paused, thoughtfully.

"Okay. So screw 'em. Run a Republican campaign and point out all the press' inconsistencies..." Connor suggested.

Lacey laughed.

"Because the Republicans are sweetness and light? No, learning to distrust the Democrats hasn't necessarily made me any more trustful of the Republicans. I mean, look at Ohio, just as an example. What a mess. Republicans didn't want poor people to vote, and Democrats wanted them to vote four times." Connor laughed out loud.

Lacey shook her head sadly. "It's all one way or all the other, and nobody's willing to criticize people on their own side, no matter how outrageous their practices. There's no incentive to tell the truth and let the chips fall where they may. Think about it. When banks or corporations hide information from the public—or just don't disclose information that's relevant to the consumer's decision-making—we consider that cheating, fraud. And the press and politicians usually scream the loudest about the betrayal of the public trust. But when the press and politicians parse what information they allow us to know, so that we make the 'right' decision as voters—how is that different? Don't they have an obligation to the public trust, as well? Why is our money more valuable, more protected, than our votes, or by extension the democratic process?"

Connor shook his head sadly. "I don't know, Lacey."

Suddenly, she laughed. "I'm sorry, Connor. I'm really on my soapbox today, I guess. Not that any of this is new, except to us. Politics and sausages, right?"

They spent a few minutes eating their lunch. Finally Connor asked quietly:

"Do you think McCracken ever had a chance?"

Lacey considered: "I don't know." She shook her head. "We thought we would wave our pithy signs and hand out our carefully researched little flyers and that would make a difference. Looking back, we were so naïve. I mean, who are we, right?" Lacey looked at Connor with a rueful smile.

"I think none of us ever sees the whole picture. I used to just think that was happenstance. Now I'm not so sure the media ever covers any issue completely or fairly. Special interests are so entrenched, so corrupt...I guess I just never realized it before," she said softly.

Connor watched the street scene. Did he agree with Lacey? He was trying to decide. With all his years in law enforcement, he'd seen some pretty shady deals go down.

"Well, even though she didn't win the nomination," he said thoughtfully, "I can't help remembering that more people actually voted for McCracken than voted for Okono. A point that the press have conveniently forgotten," he said with a laugh. "I guess I want to believe that means something."

Lacey nodded, but remained silent.

"I just read something I thought was interesting," Connor continued. "18% of McCracken supporters did not vote for Okono."

Lacey was surprised. "Wow. Really? That's more than I would have thought," she said.

"Yup. If you consider that a lot of her supporters were women, and women tend to be more liberal than men...and yet they either didn't vote or voted for the Republican? Well, that's a pretty staggering indictment, wouldn't you say?"

"I guess," Lacey replied.

"And you know what else?" said Connor.

"What?" replied Lacey.

"At the convention, after McCracken released her delegates—the press reported that Okono's nomination was unanimous?"

"Uggh. How could I forget? I was there, remember?" Lacey said, shaking her head.

Connor continued.

"It wasn't unanimous. No matter what happens for public consumption in the hall, they're required to have a paper ballot. One-third of the delegates still voted for McCracken." Connor paused. "I know it was really hard, but I think we made a difference, maybe just enough to get people to start asking questions. The American people are smart, Lacey."

Both were silent. Lacey spoke first.

"Connor did you ever wonder...?" There was a long pause.

"Wonder if we were right about Okono?" Connor completed her sentence. Lacey looked down at her salad. Connor could see she had lost her appetite.

She continued. "I guess...yeah." She paused. "We had so much damning information on him—but if it was as powerful as we thought, why didn't anybody ever run it, why didn't anybody ever print it?"

"You just said it. The press are on his side," said Connor

"But the press are still people, Connor," Lacey said. "Is there 'group think?' Absolutely. But think about it. You get forty people looking at an event, you end up with forty different versions of what happened. So why not with Okono?"

She paused as if groping for an explanation. "I mean, we've both seen it: people feel this weird, visceral, *emotional* connection to Okono, that just kind of sends their brain into neutral. It's not that they defend Okono, or justify his actions. Mostly they won't even listen to the evidence before they decide. If I say anything remotely critical about Okono, my relatives put their hands over their ears and start humming like they're three-year-olds. And on issues they care about—like FISA and gay marriage. I don't understand it. Suddenly, they all think I'm a right-wing Bircher just because Daniel and I didn't support Okono." She laughed an uneasy laugh. "Why is that? Do you ever wonder if it was us? Maybe *we* had 'group think?' Maybe we were so busy believing Okono was a bad guy we only saw the stuff that supported that? Can all those millions of people be wrong? I mean, honestly, Connor, was it us?"

Connor thought about all the time he'd served in law enforcement, more than 20 years. He thought about Antwone Green, doing a favor for a friend. He thought about Joey Ali and his indefinitely suspended sentence. He thought about the slums created by the cupidity of Okono's top advisors and friends. He thought about Okono supporters threatening and intimidating women and senior citizens at the caucuses. But, mostly, he thought about Miriam Carter. He'd never met her, but like many investigators, he'd formed a kind of post-mortem bond with the victim. It was hard not to be impressed by her canny intelligence and *joie de vivre*. He admired the incredible integrity of the way she'd lived her life. Honest, strong, fair. Miriam Carter had been the real deal, an African American hero, an American hero. It was hard not to feel he owed her something.

He turned to Lacey, and he could see she needed an answer. At some point, she had decided she needed to know more than she needed to be right. She'd put a lot on the line. They'd all put a lot on the line—because they thought they were doing the right thing—but they'd been like small voices in the Stygian darkness. Connor considered a moment.

"Naw. Lacey...the guy's a crook."

Chapter Sixty-Five

Washington, DC

Appelbaum loved to portray himself as an idealist. And the Washington press corps had mostly bought it. Soft-spoken and conciliatory, he had learned a long time ago to measure his words carefully and get a little tearful when he talked about the unfulfilled promise of the Kennedys. As The Minister (who was no fan) had pointed out, Appelbaum was the master of promoting black candidates to white voters, but really cared nothing about black voters. It was true. Appelbaum never really cared about black voters because he had always assumed black voters would take care of themselves. Campaigns for black candidates in Detroit, Cleveland, D.C., Houston, and Philadelphia had borne out the wisdom of his strategy.

But, of course, the story wasn't really that Appelbaum knew how to sell a black candidate or a white candidate; the real story, the untold story, was that Appelbaum could sell anything and did. And, his corporate clients—who wanted to build support for laying fiber-optic cable, or using coal to fire their electric plants (such a disappointment to all the public interest attorneys fighting mountaintop mining in West Virginia) or investing in nuclear power, or bidding for the Olympics—they didn't pay him the big money because he was an affable guy. It's a truism of the modern world that idealists are so rarely worth $7 million dollars. And Appelbaum, the original "red diaper baby" (his mother used to be a journalist on a communist screed), wanted the big money.

It was a mystery he would never understand, how the McCracken campaign had missed the basic strategy of the race. They had never understood the incredible importance of the caucus states or realized how vulnerable they were to manipulation. And they had given away one of their most critical advantages when they had agreed to censure Michigan and Florida. Some in the Okono campaign thought they might be able to swing Florida. Appelbaum never believed it. If those primaries had counted, it would have diffused whatever bump the campaign got in South Carolina. And, really, who were they kidding? Rural, poor South Carolina vs. the industrial might of Michigan or the wealth of Florida? South Carolina? *Shit*, Appelbaum thought. Who the fuck won Alabama? Who the fuck *cared* about those shit-kickin' Southern states? If Michigan and Florida had counted, McCracken would have been home free.

Then when the tapes of The Minister came out—Okono would have skulked away in ignominy—not quite barricading himself in a men's room like Chet Williams—not quite that bad. But bad.

Of course, Appelbaum thought with a chuckle, having his own partisans on the JournoList group and inside McCracken's campaign hadn't hurt either.

Conventional wisdom was that McCracken had run a stupid campaign, and there was plenty of evidence to support that. Journalists constantly pointed to McCracken's $30 million throw-a-way in Iowa. Appelbaum smiled to himself. What they never reported was that McCracken was herself out-spent in Iowa. Oh, yes, even in the first contest!—before anybody even knew the guy—by Okono.

As to Malloy, Appelbaum thought the race was decided when Helman Brothers collapsed in the middle of December. Insurance policies carefully indemnified themselves against 'acts of God' —hurricanes and the like—in which case the insurer was not responsible to provide coverage. Well, Appelbaum reflected, Malloy had gotten himself caught in an economic cyclone without so much as a pair of galoshes.

One of the cheerful aspects for Appelbaum had been the fall-out. It was delicious to let everyone think those arrogant Wall Street guys weren't so smart after all. Greed made people act like idiots. As the great Saul Alinsky once said of the support he (inexplicably) received from conservative industrialists: "I feel confident I could persuade a millionaire on Friday to subsidize a revolution for Saturday, out of which he would make a huge profit Sunday, even though he was certain to be executed Monday." It was all about the last laugh, the long view.

Appelbaum was still babysitting Okono. Every speech, every statement, every policy position was reviewed by Appelbaum before the president opened his mouth. He had no real portfolio, but as the senior advisor, his finger was in every pie, just where it should be. And, in a town where physical access was power, Appelbaum occupied the broom closet-like space directly next to the Oval Office—just another, in a long line of bald-headed old men pushing levers and pedals to create a myth of a Mighty Oz.

Adding to his complacency were the huge fees his firm was raking in to astro-turf Okono's policy initiatives. Of course, the press agreed with most of them—who didn't want affordable healthcare? Perhaps as a result, no one was screaming about the millions his firm was collecting. But somewhere out west, Appelbaum reflected with some satisfaction, the former Republican Vice President (who'd gotten excoriated for the sweetheart deals given to *his* former employer) must be gnashing his pointy teeth. And of course, the VP's sweetheart deal wasn't nearly as sweet as Appelbaum's. The VP's former company was publicly traded. The former vice president was only one, of many, with a large stock position. Appelbaum was the sole proprietor of his company. To the victor go the spoils.

If Appelbaum's tactics hadn't changed, the same could not be said for his hours or his wardrobe. Never an early riser, he now got to the White House by 7:30 a.m. and tried not to let anyone speak to him until he'd had his civilizing caffeinated tea. Gone were the rumpled shirts and leather jackets, replaced by a bespoke suits from a Slovakian Georgetown clothier.

For such an avowed family man, he'd made the (to some) curious decision not to move his family from Chicago. Appelbaum now saw them only twice a month. But the schedule suited him. Not having them underfoot allowed Appelbaum to channel his energies. Perhaps too much, Appelbaum reflected. Because at night, sometimes, as Appelbaum looked out the window of his apartment at the dazzling spectacle of the brilliantly lit Washington Monument; he almost felt a sense of well,... loss.

It had been too easy. He had expected more of a challenge. Appelbaum had always warned Okono he couldn't take a punch, and the truth was, Okono couldn't. The amazing thing was, he'd never had to.

They'd all cleaned up pretty well he thought. Even the formerly captious Antoinette was radiating the milk of human kindness lately. Although Appelbaum still shuddered as he recalled how it had fallen to his unhappy lot to go to her, proverbial hat in hand, and beg her she not to wear a diamond necklace with her inaugural day outfit. Appelbaum had made his pitch, struggled to make her understand that for a nation facing financial Armageddon, it was so outrageous, so inappropriate, *as a message*. Appelbaum could barely believe she was considering it. Her husband, sitting beside her on the couch in the solarium, looked bemused, but said nothing. Antoinette had surveyed her interlocutor with narrowed eyes, one eyebrow preternaturally raised above the other.

"David Appelbaum," she said in frosty tones worthy of the Red Queen, "Every dog has its day... and on *that* day, *this* dog...is wearing diamonds." As Appelbaum, crestfallen, turned to leave, the president-elect consoled him in a stage whisper: "she's scary," he'd said with a laugh.

But to Appelbaum's everlasting amazement, Antoinette had worn her diamonds (and sequins) on inaugural day, and the only muted criticism among the avalanche of raptures was that "maybe it was a *little* fancy." Appelbaum had to laugh—a diamond necklace and sequins at 11:30 in the morning—a "*little* fancy"?—*Ya think*? When he thought of previous administrations that had been crippled by endless media criticism about supposedly highfalutin expenditures for decorations and dishes—it seemed impossible! But it had all worked out, he thought with a crooked smile. It turned out Antoinette's notorious cupidity for attention, for respect, for stuff—*could* be satisfied. Of course, it took being Queen of the World to do it.

As for himself, he'd always known himself: a little sleazy, a little schlumpy, an outsider. Now he was the "in" guy. Universities he could never get into were clamoring to give him honorary degrees, teach a course, ride a little on his super-hero cape. Their frank idolatry of Okono was one thing—but him? He started to feel like the Grinch looking down at Whoville. These people were so trusting and foolish, *so good,* —it was kind of endearing in a way. And Mr. Appelbaum started thinking...thinking about a second term. Well, after all, if The Minister had been promised a few White House dinners in the second term to keep him quiet, what might not Appelbaum get? Perhaps...dare he say it? Secretary Appelbaum? *Vice President* Appelbaum. Who knew? Strange things could happen. Stranger things *had* happened. He should know. He had made them happen.

The Republicans were in such disarray, it made Appelbaum almost giddy. When he had directed the attack against their number one blowhard—the Republican rank and file had rushed to disassociate themselves from him and run for their warrens. Good, Appelbaum thought, let them stay down their hidey-holes ("Pick the target. Cultivate unity against a clearly identifiable enemy. Specifically name the foe who is to blame for the particular evil that is the source of the people's angst. Cultivate in people's hearts a negative visceral emotional response to the face of the enemy." Alinsky's Rule #5).

The problem with the Republicans, Appelbaum reflected, was that they didn't read. They didn't educate themselves. What the dean of community organizers, Saul Alinsky, didn't know about swaying public opinion wasn't worth knowing ("Ridicule is the most potent weapon. Almost impossible to counter-attack. Infuriates opposition who will react to your advantage." Rule #3). Alinsky was a genius. Appelbaum shook his head in wonder. Alinsky's tactics had outflanked these guys for 70 years. They never learned. Or more accurately, Appelbaum considered, ever cautious, they hadn't learned, yet.

And, of course, The Professor. If The Professor's role in creating the swooning, lock-stepping grassroots Okono juggernaut had been largely anonymous during the campaign, Appelbaum could at least acknowledge to himself the pivotal role The Professor's plan had played. Not, he thought to himself with a smile, that he needed to acknowledge it to anyone else. That kind of expertise in organization building was almost incalculably valuable. Unfortunately, The Professor hadn't been motivated by anything so reasonable as money—or fame.

No, The Professor was the kind of true believer that most irritated Okono—a relentless, romantic ideologue that expected the president to use the vast power base he had created for him to institute real change. Appelbaum chuckled to himself. It would be difficult to imagine misreading Okono more completely. But Appelbaum thought it was pretty simple, really. If Okono had been interested in change, the South Side of Chicago wouldn't look like Beirut.

No, after the election, all the newly created and empowered grassroots *activists* had been quietly powered-down and...*de-*

activated, consigned to the Okono-dominated DNC and given insultingly mindless tasks like sending emails to congressmen and donating money. Naturally, they complained, but O. had never been interested in catering to any interest group, even his own. He'd used them when he'd needed them, and he'd use them again without scruple. By keeping them out of the discussion, Appelbaum and Okono had rendered them powerless, entirely dependent on the administration and the scraps they might throw.

And when Okono wanted them again in the next election...? Well...? Appelbaum smiled his Grinch-like smile. Where else could they go? As he surveyed the brilliantly illuminated city below, Appelbaum congratulated himself. Of course, they would return. Of course, they would help. After all, they were people of hope.

ACKNOWLEDGEMENTS

This book has been long aborning and is often the case there are a lot of people to thank.

It goes without saying that any errors or omissions are my own.

To all my friends, Democrats and Republicans, who asked me NOT to list your names, but whose true life stories made this book sound more authentic. Thank you for trusting me.

For when Google failed me: Gayle Detamore at the Oglethorpe Public Library, Oglethorpe, Georgia and Jay Rogers of D.J.'s Ideal General Store, Ideal, Georgia for helping me to get the details right. For Alan Jasperson of Great Northern Antiques in Minneapolis, Minnesota for his time, patience and sharing his encyclopedic knowledge of early radios. Thank you.

To Oak Leaf Press, for making this happen. To Russell James at James Literary Services (who believes in creative writing and standard punctuation), for his careful editing and refusing to let me capitalize everything. To the best in the business, Tony Greco of Greco & Associates for a gorgeous cover. To Christopher Katz at Pequod Book Design for his brilliant interior design.

To all my buddies at JSND Coalition, especially: Will Bower, Diane Mantouvalos, Elizabeth Joyce, Jon Winkleman, Jon West and (the late, great) Robin Carlson. I'm grateful to you all.

To my early readers & editors; some of you loved it, some (I suspect) hated it, but all of you helped to make it better: Aimee Dunn, Jean Schepers, Linda Mahoney, Martha Gallagher, and Jill Brantley. Words cannot express my appreciation for your friendship and support.

To my constant inspirations: Marilu Sochor, Doris Bim, Janet Margusity, Nairoby Otero, Krista Duffy, Marcia Dyson, Anita MonCrief, Carolyn Cook, Patricia Lengerman, Edith Miller, Lisa King, Polly Stamatopoulos, Marielle Hermann, Betty Jean Kling, Lee Dixon, Rose Storaska, Mary Atwater, Giny Vilk, Maria Hill, Rosemary Berlin, Sara Johns, Robin Rowlinson, Cecelia & Patrick Hickey, Linda Hayes, J.D. Overton, James Hannagan, Karen Murphy, Kamala Edwards, Vinod Ghildiyal, and Alberto and Linda Garcia. You're the best. Thank you for letting me tag along for the ride.

To my little campaigners, Winthrop and Everett, thank you for your patience, and to my rock-star Goldendoodle, de Tocqueville, who sits at my feet every morning as I write, thank you for your companionship. To my in-laws Hetty and Charles Abeles, for kindnesses over the years too many to enumerate. To my parents, whom I miss every day, for everything. And always, to my beleaguered husband, Nathaniel Abeles, who thoughtfully and carefully read all ten edits of this novel, and whose enthusiasm and support for this project never faltered; *vous tenez mon Coeur.*

ABOUT THE AUTHOR

P.G. Abeles is a graduate of Smith College and the host of the popular internet radio program, "Sins of Omission" (currently on hiatus). In the 2008 election, she co-founded a group of 14,000 Hillary Clinton supporters called Real Democrats. She is currently at work on a new thriller about Wall Street, "The Madness of Crowds," scheduled to be released in November 2012. She lives in Maryland with her husband, two sons, and a seriously naughty Goldendoodle.

Book Club Discussion Questions

1. The author purposely tells the story of the two political candidates, Okono and McCracken through the prism of their critics, supporters and handlers—as opposed to allowing them to speak in their own voices. Does this make the 'disconnect' in the election process more real? The idea that voters really don't know the candidate as a person—but only a distorted image reflected either through other people or their own expectations?

2. At the end of the book, Lacey makes the point that no one person sees the entire picture—that each person only sees their pieces of the puzzle. Does the author reinforce that point by presenting the story from a number of different viewpoints, with only the reader having access to the 'whole story'?

3. At the end of the book, Connor clearly believes Miriam Carter (not Okono) is the real hero. Is it important that Miriam is a woman?

(Continued on the next page.)

4. Throughout the book, the author introduces history about African American's struggle for civil rights as a way to explain the media and liberal elite's reaction to (and protectiveness of) Okono. How does Miriam Carter's life experience shape her in a way that is different than that of the privileged Okono?

5. In the book, Lacey criticizes the news media for "parsing" the information it presents to the public about political candidates, depending on their own bias. Is this a fair criticism?

6. So much of the story revolves around tracing money (Connor looking at Okono's early campaigns, the questionable contributions to Okono flagged by the FEC, even Archie Newton's seemingly fantastical statement that Okono received funding from the Saudis). Do you think the public cares? How important is it that candidates provide the public with information on where their donations come from? Does it matter if foreign nationals contribute to U.S. elections?

14167547R00277

Made in the USA
Lexington, KY
12 March 2012